"I'm going to need you to lift your skirts."

"My skirts?" Prue balked, retreating from his touch.

Lord Savage shrugged and turned to open the case. Withdrawing the short sword, he rested the hilt on the pads of two extended fingers, the weight perfectly balanced. "How else did you imagine we would sneak this past the footmen without being detected?"

"I'm not certain," she said, trying to think. "Beneath your coat, perhaps?"

"I never thought I'd utter these words in my entire life, but this is too large for me to manage." He issued a sigh of mock dismay, but there was a rakish grin tucked into the corner of his mouth. Then he kneeled down and tugged on her green hem. "I won't even look. Well, not too much. Or, if you'd rather, I could simply *feel* my way underneath, hmm?"

"No," she said at once. "I'll do it."

Holding her breath, she gripped the silk as primly as possible and slowly, haltingly, lifted her skirts . . .

How to Steal a Scoundrel's Heart

The Mating Habits of Scoundrels

Vivienne Lorret

AVON BOOKS

An Imprint of HarperCollinsPublishers

HOW TO STEAL A SCOUNDREL'S HEART. Copyright © 2022 by Vivienne Lorret. All rights reserved. Printed in the United States of America. No part of this book may be used or reproduced in any manner whatsoever without written permission except in the case of brief quotations embodied in critical articles and reviews. For information, address HarperCollins Publishers, 195 Broadway, New York, NY 10007.

First Avon Books mass market printing: May 2022

Print Edition ISBN: 978-0-06-314301-2
Digital Edition ISBN: 978-0-06-314302-9

Cover design by Amy Halperin
Cover illustration by Judy York
Cover image © fotojagodka/Getty Images

Avon, Avon & logo, and Avon Books & logo are registered trademarks of HarperCollins Publishers in the United States of America and other countries.

HarperCollins is a registered trademark of HarperCollins Publishers in the United States of America and other countries.

FIRST EDITION

22 23 24 25 26   BVGM   10 9 8 7 6 5 4 3 2 1

For all the readers
who promise themselves *just one more chapter,*
then end up finishing the entire book in a night

Time is
Too Slow for those who Wait,
Too Swift for those who Fear,
Too Long for those who Grieve,
Too Short for those who Rejoice;
But for those who Love,
Time is not.

—Henry van Dyke

How to Steal a Scoundrel's Heart

Prologue

Prudence Thorogood drew the hood of her tattered mantle over her head and reached for the lion's head door knocker. Taking a deep breath, she rapped soundly.

There was no turning back. Not for her.

After all, the marital prospects of a penniless, ruined debutante were grim. Such a woman may have the opportunity to wed the man who'd taken her innocence. *If*, perhaps, he was forced into a proposal while being beaten about the head with a reticule and dressmaker's dummy until finally relenting with an agonized, "Very well! I'll marry her!"

She would decline, vehemently.

There was also the possibility of allowing the clergyman to introduce her to a twice-widowed farmer in need of a *healthy young wife* who could cook, clean and sew for him and his fourteen children.

Thank you, no.

Of course, if she was truly selfish, she could continue to accept the kindness of dear friends and live beneath their roof, watching as society slowly turned their backs on them.

Or . . . she could take matters into her own hands.

But it was an undeniable truth that any future would require selling her very soul, in some form or another. The least she could do to honor the sacrifice was make her own choice.

She released the air in her lungs on a resolved exhale just as the black lacquered door opened.

A stately manservant greeted her with a bland inquiry, as if it were commonplace to see a cloaked female on this doorstep in the dead of night. A shiver of trepidation skated down her spine, but she shrugged it off and simply said, "Lord Savage, if you please."

The man opened the door for her to step inside the foyer. "I shall see if his lordship is at home. Whom should I say is calling?"

"Miss Thorogood . . . ?" she said as if unfamiliar with her own name. So she repeated herself with more authority. After all, she knew who she was and why she'd come to the house of a notorious rake.

Now, if only her heart would stop beating four times faster than the golden pendulum vacillating in the curved belly of the longcase clock beside her.

The butler's footsteps on the marble floor were crisp and concise as if he led dozens of visitors to the aubergine receiving parlor each evening by rote. And before he left, he absently set a bone-white bowl of bright red rose petals on the black marble console table by the door.

She stared at the bowl. How peculiar. Was every guest escorted into this room with their own rose petals?

It was possible, she supposed. The Marquess of Savage was known for having an appetite for excess, including all manner of hedonistic pleasures. Proof of that was in the sumptuous furnishings surrounding her, the windows swathed in heavy brocade, the upholstered bronze armchairs, the scallop-back settee, mahogany tables inlaid with gold . . . and the oil painting of a voluptuous woman in repose above the mantel, nude aside from a sliver of red silk draped down her body.

Prue quickly averted her gaze and tried not to think about his other indulgences. She didn't want to lose her nerve, after all. And she needed every ounce of daring she possessed to face this man and tell him exactly why she'd come.

Distractedly, she coasted her fingertips over the cool, velvety petals. What an odd offering for guests. She could imagine cut flowers in vases. Decorative arrangements were typical in finer houses. But these?

Picking up the bowl, she breathed in the sweet aroma of the petals and felt her lips curve in a smile. They were so soft, so fragrant, so extravagant that they seemed almost romantic. And after the way their first meeting had commenced, she would never have taken *him* for a romantic.

Surely, he wouldn't have these on hand for every guest. And certainly not for every unexpected . . . guest. Like . . . her.

Prue lifted her head at once. It suddenly occurred to her that these rose petals weren't here for random guests at all, but for one in particular. The very guest he was likely entertaining right this moment . . . until *she* had interrupted.

A surge of dismay strangled her throat. She swallowed it down and began to pace, clutching the bowl to her chest.

Why hadn't she thought of this before? Of course, he was with another woman. And they were engaged in whatever activities one normally did in the evening hours. Like reading a book. Watching the flames in the hearth. Resting after a long day, and . . .

Oh, who was she trying to fool?

He was a scoundrel. He was doubtless upstairs right this instant, otherwise engaged in something that he couldn't tear himself away from. Something that involved two people, heavy breathing, perspiring, grunting . . . lots of grunting . . . And now, with her interruption, he would have to put his clothes on and—

The parlor door opened suddenly.

Prue startled like a rabbit caught in the garden with half a cabbage in her grasp. The dish went flying. Petals rained down everywhere. And gravity brought the spinning creamware down directly toward her head.

She squeezed her eyes shut, preparing for it to hit. Hard.

And yet . . . it didn't.

When she opened her eyes again, she saw the staid butler holding the bowl in his grasp. Apparently, he was much quicker than he looked.

Then, as if this type of thing happened all the time, he merely set it down on the table and said, "Right this way, Miss Thorogood."

"Actually, there's been a mistake." She shook her head and immediately crouched down to the rug, nervously scooping up as many petals as she could. The bowl may not have struck her on the noodle, but she had some sense knocked into her nonetheless. "I should never have come."

"His lordship is waiting, ma'am. There's no need to fret over the petals." He gently, but firmly, took her elbow to assist her in standing.

Awkwardly, she transferred her handful into his. "Right. Well. Be that as it may, I really must go before I disturb his lordship from whatever it is that I'm . . . disturbing."

The butler followed her hasty retreat into the foyer. "Would you care to leave a card or a message?"

"I think not."

Reaching the door, her nervous hand fumbled with the latch. And just before she could finally manage to open it . . . she heard a familiar drawl behind her.

"Leaving so soon, Miss Thorogood? Is that any way to greet an old friend?"

Chapter 1

A month earlier

If the carriage went any slower, they'd be traveling back in time.

Leo Ramsgate, Marquess of Savage, muttered a curse beneath his breath and snapped his pocket watch closed before he tapped on the hood. "What appears to be the problem, Rogers?"

"Sheep, milord."

Ah. That explained it, he thought with a glance through the rain-dappled window toward the rolling hills of the verdant Wiltshire countryside. He wondered—and not for the first time—why he'd agreed to escort his former paramour to Bath. Typically, when an affair ended, it was over and done with for good. And yet, here he was, waiting for sheep.

As they came to a complete stop, a heavy sigh drifted across the carriage. "Will I be so easy to forget, Savage? No, don't answer that. You'll only say something detached and uncaring to make me feel guilty for my part in this premature separation of ours. Yet you never take any blame for pushing me into the arms of another man."

Thus far on their journey, Lady Chastaine had held fast to two topics of conversation—the weather and their *misunderstanding,* as she put it. If she wasn't scourging the rain for frizzling her auburn coiffure and the dreary gray atmosphere for doing nothing to complement her complexion, then she was relentlessly denying any culpability for her adulterous tryst. Had her excuses been a dead horse, she would not only have beaten it but dismembered and buried it in the deepest pit from which nothing could return.

He stared back at her with the bland nonchalance he'd perfected over the years. "Am I as ruthless as all that?"

"More," she said with kittenish petulance.

He called up to Rogers again. "Any news to report?"

"There appears to be . . ." His words were drowned out by the excited barking of a dog, agitated *baahs* and the hollow clanking of a copper bell.

Leo opened the door to the drizzle and peered ahead, trying to discern the cause for himself. Unfortunately, from his vantage point, all he could see was a flock of dirty-arsed sheep.

"But I'll have you know," Phoebe continued, "I won't be jealous of your next mistress. I'm too self-assured for that."

"Glad to hear it."

"And besides. For that, I would have to suffer from the delusion that you could ever truly care about any of the women you take as mistress. But you and I both know that isn't possible."

"Are we back to calling me heartless again?" he asked, flicking an absent glance over his shoulder.

She squinted at him, pouting prettily. "Did we ever stop?"

His mouth quirked in response. He would miss Phoebe's particular brand of cynicism. Her wit could flay a man's ego at fifty paces. Her tongue was waspish to a fault, but also devilishly skilled in other more delightfully provocative ways. No, she wouldn't be easy to forget. But he would put her from his mind, regardless, as he'd always done with each paramour at the end of every affair.

The problem was, escaping the tedium of eternity that yawned before him in the meantime.

Leo had never been a man at ease with lingering in the hinterland between two places—the end of one thing and the beginning of another. He'd much prefer to continue on to London and find a new mistress to take her place. But instead, he was trapped here in this provincial hell.

His throat tightened on a growl of impatience as he called up to the driver again. "What were you saying, Rogers?"

"A woman, milord. On foot. The shepherd's drover won't let her pass. Oh, and now he's got hold of her bag with his teeth." He chuckled, clearly amused by the spectacle. "It's a right solid tug-of-war, it is."

Well, damn. Now Leo had to step out and see this nonsense for himself. If nothing else, it would serve as a distraction.

"So . . . have you?" Phoebe asked as he stepped down, the muddy road squishing beneath his hessians. "Selected my replacement, that is?"

He murmured an absent response that was neither admission nor negation.

As of yet, he'd not made a firm decision. He received more than a dozen perfume-scented requests by post each week, some even from women who lived on other continents and knew him by reputation alone. There were more who approached him at evening soirees, whispering scandalous promises in his ear while slipping calling cards into his pockets. It was only a matter of choosing one to be on his arm and in his bed.

"Not that I care a whit, mind you," she said, her skirts rustling against the bench as she scooted closer to peer over his shoulder. "Just don't tell me that it's to be Millie Sutton."

He absently pulled at the cuffs of his green coat and looked toward the convergence of dingy sheep and the barefooted shepherd boy. "No?"

"Absolutely not." She scoffed. "With that chirruping laugh of hers? And she thinks she's oh-so clever with her fan-play. Someone should tell her that she looks more like an injured parakeet with all that flailing and flapping. Not only that, but she whines constantly about the old earl leaving her nothing in his will. I've even heard that she's already ordered seven new gowns because she's anticipating your invitation and told her modiste that you would pay for them. Why, that woman would drain your coffers dry in a month if you let her."

"And here I thought you didn't care."

The truth was, he'd always known that women were attracted to what he could offer on the surface. Women liked his looks, his bedsport prowess, and especially his money. Which was perfectly fine with him.

It didn't matter much in the end, regardless. He never kept a mistress beyond four months. After that, it just felt too . . . permanent. Too confining. A lengthy affair only built expectations like a house of cards, increasing the likelihood of collapse with disappointments and betrayals. As his current former mistress had so kindly reminded him.

A large sheepdog appeared on the grassy knoll, drawing him out of his musings. The shaggy canine gamboled by in a ripple of rope-like fur, tinged a sooty black on the ends. A battered leather valise was clenched in his teeth. He stopped to look over his shoulder, one eye peeping through a thick mop of fringe, bobtail wagging as a figure approached.

And that was the instant Leo first saw the woman.

She dashed into view at a long, graceful lope, a damp gray cloak plastered to her willowy form. In her haste, the hood slipped to her shoulders, revealing an intricately braided twist of hair the color of fresh buttermilk. Loose tendrils escaped the confines of tortoiseshell combs and spilled wetly against the curve of her cheek. But she paid them no mind. Her focus was on the dog.

Just as she was closing in, the beast playfully darted from one side to the other. The young woman paused, slender hands on hips, and regarded the thief with marked determination. After a moment's consideration, she bent to pat the tops of her thighs. Then she pursed a pair of deep pink, Cupid's-bow lips and kissed the air to call the animal.

Leo felt himself take a step.

The motion must have drawn her attention. Her head turned at once and a pair of stormy blue eyes alighted on him. Framed with lashes the color of dark sand, they were set inside a heart-shaped face bejeweled by beads of dew that shimmered like diamonds in the bleary rain-soaked light.

Leo couldn't look away. A legion of trimmed tawny hairs lifted on his nape, his flesh tightening beneath layers of fine lawn and tailored wool. And when she straightened, his appreciative gaze drifted down the lithe form that the clever rain saw fit to reveal in subtle curves and shallow nooks where the dark cloak clung.

When his gaze returned to hers, there was a definite degree of coldness there. A warning to keep his distance. And since he couldn't fathom why he'd moved in the first place— when he was the last man on earth to come to the aid of a damsel in distress, no matter how fair—he merely inclined his head and anchored his boots to the earth.

"Even she would be a far sight better for you than Millie Sutton," Phoebe said.

"A wayward country waif? I think not."

"Oh, but she's one of us," she said, surprising him. "I'm acquainted with her stepmother, Lady Whitcombe. The viscountess and I were finished together."

"How delightfully sapphic, my dear. I do hope you both enjoyed yourselves."

Phoebe ignored the naughty remark. "If rumors are to be believed—and you know the delicious ones always are—this stepdaughter was caught in a rather compromising position at one of the soirees last year. Don't know the particulars, but the gentleman involved obviously chose not to marry her. Poor girl. Quite ruined, of course. Lord Whitcombe holds a seat in Parliament and summarily banished her to the country without batting an eyelash."

"Nothing like the warm embrace of a father to give one a bright start in the world," Leo muttered sotto voce.

His mood—bitter as it usually was—abruptly soured. He knew all too well what it was like to have parents who chose their own pursuits without considering the ramifications to others.

What the devil was the daughter of a peer doing out here all alone? Had she no other family to look after her?

He studied the stranger once more as she attempted to reclaim her property. He caught sight of the frayed hem and a faded blue dress that had seen better days. Yet, even in tattered muslin, there was something regal in her bearing. She kept her swanlike neck straight as she snapped her graceful fingers and ordered the dog to heel.

Surprisingly, the beast trotted toward her. But heeling wasn't at all what he had in mind.

Instead, he bounded up with his paws reaching to her shoulders, his hindquarters wagging with glee. However, since he likely outweighed her by a stone, she summarily toppled to the squelchy ground with an audible *splat*.

A huff of indignation preceded her careful attempts to stand with utmost decorum. Yet, as soon as she righted herself and shook out her skirts, the dog woofed and knocked her down again.

This was all just a game to the exceptionally enormous puppy and wasn't likely to end anytime soon with the shepherd busily trying to corral his errant sheep. So, Leo decided to intervene.

Placing the hook of his thumb and middle finger between his lips, he issued a shrill, ascending whistle. Instantly, the drover turned, ears perked like two spraying fountains beneath that tangled mop. Then he loped obediently over to Leo, sat on his haunches and dropped the valise.

Behind him, and a little muddier than before, the young woman stiffly smoothed her clothes as though she wore a coronation robe instead of a threadbare cloak. As she approached, he heard her grumble, "You couldn't have done that sooner?"

He felt a grin tug at the corner of his mouth as he lifted her bag from the ground. "I believe this is"—just then one side of the handle tore free of its stitching—"yours."

She issued a soft, barely audible growl as she reached out. But she took special care to ensure that her grip wasn't even close to coming into contact with his. "Thank you for your assistance."

"Delighted to be of service," he said and saw those stormy eyes narrow ever so slightly.

Behind him, Phoebe gave his shoulder a light shove to move him out of her view. "Miss Thorogood, what a lovely surprise to see you here. It's been an age since we've last met."

"Oh, Lady Chastaine. How very . . . kind of you to remember me," the young woman said, all politeness. But it was clear in her halting tone and shifting stance that she was eager to depart their company. "If you would forgive me, I'm not quite fit for a social visit and must be on my way. I have a pressing errand to attend."

"Isn't that forever the way of it, my dear? When we are dressed ever so smartly we hardly see a soul. But when we are at our worst, we will run into everyone we've ever met," his companion purred. "Surely you can spare a moment or two while we're waiting for the sheep to move onward. That is . . . unless it would sully your pride to associate with the likes of a fallen woman and her former protector."

Miss Thorogood straightened her shoulders, the flesh around that Cupid's-bow mouth tightening. "As you have doubtless witnessed from my current state, it is clear that I have no pride. Therefore, it must be curiosity that prompts your invitation and, for that reason, I will decline it. Thank you all the same, my lady."

This stranger was no simpleton, to be sure. And for some peculiar reason, witnessing her cool show of mettle stirred a measure of admiration within him.

Just as she was turning to leave, Lady Chastaine added hurriedly, "Settle your feathers, my dear. I meant no offense." She huffed. Though there must have been enough contrition in her voice to earn a patient pause from their guest. "Do stay for a moment, please. I promise to hold a tight rein on the ribbons of my curiosity. Your presence would be most welcome. Necessary, in fact, as Savage and I have exhausted our attempts at playing nice. Of course, you've met the marquess, haven't you? No? Well, you have now."

"Lord Savage." Miss Thorogood offered a dignified curtsy. She did not blush or simper as most young women did when introduced to him, but met his gaze squarely, like an old crone who had lived a thousand lifetimes and had yet to be impressed by anything.

The irredeemable scoundrel in Leo was half tempted to take her hand and bring it to his lips, just to see what she might do. But he tamped down the wayward impulse and merely inclined his head. "A pleasure."

"There, now that all of the niceties have commenced, I insist that you allow us to assist you in any way we can," Lady Chastaine said with the tenacity he'd once found charming. "After all, it must be a tremendously important errand for you to brave such dreary weather, and on foot. To where will you be traveling?"

"The ribbons seem to have slipped from your grasp already, my lady," Miss Thorogood responded, but without censure. Instead, she issued an undisguised exhale of resignation as the panting dog suddenly licked her hand before settling down again at Leo's side. "If you must know, I'm going to take the stagecoach to London."

"My dear, that is absolutely splendid! You'll be the toast of the *demimonde*."

"Actually, I—"

"Though in order to take London by storm," Phoebe interrupted, "you'll need a gentleman of influence on your arm. And I just happen to know of one who will soon be losing a companion. He's rich as Croesus. Generous, not only with gifts but with his—shall I say—*natural endowments*," she added with a salacious waggle of her brows toward Leo. "And he's not terrible on the eyes either. In truth, Savage has only one great flaw."

"And that is?" he interjected impassively. Like stage actors in a play that had run too long in Haymarket, he knew his lines as well as Lady Chastaine's.

As if on cue, sunlight stole through the clouds to shine a perfect ray of light on Phoebe's pout. "He has no heart."

"Then he is all the better for it, I should think," Miss Thorogood said quietly, the flesh over the bridge of her nose furrowing slightly as she glanced at him.

The instant their gazes connected, however, she looked away. It was a pity because he wanted to discern what she was thinking. Not only that, but he liked the sound of her voice. It was pleasantly textured, layers blending richly together, revealing themselves by degree upon listening. Like silk, he thought, cool to the touch at first, then warming as it lingered against the skin.

"My dear, such a sentiment makes you positively perfect as Savage's next in line," Phoebe offered excitedly. "Not only are you beautiful—and he adores beautiful things— but you would bring a bit of class to the *demimonde*, I think.

No, actually, I'm sure of it." She lifted her arm through the open doorway and held out her hand. "Come with us. We'll talk more in the carriage. Savage will drive me to Bath first, then you and he will journey to town."

The dog woofed as if in agreement. And even though this was no plan of his own, Leo found himself waiting for Miss Thorogood's response. The noises of the wayward sheep and shepherd's bell faded, and his entire focus centered on her.

But as one second ticked by—*two, three*—he thought he glimpsed something lurking beneath the surface. It was in the lowering of her lashes, the delicate movement of her throat above the tarnished clasp of her cloak as she swallowed. Something vulnerable and innocent.

In his experience, innocence usually paired with fragility. And he'd learned to keep far afield from fragile women.

He preferred a certain type—jaded, cynical and self-absorbed. After all, the last thing he ever wanted was to be embroiled in another complicated affair.

So he was glad when she withdrew a step and said, "I have no intention of taking London by storm or otherwise."

"I do not understand, then," Phoebe groused. "What other reason could you have for returning after such a ruinous scandal?"

Miss Thorogood's spine went ramrod straight. She gripped the broken strap of her valise, knuckles white through the gray layer of drying mud, and Leo presumed she was too offended to answer.

All the better for her, he thought. And yet . . . he was unaccountably curious, too. What could this proud creature hope to gain by enduring the trial that awaited the disgraced daughter of a peer amidst the *ton*?

When Miss Thorogood turned on her heel, he thought he would never know the answer.

But then she hesitated. Chin set, she issued a single-word response.

"Larceny." Then she walked away like a queen preparing for battle.

Leo stared after her, an intrigued grin on his lips. At his side, he gave his woolly friend a scratch and murmured, *good boy.*

Chapter 2

——⌒——

Prudence Thorogood knew there was no going back. Not for her. And there was no way to change what had already occurred.

She could only move forward and think about her future.

Therefore, the following morning, she marched along the muddy road with her head held high. She'd walk to London if she had to. After all, it was a better option than traveling with the vile wastrel who'd thought an unprotected female on the mail coach would welcome his hand upon her thigh and his gaze fixed upon her bosom.

Well, she'd showed him. Her hand still throbbed from the slap she'd delivered.

Now she was just east of the beatific Berkshire Downs. Although, in her opinion, it should have been named the Berkshire *Ups*, since she found herself trudging up steady inclines far more often than down any declines.

At the top of one rise, she paused to catch her breath and take in the view of the vast countryside . . . just before the heavy-bottomed clouds decided to give her one more obstacle on her journey. Rain.

Splendid.

But it didn't matter that she would soon be soaked to her chemise. She wasn't going to let a little water stop her. And she wasn't going to let another man interfere with her dreams—a lesson learned the hard way a year ago.

She'd been fooled once, believing a scoundrel's lies. But never again.

This ruined debutante was taking back her life . . . or what was left of it. And she would do it alone.

She was in control. Not her disapproving father and step-mother. Not her pious aunt and uncle. And certainly not the deceitful cad who'd ruined her.

"Besides, I'm better off on my own," she declared aloud, gripping the knotted strap of her valise tighter, and pretending she wasn't exhausted after having already walked for hours. "I don't need any— *Ow!*"

She stopped suddenly, pain pricking the ball of her foot. Lifting it from the ground, she hopped one-legged past a large puddle to the side of the road, careful to keep the hems of her cloak and skirts out of the way. Then she sat down on the grassy embankment.

A rock, of course, she thought scornfully. And not just a little pebble either. No, indeed. It was a goliath, splitting open a crevasse in the sole of her nankeen half boot.

"Blast it all!" she muttered, angrily tugging on her mud-coated laces. She wished she knew more colorful epithets. Now *that* would have been a worthwhile class in finishing school, instead of learning how to be the perfect debutante and the perfect hostess for one's future husband. *Ha!*

Perfection, at least for her, was as elusive as capturing mist in a net. No matter how hard she tried, she simply couldn't hold on to it.

Which had brought her here, to this new low point.

If her dour aunt Thorley could see her, she'd doubtless unleash another one of her delightfully condescending castigations. *Tut-tut, Prudence. I am greatly disappointed in your actions, and greatly disappointed in your shabby attire. Once again, you've proven that you are nothing more than a blemish on your father's good name.*

Prue hated that she'd allowed herself to be cowed by that woman so many times.

Well, no longer.

That was the old Prue.

The old Prue would have given up after encountering so many obstacles. Convinced herself that she didn't deserve anything better. Accepted the impossibility of moving on. And would have, ultimately, fallen back into a soul-withering existence.

But the new Prue wanted more . . . whether she deserved it or not. And the new Prue was bold, too. Determined to live a life that was hers and hers alone. The word *impossible* was no longer in her lexicon. She laughed in the face of obstacles. "Ha!"

Whipping a handkerchief from her sleeve, she shook it in her fist and glared up at the heavens, where the Fates were likely looking down upon her with smug superiority. "A rock won't stand in my way. Even if I have to hop to London through a sea of mud, nothing will stop me. I've already hit my lowest point. There's nothing else you can do to me!"

A bolt of lightning splintered across the hilly horizon. A booming crack of thunder followed.

The new Prue lowered her arm.

Perhaps tempting the Fates wasn't such a grand notion. And thinking about what they might do next made her heart gallop hard in her chest. Quite loudly, too. In fact, her entire body was practically vibrating from—

Just then, she heard the jangle of rigging behind her. Turning sharply, she realized it wasn't her heart galloping but a team of horses pulling a sleek black carriage.

Panicked, she jolted to her feet, just in time to allow it to pass . . .

But, regrettably, *not* in time to avoid the tsunami splash from the wheel hitting the puddle she'd so carefully avoided.

Before she could scramble down the embankment, a colossal wave of brown sludge rose up from the bowels of Hades and splashed her from hood to hem.

She went still. A statue frozen in midflight, arms flared at her side and . . . Dear heavens, what was that awful smell?

Her nose wrinkled as the inescapable answer seeped into her clothes.

Honestly, the only way this day could get any worse would be to have someone she knew witness her humiliation.

Behind her, she heard the gruff voice of the driver call out a command to the horses. Shortly following, the thunderous plodding of hooves went still. Warily, she turned to glance over her shoulder.

The door flew open. And the instant the occupant emerged, she knew that the Fates were, indeed, having a jolly time toying with her. It was Lord Savage!

Splendid, just splendid.

The marquess bounded out of the carriage. He paid no heed to the drizzle or mud, but strode toward her with his polished hessians dispersing puddles in sprays. Every hard-footed step accentuated thickly muscled thighs encased by buckskin breeches. His coat parted to reveal his powerful build and lean torso beneath a fitted russet waistcoat. And even though he wore no hat, his appearance did not suffer for it. The slow saturation of water turned his golden mane a darker shade, the tarnished bronze color only intensifying the emerald green of his irises.

He looked as though he were emerging fresh from his tailor's shop or a portrait sitting.

She, on the other hand, resembled a drowned cat. Which was only slightly worse than her appearance yesterday. And thinking back to that, she became irritated with him once more.

"You couldn't have stopped the carriage *before* the puddle?" Prue groused under her breath.

Lowering the dripping hood to lay on her shoulders, she

felt a clump of something she'd rather not think about dislodge itself from the wool and fall with a *splat* at her feet.

"Miss Thorogood, what the devil are you doing out here?"

Her spine instantly stiffened at the way he barked at her, his tawny brow furrowing. And she wasn't particularly pleased with his preeminent manner when he glared down the ridge of his aquiline nose either.

"I fail to see that my travel habits are any concern of yours, my lord. Need I remind you that we're barely acquainted?"

"You said you were taking the stagecoach," he added as if she hadn't spoken.

She had a good mind not to answer. However, since they were both standing in the rain like sodden nincompoops—at least on her part, *no thanks to him*—and she would hardly be able to make a grand exit into the nearby meadow, she humored him. "If you must know, the stagecoach was full. I took the mail coach instead. That conveyance hit a rut, the wheel badly bent. And when the passengers disembarked to await the repair, a country squire became a bit too friendly for my tastes. Therefore, I decided that I was better off traveling on foot."

When his expression darkened even more, she felt her own ire rise. She had reached the limit of what she would take from the Fates *and* from members of his sex. The absolute limit! And if he so much as breathed another castigation, she would lose what little remained of her patience and flog him with her valise.

"Were you"—he gritted his teeth, growling the words—"harmed in any way?"

Prue's grip on the frayed leather strap loosened at the surprisingly harsh, gravelly tone. He sounded nothing like the bored, overindulged aristocrat she'd met yesterday. In fact, he almost sounded . . . concerned.

She dismissed the foolish notion at once. There was no

reason that her circumstances should trouble him. Not only were they strangers, but a rake of his reputed caliber was hardly renowned amongst the *ton* for his chivalry. Oh yes, she'd heard of him. And a man who kept a constant parade of paramours on his arm, then discarded them with ease, was hardly likely to care about the trials and tribulations of the female population.

Even so, she noted the tight cording of his throat above the crisp edge of his cravat, the furrows of tension in the superfine wool over broad shoulders, and the jagged vein rising beneath the flesh of his clenched fists. He seemed to be waiting for her response.

"Only my toes from where I kicked him rather soundly," she said. "I believe that is how I broke one of the soles of my half boots."

Lord Savage issued a curt nod. "Good. I'm certain he deserved it."

Hmm. Could it be that some scoundrels had a line they would not cross?

She blinked at him with open curiosity as he raked a hand through his hair, slicking it back away from his forehead. On any other man, features on full display without relief, would likely look too austere or even unattractive with any potential flaws front and center—like a weak chin, a Neolithic brow, or even an asymmetrical pair of nostrils.

But not this man. As far as she could see, he had no flaws. Every angle was faultlessly chiseled, from the perfect slope of his brow to the uncompromising edge of his jawline. Even his mouth was the ideal shape. Any more flesh and it would have been too broad. Any less and . . .

She shook her head, not understanding why she'd let her thoughts drift in that manner. It mattered nothing to her that he was inhumanly attractive and broad-shouldered. She still despised all men and refused to be tempted into furthering an acquaintance with one.

As if reading her mind, Lord Savage pointed up to the sky. "Doubtless, you've noticed the imposing activity in the clouds. I'm afraid it will only get worse from here. Therefore, I gladly offer the use of my carriage."

She frowned and leveled him with a glare of warning. "At what cost, my lord?"

"None at all," he said blandly. "I consider it bad form to take advantage of soggy debutantes. No need to break another sole on my account."

She scoffed. In her experience, displays of benevolence left the door open to an abuse of power over the recipient. "I do not take charity."

"I'd presumed as much," he said, expelling a patient breath. "Therefore, what say you to an even exchange—an undisturbed ride into London for a few hours of your conversation to release me from the monotony of my own thoughts?"

Her gaze slid from him to the carriage. An unexpected tremor of yearning leached from the soles of her aching feet and traveled up through her entire skeleton, leaving her enervated to the very marrow.

Her pride and sense of self-preservation wavered.

"It's a new landau," he added with the quiet enticement that the devil likely used when whispering in one's ear. "Well sprung. Velvet upholstery. Pillowy tufted benches."

Aunt and Uncle Thorley would have sniffed with disdain over such an extravagance. They disapproved of indulgence in any form and hadn't so much as draped a horse blanket over the wooden bench in their own curricle.

Prue, on the other hand, imagined it would feel lovely to sit on something soft. The past year had been hardbacked chairs, hardwood floors and hard pillows. Even her mattress had been stuffed with stiff, horsehair ticking. She'd forgotten what velvet was like.

"I'm covered in filth," she said, her excuse as threadbare as her soaked stockings.

Those vivid green eyes scanned her in shrewd appraisal and he clucked his tongue. "Ah. So you are. Can't have that. Well, best of luck to you . . ."

Then he turned and began to walk away. Which was fine with her because she didn't need anyone.

And yet . . .

It occurred to her that she was likely thinking too much of her own charms. Renowned rogue though he may be, she was hardly irresistible, especially in her current travel-worn state with tangled hair, eyes purplish and puffy from exhaustion and a drenched cloak that smelled of . . . Well, she'd rather not think about that.

Lord Savage could have any woman he wanted, and likely did quite often. So it was ridiculous to imagine that he would want her. Not to mention, it was Lady Chastaine who'd suggested that Prue could be his *next in line*, not he.

"I'm an excellent conversationalist," she called out to his retreating form, the words spilling out before she could pull them back.

But they stopped him, nonetheless. "As you have proven with the two dozen words spoken since the beginning of our acquaintance. I've been positively riveted."

"I suppose . . . a fair trade would be a ride to London."

"It would, indeed." Without facing her, he proffered his arm and waited.

Garnering her courage, she drew in a deep breath. Then she went to him, slipping her hand in the crook of his elbow as if he were leading her to a ballroom floor instead of the uncertain confines of the carriage.

As they reached the door, he hesitated and glanced down at her in shrewd appraisal. "Much as I enjoy the robust aroma of a stable yard on a rainy morning, perhaps you would prefer to leave your cloak with my driver?"

The heat of embarrassment flooded her cheeks. Though,

if she'd needed further reassurance that the marquess had no interest in seducing her, she had it.

"Of course," she said, but fumbled with the clasp.

Before he even finished saying, "Allow me," he lifted a long-fingered hand, flicked the fastening, divested her of her cloak and tossed it up to the driver.

Startled by his degree of deftness with disrobing the nearest female, she stared warily down at the hand he offered to help her into the carriage. "I can manage on my own, thank you."

He inclined his head and lowered the hinged step. Which she would have navigated perfectly well if the broken sole of her half boot hadn't caught against the edge. She teetered for the barest second before her fingers found purchase in the warmth of his waiting palm.

His hold was firm and steady as he guided her inside. And it wasn't until she withdrew that she felt the sharp prickle of a splinter she'd taken the day before.

Prue didn't dare to look at his expression, knowing it must be filled with distaste. She knew how rough her flesh had become over the past year. He was likely used to softly pampered women who bathed with scented oils and dressed in the finest silks, instead of layers of mud and poorly mended muslin.

These thoughts were only confirmed as the luxurious interior enveloped her. He was most definitely used to the finer things.

She balked at the rich surroundings. It seemed more like a bedchamber than a carriage, imbued with the subtle fragrances of new upholstery, sandalwood and amber, and a pleasant spice of some sort. Her fingertips sank into the plush pile of brushed velvet as she sat on the edge of a bench that was softer than any sofa she'd ever encountered and adorned with rolled bolster pillows on either side. Shimmering black silk lined the hood, running in fanned pleats that gathered in the center. And the surrounding windows were swathed in tieback brocade curtains trimmed in silver fringe.

Tut-tut, Prudence. Your admiration of such frippery is sinful.

Aunt Thorley's voice in her head was likely correct, but Prue couldn't help it. She'd never seen a more magnificent carriage in her life.

It made her all the more aware of the dreadful state of her clothes.

As he climbed in after her, unfolding his masculine form on the inverse corner, she smoothed her damp skirts and sat as primly as possible. Yet, when the carriage set off, the momentum forced her back against the tufted cushion.

So she tried again to maintain a formal bearing, not only to keep herself from ruining the upholstery but to keep from relaxing her guard in the company of a scoundrel. She had vowed never to make that mistake again.

"You may as well abandon yourself to comfort, Miss Thorogood. We have a few hours ahead of us and not a single soul around to care if you slouch."

"I'm not usually given to slouching, my lord."

"You don't say," he remarked without a shred of surprise as he withdrew a handkerchief and extended it to her. Seeing her watchful hesitation, he added, "No improper advances hidden within the pressed creases, I assure you."

She accepted the offering with a nod of thanks and unfolded it carefully, not wanting to soil it in any way.

"I hope your sacrificed combs purchased a meal and a room for last night, in addition to coach fare," he said, casually easing back against the squabs.

The hand daintily blotting the droplets of dew from her face paused. How did he know? Yes, it was true. She had sold them. But surely, he couldn't have recalled such an insignificant detail in her appearance from their brief encounter yesterday.

"They did . . . for the most part," she answered. "Although, the landlady was in a delicate condition and her time had come. And since the cook was also the local midwife, they adjourned to the room upstairs. This left the kitchen without a servant. So I offered my services, such as they are, tidying up, boiling water, and readying the linens for a makeshift bassinet."

"You *offered to*—" He broke off abruptly, his features revealing bald surprise before he carefully resumed a mask of nonchalance. "How industrious."

"I know engaging in such labor is hardly common practice for young women in society. Since living with my aunt and uncle for the past year, however, I've become well accustomed to earning my keep through daily household tasks. And it was no trouble at all to lend a hand when needed."

Returning the handkerchief, she saw his gaze drift to her chapped hands and she hastily hid them in the folds of her skirts.

"Your aunt and uncle are absolute models of economy," he quipped, scrubbing the same handkerchief over his own face and through the layers of his wavy hair. "I, myself, wanted to turn all my relations into indentured servants but, sadly, I don't have any. None legitimate, at any rate."

She squared her shoulders. "I do not want your pity."

"I have naught to give. In fact, I was asking for yours. Not only do I lack a nephew to enslave, but there isn't even a single cousin to fight over his place in my will or to secretly plot my murder. Terrible shame, isn't it?"

She didn't answer but studied him quizzically in the shifting gray light. Was he truly that self-absorbed, or was he merely attempting to put her at ease?

Not that it mattered to her either way. As soon as the carriage stopped in London, their acquaintance would come to an end. Besides, she was feeling too grateful for being off her feet to want to delve beneath his surface. She would hate to discover something to like about him.

Across from her, he lifted his sculpted brows as if commencing his own speculations. Then he proved this theory correct when next he said, "So, larceny, hmm? I must give you marks for originality on your choice of professions."

"I don't mean to make a career out of it. In fact, I doubt it will take me longer than a fortnight to reclaim what was stolen from me."

"Ah. A hidden motive," he said with intrigue. "You've piqued my interest. Well, don't leave me sitting here with bated breath. You must hold up your end of our bargain or I shall toss you out of the carriage this instant."

"My quarry is far from fascinating, I'm afraid. Simply my inheritance—a collection of various objects passed down on my mother's side for generations. Or, at least . . . it had been until recently."

At the painful reminder, she glanced out the window toward the broad-leaved woodland that lined the path. The echoing rumble of the carriage beneath the canopy of oak and ash compelled her to enunciate clearly, helping her to push past the knot gathering in her throat. "But a few days ago, I received a letter from my father, informing that he had decided to allow my stepmother to dispose of those items as she saw fit. Then he concluded his note—written with utter formality to *Miss Thorogood*—requesting I cease all further attempts at communication and reconciliation, and find a situation better suited to a woman of no family. And that is all there is to know."

Prue attempted to shrug as if the event were a mere trifling occurrence. But her shoulders moved stiffly. Even so, she was glad that she could speak the words without a single break in her voice. No futile tears. No lamentations. Just a cold recitation of the facts.

When the marquess didn't respond, she dared to look across the carriage.

His face was turned toward the window, shadows flickering over his profile. His jaw was razor-edged and so tight that a muscle flicked beneath the shaven surface.

She realized her error at once. "Apologies, my lord. I've been a complete bore and not the diverting conversationalist for which you bargained."

"On the contrary," he said smoothly. And yet, when he turned to meet her gaze, his eyes were hard, startling in their intensity as if lightning were trapped behind orbs of green glass. If dragons existed, those were the eyes they'd have. "I prefer plain speaking. One doesn't often encounter that in society."

"Then I hope you won't mind me saying that I do not believe you, for your expression is clearly displeased."

"Is it?" He blinked, his tawny brows arching.

"Indeed."

"How curiously transparent of me," he said thoughtfully. Then his lips curled in something just short of a smile and his features regained a semblance of their usual mask. "However, your skillful observation was just a shade off. The displeasure was not directed at you, but at the unjustified treatment toward you."

A swell of guilt churned in her empty stomach and she looked down at the roughened, knitted fingers in her lap. "Your judgment is far too kind. I fear I have neglected to confess the whole of my own crimes that served as the impetus for all the events to follow."

She had no desire to speak her sins aloud and to be judged for them. But there was something in the ensuing silence—something in her own conscience—that demanded her to continue. Or perhaps it was simply something in her that begged to be unburdened. Either way, she knew this stranger did not truly care what she said as long as she provided him a moment's entertainment. Afterward they would part and she would be forgotten soon enough, and she felt a sense of safety in that knowledge.

Even so, it was difficult to relay to Lord Savage that, on a warm spring evening little more than a year ago, she had been swept away in a moment of fancy. And worse, guilty of allowing the advances of the very gentleman that her dearest friend had once wanted to marry.

"I let him kiss me in the gardens at Sutherfield Terrace," she confessed with quiet regret. "My father bore witness to this and sent me away shortly thereafter. And rightfully so."

"Why do you say that?"

She looked up at him in confusion. "Because I deserved to be punished for betraying my friend. Betrayal to any degree is inexcusable."

"I, myself, have uttered those words on numerous occasions," he said on a rueful puff of amusement. "And yet, in this circumstance, I find that I cannot agree. Banishment was rather severe for a stolen kiss."

"But I *gave* it to him. I am not a simpleton. I knew what I was doing. And besides, would you not have banished one of your . . . companions for such an act?"

His irreverent mouth pursed slightly in consideration. "Something to that effect. However, there is a difference of intent. A woman well versed in the art of seduction cannot claim to be taken unawares by it, then expect forgiveness. Therefore, your only crime, as far as I can tell, was in being naive. And life, such as it is, tends to dole out punishments enough for that defect."

She shook her head. The daily rebukes she'd endured for the past year from Aunt Thorley, along with the ones doled out from her stepmother for the past twelve years, had taught her that every misstep, every wrinkle on her frock, every misspoken syllable, every possible *thing* . . . was her fault. And hers alone.

"Miss Thorogood," he said. "You must learn to forgive yourself. Otherwise, you'll never get very far stealing. A conscience can be a terrible burden."

Had he spoken with the flippant indifference she was already becoming accustomed to from him, she'd have disregarded his advice. But it was his sincerity, both in his tone and in the gaze that held hers, that gave her pause. And she—as the new Prue—knew he was right.

"You are very wise, my lord."

"Merely a scholar of human nature," he said, his arm stretching out along the upper curl of the bench, his fingertips absently combing through a gather of silver fringe. "So, tell me, Miss Thorogood, was that single kiss all that has cast the label of *ruined* upon your head?"

An instant rise of unwelcome heat climbed to her cheeks, even as an icy shiver sluiced through her. She wasn't going to answer him at all. And yet, the subject seemed like an enormous gray elephant, riding in the landau with them. There was simply no avoiding it.

"No," she said, swallowing down the sour taste of bile at the back of her throat. Then to ensure that would be an end to this particular topic, she crisply added, "But I shall never endure that dreadful ordeal again."

He paused for a moment, scrutinizing her from his relaxed pose in the opposite corner, a calculating gleam in his eyes. "You seem to have a solid plan in mind for your future. In a fortnight you'll have all you desire. That is, presuming you know where to find the objects of your inheritance."

"Unfortunately, I do not," she said. "All I know is that my stepmother has a penchant for gambling and for buying her so-called friends with expensive gifts. I'm certain that a few discreet inquiries will tell me all I need. Until then, I shall cling to the only thing left of my mother, which is the miniature my father sent with his last letter."

"Ah. I'd wondered if there was something."

"What do you mean?"

"You are braving the unknown to embark on this journey," he said. "That determination must come from somewhere. In fact, I'd hazard a guess your decision to leave for London, come hell or high water, likely had something to do with seeing that miniature."

Prue felt her jaw drop. "But how could you possibly have known?"

"Mothers have a powerful hold on us, even from beyond the grave." His shoulders lifted in a shrug of nonchalance, as if his peering into her soul was nothing more than a parlor trick. He looked down at the valise on the seat beside her. "May I see it?"

She might have asked him how he knew she'd carried it with her but that seemed like a pointless question. Of course, he knew she wouldn't have left something so important behind.

With care, she reached inside the worn leather and unwrapped the wax coated paper that protected the miniature from the elements. Then she handed it to him, and she was glad to see that he was gentle, as if sensing how precious it was to her.

"Beautiful," he said after studying the portrait, then returned it with the same care.

"She truly was. There has never been anyone like her. Her smile was pure sunlight and her laugh . . ." She shook her head, embarrassed as she covered the portrait once more. "Apologies, my lord. I do not mean to drone on and on."

"Nonsense. I bartered for your conversation without stipulations. Therefore, you must tuck that apology away and don't waste it on something so trivial. Save it for when we part company."

Her head tilted in perplexity. "And why do you imagine I'll have need of it when we part company?"

"Oh, I have an inkling that you'll unknowingly deliver

a deafening blow to my *amour propre*," he said with that almost-smile. "But before that occurrence, I should like you to continue. Tell me what her laugh was like."

ꝯ₰ꝯ₰

LEO RELAXED during the last hours of their journey. Easing back into the corner of the bench, he closed his eyes and listened intently to stories of Miss Thorogood's childhood in a cottage by a lake in Bedfordshire.

The distraction helped him rein in the inexplicable anger welling up inside him toward the father who'd carelessly abandoned her, the aunt and uncle who'd treated her like a servant, and especially to the nameless blackguard who was guilty of casting the label of *ruined* upon her.

Not usually one to concern himself with the plights of debutantes, he was surprised by the desire to see these people drawn and quartered. In his opinion, Miss Thorogood should be turning the *ton* on its ear, not bargaining with a scoundrel to get out of the rain.

When they stopped for the last change of horses before reaching London, he discreetly pressed a few coins into a maid's hand and asked her to assist his companion but to pretend it was a common courtesy from one woman to another. He knew Miss Thorogood would refuse any show of charity. And he also knew that, if not for their agreement, she would have been too reticent to reveal anything about herself.

Now that it was all said and done, however, he wasn't entirely certain if he was better off knowing more about her or worse.

But before he could unearth an acceptable answer, she found him waiting at a table in the inn's common room.

She was dressed in a fresh gown of faded jonquil muslin, her face scrubbed clean and pink. She'd repaired her hair, too, every pale rope tucked away in a clever twist and secured by unseen pins. He lifted his brows in appreciation and she almost smiled back at him. *Almost*, but not quite.

Yet while he was struck again by her loveliness, she only had eyes for the steaming currant scone and brown pot of tea set before him.

Never having to compete with food for attention before, he couldn't suppress a wry smirk. "Would you care for some, Miss Thorogood?"

"I couldn't accept." She shook her head firmly, even as she stared fixedly at the rich mahogany brew that he poured into the waiting cup.

He'd known that would be her answer. But that didn't mean he was above a little deception. She didn't need to know that he'd ordered it for her and her alone.

So he furthered temptation by stirring in a splash of milk and a nip of dark sugar. And she swallowed audibly.

Smiling to himself, he set down the spoon, pushed away from the table and stood. "Well, then, if you are ready to disembark then so am I."

"But aren't you going to"—she glanced with undisguised longing to the cup—"finish?"

"Actually, I'd better not. You see, I have a temperamental chef at home. Massey would be quite cross if I arrived without an appetite. But it does seem a shame for it to go to waste, doesn't it? By all means, you are welcome." He even handed her the cup. But when she did not drink and said nothing for a moment, he added, "Surely, you aren't one of those lemon purists that are always sniffing with pinched disdain over the small indulgence of milk and sugar?"

"No. That would be my aunt Thorley," she said quietly and blew briefly on the surface before taking a sip.

Then he witnessed something quite extraordinary. Something that stole his breath.

A smile.

Her ever-guarded expression unfolded like the petals of

a rare flower—a moonflower that bloomed when you least expected. Her lush lips spread in a slow upward curl as her lashes sank down to brush the crests of her cheeks, where a soft peachy glow blossomed.

Then she exhaled a pleased sigh.

The soft sound abruptly altered the beating of his pulse, making it slow and thick and hot. His throat was suddenly dry and in desperate need of—well, not tea exactly, but something else—something far stronger. "Had I known it was that good, I'd never have relinquished my cup."

"Forgive me. My aunt and uncle are rather disapproving of sugar. I'd forgotten how lovely it is."

When Miss Thorogood blushed, it only intensified his craving. He wanted to sink into those tantalizing lips, taste the flavors on her tongue, swallow down her sighs and pleasure her body until every inch was covered in the warm glow of her blush.

In that moment, Leo Ramsgate knew he had to have her. He needed no time to deliberate. No time to consider other women or any possible pitfalls. He just wanted her.

"Come home with me," he said, his voice rough and low. Hungry. "I'll help you steal back your inheritance. All of it. Just come home with me. And by the time our contract is concluded, you'll be set in a new life of your own making. You'll never need to care about the people who turned their backs on you ever again."

She stared at him, unblinking. And, damn it all, those stormy sea-blue eyes gave away none of her thoughts. He felt an uncharacteristic rise of impatience begin to simmer in his veins as he waited for her answer.

She set down the cup. Then, reaching out, she presented her closed fist and waited for him to extend his open hand. "For you."

"What's this?" he asked as her fingertips brushed his

palm in the barest tingling caress before she withdrew. His hand closed reflexively.

"The apology that you had me tuck away before."

Leo expelled a breath. "Still some pride left, I see."

"You've helped me to find it, if that counts for anything," she added kindly.

Bloody hell. He'd always hated unforeseen consequences. But it was for the best, he supposed, as he proffered his arm. She accepted and returned with him to the carriage.

His driver reached her friend's home on Upper Wimpole Street far sooner than Leo expected. And as he watched her peer through the window glass with trepidation and uncertainty, he found himself fighting the impulse to repeat his offer. Yet, for the sake of his own pride—a man of his age and renowned prowess should never have to beg, after all—he did not give in to temptation. He did, however, reach inside his pocket and withdraw a slim silver case, opening the clasp.

"Take my card." When her wary gaze alighted on the crisp black lettering, he added, "At least allow me the illusion that you might change your mind."

A soft smile brushed her lips and there was something almost tender in her gaze. "My dear Lord Savage, I can honestly say that I am glad to have made your acquaintance and I am grateful for your generosity. But I do not believe that either of us is good at pretending. You know that I will not call on you. And I know that you will have forgotten about me and decided on another companion by the time you reach your town house."

She said nothing more. In fact, she didn't even permit him to hand her down from the carriage. She slipped away without a backward glance.

And as his driver headed toward Mayfair, Leo tucked his card away, knowing she was right.

Chapter 3

A month later

Leave it to a yipping lapdog to spoil a perfectly good heist, Prue thought as she dashed out of Lady Entwistle's bedchamber.

Clearly, disguising herself as a maid wasn't such a stellar plan, after all.

Until a moment ago, she'd been ready to give herself a pat on the back the instant she'd found her great-grandmother's roman coin diadem in the viscountess's dressing chamber. But then the furry object on the floor—which she had mistaken for a discarded muff—opened its eyes and began to growl. Then the little snub-nosed beast sounded the alarm. *Yyyyyip-yipyipyipyipyip! Yyyip-yip!*

Now, Prue was running from a dour-faced housekeeper, scrambling down the narrow back stairs. Thankfully, the orchestra playing in the ballroom drowned out the shouts of *"Call the guard! Call the guard!"*

Reaching the doorway at the bottom, Prue dashed across the corridor to make her escape. But the kitchen was in midparty chaos, a line of tray-toting footmen waiting near the door. And she collided with the first one.

"Oh! Apologies," she said hurriedly. Then cringed as she saw him bobble his dish and stumble backward into the next in line—who, in turn, bumped the man behind him—and from there it was like dominoes of doom.

The blustering housekeeper charged into the room, shaking her fist. "Did you simpletons hear me? I said to call the—"

She didn't finish. Because an artfully garnished haddock slid off the platter and slapped her across the face. Before she could recover from shock, a mountainous molded gelatin bounced atop her grizzled coiffure, knocking her cap askew. Then a tureen of turtle soup teetered and everyone held their breath. The contents sloshed back and forth, rising higher and higher. But the footman held steady. He breathed a sigh of relief . . . until he took a backward step and slipped on aspic. The tray suddenly jerked. A curling tidal wave of steaming broth surged over the creamware lip, hovering for a fraction of a second . . . then splashed down over the housekeeper's disapproving head.

And Prue stole through the door, leaving pandemonium in her wake.

Darting down the mews between rows of walled gardens and carriage houses, she slipped around the corner. Only then did she stop to catch her breath. All she had to show for her efforts were perspiration, a hammering heart, a stitch in her side and two empty hands.

"Pekingese!" she grumbled with the contempt of an expletive. The word might as well be used as a curse considering how it seemed to encapsulate all her disappointments, frustrations and setbacks in one angry little ball of fur.

Larceny was turning out to be far more difficult than she imagined.

After all, this wasn't her first failure. No, indeed. That began with her accidental attendance at a funeral . . . for a fish named Algernon.

She'd thought stealing in through the back gate of Lady Mumphrey's garden, early in the morning before the servants went about their duties, was the perfect plan. Instead, she'd found a slightly senile older lady stooped over a small mound of freshly turned earth, gripping a bouquet of calla lilies in her gnarled hands. And when Lady Mumphrey saw her, she smiled, believing that she'd found a fellow mourner who'd been touched by the short life of the happy little goldfish with a fondness for eating shiny things . . . such as Prue's great-great-aunt's amethyst ring. Which was how he'd died, apparently.

In the end, after she'd fabricated a few words of remembrance, laid flowers over the grave and helped Lady Mumphrey inside, Prue hadn't had the heart—or the stomach—to dig up the grave.

"And that makes two failures now," she said on a heavy sigh, leaning against a tall wrought-iron fence. Her breath misted in the gilded lamplight as she looked up into the bleak darkness of the heavens. The night air was cool and damp, tinged with the charred fragrance of chimney smoke and autumn leaves.

Had she honestly thought it would only take a fortnight to retrieve her inheritance and reclaim her life?

It had been four weeks now. Four! And she still didn't have a single one of the twelve items that her stepmother had maliciously discarded.

Her time was running out. The longer she stayed in London, the worse the societal scorn would become. Not that she was worried about herself. After all, she'd made her choices and she would live with the consequences. But she hadn't counted on her friends suffering because of her, or even imagined that they would have forgiven her after what she'd done.

On the day Prue had arrived in London to confess her unforgivable actions to the friend she'd betrayed, she never anticipated forgiveness. A slap, perhaps. Immediate expulsion from the house, of course. Tears and condemnation, at the very least.

Instead, Elodie Parrish had welcomed her wholeheartedly. Ellie had not blamed her for being duped by George, because he had fooled her as well for most of her life. Apparently, her blinders had fallen away after she'd met Brandon Stredwick, Marquess of Hullworth, and had fallen head over heels in love with an honorable man.

Shortly following this unexpectedly merciful reception, Prue was also reunited with Winn and Jane, who along with Ellie, had stayed by her side from the beginning of this entire ordeal. And she even found a new friend in Brandon's younger sister, Meg.

During the past month, the five of them spent their time chatting, laughing and planning Ellie's wedding as if they'd never been separated.

Prue had not encountered much constancy in her life until she'd met Ellie, Jane and Winn in finishing school. And their friendship meant more to her than they would ever know.

Which was the precise reason she couldn't go on like this.

They were enduring societal scorn because of her. It had begun innocuously enough, just little snubs here and there. For Ellie it was in the scant number of callers she'd had during her *at home* hours. For Winn, it was a dressmaker who'd turned up her nose when they were shopping together. For Jane, it was a sudden cancellation from dinner guests when Prue was to attend. And for Meg, it was the whispering matrons in the park who speculated over her chances of marrying well if she kept such undesirable company.

In the grand scheme of things, these were small slights. But it would only worsen over time as it had done for her. Because of that, she knew she had to separate herself from them before their reputations suffered by association.

It was time to leave her friends and forge the new life she'd planned the day she walked out of Wiltshire.

Heavy-hearted, she pushed away from the fence and began her walk back to Upper Wimpole Street, where she had been staying with Ellie and her aunts, Maeve and Myrtle Parrish.

Beside her, sleek carriages passed by the dozen, filled with merrymakers in fancy dress and feathered hats, bound for balls, dinners and parties. It was a world she had only inhabited for the barest blink of an eye. Had she known her time as a debutante would have been so short, she might have chosen to enjoy herself more. Instead, she'd been constantly worried about doing or saying something to incur her father and stepmother's disapproval. And of course, she had done just that, time and time again without even trying.

Pausing on the edge of the street, she gave her head a rueful shake as she waited for a black curricle and a yellow hackney to streak by. Those memories were part of her old life, she reminded herself. Her new life didn't require enjoyment, only careful footing—much like the way she had to cross this busy intersection, a fine drizzle making the cobblestone slick underfoot.

All she needed was her inheritance and the deed to the cottage that had been in her mother's family. Prue would find fulfillment in that. She didn't need society looking down their noses at her, or the guilt of having friends who supported her and risked their own reputations in the process. In fact, she didn't need anyone.

The instant that thought swept through her mind it began to rain in earnest, slanting sideways on a sudden gust of wind. She cast a rueful glance skyward, recalling a similar atmospheric response when she'd first made the same declaration on the muddy road to London.

If she were of a superstitious nature, she might wonder if the heavens were privy to her thoughts and sought to intimidate her into recanting by means of drowning. But she was resolved to keep her current course.

Quickening her step, she leapt over the gutter and landed

on the pavement, the soles of her shoes sliding to a graceless stop.

And that was when she saw Lord Savage.

A shiver coasted over her skin. For a brief moment she
simply stared, watching as a footman in blue livery rushed
from the white stone steps of a grand house to his side with
an open umbrella.

But the marquess paid no attention to the servant . . .
because he was looking at Prue.

He'd just emerged from his own carriage, the lacquered
door still in his grasp. And his gaze was locked on hers.

She didn't know why her breath caught at this mere look
or why a sudden warmth rushed to her cheeks. They were
nothing to each other. Barely acquainted. And yet, with seconds ticking by and a long stretch of pavement between them,
she felt a peculiar sense of intimacy with this virtual stranger.

It was as if they were back inside the secluded confines
of his carriage, just the two of them. And as she listened
to the hollow patter on the carriage hood, her mind drifted
back to one of their meaningless conversations.

"I like the sound of rain, don't you?" she asked.

*A bank of low-lying clouds darkened the interior and the
only light seemed to come from his watchful green eyes as
his hand passed impatiently through his golden mane. "Not
particularly. But tell me why you do."*

*Only then did she notice the stiffness of his shoulders,
the tension in his jaw. And for reasons she couldn't explain,
she wanted to soothe those roughened edges. "The way it
hits the roof, tapping intermittently, reminds me of the Au-
gust fowling parties my parents would hold at our lake cottage when I was little. The softly echoing sound—like the
distant report of flintlocks firing toward a nye of flushed
pheasants—is a happy one for me."*

*"That explains it then. My own recollections of gunfire
at dawn aren't nearly as idyllic."*

A shadow crossed his gaze—a glimpse of something lurking beneath the surface—and she found herself inexplicably curious about this man.

She wanted him to continue but he fell silent again. So she prodded, "Care to share the memory with me?"

"Afraid not, my dear," he said with that rueful half grin returning, his facade of boredom back in its proper place. "I keep all those locked in the attic behind old trunks, cobwebs and three-legged chairs."

As they stood in the rain now, with the ruffled edge of her borrowed maid's cap plastered limply to her forehead, Prue found herself wondering about those memories again. Wondering about the man who kept them locked away. The man who'd said, "Come home with me," with such earnestness that it had seemed like something more than an indecent proposal.

Through the misty silver curtain, she saw him take a step toward her.

Something inside her jolted to life, startled like a bird flushed from tall grasses. Her heartbeat rushed faster. Tingles of gooseflesh skittered over her skin beneath the drag of her hands along the sleeves of her borrowed dress. She held her breath, arrested by anticipation as if they were in the middle of an unfinished conversation, each awaiting a response.

But before he took another step, a coquettish voice from within the carriage asked, "Savage, are you going to keep me waiting all night?"

At once, the peculiar spell was broken.

Of course, he would have a woman with him. He likely never went a day without female companionship. The only woman who could matter to a man like him was the next one. And she had known that all along. So it was foolish for her to linger.

Turning on her heel, she walked away without looking back.

She had a new plan to forge, after all. And it wouldn't have anything to do with Lord Savage or his offer.

❧❧❧

LATER THAT evening, Leo withdrew his pocket watch and turned the face toward the carriage lanterns. Then he closed it with a firm click, without having paid attention to the time.

"You never said a word about my new gown," Lady Sutton said from beside him as she primped her dark coiffure, then smoothed her gloved hands down over the plump swells rising above the bejeweled edge of her low-cut crimson bodice.

Knowing he would be charged for this gown in the near future, he allowed his gaze to linger in admiration. It didn't matter that she'd been so assured of his choice that she'd ordered the frock more than a month ago. She wasn't the first to have done so. She wouldn't be the last.

He smiled. "You look ravishing, my dear."

"And I hope to be ravished very soon," she tittered and laid her hand on his thigh.

When he merely arched his brow, she inched closer and pressed her lips to his, enveloping him in a cloying cloud of gardenia perfume and dusting powder. His hands went to her waist as he angled her, delving deeper, and felt the silken slide of her hand rise higher.

She murmured hungrily as she skillfully massaged his cock into semi-arousal. "Mmm . . . yes, indeed. I'd hoped this rumor was true, but I wasn't certain until now. Oh, Savage, you must take me—take *all* of me in this wicked, black velvet coach of yours. I know you want to. You cannot pretend with me."

Her statement had the opposite intended effect. Because

the instant she spoke, he heard the memory of another voice saying, *I do not believe that either of us is good at pretending.* And just like that, a vision splashed across his mind of a pair of stormy blue eyes beneath a wealth of buttermilk hair . . . and Miss Thorogood sitting primly across from him in this very carriage. The same eyes he'd seen earlier this evening, beneath the ruffled edge of a housemaid's cap.

Though he'd tried to put the near encounter out of his mind at dinner and cards, it had lingered, festered like a thorn beneath his skin all evening.

Had she actually chosen a life in service rather than consider his offer? Perhaps he hadn't made himself clear. He could have given her everything, not just her inheritance but gowns and jewels and—

Damn it all! Why was he wasting a single moment wondering about it? He didn't care a whit about the choices made by some random woman he'd known for a few hours of his time. Not a single whit.

But now his mood turned sour.

Stilling Lady Sutton's hand, he gently pried her away. "As enticing as your invitation is, I would prefer to build our anticipation."

"And I think anticipation is highly overrated." She licked her red lips, her breasts heaving as she draped herself over him and nibbled on his chin.

"Nevertheless, I'm certain we both desire far more than a quick swive in my carriage."

She huffed in annoyance and moved apart from him, arranging her skirts in jerky movements. "You've left me waiting so long, I'd almost think you were keeping company with another woman."

At this, he went still. "Have you heard rumor of another woman?"

"Well, no. However, it has been a month since you broke

with Lady Chastaine, after all," she said petulantly. "Surely, your renowned appetite requires a little sustenance."

Ah. So jealousy and vanity were the reasons behind her remark.

She had no idea the relief she'd given him.

For the past month, he'd been wondering if his carriage had been recognized as the one to deliver Miss Thorogood to her friend. And if he'd been linked to her, she would have been labeled as his mistress regardless of her refusal. Then, he would have had no choice but to renew his offer.

He'd waited four long weeks for any gossip to reach him. Though, apparently, he needn't have worried for her sake. Not that he'd spent much time doing so. In fact, he'd nearly put her out of his mind altogether . . . until this evening in the rain when he saw her looking at him as if . . . as if she hadn't quite put him out of her mind completely either.

He shifted, plagued by the damnable sense of restlessness that had been gnawing at him of late. "As I have mentioned to you before, the reason for my delay was due to matters of business I had to attend. Let us wait until the contracts are signed and then I will take you again and again until you're so exhausted from pleasure that you'll beg me to stop."

Mollified, she tittered and coyly said, "What if I'm the one who makes you beg?"

He did not answer, but lifted her hand to press a kiss to her wrist. Then he eased back against the squabs and stared at the vacant bench across from him.

Chapter 4

The following afternoon, Prue sat at the writing desk in the parlor at Upper Wimpole Street, a square of gilded light falling on her paltry list of houses to pilfer.

Through rumors and discreet inquiries, she'd managed to discover only three names thus far. The first two—Lady Mumphrey and her dead goldfish, Lady Entwistle and her yapping Pekingese—had been utter failures. Which left only one name on her list—Viscount Holladay.

She was contemplating whether or not to try the maid's disguise again when Maeve and Myrtle Parrish bustled into the colorful room, past the red caffoy settee.

Of Ellie's aunts, Maeve was the elder and more reserved of the two. She never had an iron-gray hair out of place or a wrinkle in her sedate attire. And even though she appeared rather austere on the outside, she had a dry wit that could startle a laugh out of anyone and a fiercely devoted heart to all she held dear.

Myrtle was bright and cheerful, her nature matching her dandelion-fluff hair and plump porcelain cheeks. She was quick to smile and tease, and always smelled like freshly baked biscuits. "We've just come from the sweets shop with a pilfered recipe for the best Turkish Delight in town. Now, our Elodie's wedding breakfast on Wednesday will truly be the talk of the *ton*."

For Ellie's sake, Prue hoped that only good things were said about her wedding day.

"Had we known you were here alone, we'd have taken you with us," Maeve said, steadily plucking her gloves from her fingertips, one after the other.

Prue shook her head to release them of any sense of obligation. "Lord Hullworth and his sister dropped by to take Ellie to Gunter's. His aunt has just arrived in town for the wedding and I didn't want to intrude on their outing."

"My dear, you could never be an intrusion. Why, Myrtle and I were just saying last night how lovely it would be if we all took a holiday together, while Elodie and Brandon are on their honeymoon."

Myrtle carelessly stripped off her gloves inside out and tossed them on the nearest wine table. "We've never toured the southern coast before or sampled the food. And just because our Elodie is getting married, doesn't mean our careers in recipe espionage need to be over."

"Recipe espionage?" Prue parroted.

"Stealing all the best recipes. Soups, puddings, pastries, confections—oh, the list is endless. *And* delicious," Myrtle added with a grin.

"We've been gathering these for years in preparation for Elodie's long-awaited wedding breakfast," Maeve added, and there was a small grin on her lips, too. "Not to boast, but we're quite good at it."

Myrtle nodded proudly. "I doubt many realize that there is an art to subterfuge."

"Indeed," her sister said. "The key to success is to believe that the recipe belongs in your possession. And that you are among a select few who can truly appreciate its worth. I've known for most of my life that Myrtle and I have been blessed with a superior palate. It would be selfish to squander such a gift by letting all the delicious foods we've tasted remain unsampled by our loved ones."

Prue pressed her lips together, hiding her own smile at

the unapologetic reasoning. "Have you never worried about being caught?"

Maeve exchanged a look with her sister. "In such circumstances, one must never appear to have all her wits about her. I prefer to deploy the subtle, vacant blinking method when I am nearly caught in the act."

"And I flit my hands like a clipped-wing bird in a dither and sigh with great distress as I mention my poor nerves," Myrtle added, demonstrating.

Recipe espionage? It might have been the oddest thing she'd ever heard. And yet, such experience might prove handy for her own endeavors. "Have you ever tried to, perhaps, disguise yourself as a maid?"

"That would never work," Maeve said with a purse of her lips. "Maids are overseen by housekeepers and housekeepers are, as a rule, far too sharp-witted. They excel at keeping things in order."

Myrtle sighed, nodding in agreement. "So true, sister. A lesson learned the hard way when we first set out on our quest and tried to insinuate ourselves into a house where a ball was underway. We'd had no invitation, you see," she said to Prue.

And Maeve interjected, "Indeed, and that particular housekeeper had been ready to call the guard."

"That's hardly fair," Prue said in commiseration. "What should it have mattered to her? That housekeeper was clearly overreacting and thwarting your attempts to reclaim something that was rightfully yours." When that earned puzzled expressions, she made a hasty amendment. "I mean . . . um . . . you must have been frustrated to have been so close, as well as terrified about being caught. Whatever did you do? Dash to the door?"

"Heavens, no," Maeve said. "That only makes one look guilty."

Myrtle cupped her hand beside her mouth and said in a

stage whisper, "Not to mention, running wreaks havoc on the corset laces."

"Thankfully, it was a masquerade ball and we merely claimed to have lost our way. And speaking of masquerades, I heard that Lady Lewis is planning to host one at the end of next month. She's doing everything she can to marry off her son." Maeve passed a meaningful glance to her sister.

Instantly picking up the baton, Myrtle came to Prue's side, eyes bright with enthusiasm. "There are sure to be dozens of eligible gentlemen there. Oh! And do I spy Lord Holladay's name on your list? Excellent choice, my dear. The viscount is quite the well-to-do bachelor."

Reflexively, Prue shielded the list, then folded it for good measure. "It isn't what you think."

The aunts prided themselves on knowing the comings and goings of every bachelor in England and Prue had a sinking suspicion that they were going to attempt a bit of matchmaking.

Yet, even though they remembered the names of every eligible male, they couldn't quite seem to recall that she was ruined and, therefore, unmarriageable.

"I do believe he's hosting a party this evening," Maeve added, sparking Prue's immediate interest. But then she clucked her tongue in dismay. "It is a shame that we did not receive an invitation."

"Indeed, sister! Oh, and he's having a gathering for the visiting Duke of Merleton, who is also a bachelor. A duke! Imagine the wedding breakfast we could host for a duke and duchess!" Myrtle, single-minded in her excitement, rushed over to snatch up her discarded gloves. "We'll need more recipes posthaste!"

"I do recall that Lady Cheshire serves a splendid trifle."

"The one with the lemon savoiardi. Absolutely divine! We should definitely pay a call on her first, sister."

After gathering up her own neatly folded gloves, Maeve

paused at the door. "Would you care to come along with us? We could always use a lookout when we slip into the cook's office to pilfer recipes."

Prue smiled but shook her head, her thoughts distracted. "I need to finish my list."

Myrtle popped her head back inside for an instant. "Don't forget to add the Duke of Merleton, dear."

A wistful smile brushed Prue's lips as the aunts left the parlor. She was impossibly fond of them, which made retrieving her inheritance without any further setbacks all the more necessary.

Therefore, this evening, she was going to invite herself to a party.

✦✦✦✦

ON THE bright side, Lord Holladay did not have a dog.

Brighter yet, he had her great-great-grandmother's miniature, among a cluster of others on display in the library. It was still just as lovely as she remembered—her grandmother's beatific face above a high-ruffed collar, the portrait surrounded by a frame of silver, studded with diamonds and pearls. A veritable treasure, and one that she intended to use for her own means of support. All she truly cared about keeping was the likeness itself.

On the not-so-bright side, however, she was no longer alone in the room.

She heard the creak of the floor behind her an instant before she heard a low voice say, "Good evening."

Prue snatched her hand away from the miniature and turned with a start to see a tall, lean, dark-haired gentleman dressed in tailored black evening clothes, the white of his cravat accentuated by his olive complexion. He entered the long room with his attention fixed on her, his steps as silent as the footpads of a cat.

Trying not to look guilty, she attempted a smile and greeted him in kind. "Good evening—" She hesitated mid-curtsy, unsure if this man was Viscount Holladay, the Duke of Merleton, or any number of others she'd never met during her short time as a debutante. However, since he seemed to possess an aura of authority, as if he owned every brick, board and book around him, she concluded that he must have been the viscount. "—my lord."

Behind a pair of wire-rimmed glasses, dark eyes studied her like a mathematician discovering a new number and deciding whether to put it between six and seven or simply to throw it onto the string at the end of infinity. "I see you are an admirer of Samuel Cooper."

Was that a name she should know? Someone in attendance, perhaps? Or no—she saw the way his gaze shifted to the wall of miniatures and realized he was referring to the artist.

"Mmm," she murmured with a scholarly nod as she turned to study them. Only then did she see that her grandmother's miniature was hanging at an odd angle. Her heart lurched to her throat. "I . . . um . . . particularly like the way he captures the essence of his subject."

He came to stand beside her and she did her best to hold still and not shift nervously. "Then perhaps that is the reason for Lord Holladay's collection."

She swallowed, realizing that he wasn't the viscount. After all, he wouldn't refer to himself in the third person. Which meant that this imposing man was very likely the duke. And anyone who belonged at this party would have referred to him as "Your Grace."

Oh, Pekingese, she cursed inwardly.

"Or perhaps," he continued, "it is because Cooper was a great favorite of King Charles II. There are even some who believe he was a spy for the crown and used to paint secret messages in these miniatures. They travel quite easily, you know. There are few who would ever suspect subterfuge if caught with such an object."

As he spoke, she started to feel like a spy. Her hands felt slick and clammy beneath her borrowed gloves. Perspiration collected along her hairline. Inside her mind, she was already waving a white flag, confessing everything. *It's me. I am guilty. Guilty of subterfuge, of slipping in through the terrace doors, of intending to steal that crooked portrait! I'm even guilty of borrowing Ellie's primrose gown and slippers without asking . . .*

Keeping her attention fixed on the miniatures, she felt his stare burning into her profile and she wondered how an innocent person would respond.

"Fascinating," she croaked and slowly took one step to the side. "Oh, but look at the time. I really must be getting back."

"*Back* to where, precisely?"

"Well, to the party, of course. My escort will wonder where I've gone."

"I'm afraid that isn't possible. If you had been escorted here, I would have seen you in the room."

"Not necessarily. You see, I have an unassuming presence. I'm quite easy to overlook," she said with the absolute certainty acquired from many balls where not a single gentleman had asked her to dance.

His dark brows lowered into a flat line. "I think not."

"No, truly. I've often escaped the notice of—"

"The reason I am certain," he interrupted, his voice low and direct with indisputable authority, "is because this is a *gentlemen's only* party. And therefore, I must insist that you explain what you are actually doing here."

Pekingese! Leave it to her to crash the one party with no women in attendance.

Remembering Maeve and Myrtle's advice, Prue blinked

as if she were lost and fluttered her hands as she sighed dramatically. "What an embarrassing blunder. I must be at the wrong soiree. No wonder I feel quite out of place. Like you, I wear spectacles, but I left them at home this evening. I'm sure you can understand."

But with her perfect vision, she could clearly see that he wasn't fooled for an instant.

He took a step toward her. "Who are you?"

"I—"

"She's with me," a familiar, deep voice drawled from the doorway. As Prue turned her head, she could have wept with relief at the sight of Lord Savage. He moved into the room with prowling grace to stand by her side. Then his hand rested at the small of her back—a gesture not missed by the sudden jolt of awareness beneath her skin or by the man who scrutinized them with suspicion. "No need to call the guard, Merleton."

"You brought a guest to *this* party?"

"Of course not. Clearly, my wayward companion is of a jealous nature and wanted to ensure that there were no women here, even though I already told her as much." He looked down at her with hard green eyes and tsked. "For shame, my dear, you should have accepted my offer"—he paused for a beat—"to take you to a rout later. But because you did not trust that I could uphold my end of the bargain, I will have to send you home without your prize."

The duke moved around them, stopping when he was between them and the door. "And what prize might that be?"

"Why, *me*, of course," Lord Savage said with an unabashed shrug as if the answer were staring them all in the face. Lifting his hand, he brushed the curve of her cheek with the backs of his fingers. "This one has been dogging my heels—hounding me like a drover—since the day we met. Isn't that right, my sweet?"

"You are hardly an innocent lamb," she said, her tone

disapproving as she recalled how long he'd stood and watched her in a comic struggle with that sheepdog.

He grinned, his gaze warming as it drifted to her lips, making them tingle in response. "A truer statement has never been uttered."

Prue felt her cheeks heat beneath his touch. Felt how close they stood. Felt her borrowed skirts press against his dark trousers. And she wondered if he intended to kiss her, right here in the library, in order to make their story plausible.

"I see that I was mistaken," the duke offered and cleared his throat. "This woman is clearly here for you, Savage. However, I suggest that she depart before the others catch wind of her unexpected interruption."

Prue drew his hand from her face, her breaths oddly quick and shallow. "I'll just hail a hackney, then."

"No," the marquess said, already guiding her through the doorway. "My driver will take you home."

He walked with deceptive ease. No one around them would ever imagine that the proffered arm beneath her fingertips was exuding so much tension that she feared for the stability of his seams.

As they approached the paneled foyer, a footman lifted his eyebrows in surprise but quickly jerked to attention and rushed to open the door.

They crossed the threshold without a word and stepped out into the cool night air, the lamplit street lined with waiting carriages.

"You see mine, there, do you not? Good," he said, his tone clipped and not at all the teasing drawl she'd come to know during their short time together. "Had I not come along when I did—" He expelled a slow breath, his jaw hard as granite. "It was a fool's errand to come here without knowing what you might encounter. Your evening, and any plans you might hold for your future, might have been altered drastically. I trust you understand that."

She nodded, duly chastened. "My conveyance likely would have had bars instead of black velvet. But, for curiosity's sake, just what type of party did I interrupt?"

He opened his mouth to reply. Then he must have decided against it, because he merely inclined his head, turned and walked back inside.

She didn't even have the chance to thank him for his intervention.

But she couldn't stop thinking about how close she'd come to ending up in irons and shackles . . . if not for him.

The thought stayed with her all that night and into the morning hours as she paced sleeplessly in her bedchamber. In the end, she had concluded that her steadfast friends would have remained by her side through whatever new calamity she would have brought into their lives.

Her presence already threatened to rob them of their social standing and put a black smudge on their reputations. It was only a matter of time before the smudge turned into an indelible stain.

Unless . . . she cut ties with them.

Unless . . . she made a decision that not even they could support.

Prue stopped short, shocked by her own thoughts and how quickly they turned back to Lord Savage and his scandalous offer.

Come home with me. I'll help you steal back your inheritance. All of it. Just come home with me. And by the time our contract is concluded, you'll be set in a new life of your own making . . .

Standing there, her stockinged feet dug into the thick-woven pile of the rug. There were so many reasons she shouldn't even consider such a proposal, not the least of which was that it had doubtlessly expired. And yet, there was something in the way he'd spoken to her last evening that suggested he might still—

A knock fell on the door, interrupting her thoughts.

Ellie's dark head and beaming face appeared, her eyes bright and shining as if she'd swallowed the sun. Floating into the room in a gossamer night rail, she spun in a circle as she clutched a paper parcel to her bosom.

"Guess who's getting married today? Oh, I'm so happy, Prue, I could positively burst!" Abruptly, she spun to a halt and blinked warily. "You don't think it's possible that a person could actually explode from happiness, do you? Because that would be a dreadful way to die."

"I think you'll manage to survive it," Prue said with fondness. "Lord Hullworth would surely stitch you back together."

Ellie smiled again and sighed. "He would, wouldn't he? Oh, and I nearly forgot. This came for you just now."

She handed over the parcel and Prue took it hesitantly. "Are you certain it's for me?"

"That's what the messenger told Mr. Rivers at the door. There was no name given, so that part is a mystery. Until you open it, that is. Well, go on now. Don't leave me in suspense."

Inside the paper wrapping was an ebony box. She gasped when she lifted the lid to find the miniature of her great-great-grandmother on a bed of black velvet.

Beneath it was a card that read:

The artist who painted this was a lucky man, indeed. Clearly, beauty runs in this woman's family.

"No signature," Ellie said, peering over her shoulder. "But you're blushing, so I gather you know who sent it."

Prue dropped the card and hid her cheeks behind her palms. "Don't be ridiculous. I am not blushing. It's warm in here with the fire"—she glanced over to the cold ashes in the hearth—"blazing."

Her friend laughed. "Very well then. Keep your secrets . . . for now. But by the time I return from my honeymoon, I am determined to see you married to a man who makes you blush and keeps you blissfully happy."

"Ellie, you know that I will never—"

"Uh uh uh," she interrupted, her index finger oscillating back and forth as she glided to the door. "No arguing with the bride on her wedding day. Now, come to my chamber and help me with my hair. You always were cleverer than I with braids and twists and combs."

Prue nodded. "I'll be right there."

When the door closed, she looked down at the miniature once more, Ellie's words ringing in her head. But Prue no longer wanted to marry and become some man's wife. At one time she did, perhaps. However, after her excruciating—though, thankfully brief—introduction into what was expected of a wife, she knew it was not for her.

What she wanted was to be her own woman. In order to do that, she needed her inheritance. And, thus far, the closest she'd come to reclaiming any of it was with the assistance of Lord Savage.

It was apparent that she had only one real option. In order to take possession of her own life, she would have to leave this one behind.

$\sim\!\!\sim\!\!\sim\!\!\sim$

THE FOLLOWING evening, Prudence Thorogood drew the hood of her tattered mantle over her head and reached for the lion's head door knocker. Taking in a deep breath, she rapped soundly.

There was no turning back. Not for her.

Chapter 5

Leo sat in his dining room amidst walls painted in the deepest greens and shadowy grays of a woodland at night. The bank of mullioned windows behind him and black marble hearth along the far wall blended seamlessly into the mural that was commissioned by one of his former mistresses.

Redecorating his house was something they all did. He never minded. After all, if they were occupied with changing his rooms, then they wouldn't turn their *fixing* intentions on him.

But this evening, he found himself thinking that there was something wrong with the table. It stood out like a sore thumb. Down the long expanse of mahogany, the light from three silver candelabras gleamed off the polished surface, accentuating the grain and every vacancy. Perhaps it was too large for this room. Or perhaps a darker wood . . .

"Are we still expecting Lady Sutton this evening, my lord?" his head butler asked in a droll monotone, interrupting Leo's musings. Standing at the buffet, he decanted a bottle of wine with a steady hand and continued without pause. "The carmine red rose petals have been plucked and await your plans."

"I've no plans for this evening, Grimsby."

"Then tomorrow. I shall ensure the usual arrangements are in place—a *fresh* carpet of rose petals leading up the stairs to your chamber, the selection of bath oils by the copper tub. Oh, and the peacock feathers were just delivered today," he added with the unflinching efficiency born of decades in service to a libidinous rake.

And Leo wondered when his dalliances had become merely a matter of scheduling.

His affairs began with a pursuit of pleasure, flirtations with a variety of women who appealed to his extensive appetite. After that, he would give a name to Jones, his loyal valet—who, in turn, would keep an ear tuned to the servant rumor mill—and to his personal investigator, Mr. Devaney—whose inquiries were more in-depth. Then came the formal invitation to become his mistress, followed by the meeting with his solicitor, signing the contract, and . . .

Leo expelled a lengthy exhale, suddenly enervated by the entire process.

"No. Not tomorrow either," he said in response to Grimsby's query.

A beat of silence followed. "I beg your pardon, my lord. I was unaware of a prior engagement. Shall I inform the kitchen that you'll be dining elsewhere?"

"That won't be necessary."

Grimsby brought the decanter to his side, his long jowly face resembling a tallow candle that had been left too close to the fire. A complete want of surprise was permanently etched into his expression. "Again, I beg your pardon. I had assumed, with the visit from your solicitor this afternoon, that the contract had been prepared."

"Indeed, it has been."

"Is Lady Sutton out of town, then? That would certainly explain the reason you haven't entertained a guest in more than a month."

"This is sounding like a bloody inquest." He flicked a glance to his butler. Grimsby made it seem as though any diversion from his usual activities was cause for alarm. Leo suppressed the desire to tell the man that he did have other interests aside from fornication.

Lifting the glass, he took a fortifying swallow and felt the dry pucker of wine on his tongue. "If you must know, the delay is my own and for no particular reason. I might be considering taking a holiday. Perhaps another grand tour."

Without a modicum of surprise at either the uncharacteristic terseness or the announcement, Grimsby merely inclined his head. "I shall have the portmanteau brought down from the attic."

"Fine. That will be—"

The abrupt sound of the door knocker interrupted him and his attention swerved to the ormolu clock on the mantel. He wasn't expecting anyone at this hour. Then again, perhaps Millie Sutton wasn't playing by the rules and thought to skirt around the contract. After all, she had tried to bargain for a longer duration, wanting an unheard-of six months.

"If it is Lady Sutton, inform her that I've gone out."

As Grimsby disappeared to tend the door, Leo shifted in his chair, plagued again by that peculiar restless irritation. It clung to him like tree sap. Why couldn't he rid himself of this?

Gripping the decanter, he poured himself another glass. But he wished the vintage had a more numbing effect on his senses. In fact, the more he looked down the length of the empty table, the more restless he felt and the more he realized that he wasn't much in the mood for dinner at all.

Tossing down his napkin, Leo pushed back his chair. He would rather spend the rest of the night at Sterling's, losing a fortune at the hazard tables.

Grimsby reappeared and Leo was half standing when the butler announced, "A Miss Thorogood to see you, my lord."

A jolt rifled through him, rooting him to the chair, strong enough to shake his knees. "Did you say 'Miss Thorogood'?"

"Indeed. Shall I tell her that you are out for the evening?"

"No," he said quickly. "Show her in."

"To the dining room, my lord? Or would you prefer the drawing—"

"Here." He reached for his glass. Then set it down again, noting that his pulse was racing, rushing in his ears. Glancing down to his wine with suspicion, he asked, "Was that a fresh bottle you opened?"

"As always," Grimsby said with a sniff of affront. "Would you prefer another vintage from the cellar?"

"No."

"Then perhaps a place setting for your guest?"

He pushed the glass away. "Just show her in. I'll inform you if I require anything further."

When the butler left, Leo stood and moved to the carved mahogany sideboard. Inspecting the cork and the bottle, he sniffed and held them up to the light. Then he did the same to the decanter. Hmm . . . He didn't detect acrid bitterness, but that didn't necessarily mean someone hadn't tampered with it. He'd learned that lesson the hard way years ago.

After that, he'd destroyed every bottle in the cellars of all his houses—including a dozen of the 1787 Lafite, which had been particularly divine and his favorite Bordeaux— and vowed to never again fall for the cunning manipulations of a woman who pretended to be in love with him.

But there was no reason for anyone to poison him now. Well . . . unless it was Grimsby because Leo had been such an arse this evening.

Distracted, he looked to the vacant doorway. Where the bloody hell was Grimsby, anyway? Surely, it shouldn't take this long to escort a guest to the dining room.

Not unless . . . the guest in question was someone who tended to suddenly appear out of the blue and disappear just as quickly.

Bloody hell! She was bolting, he just knew it.

Leo strode through the doorway, determination in every long stride. He wasn't about to let her slip through his fingers this time.

He just reached the foyer when he saw the willowy figure with her back to him, and her hand on the door latch. "Leaving so soon, Miss Thorogood? Is that any way to treat an old friend?"

She went still and, without turning around, said, "I did not mean to intrude. Please, return to your company and pretend I was never here."

"You're not intruding." As he stepped closer, he watched as she straightened her proud shoulders and regally lowered the hood of her cloak. "Come. I was just about to have dinner. There's plenty enough for . . ." He paused, a grin tugging at his lips. "Why are you covered in rose petals? Not that I mind, of course. It's just that my guests normally don't arrive with such fanfare."

Her brow furrowed as a pair of delicate hands in fingerless mitts lifted to her pale coiffure. Discovering the wayward petals, she blushed and looked askance as she collected them, one after the other. "Coming here was a mistake. I'm sure you'd prefer to continue . . . whatever it was that you were doing when I arrived."

Her mortified glance toward the stairs and the deepening color of her blush told him precisely what she was thinking. As if his name had become synonymous with bedsport and debauchery.

His grin fell flat. First Grimsby and now her?

"Grant me one moment of your time, if you please," he said curtly.

Without giving her time to argue, he took the petals from her and gave them to his butler who'd been standing stoically off to the side. Then, still in possession of her hand, he began walking toward the far end of the hall at a clipped stride, keeping her beside him.

"I can assure you that I have no desire to bear witness," she proclaimed, but all the while keeping pace beside him. So there must have been some curiosity on her part.

"If what you see disturbs you in any way, you are free to leave."

Entering the dining room, he stopped just inside the door.

"As you can clearly see, I have no guest with me this evening." He released his hold as her eyes widened in blatant astonishment at the single place setting at the head of the table. "Contrary to your apparent belief, I do take time away from fu—*sexual congress*," he amended for her sake, "to eat. At least, on occasion."

"Then your companion is . . . out for the evening?"

"Something to that effect," he said dryly.

Standing beside her, his empty hand tingled uncomfortably as if in want of occupation. So he moved toward the sideboard to flex his fingers around a fresh glass of wine.

"But now that you're here, join me," he said. "I should like to learn what you've been up to of late. That is, other than taking a position as a maid, then burglarizing houses on your off-days."

Wearing a chagrined expression, she took tentative steps deeper into the room, her skirts rustling softly. "The service dress was borrowed in a failed plot to steal back my great-grandmother's diadem. The same with the evening gown from the other night. In fact, these clothes are borrowed as well, aside from my cloak."

Ah. So then, she hadn't chosen a life in service over becoming his mistress, after all?

A hard band of tension along his shoulders seemed to relax at the news. Strange, but he hadn't even realized that thought was gnawing at him until now.

"I must say, I'd hoped to have seen the last of this garment," he said with a casual gesture to the threadbare wool. "Haven't you put the poor old thing through enough? I believe it's time to shoot it, then bury it beneath the rose-bushes."

She graced him with one of her rare smiles, leavening his mood instantly.

"The truth of the matter is, I didn't expect for you to see it, *or* me, again," she admitted. "But I needed to thank you for your intervention on my behalf and, also, for the miniature. I wasn't certain I would see it again either."

Was that the only reason she'd come? His lighter mood suddenly deflated, his pulse slowing noticeably with disappointment. "I couldn't allow you to go through so much trouble without a reward for your efforts. Now, could I?"

"Well, it was very kind of you. In fact, it has been the only item reclaimed thus far. Regrettably, I have discovered that larceny is far more difficult than I first imagined." She drew in a deep breath and glanced down to the knitted fingers. "Which brings me to the second reason for my untimely visit."

A *second* reason? The peculiar hammering of his pulse returned at once.

As he took a swallow from his glass, Leo was forced to acknowledge that there had likely been nothing wrong with the wine at all. Apparently, the reaction was entirely the fault of Miss Thorogood.

Bemused, he took out a fresh glass from the lower cabinet and poured one for her, waiting for her to continue. As the seconds ticked by and still no utterance erupted from his unplanned visitor, he went to her. "Bad as all that, is it? Here. A little liquid courage."

She surprised him by accepting with eagerness. Gripping the goblet by the stem, she lifted it to her lips and gulped down the contents like a desert nomad.

When she shivered, her face pinched in distaste, he inquired mildly, "Do you not find the Bordeaux to your liking? Alas, it is no 1787 Lafite, but *needs must*, as they say."

"It isn't that. My apologies. I normally do not abandon all decorum. It's just that I . . ." She didn't finish. Pressing her fingertips to her temple, she closed her eyes briefly. "The wine seems to be going right to my head."

"Would you like to sit, then?"

She shook her head and squared her shoulders. "I feel I must stand for this."

"We all must stand for something, I suppose. It might as well be this. Whatever *this* is."

Looking askance at him, she said, "You're right. I should simply say the words and be done with them." Then she nodded succinctly. "Very well. Here it is—I should like to be considered for your list."

"List?"

"The list of candidates for your . . . paramour," she finished on a dry whisper as if sin-tallying angels were eavesdropping nearby. "I know it has been over a month since you made your offer. Whether it was out of pity or charity, I know not. However, I am wondering if, perhaps, you might still . . . want me."

A sudden, heady surge of blood rushed in his ears. Did he still want her? Did horses have four legs and a tail?

"What happened to your pride?"

"A shred of it remains," she said ruefully as she stared down into the glass, the light of the candelabra gilding the tips of her lowered lashes. "However, I've discovered that there are some things worth the sacrifice."

"Even enough to engage in—I believe you called it—the *dreadful ordeal* you've foresworn never to repeat?"

She shifted, the soles of her shoes rasping restively against the hardwood floor. "That actually brings me to my proposal. What say you to a continuation of our previous bargain—my conversation in exchange for your assistance? It would be satisfying for both of us, I should think."

"Let me see if I have this correct. You want to be my

mistress in name only?" He nearly laughed until he saw her nod eagerly. Apparently, she was serious. "No. As much as I enjoy your conversation, I desire your companionship in *all* ways. And that is still my offer. My only offer."

"I'd thought as much." She issued a resolved exhale, looking very much like a martyr tied to a pyre and staring at the torchbearer. "Very well, then. I accept. However, if all goes to plan, we should only have to suffer through it for a fortnight."

"Oh, how you flatter me, child." He returned to the sideboard to pour his wounded ego a drink.

"I intended no insult. In fact, given your reputation, I'm certain you are adept at . . . what it is that you . . . do." She swallowed audibly. "I speak only of my own failings and inadequacies."

Over the rim of his glass, he glimpsed that innocence he'd seen before, lurking beneath the surface of her carefully reserved countenance. It was abruptly clear to him that her prior experiences had not left her with a favorable outlook on future intimacies. And while he normally remained far afield from anything that reeked of naivete, he found himself oddly drawn to hers.

In fact, it only made him determined to amend her opinion.

And yet, he sensed that it would not be a simple matter of verbal reassurance. No, indeed. He would need to bring her own desires to the surface, much like the way he'd offered her a cup of tea that day in the coaching inn. She never would have taken a sip otherwise.

"I shouldn't be concerned in that regard," he said in an easy drawl as he came back to her. "Besides, I've always found pleasure to be rather basic. One simply does what feels natural in the moment, like drawing in a breath and letting it go. One doesn't think about it. Just as you're not thinking about your hand holding this goblet, with your fingers curled around the bowl so that it doesn't slip. And when

I reach out to take possession of it"—he did just that—"your hand reflexively releases. Your mind instinctively knows, perhaps even trusts, that I won't let it fall."

He set the glass on the table beside them. Then slowly, carefully, he lifted his hand and reached for the clasp of her cloak. She held perfectly still, brave but watchful, her unflinching gaze searching curiously.

He had no wish to startle her and make her run for the hills. So he moved slowly, taking in every nuance of the moment. His fingertip barely grazed the tempting V-shaped hollow at the base of her throat before the fastening came undone with a delicate flick. And even though the touch only lasted a mere fraction of a second, he saw her skin react in a sudden rise of gooseflesh. Watched as her lips parted, and her breasts rose and fell on shallow, ragged breaths.

Damn, but she was sensitive. So receptive. She made it positively irresistible to be the man who awakened her appetite.

"You're wrong, you know," she said, her voice hoarse. "I *am* the sort who thinks about breathing. At least, some of the time."

"Like now?" he asked from behind her.

"Mmmhmm . . ." she murmured as he peeled the cloak from her shoulders.

The neckline of her dress was modest, prim even. But exposing those scant few inches of tantalizingly creamy skin made his mouth water.

He felt the warmth rising from her body, a subtle fragrance teasing his nostrils. The exact same scent that she'd left behind in his carriage that day. He'd never smelled anything so pure and sweet, like a blend of autumn rain and vanilla orchids. He wanted to bottle it. Bathe in it. Pour it over his bed linens and climb inside . . .

For the moment, however, he settled for a slow inhale, drawing it deeper into his lungs.

"And I never know what to do with my hands," she added nervously.

He draped the tired garment over the back of a chair and faced her. "Then simply give them to me."

Her brow furrowed as she looked skeptically at his waiting palms. "What do you intend to do with them?"

"Merely take you—"

"Here?" She balked. "Now?"

"—to the study," he concluded with a slow grin. "However, if you'd prefer to put this table to better use . . . No? Well then, perhaps we shall discuss the details of our contract in more comfortable environs."

"*Our* contract? Does that mean you're adding my name to your list?"

"There is no list."

"How very politic of you," she said with a charmingly disenchanted roll of her eyes as he guided her out of the dining room. "But you needn't spare my feelings. I know perfectly well that I'm not the first woman to cross your threshold and I certainly won't be the last." Walking by his side down the corridor, she glanced at the chiming longcase clock. "Nevertheless, I cannot linger too long. My friends do not know where I am and I shouldn't wish them to worry."

"Are they shredding the carpet underfoot with all their pacing as we speak?"

"No," she said with a small laugh, the sound raspy like the pages of a new book that needed a thorough reading. "Actually, after the grand production of the wedding breakfast, then bidding Ellie and Lord Hullworth bon voyage on their honeymoon, they will all likely sleep for days." She looked up at him. "Are you acquainted with Lord Hullworth?"

"Old school chums, as a matter of fact. I seem to recall having received an invitation from him recently. Must have been the wedding you mentioned. However, I left instructions with Grimsby long ago to set fire to anything that reeks of nuptial bliss the instant it crosses the threshold."

He intended her to laugh again, because he liked the sound of it. But she did not. Instead, she stared stoically straight ahead as they approached the study. "I've come to learn that there is little incentive for a man—at least those of a certain nature—to commit to one woman when he can always replace her with another."

"The same truth applies to women. Which is why I insist on fidelity for our brief interval." Seeing her dubious glance, he added, "I adhere to that rule as well. Nevertheless, affections can be changeable and if either party finds companionship elsewhere, then the contract will be terminated."

She frowned. "So matter-of-fact. You make the prospect of selling one's soul as unfeeling as haggling over the price of turnips at market."

"Is such a thing done? I thought turnips were simply thrown at bystanders just to be rid of them."

When they entered the study, he led her to the sofa that sat cozily in front of a blazing fire in the hearth. Good old Grimsby, anticipating this very moment. Was there anything more relaxing—or persuasive, for that matter—than an early autumn evening by a fire?

He crossed the room to a tall secretaire of rosewood, inlaid with bronze and mother-of-pearl marquetry. Slipping the key from his waistcoat pocket, he unlocked the hinged door and lowered it. Then he poured two generous snifters of apricot brandy. Just enough to put her at ease and to keep her gaze from shifting to the door like a doe caught in the clearing.

"Here, my dear. You'll like this one. Much sweeter on the palate," he said, swirling the amber liquid so that it caught the light as he handed it to her. But, seeing her mitts, he hesitated. "No. This won't do at all."

For the moment, he set their glasses on the mantel. Then

he returned to her and sat on the cushion beside her. "The only way to truly appreciate the flavor of brandy is to warm it with the heat of your hands."

As he spoke, he reached over and deftly unfastened the twin pearl buttons on the side of her wrist. Knowing how wary she tended to be, he worked with efficient quickness. Nothing untoward.

Even so, she held her breath as if she thought her dress would be the next to go. But he was not deterred. He wanted her to become comfortable with him in all ways. And if that meant taking these small steps, so be it.

"Breathe, Miss Thorogood," he said, not unkindly as he slipped the second mitt free with a gentle tug, then released her. "Or I shall have to resort to doing something truly shocking in order to fill your lungs."

She dutifully obeyed, her lashes lifting from her blushing cheeks. "I suppose it would be rather unnecessary to say that I am nervous."

"The two of us are only here to talk. Nothing more," he assured her as he stood and moved to the mantel. "We are learning more about each other, not plotting war strategies."

"You might want to tell that to my heart. It's racing as if I'm heading into battle."

He smiled without giving an answer. When he returned her glass, she immediately took a hearty swallow. "Careful now. You'll want to go slowly with that."

Her eyes watered. Splaying a hand against her throat, she croaked, "It burns."

"Only at first. It's best to take in the aroma. Warm the liquor inside your mouth first. Coax out the flavors. Let them caress your tongue," he said, lowering his frame onto the cushion beside her. As he rested his arm along the curved back, she lifted the glass for a tentative sniff.

"It smells a bit smoky like charred sugar, and there is the barest hint of apricot," she said with a surprised lift of her brows. Then she took another sip. This time she held the liquor in her mouth behind her pursed lips before she swallowed. Her eyes cleared, brightening. She hummed with pleasure, the throaty sound sending a spear of heat straight through him. "Oh, that's lovely. Much sweeter now. I feel warmed by it as if it were a liquid ray of candlelight."

Taking another sip, she eased back against the cushions. His fingertips were within easy reach of the fine wisps of downy hair against her nape, but he resisted the temptation to touch, to explore, to curl his hand around her nape, draw her close and taste the glow of delicious fire inside her mouth.

"How long do these affairs"—she paused to take another long pull as if she imagined the brandy was akin to sand in an hourglass and she might expedite matters if she consumed it with utmost haste—"usually last?"

"Four months is usually sufficient to satisfy both parties."

"Four months?"

"Although, if you would prefer a longer duration, I'm certain we could—"

Before he could finish his unprecedented offer, Miss Thorogood was adamantly shaking her head. "I won't need that long. With your assistance, we should be able to steal back my inheritance in the matter of a fortnight. Perhaps even sooner."

He felt the flesh over the bridge of his nose crease. Typically, women were begging him for *more* time, not less. "It will take at least a month for the modiste to fashion the majority of your gowns. No, my dear. I'm afraid you'll have to endure my company for four months, no less."

"I'm certain you'll tire of me before then."

Ah. He understood at once. "Is this where I shower you with compliments and assure you of my regard?"

"I wouldn't believe you if you did," she said, the words sharp, her chin notching higher as if daring him to refute her claim. When he didn't, her gaze shifted to the fire, the flames reflecting in her eyes. "I'm just eager to start over. You likely don't remember what you said to me in the coaching inn a month ago. But ever since, your words have been spinning inside my mind like scattered leaves caught in a whirlwind. *A new life of my own making.* You made it seem so simple, so liberating. I want that life. I want it more than I have ever wanted anything before."

She spoke with such yearning that he actually felt the ache spur a need inside him to find a solution for her. That was one of the reasons he'd been compelled to make his uncharacteristically impulsive invitation.

But she was wrong about one thing. He remembered everything about that day. "Then four months it is."

She looked askance at him. "You didn't answer my other question. What happens when you tire of me? Will I be released from the contract?"

He expelled a patient breath. "Would it suit you if I were to add a codicil that allows *tedium* to be a factor of our early separation?"

After a moment, she nodded.

"Splendid. Now, time for a bit more information," he said. "How many lovers do you currently have? Oh, come now. No need to avert your face in embarrassment. Our contract—if we should come to amenable terms, that is—will call for far more intimate acts than mere conversations."

She took a hearty swallow before she quietly confessed, "I have had but one."

"Still the innocent," he said with a tsk.

She stiffened, her posture rigid, her hiked chin encased in steel. "Not so naive as to be ignorant of mockery when it is aimed at me."

"My dear, pray, sheath the icy daggers in your gaze. I meant no insult. It has only been my experience that some women profess to a much smaller number than the truth later reveals. It matters not."

She scrutinized him over the rim of her glass for a moment. "I imagine that such an experience would diminish one's ability to trust."

"Oh, it's far worse than that. I'm positively jaded to the core."

"I am, too," she said with a sigh, easing back against a gold fringed pillow, unconsciously teasing his knuckles with a brush of fine, silky tendrils. Tilting her wrist to take another sip, she blinked slowly, perplexedly, at the empty contents of her glass. "That's odd. I could have sworn there was more."

He hid his amusement and remedied her conundrum by exchanging her snifter for his own. This earned him a sleepy smile and a polite "Thank you."

Recalling their initial meeting and the broken valise, he inclined his head. "Delighted to be of service."

She giggled then quickly slapped a hand over her mouth. Her eyes went wide with surprise as if she had no idea how that pealing sound erupted from her own body. Then it happened again, and finished with the most delicate little snort he'd ever heard.

Blushing profusely, she tried to hide her face in her free hand.

A grin toyed with his lips as he drew her hand down. "Are you foxed, Miss Thorogood?"

"I'm not entirely certain. I've never imbibed brandy before. How much must one drink before one is actually in her cups?"

"Well, in your case, I'd say half a glass. Here now, I'm cutting you off." Dutifully, she handed him the snifter. "Let us finish our discussion while you still have some sense about you."

"I'm completely sensible." Her offended sniff was less

effective when she slurred the last word. But he wasn't about to tell her.

He also wasn't going to point out that she hadn't bothered to slip her hand free of his. That she was allowing the casual caress of her soft skin, across the tender protrusions of her knuckles, along the length of her slender fingers and over the rounded ridge of her neatly trimmed nails.

He was glad that the chapped, labor-roughened flesh he'd witnessed when they'd first met had become pale and supple. Not for his own sake, but for hers. She was too delicate a creature for pot scrubbing, he mused, soothing the pad of his thumb over the two tiny calluses that remained at the base of her fingers. Before they parted ways, he would ensure that she was pampered from head to toe, her hands as silken as her voice.

"Good then. We'll continue," he said. "Am I correct in assuming you have no maid of your own? No need to fret. I'd presumed as much. Therefore, I will employ one for you. You'll also have an open account at whatever dress shop you favor. Just make certain your modiste is capable of supplying the quantity of clothing needed in a short amount of time. I cannot have you gadding about on my arm in borrowed dresses or your shabby cloak, after all. Of course, you'll have pin money. And I'll ensure you have an array of combs for your hair, jewels for your lovely throat, and—"

"I don't want any of that," she interrupted, slipping her hand free and covering it with the other. "I have no need of a maid. I've managed quite well without one this past year. I don't want jewels or money. I have clothes of my own. Lovely gowns and dresses. I did try to reclaim them, but the servants at my father's house had been told not to bid me entrance for any reason. Though perhaps, with your assistance . . ."

She looked up at him with so much undisguised hope in her eyes that it caused a sharp twinge in his chest, as if his tailor had just stuck him with a needle . . . and drove it deep beneath his rib cage. All he could think about was how wrongly she'd been treated and abused. And he was furious as he imagined her on her father's doorstep, being turned away like a beggar. His own father had been guilty of many crimes, but never that.

Leo managed to keep his expression bland, and he tossed back the last of the brandy in one scalding swallow. "I'm afraid that won't do. You'll need to be dressed in the height of fashion on my arm, not wearing last Season's togs."

"Oh," she said, the single syllable uttered with such despair that it was almost comical.

"Miss Thorogood, you're the only woman I've ever known to be disappointed by the prospect of being spoiled."

"I did not come here for your money or for frivolous pampering. I came here for you." Her expression was so earnest that his breath stalled for an instant. "I came here because I need something only you can give. I need your help in reclaiming my inheritance. It's the only way I'll ever find contentment in this life. I need only this from you and, in exchange, I will give you what you ask of me."

He studied her in the flickering firelight as he exhaled slowly. His deep-seated cynicism warned him not to be taken in by those guileless eyes. People often professed to desiring nothing more than a few trifling things at first, but their true motive eventually showed itself.

Miss Thorogood's pretty speech didn't persuade him to believe otherwise. Not in the least.

Chapter 6

Somewhere in the distance, Prue heard the rap of a door knocker. The sharp clap of footfalls followed. Gradually, the low, indistinct murmurings of a conversation reached her, but she paid no attention.

Most likely, it was only a caller speaking to Mr. Rivers, the aunts' butler on Upper Wimpole Street. And since no one ever called for her, she went back to sleep.

Besides, she was too comfortable to wonder about anything. She was so warm. And her cheek had found the perfect placement on a pillow that smelled enticingly of sandalwood and amber. Drawing in a deep breath, she cuddled closer, then released an exhale on a contented *mmm . . .* that tingled her lips.

"Good morning, Miss Thorogood."

The words were so deep and low that she felt the vibration of them beneath her cheek, like the purring of a very large cat.

Her brow furrowed in confusion. The voice was decidedly rich and pleasant, but it wasn't one she expected to awaken to. As far as she knew, Maeve and Myrtle Parrish only employed one butler on Upper Wimpole Street and this didn't sound like Mr. Rivers. Then again, her drowsy mind reasoned, perhaps he had a cold.

"Good morning," she said, trying to rouse herself. But her head felt heavy, her thoughts muddled and hazy as if submerged in a bog.

Blinking bleary eyes, she stared curiously at her pillow. Or rather, *not* a pillow. After all, pillows weren't usually covered in cashmere with a row of embossed brass buttons.

Her drowsy attention drifted to the gold chain in repose between the fixed points of a buttonhole and the smooth raised circle tucked beneath the slash of a pocket. A quiet ticking sound reached her ears. Curious.

Further down, she saw dark wool drawn taut over a heavy form before separating into what looked to be a pair of trousers over . . . thickly muscled . . . widespread and—she swallowed—inescapably male thighs.

And Prue wasn't sure that she was in bed on Upper Wimpole Street after all.

Her disoriented gaze blinked up at a pair of familiar green eyes, but ones that were looking back at her in a rather unfamiliar way. They were warm and slumberous. And there was a light furring of amber whiskers along his jaw and chin that softened his countenance. *"Lord Savage?"*

"Were you expecting someone else?" he inquired, arching a single gilded brow.

She shook her head, but stopped when the contents within swished in a dizzying wave, like the tide slamming against one side of her cranium and then the other. So she closed her eyes to stop the motion.

"I think I must still be dreaming," she said. Though this was far different from the nightmares she'd been having of late.

A recurring theme was seeing herself on a bed in the middle of Rotten Row, wholly naked, with every member of the *ton* dressed in their finest and lined up with opera glasses to examine her lack of maidenhead. And Aunt Thorley usually made an appearance on a golden chariot, whipping her horse as she drove around the bed in circles, and shouting, "Tut-tut, Prudence. Tut-tut."

Of course, she preferred this current dream . . . even if it left her rather muddleheaded.

"You are quite a sound sleeper," Lord Savage drawled. "Affectionate, too."

Only then did she become aware of his hand caressing her back in gentle passes up and down her spine, the warmth of his lips coasting over her brow in soothing sweeps from temple to temple, and the faint scrape of his whiskers.

Only then did she become aware of her own hand splayed over his chest, her breasts and torso molded intimately to him.

Though, strangely enough, it was the sight of the coat draped over her curled-up knees—the same dark gray evening coat he'd been wearing when she arrived—that made her aware of how inappropriate her current position was. He was, after all, only in his shirtsleeves.

She pushed away from him and sat as primly as possible on the edge of the cushion. Carefully, she folded his coat and set it off to the side before smoothing her skirts. And yes, she was aware that her prudish display must appear rather comical considering that she'd agreed to be put on the list to become his future mistress *and* apparently had fallen asleep at some point . . . during the . . .

Her gaze shot to the sliver of golden sunlight slicing in through the part in the dark green brocade drapes. At once, her heart thumped in a wild, ramshackle rhythm. "Did you say, 'good morning'? And did I actually sleep here *all* night?"

"One occurrence usually follows the other," he said with a slow grin.

"Oh no. Oh dear. Oh . . . The aunts will be worried sick." She shook her head and stood up. Too fast as it turned out and she wobbled—

He was there at once, holding her steady with his hands curled securely around her shoulders. "No need to fret, my dear. I sent word last night."

She wasn't certain if that was better or worse.

"I never intended to stay here. At least, not until our arrangement began. Now there isn't any possible way I could go back, to live beneath their roof. They would never understand the reason for my decision. Even though they know I am ruined, they were still planning to find a husband for me. Can you imagine? And you thought *I* was naive." She realized she was rambling in a nervous rush. Realized that he was patiently listening while his thumbs and fingertips gently eased the stiffness from her shoulders in small, wondrous rotations. And she couldn't fathom why she wasn't trying to move away.

Perhaps she was simply too tired. Yes, that must have been it. All of the strain in her overwrought nerves made her stockinged feet sink further into the plush pile of the woven—

Wait a minute. *Stockinged* feet?

She shrugged away from him and stiffened her spine. "And just where are my shoes?"

"The regal affront in your tone suggests that I should deny any knowledge and blame cobbler elves instead," he quipped. "Nevertheless, since I am responsible, I'll tell you that I only wanted to make you more comfortable after you fell asleep, shortly following your charming anecdote about a fish named Algernon."

And suddenly she remembered everything—every conversation, every debate over the terms of the contract, every piece of her inheritance listed in as much detail as she could provide. And he had unblinkingly promised to live up to his part of their bargain without fail. He'd even offered to hire an investigator to uncover the whereabouts of the rest of it, which included finding out who now held the deed to Downhaven Cottage.

And thinking back now, she'd likely talked too much. She did that on occasion when she was nervous or trying to

avoid thinking about something else . . . like agreeing to become a man's mistress. *Oh, Pekingese!*

The heat of embarrassment rushed to her cheeks. "Why
didn't you wake me and send me away?"

"I saw little point in rousing you, considering this is
where you'll reside for the next four months."

"But surely you don't mean straightaway? Directly? This
very instant?"

The corner of his mouth twitched. "I mean forthwith.
Promptly. And, dare I say, *at once.*"

"But you're already with that other woman, the one
who spoke to you from within the carriage the night I was
dressed as a—"

"I remember, and no," he said simply. Keeping any further details to himself, he reached into his waistcoat pocket
and withdrew a gold watch.

Prue shook her head in disbelief. Her lungs strained
against her corset lacing, breaths shallow and quick. In the
back of her mind, she'd imagined that she'd have time to become better acquainted with him before their arrangement
began . . . and perhaps time to come to her senses and think
of a better plan.

She'd never intended to fall asleep. She'd only wanted to
close her eyes for a minute in order to gather her courage to
finish their discussion. She'd kept skirting far afield of the
topic most preeminent in her thoughts: *Sexual congress.*

But she'd been cowardly and now it might be too late to
tell him that—

A knock fell on the study door. "I beg your pardon, my
lord, but Mr. Godfrey has a question regarding the codicil."

"I'll be there directly," Lord Savage said. Then he took a
step toward her again. "Mr. Godfrey is my solicitor, here to
draw up the contract."

"So soon? Surely it's far too early in the day for matters

of business," she said, knowing she was grasping at straws and seeking any sort of delay.

The thought of signing an actual contract seemed so final. Like there was no turning back. And yet, after spending the entire night here and with the aunts knowing—and soon word would spread to her friends as well—hadn't she already sealed her fate?

Tut-tut, Prudence.

"I pay him handsomely enough to compensate for the inconvenience," Savage said. "Besides, the sooner it is settled, the sooner you can stop rethinking your decision. Ah yes, you're quite good at keeping your countenance from revealing that inner turmoil, but this spot right here"—he brushed the crook of his finger against the rabbiting pulse beneath the susceptible skin of her throat—"betrays you. And so do your panicked eyes. But you've nothing to fear, Miss Thorogood. We'll be good together. I'm certain of it."

Was he trying to soothe her fears or increase them tenfold?

What did she know about becoming a mistress? Nothing. Nothing at all, other than the fact that the intimacies between a man and a woman were unbearable and excruciating, and that, in the end, she'd only leave him vexed and disappointed. Just like she had with George.

At the memory, a sick feeling churned in her stomach.

Savage tilted up her chin and looked at her with something between amused pity and understanding. "I'll have a maid show you to your bedchamber. Take as long as you need."

She watched him cross to the bellpull, every step lithe and confident. George tended to lumber and plod along as if his boots were too heavy. But Savage had a certain swagger about him. It was in the cut of his clothes and in the movement of the muscular form shifting beneath fine lawn and wool. The man fairly exuded masculinity with every fiber of his being.

She swallowed. And realizing that her gaze dipped lower in admiration of his taut backside, her cheeks heated. A wayward *flip* replaced that churning in her stomach.

Splaying a hand over the peculiar sensation, she abruptly turned her head, needing to focus on something more ascetic. Her attention was caught by the gilded mantel clock as it chimed the quarter hour. A bronze dial was set against a circle of jade behind an arched door of beveled glass, and flanked by a pair of nude lovers in white porcelain.

She swallowed. "Will you . . . um . . . tell Mr. Godfrey about Downhaven Cottage?"

"Of course," he said. "You'll have your cottage before our contract expires. I'm always generous with my parting gifts."

She wanted to trust that he would keep his word about everything. But trust was hard for her to give.

Everything depended on Downhaven Cottage. It was where she planned to live the rest of her days. Without it, she would have nothing—no future and no possibility of living a reasonably contented life.

Another knock fell on the door an instant before a cheerful housemaid appeared.

Numbly, Prue turned away from the ticking clock. But before she reached the door, Lord Savage spoke.

"Oh, and Miss Thorogood," he said, and she looked over her shoulder to see him crossing the room toward her, carrying her shoes. "You wouldn't want to forget these. However, I'm tempted to hold on to them to keep you from slipping away again."

A stilted, nervous laugh erupted in her throat, betraying her guilt. The notion had crossed her mind once or twice . . . or a hundred times in the last minute.

He eyed her perceptively. Then as he handed them to her,

he leaned in, his scent tingling her nostrils as he whispered, "But we both know that the woman who knocked on my door is far too determined to let a little thing like nerves stand in her way."

He left the room, leaving her to contemplate her fate.

She exhaled and considered his argument. He was right. She had made the choice to come here last night. And it was time she reminded herself that she was no longer the old Prue.

"I'll take those, Miss Thorogood," said a young woman with a pixie-like smile and brown hair tucked beneath a white mobcap. Plucking the shoes out of her grasp with alacrity, she bobbed a curtsy, then led Prue across the hall and up the stairs. "I'm Dottie, by the way. I can't tell you how happy I was when the housekeeper called upon me to assist you. After all, it isn't often one of his lordship's companions arrives without a maid of her own. In fact, one lady had three maids. It was fair crowded in the attic for those months, I can tell you . . ."

Dottie continued to chat away as she escorted Prue up the stairs. The next floor opened to a long Carmelite brown gallery, trimmed in white plaster and rich in adornments— polished tables, marble urns and molded mirrors, priceless vases and oil paintings that one usually only saw hanging in the London gallery.

After spending a year secluded with her aunt and uncle in a spartan country house, her current surroundings left her more than a bit gobsmacked. She was most definitely not in Wiltshire anymore.

She did her best not to appear slack-jawed as they walked through an archway at the far end toward a corridor that split off in two directions.

Peering down the path to the left, she saw a pair of white-glazed French doors, adorned with intricate scroll-work along the hinges and gleaming brass doorknobs. *The ballroom*, she was told before Dottie led her in the opposite direction, up another set of stairs.

This next corridor was wide and bedecked in panels of rich, glossy wood that seemed to harness the golden light sifting in through the broad mullioned windows at the far end, without any need to light the crystal wall sconces. They passed a series of recessed doorways before reaching the last. And there, Dottie escorted her into a lavish bed-chamber that stole Prue's breath.

She'd never seen anything like it.

Decorated in the deepest pinks and violets, silks and vel-vets with a plush piled rug so soft it left an impression un-derfoot, the chamber enfolded her in feminine luxury. Even the furniture was gently rounded and warm-hued. It was a sensual room. And yet, at the same time, it was soothing. A balm for the senses.

Unlike the other rooms she'd seen thus far, it possessed fewer embellishments—a carved walnut dressing screen and washstand in one corner, a peculiar arrangement of three standing mirrors in another—as if the one who deco-rated it had simply decided it was enough.

Then again, perhaps the decorator in question had sim-ply been too tired, Prue thought when her gaze fell on the massive canopied bed. The mattress was large enough for a family of four. Or, she gulped, just one ardent marquess and his latest courtesan?

She turned her head. Better not think about that now.

As she was being unbuttoned and served some gossip pertaining to the previous inhabitants of the house, Prue be-gan to feel somewhat surer of her decision. After all, high-born women did this sort of thing all the time. Right? They had to make bargains with men in order to secure their own futures. In some instances that meant marriage. In oth-ers, becoming a man's mistress. One gave a person respect among her peers. The other provided more independence.

So, it really came down to a matter of duration, with one lasting until either party died . . . and the other just a blessedly short interval in her life. And from her prior experience, she was most definitely in favor of the latter.

Besides, after having spent last night with him, her options were even more limited than before. She had nowhere else to turn.

Four months. Surely, she could manage that.

She gave a sideways glance to the four-poster behemoth in the room. Four months . . . unless he tired of her. And he most definitely would tire of her the instant he discovered her secret. Therefore, they must reclaim as many pieces of her inheritance before he did.

In the meantime, perhaps she could distract him or stall his pursuit by pretending an ailment. But the instant the thought crossed her mind, her conscience niggled at her. As much as she had convinced herself that stealing back what belonged to her was perfectly within reason, she couldn't abide lies or deceptions.

A fine time for your scruples to make an appearance, she thought ruefully. And was it really fair of her to enter into this arrangement without confessing her terrible truth?

᪥᪥᪥᪥

Leo paced impatiently in front of the sofa in his study. He opened his pocket watch. Closed it. Looked to the mantel clock, then to the open doorway. The *vacant* open doorway.

In the past thirty-four minutes, he'd gone over the finer points of the bargain with his solicitor, had a fresh shave, changed into his riding clothes, and gave instructions to his valet to discover whatever he could find about Miss Thorogood's recent beaus through servants' gossip. But he was still left with too much time on his hands. Thirty-five minutes now.

What the devil was taking her so long?

This was new for him. He was never kept waiting when a contract was ready to sign. His previous companions had been all too eager.

Then again, he reminded himself that Miss Thorogood wasn't familiar with these arrangements. He knew her father to be a puritanical, stiff-necked sort of fellow. So, it stood to reason that any daughter of his would have been somewhat sheltered from the more scandalous aspects of society.

At least, until a year ago. Then she'd had a rude awakening, and the world she knew had crumbled beneath her feet.

Leo understood what that felt like. He remembered when his own life had disintegrated into dust. When the ones he'd trusted implicitly had betrayed him. It had taken him more than a year to climb out of the rubble and forge onward. Therefore, he could understand Miss Thorogood's hesitancy to commit to this new path she was choosing.

But knowing that made him all the more impatient to have this contract signed and settled. Sooner rather than later.

He glanced again at the mantel clock and frowned. The minute hand hadn't moved. He was sure of it. Time seemed as frozen as the porcelain figures with their arms outstretched toward each other.

He'd never really liked the clock. It was just another of the countless *objets d'art* purchased in a decorating frenzy from one of his former lovers. But he still expected the bloody thing to work.

Frustrated, he took the heavy bronze base in hand, opened the door of beveled glass and tapped on the dial.

"I'm here," came the soft rasp of a voice from the doorway.

He turned instantly to see Miss Thorogood lingering on the other side of the threshold. She stood regal and poised. Any remnant of their night on the sofa together had been ironed from her borrowed muslin. Her becomingly disheveled coiffure had been tamed and smoothed into a neat chignon away from her face. Her cheeks were scrubbed pink, her eyes alert, if not a bit wary.

Without delay, he crossed the room only to realize he was still carrying the clock. Pausing briefly, he set it down on the blotter by the waiting papers. And since she seemed to be glued to the floor on the other side of the threshold, he went to her.

"The contract is on the desk, my dear. We could walk over there together or I could drag that claw-footed monstrosity over to you. Which would you prefer?"

"I wasn't certain it was finished. I didn't want to rush and put undue pressure on your solicitor," she said on a frayed breath that immediately quieted Leo's impatience and spurred a need to soothe her.

He held out his hand in offering. "Not to worry, Mr. Godfrey is exceptional at what he does. I'm sure he would be the first to tell you that I don't pay him nearly enough."

"Not true, my lord," Godfrey said, stepping out of the small parlor across the hall. As he approached, his eyes glinted with good humor behind round spectacles. He whipped a handkerchief from where it had been tucked into his umber cravat, then stuffed it into the pocket of his brown coat. "You've always been exceedingly generous, even with your own breakfast. Much obliged, by the way."

Leo issued a short nod. He had, indeed, given up his own tray of kidneys, ham, coddled eggs and buttered toast, discovering that he had no appetite. Which was puzzling since he hadn't supped on anything the previous evening either.

But that changed the instant Miss Thorogood's fingers settled tentatively into his grasp just then. His hunger awakened on a heady jolt, his gut clenching on an empty ache as his hand closed reflexively on the cool, delicate fingers curling into his palm. And all at once, he . . . was . . . ravenous.

He drew her deeper into the room. All of his appetites

were in want of sustenance, and temptation was near enough to taste. However, his needs must wait for the time being. Mr. Godfrey followed them inside, and after a brief introduction, he gave a bow. "A pleasure to make your acquaintance, Miss Thorogood."

Stopping at the edge of the desk, she inclined her head and greeted him with utmost decorum, likely making Godfrey feel like he was in the presence of a queen.

Leo reluctantly released her and offered the page for her perusal. She skimmed the document, the paper fluttering ever so slightly from a nervous tremor in her hand.

After a brief hesitation, she said, "Can any of this actually be legally enforced, my lord?"

"My dear, I'm a marquess with a propensity to get what I want through any means. Do you believe I couldn't find *someone* in the courts, willing to declare that this was the most law-abiding document they'd ever clapped eyes on before?"

"Fair point," she rasped and delicately cleared her throat.

"Fear not, I always own up to my end of the bargain as a matter of honor." Since his own father hadn't possessed a shred of honor in any of his dealings, Leo always made it a matter of pride to hold true to his word.

He expected the same of others, but he was often disappointed.

Watching her lips purse as her eyes carefully surveyed every single word, he felt another uncharacteristic rise of impatience.

That pink, Cupid's-bow mouth had haunted his dreams for weeks, and not only while he'd slept. No, he'd had plenty of *wide-awake, fully aroused at midday* thoughts of her, too. Did she have any idea how much she was taunting him with that ever-so-slight pucker? How many ways he had imagined what her mouth could do?

He gripped the side of the desk, silently imploring her to sign and end his torment.

"We agreed to no pin money, no jewelry and only the required number of gowns in exchange for the cottage as my parting gift." She pointed to the paragraph in question.

"No. *You* agreed," he clarified. "I, however, am making your acceptance of all that you see here a condition of my agreement to assist you in committing larceny. I do have my integrity to consider, after all."

She slid him a dubious glance. "That makes absolutely no sense, and you're being far too generous. This arrangement is one-sided. I am getting everything, while you're only getting—"

Having a sense that she was about to utter something self-disparaging, he pressed a finger to her impossibly soft lips and didn't allow her to finish. He held her gaze unswervingly and said, "I assure you that I will soon have everything I want."

Then, before she could ferret out another argument, he plucked the contract from her grasp and laid it down to sign. Picking up the quill, he reached toward the open bottle of ink and—

"Wait." She stopped him with a hand on his sleeve. "There is . . . something I need to tell you first."

He closed his eyes briefly, a familiar coldness creeping into his veins.

I should have known, he thought, imagining all sorts of admissions she might utter, all the duplicities to which she would confess.

This was the precise reason he kept an investigator on retainer to ensure that unexpected issues didn't arise. He'd learned long ago that being a wealthy marquess—even one with a smeared title and scandalous reputation—made him a prime target for women who weren't always honest with him. Thankfully, because of his investigator, Leo had avoided prior traps.

This time, however, he hadn't waited. And he hadn't waited because he knew that—if he'd let Miss Thorogood walk away again—she would slip through his fingers for good.

He looked over his shoulder to his solicitor. "Leave us."

Godfrey inclined his head and left without a word, shutting the door quietly behind him.

Leo set down the pen and, in as patient a voice as possible, said, "And what's all this about?"

"Before we continue, I have a confession to make."

"I'd gathered as much."

"My lord, I've been keeping a secret from you, and it would be unfair if I did not reveal the truth about myself."

"Go on then," he said, hearing the crunch of his molars grinding together.

"Very well. It is only right that I tell you"—she drew in a deep breath and met his gaze—"that I do not possess a passionate nature. I am quite reserved and disinclined toward displays of affection of any sort. In fact, they make me rather uncomfortable."

"And . . . ?"

She pressed her lips together as if to shield them before she continued in a nervous rush. "And the reason I'm telling you this is because . . . well . . . because I have no idea how to become your mistress. Absolutely none at all. You are likely used to women who were born with certain appetites that are absent in me. My attempts at pleasing a man were labeled as *awkward* and *inept*. I cannot even list all the things that I unknowingly did incorrectly and because of that I am guaranteed to be a disappointment, especially to a man with your reputation." Her shoulders sagged from exhaustion as if she'd purged the contents of her soul. "There. I've said it. And I must apologize for misleading you by my display of assuredness and worldliness last evening. Of course, I completely understand if this ends our agreement."

He felt his jaw slacken as he stared at her. It wasn't often a woman surprised a jaded cynic like him. But she just had.

As he absorbed her confession, a rush of relief swept through him. But also irritation.

Apparently, some complete cad—who ought to be shot, in his opinion—had been most unthinking in his words to her. And because of an idiot, this lovely creature was unsure of herself.

Well, Leo needed to put a stop to that immediately.

"Allow me to address your concerns from last to first and begin by saying that I have no wish to end our agreement. Secondly, you needn't apologize for any part of last night. Not for boldly knocking on my door, and especially not for dusting yourself in rose petals."

"Those petals were completely your fault. You shouldn't leave bowls of them lying about in unexpected places," she chided on a whisper, averting her gaze.

He grinned at the way she blushed when she was flustered. "Regardless, I rather liked that part."

"You're incorrigible."

"Undoubtedly," he said and continued. "Thirdly, there is only one thing that ever disappoints me—betrayal."

That snared her attention. In her astute gaze he glimpsed the pain of past betrayals of parents, friends and lovers. It stretched between them like fibers of a threadbare garment in need of mending, connecting them. Then she nodded and so did he.

"And finally, if you are still harboring any ludicrous uncertainty about whether or not you will please me, here is one sure way to find out," he said. "Come here, Miss Thorogood."

When he slowly reached out, her eyes went wide as Wedgwood saucers. "What do you intend to do?"

"Nothing untoward," he said, his tone soothing as he gently grasped her fingers. "Just draw you a bit closer. There. That's about right."

She shuffled to a stop. "I will only disappoint you."

"Nonsense," he crooned and settled his hands on the narrow span of her waist.

She sucked in a breath. Beneath the thumbs resting against the firmness of her belly, he felt her tense, her body coiled like a spring. And yet, she didn't bolt or shy away.

He rewarded her bravery with a kiss to her temple. As he lingered, she took in another breath, slower this time, gradually becoming used to this close proximity.

He was doing the same. The women he was accustomed to were pampered and softer, gently rounded and cushioned, perfect for gripping and sinking into. But she was willowy and Leo, as a sturdily built, athletic man, felt as though he might break this fragile waif if he unleashed *all* his passions. So he held her with care, his lips grazing the tender shell of her ear, to nuzzle the fragrant skin beneath the petal-soft lobe.

He felt her responding quiver. It tumbled through him as keenly as if it had been his own. And when her spine bowed toward him, ever so slightly, it was impossible to resist flexing his fingers into the supple cushion of her hips, bringing her an inch closer.

He continued his exploration of the milk-white column, nibbling softly against the harried pulse. *Mmm . . .* he knew her skin would taste divine, cream and honey on his tongue.

She shivered, a sensual ripple that made her throat arch and her breath come out on a slow shudder as she gripped the fine wool of his sleeves. "I do not know what to do."

"Whatever pleases you."

"Rushing to the door, then?"

"Anything but that," he said, his lips coasting higher,

smiling against her cheek as he drew her slender form against him.

The instant their bodies fell into seamless alignment, she emitted a startled gasp. "I . . . I've been told that I'm rather wooden."

"Not every fire is quick to ignite. Some need to be coaxed."

Lifting her hands to drape around his neck, he felt the enticing weight of her high, firm breasts. The gradual yield of her soft curves and slender valleys as he pulled her closer into the shelter of his embrace, his legs bracketing hers.

His breath left him in a rush. Holy hell, but she felt good. Better than he'd imagined.

"And that I'm cold and unresponsive, as well."

She may have been stiff and uncertain at first. He expected no less from someone so proud. But now she was unfolding slowly for him, her hands tentatively gliding over his broad shoulders.

His lips coasted over her brow and temple, her heart thundering against his own.

Unresponsive? Hardly. "We must suffer fools gladly."

"I've never understood that phrase. Why should we be glad to suffer at all, but especially fools?" she asked distractedly as her delicate fingertips shyly skimmed higher above his cravat, teasing the short layers of hair at his nape.

He closed his eyes on the pleasure of her touch, his nose skirting along the length of hers. "Because we know what they cannot fathom."

"And that is . . . ?"

"This, my lovely moonflower," he said and finally—*finally*—eased his mouth over hers.

Chapter 7

The instant Savage's lips found hers, Prue went completely still. Well, at least on the outside. *Inside* was an entirely different matter.

It was chaos in there. Every nerve ending ignited at once in a sudden explosion of heat. Her heart flung itself repeatedly against the cage of her ribs like a wild creature trying to escape. Her mind raced, frantically searching the stored archives on decorum for the proper method of procedure. But she couldn't think. She could only feel.

And was it any wonder? He held her so intimately against the firm length of his body as his mouth coasted aimlessly over hers, she was surprised she didn't catch fire. But she did melt. *Oh yes, indeed.* With every searching pass, she felt her blood burn, dissolving her inner workings into a hot, syrupy liquid.

She wasn't entirely sure what was happening to her. Thankfully, her last shred of rational thought reminded her that this was a test. Only a test.

It wasn't really a kiss. Certainly, not the way George had shown her. His had been hard and wet. Hasty pushes of mouth to mouth that always ended with his frustration at her inability to return the requisite amount of passion. But this wasn't like that at all.

Lord Savage grazed over her flesh, slowly winnowing out sensations, drawing them to the surface until her lips felt plump and tingly beneath the vulnerable skin. And she held still, waiting for the hard press that would bring an end to this assessment of their compatibility.

But instead of pressing harder, Savage nuzzled invitingly into the hinge of her mouth, making her eyes flutter closed. Then he teased her with another unhurried and tingly sweep as if all he wanted was to hold her in his arms and brush her lips with his own. As if this mere contact was enough for him.

This must be another part of the test, she thought, because she knew that a scoundrel would want more. Knew that she would soon see disappointment in his gaze.

Undeterred by her cold nature, he nibbled softly with maddening patience until her lips were overripe and achy. Until the need to press her tender fullness against his enticing firmness overwhelmed her. Until nothing else would do.

So she did. She issued a hard press to quell the ache.

Prue planned to draw back at once.

But she never expected to feel the rush that flooded her senses, the frisson of awareness that shook her to the very core. Never imagined a sensation washing over her skin in a sudden rain shower of gooseflesh that descended swiftly to her breasts, drawing her flesh taut and tender where she was molded against his tailored waistcoat. Never dreamed that his gruff grunt in response would steal her breath, the sound burrowing deep into the pit of her stomach on a sweet clench.

And all from just a test.

Alarming to say the least. The man was the embodiment of seduction. Doubtless, he knew untold ways of drawing out pleasurable responses, whether she liked it or not.

And yet . . . she did like it. Quite a lot, in fact.

Shocked and breathless, she turned her head to absorb this realization and come to terms with it . . . only to have his hand cup the delicate shape of her jaw.

Gently, he drew her back to the pleasure of his lips with a single, husky command. *"More."*

The visceral need in that one syllable tunneled inside

her, taking root, deep in the pit of her stomach as his mouth claimed hers.

Befuddled by this foreign sensation, she surrendered without thinking or hesitating. *More* seemed like a perfectly sound argument for another kiss.

He nudged her lips apart with small insistent sips of her top lip, then the bottom, the warm tip of his tongue drifting along the inner seam. She gasped at the startling feel of it, the intimacy of his flesh stealing inside the humid interior.

She'd never been kissed like this either.

Then he licked into her mouth—a teasing flick, a slow sinuous slide. Sampling her. Tasting her. And when she welcomed him deeper, he made a new sound. A raw and hungry sound that sent a thrill trampling through her, exciting every pulse point along the way.

Strong hands gripped her hips, hauling her closer. He kissed her with languorous thoroughness. Kisses that kept changing, deepening, probing past her defenses until she was trembling. He tasted of heat and salt and spice and she found herself wanting—no, *needing*—more.

She had never felt this way, filled with an inexplicable craving. And her head spun, caught in an irresistible, dizzying thrall.

Dimly, she reasoned it must be him. This renowned rake with a reputation for hedonism knew how to draw out the slumbering wanton in any woman he encountered. Even one as cold and reserved as she. Yet, in this moment, she didn't care about any of that.

She boldly brushed the tip of her tongue over his lower lip just to know what it was like. *Decadent,* she thought, the texture of him all silk and heat. Something inside her unfurled in a warm, liquid rush. Slanting her mouth beneath his, her fingers stole into the heavy locks of his hair, keeping him close.

This was bliss. Otherworldly. It was like discovering a new melody that no one had ever heard before.

A hum vibrated in her throat as she explored him in return. He growled in response, gripping tighter. And she clung to him, her body fitting precisely to the hard terrain of him as his lips skimmed along her cheek to the underside of her jaw.

Then he shifted, his hands drifting lower, lifting her until she felt the desk against her backside and—

Crash!

The harsh sound of shattering glass filled the room. A startled yelp left her and she clutched his shoulders. In response, he cinched his arms around her, his splayed hand tucking her face into the warm shield of his neck. Then she heard him curse.

"What was that?" she mumbled, her nose buried in his cravat. But she didn't mind. He smelled so good. She breathed in the scents—deep sandalwood, fresh linen and the warm, masculine spice of his shaving soap—in long, unabashedly gluttonous inhalations.

It took him a moment to answer. His lungs seemed to be laboring as hard as her own. Harder. And even though it was clear that they were in no danger of the house falling down around them, he still held her tightly.

That was when she noticed her heart pounding hard in her chest, beat for beat against the hard pounding of his. She realized—with no small amount of befuddled dismay—that she was perched on the edge of his desk with his hips pressed intimately against the juncture of hers, and her skirts bunched between them. How had this happened?

Lord Savage lifted his head, his eyes heavy lidded and dark with a penumbra of brilliant green that looked almost feral and hungry. Very hungry. And even though he released his fiercely protective hold, his hands still lingered on her, the backs of his fingers brushing her cheek, soothing the rabbiting pulse along her throat.

"My clock," he said, his voice husky and deep. "It toppled over the edge."

She glanced down at the pieces of his broken clock littering the floor. At once, she heard familiar accusations inside her head, telling her how ungainly she was. Savage didn't say the words, but he didn't have to.

Prue stiffened, her stomach churning. "I apologize. I wasn't paying attention."

"See here," he said, tipping up her chin. "If anyone is at fault, then I am for putting it there in the first place, then completely forgetting about it. My attention was far more agreeably engaged. So if you are determined to take the blame for something, make it the temptation you create and nothing else." His gaze drifted to her lips, the pad of his thumb tracing the underside of the tender, swollen flesh. "Regardless, I believe any questions about our compatibility have been answered."

With the way he was looking at her, she thought he might take her mouth again and further cement his point. But the first kiss was so startling that her overwrought senses couldn't possibly take any more.

Needing to gain her bearings, she slid her hands to his chest and tried to extricate herself with as much decorum as possible. "All this test has proven is that you're capable of scrambling my wits."

"Then, by all means, let us sign without delay before your wits return. Besides"—he paused to help her down and waited until she was steady on her feet—"I have many errands to attend, as do you."

"Me?" Her hands stilled in the process of smoothing her skirts.

He nodded absently as he dipped the quill in the ink and scratched his name and title onto the bottom of the page. "Indeed. My housekeeper will take you on a tour of the house after you've breakfasted. Additionally, I've already sent for your modiste to begin your trousseau."

Prue blinked at him and then at the quill he was offering.

The flesh of her brow puckered. Everything was happening so fast. She hardly knew which end was up.

Coming here last night, she'd only expected to leave her name and ask to be put on his list. Instead, she'd fallen asleep, awakened in the arms of a scoundrel, gained a maid and a new bedchamber, was kissed utterly senseless . . .

And all before she'd even had her morning tea.

"I see you need further convincing," he said and slid his hand to her nape, his intention clear.

Her gaze darted to his lips and her traitorous pulse leapt with excitement. But before she allowed him to kiss her again, she hastily turned away, took up the quill and scrawled her signature below his.

"There. It's done," she said on a rush of breath. Her hand was shaking as if the feather weighed ten stone and he gently took the quill from her, setting it aside before sanding the ink to dry. "In four months, or likely less, I'll begin my new life."

"For four months, four *full* months," he said pointedly, "you'll be mine."

She shook her head and squared her shoulders, matching his certain expression with one of her own. "I shall still be my own woman. This is a choice I have made, not one made for me."

It wasn't until his lips curved in a satisfied grin that she realized he'd wanted her to make such a declaration. As if he knew she needed the reminder in order to feel in control again.

And it worked, too. *The sly devil.*

Picking up the contract, he let the dusting sand fall and headed to the door. Then he stopped and looked over his shoulder, a glint in his eyes. "By the by, Miss Thorogood, I haven't even begun to scramble your wits. But I will enjoy every single moment of doing precisely that."

Just when she thought her heart would stop racing, he sent it galloping again.

Chapter 8

As soon as the contract was signed, Leo left the irresistible lips of Miss Thorogood while he still could. In his current ravenous state, he knew she was better off in the capable hands of his housekeeper, Mrs. Crumb.

Additionally, he had a number of errands to attend. Not the least of which was speaking to Lady Sutton about the sudden alteration of their arrangement.

The moment he arrived at her flat, he was escorted to her dressing chamber. She received him with a warm embrace, garbed in a gauzy peignoir that hid nothing from view.

Discerning that she misunderstood the purpose of his visit, he delicately pried her away and explained the situation, giving a brief summary of events.

"In short," he continued, "I had unthinkingly presented an offer to another party weeks ago. Because of this, I felt honor bound to keep my word to her. So you see, my hands are quite tied."

"And yet you never once mentioned a word of this other party to me." She sniffed and deliquesced artfully in a puddle of silk and feminine curves to the chaise longue. Reclining back, she draped a distressed arm over her forehead and accused him of toying with her affections.

"Be that as it may, the circumstances remain unchanged."

She sighed and sat up. Perched on the edge of the cushion, she pouted up at him through her dark lashes. "Do you know what I think, Savage?"

By the cunning gleam in her eye, he could just about imagine, but he said, "No. Tell me."

"I think you're merely here to whet my appetite. Shame on you." She swatted him on the knee playfully, before she began to walk her fingers higher, her tongue darting out to lick her lips. "Perhaps, you'd like a little enticement to keep our bargain instead?"

His kiss with Miss Thorogood had ignited his ardor, and far more than he'd anticipated. It also left him in a frustrated state. And because his decision to keep her had been spontaneous—without compiling his usual research beforehand—he knew it could be quite a while before he eased the burden of his aching flesh.

But the fingers searching the fastenings of his front fall and the saucy mouth grinning with wicked delight were not Miss Thorogood's.

So he stayed Millie Sutton's hand and bent his lips to her knuckles. "Alas, my dear lady. Though you have indeed enticed me, I cannot give in to my desires until I am at liberty to do so."

A flash of temper flared in her eyes as he helped her stand. "And what's to keep me from taking another lover in the meantime?"

"Nothing at all." He shrugged, wholly unaffected by her threat.

"Perhaps he'll replace you in my affections."

"Then I will undoubtedly be forlorn," he said, playing the game of the consummate flirt as he did with her and all the others. "And, just so you are aware, I've received a bill from your modiste this morning."

She colored. "As you know, my husband left me penniless . . . and I'd presumed that by now you and I would . . . well—"

"Think nothing of it," he interrupted smoothly. "I am more than willing to pay it. In fact, I shall consider it my obligation to do so because of this unexpected delay."

After his pretty speech, she recovered instantly and didn't seem at all bothered by the fact that she'd been spending his money before they'd reached an agreement. She even batted her lashes. "And I shall look forward to the next time we are able to meet privately. Then you will wish you had never made me wait."

Her words were likely meant to incite his interest in her. And yet, as he left her flat, the only woman in his thoughts was Miss Thorogood.

He could still taste her kiss. Still feel the supple press of her body, the touch of her fingertips . . . *Damn. That was a bloody good kiss.*

Swinging his leg over the saddle of his gray, he wondered if his valet, Jones, had discovered anything yet. It wasn't likely. Miss Thorogood had spent so little time in society that the rumors would be few and far between. Therefore, he'd also sent word to his investigator, Mr. Devaney, to dig up anything he could.

Leo was normally detached about these things. They were temporary affairs, after all. He paid no mind to his paramour's incidental encounters, the trifling flirtations she might have had over the course of her life. Those meant nothing. All he cared about was ensuring their fidelity *during* the arrangement.

But with Miss Thorogood, he wanted to know it all—everything from the day of her birth up to the very minute they met, leaving nothing out. The more he knew, the less likely he would be taken off guard by her again. He felt as though she'd been doing just that from the very instant he'd seen her, and he did not like surprises.

In fact, he *loathed* surprises, as any man who'd once been poisoned by his betrothed would.

In the meantime, he had more errands to attend and rode directly from Lady Sutton's to the jeweler. He gave the shopkeeper carte blanche to put together a selection of ear-bobs, bracelets, brooches and necklaces and ordered them delivered to his town house.

It would cost an exorbitant sum, a veritable king's ransom. But it didn't matter. All Leo could think about was Miss Thorogood's delight when she opened each box. If a mere sip of sugar in her tea could bring a smile to her lips, he wondered what radiance he would behold with these trinkets.

As he left the shop, a feminine voice called out, "How dare you, Savage!"

Recognizing the lilting tone, Leo stopped at once and turned on his heel.

"Have I offended you, ma'am?" he asked, his right brow arched in inquiry as his gaze rested on Helene Marchand, Countess Babcock.

Her wizened hazel eyes glinted beneath the brim of a hat situated at a jaunty angle over her grizzled coiffure. And, try as she might to appear disapproving, her creased grin gave her away. "My dear boy, you strode right by me without even a blink. Either it has been far too long since you've visited and you've forgotten me—"

"I was just in your parlor the day before yesterday," he interjected, nearly rolling his eyes because she'd been uttering this same complaint for most of his life.

"—or you have something so pressing on your mind that it has made you insensible to your surroundings," she tsked with affection.

Taking two steps to reach him, she proffered her cheek. He kissed the soft vellum skin dutifully, her familiar powdery lilac fragrance lingering in the air. The scent was reminiscent of his boyhood when she'd lived openly as his father's mistress, in the years following his own mother's abandonment. And even though his late father's mistresses had been treated with the same callous disregard, Lady Babcock had never deserted Leo. For that, and countless other reasons, she would always have a fixed place in his affections.

"I do have a small matter on my mind," he admitted. "But nothing I cannot conquer."

She eyed him shrewdly. "Is that Millie Sutton beleaguering you already? I knew you shouldn't have taken her. There's just something about her that is a little . . . Oh, I cannot put my finger on it . . . But I'm not certain I like her. In fact, if she's put you in this state then I'm certain I don't."

"It is not Lady Sutton," he said. "I have actually taken a different mistress for the time being. And before you can chide me for not mentioning this during our last visit, I'll say that it came about rather unexpectedly."

"That is unlike you."

"Of that, I am well aware," he said with rueful chagrin. "Nevertheless, I still intend to have Lady Sutton in the future, so make your peace with whatever it is that you cannot put your finger on."

She sighed and offered a nod, slipping her arm into his. As he walked her back to her waiting carriage, he gave her a truncated summary of events that led to his decision, ending with the same excuse he'd given Lady Sutton—that he was honor bound to uphold his original offer to Miss Thorogood.

Helene scoffed. "Rather bold of her. Obviously, after refusing your offer she soon discovered that it far surpassed anything she could expect from any other man of means. Greedy, like all the others. I already hate her."

Leo was typically inclined to agree with the opinion. It was true that his paramours tended to use their wiles to manipulate as much out of him as they could. And yet, there was part of him that wondered if Miss Thorogood was capable of such deception.

There was something altogether guileless in her that he didn't usually encounter in his circles.

I did not come here for your money or for frivolous pampering. I came here for you.

At first, he had believed her simple declaration, even though such faith in a virtual stranger was laughable, not to mention wholly unlike him. For some inexplicable reason, his inner cynic was subdued around her. Or, at least it had been until this morning.

But after experiencing the pleasure of her kiss, it was all too clear that she wasn't the cold creature she'd professed to be. No, indeed. Beneath the cautious layers of her armor simmered a passion so alluring that it had made him forget himself. Hell, had their kiss continued much longer, he'd have taken her on his desk. And that realization had sent alarm sluicing icily through him.

She was either the craftiest and most cunning of all the women he'd ever encountered. Or she was as unsure and innocent as she seemed. But he didn't know for certain. Not yet.

"Don't hate her," he said to Helene. "You taught me to look after my own interests, and my *only* interest is in having her. No matter what her motives might be."

She inclined her head in negligent acquiescence. "Very well. Just make sure she isn't with child and expecting to label you as the father. Believe me, I know all the tricks."

"And you've taught me well. Fear not, I already have my men on it and will surely discover something by the end of the day."

❦❦❦

"WHAT DO you mean, you've found nothing?" Leo asked his valet that evening as he dressed for dinner. Normally

Jones was quick as a flash at ferreting out rumors in the servant mill. His investigator, Mr. Devaney, on the other hand, was more methodical, taking longer with his reports.

But Savage wanted to know more now, not later.

"Just what I said, my lord." Jones's lean, nose-heavy face was marked with self-recrimination as he tied the snowy cravat. "According to the Upper Wimpole Street gossip, Miss Thorogood hasn't been seen with any men at all. At least, nothing to warrant speculation. She has married friends and has gone on outings with those women and their husbands, but nary a whiff of impropriety."

Leo had learned the same from Lady Babcock when he'd received a summons from her to drop by her town house a short while ago. He should have known that the countess would have had her own spies diligently checking into the past of the woman keeping company with *her boy* as she affectionately called him.

"The servants at the Parrish household are annoyingly loyal and tight-lipped," Helene had said with a huff. "And they don't send out their laundry either. So there is no laundress to bribe for the information on whether or not Miss Thorogood has had her courses since returning to London. My spies did hear of a brief mention at one of the confectionary shops Maeve and Myrtle Parrish frequent, however. And according to the clerk, the ladies were recently chatting about finding a good match for their charge in the hopes of hosting another wedding breakfast. Though, considering the girl's sullied reputation, their false hope fairly reeks of a marriage plot, if you ask me. My boy, stay on your guard. She may very well be with child."

The news had been unnerving. It wasn't definitive proof of duplicity on Miss Thorogood's part, of course. Nor did it alter his plans. She would remain his companion. However, until he knew what ulterior motives she might have, the palpable desire that he'd felt for her from the beginning—and that had nearly consumed him during their kiss—would not be assuaged. *Bollocks.*

A glower stared back at him in the standing mirror as he shrugged into his superfine coat. The black seemed fitting for his current mood.

Leaving Jones, Leo went down to the drawing room. At the very least, he would enjoy a fine dinner with his companion. But she wasn't there.

When he'd first returned more than an hour ago, he'd been informed that she was dressing for dinner. So why the devil wasn't she downstairs yet?

Having no desire to be kept waiting again, he rang the bell. An instant later, the butler appeared in the wide doorway, his jowly countenance as expressive as a corpse. "Grimsby, would you send someone up to inquire after Miss Thorogood?"

"No need, my lord. I have just had word from her maid declaring that Miss Thorogood sends her regrets and will be unable to join your lordship for dinner this evening."

"Unable?" That sounded rather ominous. His irritation was stifled beneath a wave of concern. "Is she unwell?"

"I believe her reasons have something to do with her attire for the evening."

"Her attire?" Leo shook his head. He was starting to sound like a sodding mockingbird. And now that he knew it wasn't illness but something altogether trifling that kept her away, his accumulating frustration swiftly gathered in tight bands around his neck.

But he refused to lose his temper. He was not, after all, his father.

So he calmly addressed his butler with a gritted smile. "I was informed that Madame LeBlanc discovered a gown in her shop that would suit Miss Thorogood for this evening."

Not only that, but there were a slew of seamstresses working on this trousseau. The timing was rather fortunate.

Since it wasn't the height of the standard Season, Miss Thorogood would have her entire armoire stuffed to the hinges within a fortnight.

"Indeed, my lord."

He waited for his butler to elaborate but Grimsby merely blinked slowly as if all the words in his lexicon had been bled from his aging body and were now pooling at his feet. Apparently, the fount of information had gone dry.

Left without another choice, Leo went upstairs.

Chapter 9

Prue knew what was expected of her when she'd signed the contract. She had resigned herself to enduring that dreadful ordeal for the next four months—or whenever Lord Savage tired of her—in exchange for his help.

But she wasn't about to go down to dinner looking like this!

Even desperate women had to draw the line somewhere.

She took one final baleful glance in the mirror—or *mirrors*, rather—then turned away and wondered how difficult it would be to smother oneself with a pillow. There were mountains of them on the bed, after all . . .

The hard rap of knuckles on the door interrupted her dire thoughts and startled a squeak out of her.

"Miss Thorogood," Lord Savage said from the other side of the locked door. The easy drawl she knew was replaced with something harder, edgier. "Apparently there's been some miscommunication. You see, when a gentleman chooses a companion, it is generally understood that he desires to spend time in her company. The same might even be said of the companion in question. Shocking, I know."

Prue nearly smiled at his surly quip . . . until she remembered how much she hated him. "You left me with that horrible woman!"

"I know my housekeeper can be rather abrupt at times, but Mrs. Crumb is a good sort."

"Not Mrs. Crumb . . . *Madame LeBlanc*. She's positively diabolical and *you* hired her!"

The modiste had tutted and chastised her for hours on end, accusing her of being a street urchin after seeing the threadbare state of her underpinnings. If that wasn't bad enough, Prue had been scrubbed raw, slathered with oil, brutally manicured, measured to within an inch of her life and—she cringed at the memory—*rouged*.

Though why on earth Madame LeBlanc would put rouge on her nipples of all places, she would never know. Or rather, it was something Prue wished not to know. Just thinking of it, she crossed her arms over her breasts. Which, as it happened, made them nearly spill out of her low-cut bodice.

"Am I to assume you don't like your dress?" he asked dryly.

"*This* is not a dress. Not even remotely."

"What is it then, a handkerchief? If that is the case then I command you to open the door at once."

"No. Absolutely not!" She looked down at herself and shuddered.

The cream satin underdress was a shade that perfectly matched her skin tone. It was topped with a fine, shimmery netting of pale primrose. A lovely creation . . . until she looked in the mirror and realized it gave her the appearance of being completely nude beneath a lustrous fall of her own hair.

"I'm told Madame LeBlanc is the best in London, so I'm sure it isn't that dreadful."

"Your valet's eyes nearly fell out of their sockets and tumbled into his gaping mouth when he glimpsed me through the door earlier."

"The fact that Jones made no mention of this to me suggests that you are being ridiculous. Do you truly think that anything you might be wearing—or not wearing as I dearly hope—could ever shock someone like me?" he asked. "Try to remember the brave young woman who came to my town house and boldly set all this into motion."

Drat it all, he was right.

Hiding in here until she had decent clothes to wear wasn't the answer. And, perhaps, the dress wasn't as revealing as she thought.

"Very well," Prue sighed.

With each step she took across the room, she reminded herself that this was merely a means to an end. A plan to take control of her own life. Hiding wouldn't help her in the long run.

She opened the door.

Through the crack, she saw the twitch of a muscle at the hinge of Savage's jaw as he expelled an impatient breath. And she stiffened at the sight of his sour apple–green glare. How dare he look at her that way after all she'd been through!

"At last, she makes her grand appearance," he said dryly. "I do hope I will not be required to coax you out of your bedchamber for every—"

She flung open the door and stood before him with her shoulders squared and her hands on her hips.

His mouth fell slack. Then he closed it and swallowed, his gaze warming considerably as it raked down her form.

"I stand corrected," he said, his voice hoarse. "My apologies, Miss Thorogood. You were quite right. Grimsby would have had a heart seizure had he seen you walking down the stairs to dinner. I'm feeling rather faint myself. Is this"—he cleared his throat, his hand gripping the door—"the *only* gown Madame LeBlanc left you?"

"Would I be wearing it otherwise?"

"What about your other dress—the one you wore upon your arrival?" he asked with a comical degree of hope.

Prue shook her head. "Gone. She said she wouldn't allow a dog to wear it and took it with her to toss in her hearth."

"I was afraid you'd say something like that." He began shrugging out of his coat.

Prue forced herself to remain perfectly still, even though she had every wish to hide under the bed. Or rather, anywhere else aside from the bed.

"Two things have become patently clear, my dear," he continued and stepped toward her. "First of which is the fact that I'm going to have to murder my valet. And second, I'm not paying Madame LeBlanc nearly enough for her services. There," he said, settling his coat over her shoulders in a gesture that surprised her.

She blinked in confusion. "You . . . you're giving me your coat?"

"Aye. Now we can go down to dinner without inciting a riot among the footmen. I'm simply too weak from hunger to fend them off for your sake."

The fine wool enveloped her in his scent as she slipped her arms into the sleeves. Her lips parted on an unconscious sigh as the warmth seeped into her stiff limbs. Before he withdrew, he brushed his lips against her cheek, and the flesh beneath it warmed even more.

"Of course," he mused, "if you insist upon being ravished, I'm certain I could—"

"No. That won't be necessary," she said hastily, stepping quickly past him and through the door.

His low chuckle reached her side as he took hold of her hand and curled it around his arm to escort her down the stairs.

She studied him out of the corner of her eye, noting that he was still far too handsome in his pristine cravat and tailored aubergine waistcoat. Even so, he likely never went to dinner without his formal attire. As she looked down at the voluminous coat that fell all the way to the middle of her thighs, an overwhelming burst of gratitude bloomed inside her.

"Thank you," she said softly and he inclined his head as

if he did this sort of thing every day. "Though, doubtless your servants have witnessed far more scandalous things than my gown."

"Quite true. However, my town house is only transformed into a den of iniquity on every other Friday. You happen to be here on an off week."

At the sound of his droll tone, she felt the tug of her cheeks lifting in a grin where she could still feel the tingling pressure of his kiss.

❦❦❦

DINNER WITH Lord Savage was nothing like Prue had expected.

For a man who presented himself as unconcerned with the trivialities of life, issuing a nonchalant shrug of his shoulders at whatever came his way, he was certainly particular about the decanting of his wine. But he seemed to regard the thorough scrutiny of the process—from the corked bottle to the glass—as commonplace. Therefore, she dismissed it as an idiosyncrasy and didn't think any more of it.

As the first course arrived and they were left alone, she'd thought he would turn the conversation to matters of carnal pleasure. A sybaritic rake would surely embed each statement with scandalous double entendres that would make her blush whether she understood them or not. But he surprised her.

They spoke of ordinary things—the foods they enjoyed, the books they'd read, music, dancing and their shared enjoyment of the opera.

"Of course, I've only attended once in my first Season," she'd admitted, feeling rather gauche. "But it was delightful."

Savage's silverware didn't clatter to his plate. He didn't pause in the cutting of his lamb or look with either shock or pity at the *naif* in his presence. He merely acknowledged the remark, stating, "I hold a box. If you like, we'll attend next week."

Prue eagerly agreed, refusing to think about what it would actually feel like to be seen on his arm in public. It didn't matter what anyone else thought of her. She would soon be away from society and living life by her own rules, and that knowledge always eased her mind.

They sat in each other's company, with her gold-rimmed plate to the right of his, simply talking for hours. It was delightful. She'd never sampled such delicious fare—flaky haddock, butter-poached lobster, suckling pig, roast mutton, boiled potatoes, green beans in white sauce, along with various cheeses, nuts, candied oranges and tarts—and she was certain to burst the seams of her gown.

Just as it had been that day spent traveling in his carriage, she found herself inexplicably relaxed in his company. And, stranger still, she wasn't plagued by the need to be perfect.

There she was, wearing his coat with his sleeves rolled up several times to liberate her hands and to keep her from dragging the cuffs through the rich sauces, and he never once made her feel inferior or as though she needed to apologize. Had he been any other way, her stomach would have been twisted in knots, with Aunt Thorley's voice ringing in her ear.

"You have a lovely dining room," she said after the pudding flambé was served with a sweet syrup that tasted of brandy. She couldn't eat another morsel. "And I admire the superb skill of your cook, as well as the efficiency of your serving staff."

He arched a brow as if in amusement, though she couldn't imagine the reason. "However?"

"*However . . . ?* Was I supposed to mention something else?"

"This is where you offer little suggestions of ways in which all that you admire so greatly might be improved upon with your feminine touch."

She understood at once. "Ah. You must have had mistresses vying for a more permanent position. Rest assured, I have absolutely no designs on you, your house or your servants," she added with a laugh. "You are safe from my clutches, Lord Savage."

He considered her for a moment, easing back against the heavy mahogany armchair, his large hand holding the bowl of the wine goblet with incongruous delicacy. There was something thoughtful or, perhaps, amused in his expression, but she could not discern what it was without knowing him better.

After a moment, he took a drink, then asked with his usual indifference, "You don't find the table too big?"

As if it were a genuine inquiry and her input was actually desired, she humored him and stared down the length of glorious dark wood, polished to a mirror shine beneath the flicker of candlelight.

"It is impressive. Eight chairs on either side could easily become sixteen for a party. Are there leaves, as well?" she asked and he hummed a wordless sound of acknowledgment, leaving her to speculate as to the additional length. "I gather it is quite extensive when turned out for a grand affair. However—"

"At last, the *however* has arrived."

She ignored that remark. "For a man like you who routinely changes out one companion for another, I imagine it could seem quite tedious, sitting in that particular chair night after night. There are likely evenings when you look to your right and can hardly recall the name of your paramour du jour." She pointed to herself. "Miss Thorogood, by the way."

"Ah. I knew you looked familiar." He snapped his fingers, but then narrowed his eyes in reproof. "I am hardly that callous."

"Your future mistresses will greatly appreciate that."

She, on the other hand, didn't believe it for a moment.

The only woman who could possibly hold his interest would be the next one, and the next one after that.

"Then what is your cure for tedium?" he asked as if he'd been reading her mind and was ready to move on.

She shrugged. "For you, I'm sure I do not know. But when I was young and had nightmares about monsters lurking under the table skirt, my mother started to make a game of visiting the dining room. At teatime, there would be a silver dome over each place setting. Then she would hum a tune as we both walked around the table and, when she stopped, that was where we would sit. Whatever was beneath the dome was our special treat and I eventually forgot about the monsters."

"Let me see if I have this correct," he mused. "In order to forget how tedious my table is, I'll need a dome over the delicacy I most want to sample. By the by, just how tall are you?"

She tilted her head in perplexity for an instant . . . Until she saw the devilish glint in his eyes as if he were imagining a Prue-sized dome.

As the image of herself lying on a platter in this dress—or completely nude, since they were nearly the same—flashed in her mind's eye, her cheeks turned hot. She averted her face so he could not see how easily he affected her.

"Such a pity," she tsked. "You were doing so well until just now. Truly, there is no need to play the part of the libidinous rake for me."

"Then what role am I to play?"

"The kindhearted gentleman who has sympathy for his guest and allows her to retire early?"

He seemed to consider this as he stood and slowly walked around to the back of her chair. As he bent down, his hot breath fanned against her skin in a shivery caress when he said, "Then, by all means, let's go to bed."

Chapter 10

Leo felt the change in her instantly, the stiffness in her limbs, the wary sharpness in her eyes as he led her over the threshold of his bedchamber. She was back to being skittish, leaving him to wonder once more if this was a role she'd perfected or if she was really a ruined debutante with only one lover.

"This room is lovely, too," she said politely, but her gulp was audible, throat working in a tight constriction. "It reminds me of your carriage, all silk and black velvet. The only things missing are my soggy cloak and muddy boots."

"I will have them brought in straightaway if they will help you relax. Truly, there's no need to cross your arms over yourself as if I'm a lecher, Miss Thorogood. Here, let me take that coat." As he did, he looked her over with renewed appreciation. "Don't let me forget to murder my valet in the morning."

She gasped and snatched the coat from his grasp, holding it in front of her. "In the morning? Am I to sleep here all night, then?"

"You'll be here nearly every night."

"Nearly?" she asked with comical hopefulness.

"Not when your courses come, of course. And, incidentally, when might that be? Oh, come now, none of that blushing over mere words, or you're likely to turn aubergine by the time we get to the rest of it. Besides, I thought you preferred frank speaking."

"I do. I just wasn't expecting it to be so very frank." She paused for a moment, her brow knitting as she lowered her voice to a whisper. "They are due within a sennight."

He accepted the information with a nod, gently took the coat and draped it over the arm of a leather wingback chair that was angled near the fire.

"And otherwise, we will be"—she swallowed and glanced despondently at the bed—"together each night?"

"Every night," he said and at her look of utter horror, he couldn't help it, he chuckled. "You might actually come to enjoy—" He saw her shake her head before he even finished. What a very strange play they were in. He hardly knew his next line. Walking to the sideboard, he improvised. "Believe it or not, people do this sort of thing all the time because it feels good. Even, I presume, your very own friends. Brandy, my sweet?"

"Thank you," she said as he unlocked the cabinet door and began pouring two glasses. "But there is a difference. My friends love their husbands and, I imagine, it is because of their affection that they endure the pain."

"Come now, a virgin's pain only happens once and briefly." Surely, even a young woman who professed to having only one lover would know that.

"What I endured was not fleeting in the least." She scoffed then muttered quietly, "I was unable to sit without supreme discomfort for days, and the bruises lasted much longer."

"Bruises?" He turned so sharply that liquor sloshed over the rims and dripped onto his fingers. "What the devil did the blackguard do to you?"

Standing by the hearth, she was pink-cheeked with embarrassment. "Exactly what you plan to do to me."

As he crossed the room, he saw that telltale wariness in her eyes and did not believe any of it was pretense.

"Darling," he said when he reached her side, "trust me when I tell you that bruises are not normally left behind."

Taking the glass he offered, she gazed down at the amber liquid thoughtfully. "Then it's true. I *was* doing something wrong. He kept telling me that, over and over. I tried to correct my error, but my skirts were tangled around my legs, along with the tall grasses, and I couldn't—"

"He *forced* himself on you in a field?"

"No. He'd just explained that he'd taken a house for the two of us. And I thought that meant we would be married soon, so . . . why not?"

Her shrug of indifference wasn't fooling anyone.

Leo was livid. Horrified. Ready to commit murder. Whether the blackguard was merely inept or blatantly cruel, it mattered not. He wanted to wipe the earth clean of his presence. Just imagining what she'd gone through made him want to . . .

"It was still my choice," she continued, having no idea of the medieval tortures he was devising for this faceless man. "I just wanted everything settled, decided. I could endure anything once I knew what to expect."

Endure. There was that word again.

She'd used it last night when agreeing to his proposal. Which meant that she was willing to *endure* bruises in order to have the freedom her inheritance would bring.

It suddenly became clear to him that she was more determined and even braver than he'd given her credit for. Any concerns he'd had earlier about her motives were gone. Obliterated. All that mattered now was her. She deserved far better, and he would ensure she had it.

Setting his glass on the mantel and then hers, he expelled a calming breath.

"Come here, my dear," he said, then gave in to the overwhelming desire to put his arms around her. She stiffened at first, her heart thumping against the wall of his chest. But gradually she relaxed to the soothing passes of his hand along her back. "You should know that I won't permit you to *endure* a single minute of your time with me. If it doesn't bring you pleasure, then tell me at once. I shall do the same. Agreed?"

She looked up at him questioningly, skeptically, but nodded.

"Good." Leo cemented this pact with a kiss to her forehead. "During our time together, you will come to know me, as I you, and I hope you will feel more at ease in my arms. In fact, I'll prove it to you. I'm going to do something I've never done before."

"And what could that possibly be?"

"I'm going to sleep with you."

She rolled those stormy eyes and said dryly, "How magnanimous."

"I mean sleep, my dear. Only sleep," he repeated before he took her hand and led her to the bed.

Stopping at the side table, he lifted his hands and slowly unpinned her lovely hair. She watched him warily as long locks of pale silk fell around her shoulders in soft spirals. He wanted to delve into the sumptuous layers and take her mouth again so badly that he ached with desire.

But there was something else he wanted even more. Her trust.

So he resisted temptation. Placing her pins on the white marble, he then drew back the coverlet, all the while feeling her silent gaze on him.

"Would you like me to loosen your corset? It will help you breathe easier."

She shook her head and then told him the one thing that would make his night—and other things—all the harder. "I'm not wearing a corset."

He closed his eyes briefly and tried not to think about it. He failed, of course. His mind conjured her slipping out of this dress that she wore like a second skin. And after this morning's kiss, he knew how very wrong he'd been about worrying she was too slender, too fragile.

She fit him perfectly, her body willowy but strong and supple. He couldn't wait to take her.

But he would wait, nonetheless. At least for now.

She was quiet as he settled her against his side, blinking to keep her eyes on full alert. "I imagine these bedcurtains have seen a great deal."

"So much wickedness. That's why they're black, you know. They were virginal white once upon a time." He felt her smile and pressed his lips to her forehead again. "Go to sleep, moonflower. I won't ravish you tonight."

⚜⚜⚜

PRUE WAS having that dream again—the one where she was on a bed in Hyde Park with the entire *ton* watching her.

But this time it was different. It didn't feel like a panic-inducing nightmare at all . . . and she wasn't alone.

Lord Savage was with her, holding her close against the simmering warmth of his body. His lips were doing tantalizing things to her neck, distracting her from everything else. He nibbled lightly on the underside of her ear and she felt a hum of pleasure expand in her chest, exhaling on a sigh as she curled closer.

"You like this, do you?" His voice was husky and deep, rasping against her skin.

She hummed again and dozily asked, "Aren't you bothered by all the opera glasses aimed at us?"

"Not a whit," he answered and pulled her atop the length of him, nuzzling the curve of her throat, his chest rising beneath her as he inhaled. "Your scent is intoxicating, especially in the morning when you're so warm from sleep. By the way, I think you might be dreaming."

From somewhere nearby, she could hear a steady *tha-*

thump, tha-thump as a leisurely caress drifted down the ladder of her spine in lazy passes, making her want to stay in this place forever. She didn't care who was watching.

"Of course I'm dreaming, Savage. Why else would we be in bed in the middle of Rotten Row?" She drew in a deep breath of amber and wood and that unidentified, but indescribably appealing spice. "Hmm . . . You smell nice, too."

The decadent scent filled her lungs and pooled warmly, down in her middle where she felt another *tha-thump, tha-thump*. She wriggled against it with drowsy, tingling curiosity. The stroking hand on her back descended to the curve of her bottom, cupping it through the layers of satin and cambric, pressing her hips onto the enticingly firm shape.

And yet, in the dark recesses of her mind something warned her that this feeling, though pleasant at the moment, would soon become decidedly painful and turn this dream into a nightmare.

Before that could happen, she gradually opened her eyes on a blink and lifted her head to orient herself.

She did not expect to find a pair of hooded green eyes staring up at her.

Surely, this couldn't be right. So she blinked again, her head foggy and her body still tingling.

"Good morning, Miss Thorogood," Savage said with a decidedly sinful grin. "Have any interesting dreams lately?"

She startled awake with a jolt. Reality crashed upon her in hot rushes of embarrassment coupled with cold shivers of dread. And she tried to scramble away but he held fast to her writhing body.

"Be still," he groaned, wincing. "By bolting off in a panic, you'll only injure one of us, especially considering the precarious position of your knee. Rest assured, I wasn't planning to take you."

She scoffed, keeping her arms bent at the elbow and propped between them. "Oh? Then what were you doing?"

"Merely playing." And there was that grin again. He lifted his head to press a kiss to her chin and tuck a stray flaxen lock behind her ear. "My darling, if you choose to spend the entire night sprawled over me, fondling me with your delicate hands and soft curves, I cannot be held responsible for how my overstimulated body reacts come morning. You've put me in quite a state."

As if he imagined she'd forgotten, he rolled his hips against her, drawing out her gasp and proving that her arm-barrier was quite ineffectual. Her throat went dry at the feel of him. And, heaven help her, her hips hitched reflexively.

She attempted to collect herself. "It wasn't my intention. I'm not at all inclined toward any displays of affection and certainly not"—she swallowed—"to fondling."

"When your mind is fully alert and in control, perhaps. But twice now I've learned that your sleeping body has other inclinations altogether."

He pressed his mouth to the vulnerable underside of her jaw where her rabbiting pulse fluttered in response, and her eyes drifted closed of their own accord.

Well, perhaps, a minute more of this wouldn't be too terrible, she thought.

Her bones felt liquid, her muscles like wet clay, perfectly willing to obey his urging to move her arms aside. Then he held her flush against him and turned them to their sides, sliding against her with exquisite friction.

A satisfied *Hmmm . . .* purred in her throat, her fingers sifting greedily through the warm locks of his hair as his lips dragged down her throat in scorching kisses. He smelled delicious. Every deep inhalation of his scent made her stomach clench. And his mouth and tongue were doing wondrously sinful things as he bent his head, his splayed hand drifting higher over the cage of her ribs to the underside of her—

A knock sounded on the bedchamber door, jolting her out of this fugue state.

Her pulse was pounding, limbs tangled, and there was a hand on her breast. *His* hand, to be precise.

"Beg pardon, my lord," a voice muttered from the corridor.

"Not now, Jones," Savage growled, the soft scrape of his whiskers just above the line of her bodice.

Through the satin, his thumb coasted over the crest of her nipple, spurring it to a tender peak, and a mewl of distress left her as she arched into his touch. A tumult of undeniably enthralling tingles spiraled through her, looping inside her stomach in a hot liquid rush.

She didn't know what was happening to her. Shouldn't she be pushing him away? Shielding herself?

Apparently, her pleasure-drugged body didn't agree because she held him closer, sliding against him and—*oh yes*—that felt good. Really good.

This man was a spell caster. A sorcerer. A veritable devil. And, try as she might, she couldn't resist him.

Though, to be perfectly honest, she wasn't trying that hard.

The knocking came again and this time she was the one who growled, "Not now, Jones."

The instant the words were out, she clapped a hand over her mouth. Wide-eyed, she stared at Savage's raised brows, mirth glinting in his eyes. She didn't know what had come over her.

"There's a visitor to see Miss Thorogood," the apologetic voice said in a rush. "And she's rather insistent, too. The young woman claims that she will storm up here herself to collect her friend out of your depraved clutches."

Savage rolled to his back on a vexed grunt and cursed. "Who is it, Jones?"

"Miss Margaret Stredwick, my lord."

Prue sat bolt upright. "Meg!"

Chapter 11

Prue scrambled out of Savage's bed with all the grace of a drunkard from an alehouse. But to be fair to herself, it was all his fault. He was the one who'd turned her knees to jelly.

Leaving him beneath a mound of rumpled linens, she staggered stocking-footed out the door. Then she dashed down the hall to her own chamber and yanked on the bell-pull at once. Hurrying toward the washstand in the corner, she caught sight of her reflections in the trio of standing mirrors and jerked to a sudden stop, poised like a caricature sketch in a print shop window.

A stranger stared at her from the looking glass—a woman with a tousled tumble of pale hair, bright eyes and flushed cheeks. The flesh along her throat was slightly pinkened from the soft scrape of his whiskers and sensitive to the bewildered brush of her fingertips.

It was difficult to reconcile the vision of this wanton with everything that prim and proper Prudence Thorogood knew of herself. She couldn't recall ever being a particularly passionate person. While she had been a rather rambunctious child, she'd learned through the criticisms of her father and stepmother to subdue any wildness from her nature.

The same had been true with George. She had thought their kisses were pleasant enough. However, after he'd complained about her perfunctory responses nearly every moment they'd spent together, she'd become distracted by concerns for her own improvement.

But in Savage's study yesterday morning, she hadn't thought once about her performance, which direction to tilt her head, how much to purse her lips, or when to take a breath. In fact, she hadn't thought at all. She'd only . . . felt.

And it had felt good. So very good that she wouldn't have minded if he'd have kissed her again this morning, too. In fact, she likely would have welcomed it. Eagerly.

It was all quite alarming, to say the least.

He seemed to be drawing out aspects of her nature that she'd never known existed before. And it wasn't just the passion she'd experienced this morning, but the way he made her feel comfortable with him as if she could say anything—*do* anything—without censure or judgment.

Mystified by all this, she stared at her own reflection, feeling as though she were slipping into a new skin. The abhorrent gown that Madame LeBlanc had left her wasn't quite as abhorrent as before. Oh, it was still scandalous in cut and color. But after the surprising night she'd shared with Savage, she almost felt fondness for the garment.

Even so, she wasn't about to wear *this* to greet Meg. And when Dottie arrived to help her out of it, she begged to borrow a change of clothes.

Then, shortly after splashing water on her face, hastily fixing her hair, and dressing in her maid's spare service dress, she hurried down the stairs.

Prue was out of breath when she stepped into the receiving parlor to find her young friend regarding the nude oil painting over the mantelpiece. "Meg, what in heaven's name are you doing here, of all places?"

"I might ask the same of you." She turned, her pale blue eyes flashing with a mixture of reproof and concern, and then startlement as she glanced at Prue from head to toe. "Does he have you working as a maid in addition to"—she flitted her hands in a muddled gesture—"everything else? Whatever that entails."

Before Prue could answer, Savage strolled in as if he didn't have a care in the world.

He was dressed in a blue morning coat and camel trousers. Freshly shaven, combed and fitted with a neatly tied cravat, he looked the part of a respectable gentleman at his leisure. Certainly not like the tousled rogue she'd left a few moments ago. But appearances were often deceiving.

His eyebrow arched in curiosity as he looked her over. He lingered at the gray hem that was too short, exposing her ankles, and at the too-snug bodice, the fit accentuated by the apron tied beneath. And she could practically hear the salacious turn of his thoughts. A fact that was confirmed when he met her gaze and his green eyes glowed with slumberous warmth.

The sight caused her pulse to quicken. But not in alarm, she realized with a small degree of dismay. After waking up this morning in his arms, her pulse quickened for an entirely different reason now.

She was still trying to come to terms with it.

"What do you have to say for yourself, Lord Savage?" Meg demanded, hands on hips.

"And a good morning to you as well, Miss Stredwick," he drawled pleasantly. "How is your brother?"

"Likely to take you by the throat once he learns what you've done to corrupt my friend and the dearest friend of his wife."

Even though Meg was an accomplished woman of one and twenty, the roundness of her face gave her the look of someone far younger. At the moment, she resembled a dark-haired and furious cherub.

Prue felt a wash of guilt that her own actions had brought such a lamb to this sinful lion's den. She should be with the aunts, where she was staying until Ellie and Brandon returned from their honeymoon.

"I must apologize, Meg," she said in earnest. "Truly, you

needn't have come. Shouldn't have come, as a matter of fact. What if someone were to have seen you? Your reputation would be in tatters."

"Shall I have Grimsby paint the words *House of Ill Repute* above the door, do you think?" Savage asked dryly.

"I came in through the servants' entrance," Meg said to her, then directed a scathing remark to him. "And I'm sure no such marking is necessary. Everyone knows what you're about."

Unconcerned, he eased into an upholstered armchair and extended his long legs, crossing them at the ankle, his hands clasped casually over his flat stomach. "And to think, I used to give you pony rides when I came home with your brother on holiday from university. You were much more agreeable at that age."

"So were you, before your heart turned black. Then afterward, you stopped caring about anyone other than yourself."

Afterward? After . . . *what*, Prue wondered, and how had he been different before?

Apparently, something had brought about a change in him. Was it the same thing that made him a man who only desired four-month affairs instead of any permanent attachment?

She gazed at him, hoping to find an answer to these questions. He did not look at her, however. He merely smiled pleasantly at Meg. There was no sardonic rejoinder or even a nonchalant quip, which was unlike him. At least, as far as Prue knew.

Then again, what did she truly know of him? Not much at all.

And yet, she wanted to know more.

She blinked, startled by the realization. Why should she wonder about a man she'd never see again after their temporary bargain ended? It would be far better if she subdued any wayward curiosity about him. Giving in to the desire to find answers would only lead to more questions and, before she knew it, they'd become friends.

But she did not want that. Forming any kind of attachment with him would only bring pain when they went their separate ways. She'd experienced enough torment from being separated from those she cared about, and she didn't wish to add another person to the list.

Therefore, she decided in that very instant that, whatever her body might experience during their temporary bargain—because she clearly had no control over that—she would not allow it to affect her heart.

Turning back to Meg, she was sympathetic to the concern that brought her here.

"How are the aunts?"

"Oblivious," Meg said. "Thank goodness, I intercepted Savage's missive. I was waiting up for you and worrying my thumbnail to the nub, I might add"—she held out said thumb as proof—"when I heard the knock on the door. I peered through the window and recognized the groom's black-and-silver livery. So I answered the door before Mr. Rivers was roused from bed, and saw a familiar seal pressed into the wax."

Prue blinked in surprise. "Do you mean they don't know?"

"No one knows. Not Ellie, Jane, Winn or the aunts. I spun a tale that you had to stay with your grandmother because she was ill. Unless . . . Oh no! You didn't send out letters to them, too, did you?"

"I meant to . . ." She sighed, still unsure of how to tell them of her decision. "It seems that finding the words to bid farewell to one's dearest friends and staunch supporters is impossible to put to paper."

"Well, now there's no need. We'll return to Upper Wimpole Street together and no one will be the wiser." Meg offered a smile of encouragement.

But Prue shook her head. "It's too late for that. I am a fallen woman. And each time I'm seen in the company of the people I care about the most, the more society turns their backs on them. I cannot bear hurting any of you more than I've already done."

"Then we'll go to Crossmoor Abbey, away from the *ton*'s prying eyes."

"Please forgive me, Meg. I know you mean well. But that isn't the life I want. Lord Savage has been generous enough to offer his assistance, so that I may have something of my own."

Meg squinted at him. "He's hardly *Saint Savage*. And 'generous' is not at all how I would describe him when his only concern is taking everything he wants."

"Oh, but that isn't true," Prue said softly, hoping to ease her friend's irritation. She didn't want to become a reason there was a wedge between Meg and her brother's old friend. "He is quite considerate. A gentleman in his own way. And he gives far more than he takes. In fact, he is giving me a chance to find contentment on my own terms. It is everything I could ever ask for."

As she spoke, she felt his gaze on her, the intensity of it as palpable as a waft of heat blazing from a hearth. She turned to glance across the room and met those watchful green eyes, his expression inscrutable. She couldn't fathom what he was thinking in that moment.

"I only want your happiness," Meg said, drawing her attention. "I believe I can speak for all of us when I say that every one of us wants the very best for you."

Prue nodded. "I know. And I will be happy as long as my friends are surrounded by their loved ones, safe from society's scorn, and their book on the Marriage Habits of the Native Aristocrat becomes a raging success."

Shortly following Prue's expulsion from society, Winn, Jane and Ellie had decided to write a book to help naive debutantes avoid scoundrels and to find marriage-minded gentlemen instead. They had even asked her to contribute her thoughts.

But she knew—especially considering her current situation—that she was the last person to offer advice to anyone.

Meg issued a perturbed huff. "You're trying to force them—*us*—to turn our backs on you, but it won't work. You'll see." Then she reached out and took her hands in a beseeching grip. "Just so you know, I'll continue to maintain the pretense that you are visiting your grandmother for as long as it takes."

The instant Prue appeared in public on Savage's arm, that plan would be moot.

Besides, her grandmother was suffering from dementia and didn't recognize her at all. She had a nurse named Annie whom she referred to as her granddaughter, and any visits from Prue caused her to become confused and frightened. So there was no possibility of staying under her roof. But she said none of this aloud.

Prue had entered into this agreement with her eyes fully open. She knew that society held the same views as her father—the duty of a daughter was to be perfect, pure and to marry well—and because she was no longer a virgin, her value was gone. At least, in their opinion. There was no pretending otherwise.

The lessons she'd learned from her father and society were that she was imperfect, unlovable, replaceable and ruined. But Prue was determined to use the crumbled stones of her old life to forge a new one.

She squeezed Meg's hand before releasing her. "You are a good friend with a forgiving nature. That is why I know you won't hold any of this against Savage."

"That's 'Saint Savage,' my dear," he said, rising from the chair with a grin on his wickedly charming countenance. "It has a nice ring to it, don't you think?"

Prue rolled her eyes as he sauntered over and stood beside her. His nearness made her skin prickle with awareness beneath the coarse fabric of the maid's dress.

To their guest, he inclined his head. "Miss Stredwick, it is always a pleasure to see you, whether you choose to despise me or not."

Meg refused to give up her glare whenever she looked at him. "The odds that I will ever think fondly of you again are slim indeed."

She embraced Prue and whispered another urgent plea to return to Upper Wimpole Street. Then, she left.

Staring at the vacant doorway, Prue felt the brush of Savage's hand against hers. She didn't startle, but looked down to see his fingers thread through her own, pressing their palms together, flesh to flesh. It wasn't the salacious gesture that one might expect from a rogue. In fact, it was peculiarly comforting.

Her puzzled gaze lifted to find his expression looked rather grave. His mouth formed a flat line and the flesh above the bridge of his nose was drawn together in vertical lines like mortared bricks over a fireplace.

"It isn't too late," he said. "I would release you from our contract, if you wish."

For some insensible reason, she was wounded by the offer. Had she disappointed him already? Had her responses proven that she didn't possess the requirements to appeal to this rake, even *before* they'd begun collecting more than a single piece of her inheritance?

She licked her dry lips. "Is that what you want?"

"What I want is to take you back upstairs, bolt the door of my bedchamber, and spend the entire day becoming better acquainted. Much better acquainted."

As if he meant to settle her doubts with proof, he tugged her close, slid his hand to her nape, lowered his head and—

"Apologies, my lord," the butler intoned from the doorway.

Savage dropped his forehead to hers. "What is it, Grimsby?"

"Madame LeBlanc has arrived for Miss Thorogood. She is waiting in the blue parlor. Two messengers are waiting in the foyer; one from Lady Sutton in regard to your plans for the evening, and the other from Lady Babcock, regarding the same."

"A rendezvous with two women and a third in your arms?" She remedied the last by pushing away from him and muttered under her breath, "How accommodating. Apparently, there's a bit of room for interpretation when considering the fidelity clause."

He gave her a curious look, and without breaking eye contact, said, "Grimsby, send Lady Sutton's messenger away without a response, a confirmation to Lady Babcock, and a tea tray to the blue parlor."

"Very good, my lord."

As the door closed behind the butler, Savage took one step toward her. And Prue's heart began to beat in a disorderly rhythm, her lungs cinching tight, skin tingling in anticipation.

Yet, after hearing how easily his attention could shift from one woman to the next, she became frustrated by these uncontrolled responses. And angry at herself for forgetting, even for a single second, that a man like him could easily replace a woman like her.

They were nothing to each other. A means to an end. She only wished her body would remember that.

She squared her shoulders and coolly held his unswerving gaze.

"As for you, Miss Thorogood," he began. "Since you've made the irrevocable decision to stay, you'd better hope that Madame LeBlanc has brought a finished gown because we are going out tonight. And as for your peevish display of jealousy just now—"

She scoffed. "An absurd accusation!"

"—while I find it somewhat amusing, there is no cause for it." He lifted his hand and took her chin between his thumb and the crook of his forefinger. "Because there is absolutely no room for interpretation in the fidelity clause. For either of us. I hope I've made myself clear."

His penetrating gaze drifted to her mouth and he looked very much like a man who planned to cement his statement with a hard, thorough kiss. And, apparently, her mind was still sleep-addled and her body still in control because she eagerly tilted up her face in anticipation.

Her hand curled over his wrist, his pulse strong beneath her fingertips. A breath left him, the heat of it rushing against her lips just before—

Another knock fell on the door.

One of them growled, she wasn't sure which.

"Begging your pardon, milord," said Mrs. Crumb from the other side, her brogue leaving wayward *G*s to fend for themselves. "The kitchen would be wanting to know if Miss Thorogood has any particular preferences for her morning tray. And I should like a moment to speak with her about the menu for the week, whenever is convenient."

Prue let her hand fall, wry amusement in the upward flick of her brows. "It appears as though we are both in demand this morning. You with your harem and me with mine."

He drew in a breath to respond, but before he could, another interruption came from the other side of the door.

"Apologies once again, my lord," Grimsby said. "Mr. Devaney is here to see you. I've shown him to your study."

"I'll be there straightaway," Savage said through gritted teeth. Then to her, he said with a long, scorching look, "We'll finish our discussion later."

The words were so heated, the air so charged with promise, that she had to clutch the back of a chair for support as he strode out of the parlor.

And this, she reminded herself, was only the second day.

Chapter 12

Leo stood behind the desk in his study and perused the document that his investigator handed him.

Apparently, the Marquess of Nethersole was the blackguard who'd kissed Miss Thorogood one evening in the gardens at Sutherfield Terrace. The same blackguard who'd pursued her during her indentured servitude in Wiltshire, taken her in a field, then left her with the opinion that *she'd* done something wrong. The same blackguard who, quite honestly, deserved to be ripped apart finger by finger, toe by toe, before his limbs were slowly and painfully severed from his body.

"Thank you, Devaney," Leo said, tossing the page into the fire and watching flames engulf Nethersole's name. "Excellent work, as always."

The investigator issued a barely perceptible nod of acknowledgment, revealing neither emotion nor opinion in his mien. If not for the jagged scar on his forehead, he would have been the very definition of *nondescript* in both face and form. His hair was a shade somewhere between blond and brown, and he had the softer features common to many Englishmen. Given a change of wardrobe, he could play the part of an aristocrat, or even a vagrant, to suit his purpose. And his ability to blend in made him excessively good at his job.

"As for the rest," Devaney said, shaping the brim of the beaver hat in his grasp between his thumb and forefinger,

"I've found no evidence of Miss Thorogood engaging in any trysts with other men at all. But I'll keep looking."

Then he put his hat on at an angle to conceal the scar, and left without another word.

The news should have settled some of the questions in Leo's mind. But that damnable restlessness returned. That sense of lingering between two places. He hated this feeling. And he'd presumed it would have stayed away after the contract was signed.

But it had returned a short while ago . . . right around the time of Miss Stredwick's untimely visit.

He'd always liked Meg. She was affable, intelligent and pretty in a little-sister sort of fashion. But he never took her for a meddler. In his opinion, she'd gone a step too far in trying to lure Miss Thorogood away.

That cheeky girl had quite a bit of nerve, concealing Miss Thorogood's actual whereabouts from the others. Plotting to give her friend the opportunity to return to her other life, such as it was. But really, what kind of life was that? Miss Thorogood had said it herself—she was a fallen woman and there was no place for her in polite society.

Even so, he'd heard the strain in her voice when she'd spoken the words. And it had been that ever so slight tremor, that hint of vulnerability in an otherwise determined woman, that had compelled him to make an unprecedented offer to cancel their contract.

It hadn't been easy for him. He believed that when one entered into a binding agreement, one held it to the highest standard. It was a matter of honor. And after having been raised by a man who didn't possess a shred of honor, these contracts meant something to Leo. So he was relieved when she refused to renege.

But he would feel more at ease once she appeared on his arm tonight. That simple act would remove any doubt, and ensure that all of society knew she was with him. That she was his.

❧❧❧❧

LEO PROWLED at the base of the stairs, impatient for the evening to begin.

He'd just fished his pocket watch from his waistcoat for the tenth time when he heard the soft rustle of silk against silk, and felt the downy hairs on his nape stand at attention. *At last,* he thought.

However, not wanting to reveal any of the restlessness teeming through him, he presented his usual aloof manner. Without looking up, he closed his watch with a snap and tucked it away. "And here I thought you'd have been far more eager to attend Lord Tilford's soiree after I told you that my investigator discovered that the viscount is in possession of that sword on your list."

"Of course I am. The sword belonged to my grandfather. It was presented to him after his heroism in the Royal Navy when he . . ."

As she spoke, Leo swept a casual glance up the stairs and then time stopped.

Every breath in his body, every beat of his heart paused at the sight of her, poised at the top with her slender gloved arm extended along the polished railing.

She was a vision in shimmering deep green. The creamy white perfection of her shoulders and throat lay bare. The cut of the décolleté flirted with modesty but seduced in the way it embraced the perfection of her form. And just below the narrow span of her waist, her skirts flared, full and lush and long with the barest flash of gold lace at the hem, only enough to draw his eye from head to toe and back up again.

Worth the wait, he thought, his heart starting up with a heavy hammering beat.

She held his gaze as she descended, and his skin felt strangely sunburned and tight, his lungs laboring beneath his shirt and tailored waistcoat. He hadn't been this intensely attracted to a woman in . . . well, he wasn't sure when.

As she neared, an uncertain pucker rumpled her brow. "I've never worn such a bold color before. It is a far cry from a debutante's palette of pale shades and I'm not sure—"

"It suits you," he said with unquestionable authority, his voice husky.

His nostrils flared on her sweet scent, the pure essence undiluted by cloying perfume, and he was unable to resist the urge to lean in, to take a deeper breath, to fill his lungs with her.

Her breath hitched. "Surely, you're not going to kiss me in front of the servants."

"Merely admiring," he said, trailing a fingertip along the curve of her neck, her tiny pulse fluttering against the pad of his thumb. "Of course, I wouldn't have access to all this lovely skin if you were wearing the jewelry that I sent up earlier. It was part of our agreement that you accept my gifts, after all."

Her cheeks were flushed as she drew his hand away and met the challenge in his gaze with one of her own. "And I told you that I did not want any jewels. Nor do I want to be paraded about town wearing that emerald collar. I was certain it came with a leash."

Ah. So, this was an act of rebellion on her part. He fought a grin. "And the earbobs?"

"They pinched."

The stubborn little minx. But he wasn't willing to give in either. "Hmm . . . You do have plump little lobes. Perfect for sinking my teeth into."

He leaned in again as if he intended to do just that.

She gasped, her hands drifting to his satin lapels to put up a blockade. "Don't you dare!"

"No?" he asked, all innocence.

"My nerves are on tenterhooks as it is."

"Well then, perhaps you should wear the jewels, for I will surely behave better if one of us were wearing the collar. And I'm afraid my neck is too large."

She notched her chin higher, refusing to concede. "I'm not given to ostentatious displays."

He arched a brow and looked pointedly at her hair. "Then all these lovely twists and plaits tucked into an elaborate coiffure is your notion of modesty, I take it?"

Her pretty white teeth sank into her bottom lip as she tried not to grin. "Very well. I suppose I've become a bit ostentatious in that regard. Although, when I was young, I felt out of place for being so pale and washed-out . . . as my stepmother so kindly reminded me every day. But it was my grandmother who told me that a woman should never be ashamed of something she cannot hide. That it is better to show the world she fully embraces her flaws and they can all go—" She hesitated, color rising again to her cheeks as she glanced at Grimsby who was holding the door open for them. So she whispered, "Well, she would say, 'they can all go hang.'"

"She's quite right. Let them all hang. But more to the point, I don't want you to ever think of yourself as pale and washed-out again." When she averted her face as if refusing to hear him, he stopped and lifted his hand to cup the delicate line of her jaw. "You are lovely. And your hair gives you an ethereal, untouchable quality, that has beguiled me from the instant I saw you."

He heard her breath catch as she stared up at him with those unfathomable, guileless eyes. And he had the distinct impression that she was not used to such compliments. After knowing his fair share of vain women, and some who merely pretended to be modest, this was altogether foreign to him.

It still boggled his mind that she hadn't been touted as a raving beauty—a diamond of the first water—during her Season. That those poor marriage-minded sods simply let her slip through their fingers. Idiots, the lot of them.

His thumb caressed the velvety underside of her bottom lip, and Leo wanted nothing more than to lower his head, take her mouth and prove how much he meant every word. However, if he did that, they'd never make it out the door.

So instead, he took her across the threshold and headed toward the carriage.

"I meant what I said about the jewelry," he said as he settled his form next to hers on the black velvet bench. "It is important that you wear it, otherwise it will be seen as a slight, as though I haven't provided you with any because I am displeased with you."

"Of the two of us, I should have thought I would be the one more concerned with society's opinions this evening. Had I known your *amour propre* was in such a fragile state, I would have showered you with compliments the instant I saw you waiting at the bottom of the stairs."

"And what would you have said?"

She lifted her shoulders in a graceful shrug. "The moment has passed. Now we'll never know."

Mirth tugged at his lips as they set off. He was already looking forward to their future debates.

It was strange how much he enjoyed talking with her, even when on opposing sides of an argument. He wasn't certain if it was the quality of her voice, the candor of her thoughts or something else altogether, but he felt an inordinate amount of pleasure in their conversations. So much so that he was disappointed when they arrived at Viscount Tilford's estate, because now, he would have to share her.

Leo exited the carriage first and extended his hand. "Are you ready, Miss Thorogood?"

"I've come this far, haven't I?" she said, the words slightly frayed around the edges. Then she cleared her throat and set her fingers into his palm. "Only a coward would turn back now."

This woman had more courage than some military men he'd known. And she was facing her own battle, after all.

Admiration was not something he gave lightly, but she had his.

"Fear not, my dear. I shall be by your side, offering my full support. Think of me as your corset for this evening."

A glint of humor replaced the wariness in her eyes as they mounted the stairs toward the column-lined portico. "Cinched and suffocating?"

"Sturdy and whale-boned," he countered.

"Given your tone, that was doubtless meant as some sort of rakish comment. But it sounds dreadfully uncomfortable and something better off left in the armoire."

A cough of laughter took Leo by surprise. He did his best to hold it in, but his shoulders were shaking when he heard someone hail him as they stepped past the liveried footmen on either side of the wide French doors.

Then Lady Babcock appeared. She cast an appraising glance over him, her head tilted in speculation. "Surely that isn't a smile, my dear boy? I don't think I've seen one of those on your countenance since you were in nappies. Ah, and there is the glower I know and love." She tapped his cheek with her closed fan and blew him a kiss from her rouged lips. "I've been awaiting your carriage for an age. Now, I demand to meet the creature who has surprised us all with her sudden appearance in your life."

He expelled a breath through his teeth but decided not to remind her how much he abhorred it when she brought up his childhood, especially in front of others. "Ma'am, I should like to introduce you to Miss Thorogood. And Miss Thorogood, I give you Countess Babcock."

"Lady Babcock." His companion curtsied by rote. Then

her eyes widened in sudden awareness as if recalling the name from Grimsby's announcement this morning. "My lady, it is a pleasure to make your acquaintance."

"I believe I'm beginning to understand Leo's uncharacteristic haste. You are quite lovely, my gel," she said, passing an appraising eye over her. Then she slid Leo a disapproving glance. "But did you have to be in such a hurry that you couldn't have purchased a few baubles for her to wear? You know very well her lack of jewels will be the first thing on everyone's lips come morning. And the second will be speculation that she's already earned your disfavor."

He looked down at Miss Thorogood, his brow arching with challenge. But the instant he saw the uncertainty in her expression, his first impulse was to soothe her.

He covered the dainty hand that was on his sleeve. "She has done nothing to displease me. Quite the contrary. Then again"—he cleared his throat, unable to resist pointing out that this could have been avoided—"I would have preferred her to wear the emeralds I gave her. But she refused them."

"Refused jewels?" Helene gasped. "My dear, are you unwell? Pray, do not inflict such a sickness upon me."

"In my own defense, they were too large—"

"I feel rather faint," Lady Babcock interjected fanning herself dramatically.

"—and far too numerous to be worn comfortably," she said with stiff resolve. But when the countess issued a plaintive groan, the hand on his sleeve relaxed its grip. There was a hint of a grin on her lips when she said, "It is his lordship's own fault. From the beginning, I've told him that I did not want such extravagance."

"Well, every woman says that, but we never mean it."

"Miss Thorogood has been rather stubbornly insistent that all she desires from our acquaintance is my assistance in a certain matter, followed closely thereafter by my absence from her life."

Lady Babcock's brows inched toward her grizzled hairline. "Quite singular. That boot is usually on the other foot. Tell me, Miss Thorogood, what is this *certain matter* that has such an apparently irresistible appeal?"

"Well, I really could not say."

"Larceny," Leo answered at the same time.

His companion gasped and withdrew her hand to swat his arm. "You shouldn't have mentioned it aloud."

"And whyever not? After all, that was the exact word you left ringing in the air like a gong when you walked away from our first meeting. I'll never forget it."

He looked to Helene to share the story but found her gazing at him with an oddly bemused expression he'd never seen before. But before he could discern the cause, she shook her head and turned her attention back to Miss Thorogood.

"My darling gel, should you ever suffer any future qualms over jewels—emeralds, sapphires, diamonds, what have you—please do send them to me. And if you require a partner in crime," she whispered behind her fan as they entered the ballroom, "just know that I've always been willing to try anything once. I'm famous for that, actually. Remind me to tell you about a wager for 500 guineas, involving a hot air balloon and Lord . . ."

Thankfully, her words trailed off as their host approached. Leo was sure that Miss Thorogood wasn't prepared to hear the scandalous end of that particular story.

Tilford clapped him on the shoulder and shook his hand. "A little bird told me that you were bringing someone new to our little soiree. And I must know at once who this stunning creature is."

When the viscount raked an appreciative gaze over Miss Thorogood, Leo settled a proprietary hand at the small of her back as he made the introductions. He wasn't threatened, of course. Even so, he would have preferred it if she were wearing his jewels—something that would tell everyone in attendance that she was his and fully embraced her place at his side.

Having only been out in society for such a short time, Miss Thorogood was unfamiliar with the two dozen or so guests in attendance. As the evening went on, he discovered that this fortunate happenstance allowed her to loosen the firm clutch she kept on her guard. So instead of coolly staring them down, as she had done with Phoebe and him when they'd first met, she was cordial and engaging, her poise and grace speaking for her even when she spoke little.

Standing with Lady Babcock near the garden terrace, Leo kept his gaze on Miss Thorogood as she chatted with their host across the room. But he wasn't worried about Tilford. The viscount was an old dog, married now these past seven years.

"This tame gathering is the perfect way to introduce her on my arm," he said to Helene.

"And since when do you worry about overwhelming your paramours with lively parties?"

He scoffed at her tone of intrigue. "I'm hardly a mother hen. As you know, I only think of myself. And it would be a right solid bore to suffer through her clinging to my side for the remainder of the evening."

"Such a relief," Helene said, opening her fan with a flick of her wrist. "At least, I know you'll forgive me."

"Forgive you? Whatever for?"

"Well, from our previous conversation, I had the distinct impression that you felt obligated to keep her. And I wanted to save you the trouble of unloading the bit of baggage. When you mentioned you were coming here, I recalled hearing a rumor that Tilford intends to take a mistress since his wife is in the country for her confinement. So I might have mentioned it to him, in passing of course, when I first arrived." She fanned herself casually, apparently oblivious to the swift alteration in his mood and the dark cloud gathering inside him. "But then I saw the two of you together, getting on quite exceptionally well, and I almost felt guilty for my small interference. As you know, I'm never one to interfere . . ."

Leo didn't hear the last part of what she was saying because he was already striding across the drawing room.

Miss Thorogood saw him, her watchful eyes searching his expression as he approached. He made an effort to adopt a smirk of boredom, but that only made her brow furrow in perplexity.

"Ah, there's my good man, Savage," the viscount said affably as Leo stopped beside his companion. "Miss Thorogood and I were just talking about fowling parties and I've decided to host one in a few weeks at my hunting cottage up north. What do you say to that? The two of you must come, of course."

At the mention of fowling parties, Leo stiffened, remembering their trip in the carriage and the quiet memories she'd shared. At the time, it had seemed private, like a glimpse into her soul that she did not reveal to just anyone.

Apparently, he was wrong. Clearly, Miss Thorogood spoke on that very topic when first acquainted with *any* gentleman. She likely kept a script on hand and knew precisely when to peer off into the distance with a look of such beseeching poignancy that it compelled even the most jaded of men into thinking she was not like all the others.

"My apologies, Tilford," Leo drawled with overly effusive geniality, making sure to unclench his jaw. "But I must steal my lovely companion for a moment or two."

His host blinked in surprise, though he recovered quickly with a bumbling, "Of course. Of course."

Without another word, Leo set Miss Thorogood's hand in the crook of his arm and left the drawing room.

As she walked beside him down the corridor, she flicked a glance over her shoulder. "That was rather abrupt."

"Was it?"

"Our absence will only seem suspicious when he discovers the missing sword."

Earlier, they'd been fortunate enough to arrive in time for a rambling recitation on the viscount's latest travels. Leading his guests to the map room, he enhanced his tales by means of visual aids. And there, while Tilford had been gesticulating animatedly over a map of the Amazonian jungle, Leo and Miss Thorogood had spotted the sword, tucked away in a glass display case.

"Fear not, my dear. I've already thought of that," he said. "Besides, I'm certain Tilford presumes we merely stepped out for a tryst."

Her steps faltered. "Do people actually slip away for . . . *that* . . . during parties?"

"More often than you might think."

"I couldn't imagine having any appetite for dinner afterward," she muttered with undisguised distaste, her color going a bit green. Then she peered up at him, the flicker of sconce light illuminating the uncertainty in her gaze. "But, surely, you do not mean to . . ."

"To have my way with you on top of the Nile? No. Not this evening, at any rate."

A heavy sigh of unmistakable relief left her. Were he in better humor, he might have made a quip about it. Instead, he kept silent as he led her inside.

Leo closed the door behind them, shutting out the sconce light from the hall. The fire in the hearth had burned to embers, leaving only a pale orange glow.

"Even so," she said, "I've no idea how I'll look our host in the eye when we return."

"But you plan to leave society altogether, do you not? If that is true, can Tilford's opinion matter so much to you?"

As he waited for her response, he became aware of a heat collecting in his lungs, scorching the inner lining as if he'd swallowed the coals left on the grate. His exhalation was hot, his pulse labored. And it felt very like a sense of madness was overtaking him.

"Hardly," she offered, moving quietly across the room toward the glass case against the far wall. "Even though the viscount is affable, his nature seems to bend toward condescension. And I have had my fill of condescension. Can you believe that the entire notion of his hosting a fowling party came about because I remarked on the landscape above his mantel? For want of conversation that did not revolve around his wife's upcoming confinement, I decided to admire the artistry of the pheasants. To which, he replied with authority that they were quail. I politely suggested that they might actually be pheasants, considering the engraved placard beneath the painting read, *Pheasants in a Meadow*. But he chuckled in that superior way that men often do. Then the next thing I knew, he was planning a party for the purpose of showing me what quail look like in the wild."

A sardonic puff of amusement left her lips.

In that same instant, all of the fiery tension inside Leo suddenly dispersed. He knew enough of Tilford's pompous loquacity to believe her account. And now he felt rather foolish for his own presumption.

Miss Thorogood and Tilford? Absurd!

Leo didn't know what had come over him. In the past, if his paramours had chosen to encourage the advances of another man, he would have merely shrugged his shoulders at the entire affair. Flirtations were expected. More times than not, they came to nothing. And if they did cross a line, well, it was a simple matter of ending their arrangement.

But what he'd felt tonight was almost . . . territorial. Possessive. At one point, he'd even had a rather primitive urge to toss her over his shoulder and snarl at anyone who dared look at her. And for a man who had never entertained any such notion over any of his paramours, it was alarming.

"Thankfully," she continued with a soft grin over her shoulder, "you arrived just when I needed you. Though, you did appear quite intimidating as you marched across the room with your lowered brow and dragon-green eyes. My first inclination was to wonder if I'd displeased you in some way."

Stopping at the glass case, he looked down at her questioning gaze. Then he lifted her hand and pressed it to his lips. "I'm beginning to wonder if such a thing is possible."

"Even if I am the reason we're about to commit a crime?"

"I've given you my word of honor and, to me, that ranks higher than any law."

She accepted this with a nod and turned her attention back to the case, her delicate hands splayed over the glass. "Honor was important to my grandfather as well. And he was brave, too."

"Rather like his granddaughter, I imagine."

"Well, I'm not too sure about that," she said ruefully. "But it is a beautiful sword, is it not?"

Miss Thorogood lifted her gaze to his once more and smiled at him in such a way that, if she'd said the same about the crown jewels, he'd have agreed to steal those, too.

Unable to help himself, he reached up to cup her jaw and brushed the pad of his thumb along her plump bottom lip. "You should take better care of how you unleash this weapon. It makes me quite impatient. Now, my dear, I'm going to need you to lift your skirts."

Chapter 13

"*My skirts?*" Prue balked, retreating from his touch.

Lord Savage shrugged and turned to open the case. Withdrawing the short sword, he rested the hilt on the pads of two extended fingers, the weight perfectly balanced. "How else did you imagine we would sneak this past the footmen without being detected?"

"I'm not certain," she said, trying to think. "Beneath your coat, perhaps?"

"I never thought I'd utter these words in my entire life, but this is too large for me to manage." He issued a sigh of mock dismay, but there was a rakish grin tucked into the corner of his mouth. Then he kneeled down and tugged on her gold hem. "I won't even look. Well, not too much. Or, if you'd rather, I could simply *feel* my way underneath, hmm?"

"No," she said at once. "I'll do it."

Holding her breath, she gripped the silk as primly as possible and slowly, haltingly, lifted her skirts . . .

Until he began a randy commentary on every inch she exposed.

"Mmmm. Yes, my darling, do tease me with that glimpse of trim ankle and a peek of shapely calves. Oh, and the lace of your petticoat is giving me all sorts of wicked ideas . . ."

The outrageous scoundrel had her blushing seventeen shades of red, she was sure. On a huff, she hiked the gown and petticoat up to her knees, bracing herself for what he'd say next.

But he fell silent. In fact, it was a full minute later before she heard him whisper hoarsely, "I may become undone by a pair of pink garter ribbons."

She didn't know what he meant, but in the next instant, it didn't matter. Because she felt the first brush of his fingertips, trailing along the exposed skin just above her folded stockings.

"I'll need to tie the sword to the outside of your uncommonly lovely thigh, next to your skin so that it won't slip, hmm?"

She murmured her acquiescence, the sound strained. Closing her eyes, she tilted her head toward the ceiling and tried not to think about what he was doing. But with every touch, her senses seemed to come to life.

She felt the cold press of the enameled hilt. The rasp of the linen handkerchief against her skin. The hot drift of his breath searing through the lacy hem of her drawers. And when his hand encircled the bare skin above her stocking as he tied the knot, pulling it tight with his teeth, she felt the gentle tugs ascend higher, as if they were happening deep in her middle. Her hands clenched around her silken skirts. Heat pooled between her thighs, flames licking the inner seam of her drawers.

By the time he was through, she was giddy, her head spinning. Then he lowered her skirts and rose, steadying her with his hands on her hips.

Prue looked up at him, her breaths coming in shallow and quick. "What are we going to do about the empty place?"

"Hmm?" he asked, his eyes warm and drowsy. His grip pulled her a fraction closer. But as he glanced down to where she gestured to the glass case, he said, "Ah, *that* empty place. For a moment, my mind was quite happily preoccupied with filling all sorts of other places."

He released her on a reluctant exhale. Reaching inside his coat, he withdrew a dagger with a bejeweled hilt. Then, as if this were an everyday occurrence, he simply laid it on the black felt where her grandfather's sword had been and closed the drawer.

Even in the dim light, the red gemstones shimmered as if filled with fire. Mystified, she asked, "Where did you get that? And are those actual rubies?"

"Merely one of my father's things, and yes." Taking her hand, he began to walk to the door.

She slipped free. "Surely, you don't want to leave it here."

"I'm sure Tilford won't notice the difference."

"But it's a family heirloom." When he shrugged and took her hand again, she planted her heels, refusing to budge. "I cannot let you give it away for my sake."

"It is mine to give." Though his tone was cavalier, his jaw was tight. She caught a glimpse of something haunted in the gaze that had been so warm a moment ago, but now turned so cold. "If you must know, my father used to flail that blade around when he was in one of his rants. He delighted in tormenting the serving staff. I'm happy to be rid of it."

As she stared at his closed-off expression, she wondered, if his father had tormented the people who lived and worked in his house, then what might such a man have done to his own son?

But before she could ask, Savage tugged her out the door, leaving the topic firmly behind them.

When they were just outside the drawing room and about to rejoin the party, he paused and shook his head. "This won't do at all. Your countenance is hardly that of a woman who's been aptly pleasured. Shall I kiss you to remedy that?" Without giving her a chance to reply, he leaned in to whisper, "Or if you'd rather have my hands beneath your skirts again, just speak the word." At once, her cheeks heated and he grinned. "Much better."

"You are incorrigible," she whispered, swatting him on the shoulder before they went inside. As the weight of every eye and snickering expression fell on her, her cheeks flamed more. "Splendid. Now they all believe we were . . . otherwise engaged."

"Precisely the point," he said to her as they strolled the perimeter of the room. "Since you refused to wear my jewels, you've forced me to ensure that you wear something I've given you. So you'll simply have to resign yourself to blushing for the entire evening."

Prue kept a tight grin pinned to her lips as she retorted with, "You're being ridiculous. After all, you've given me every stitch of clothing I'm wearing this eve—"

She stopped at once. The instant she saw the wicked gleam in his eyes, she knew her mistake. Leave it to her— someone who'd never practiced, let alone, mastered the art of flirting—to hand a venerated scoundrel such an irresistible tool to use to further scandalize her.

Thankfully, she was saved from his salacious response when the butler rang the dinner gong.

❧❧❧

RETURNING TO Savage's town house later that evening, Prue had thought the discussion of the jewels was over. But she was wrong.

As soon as they walked through the door, he asked her to humor him by putting them on. Apparently, he needed to see the supposedly gaudy collar for himself.

After enduring hours of blushes because of those emeralds—not to mention the time spent in the map room and again in the dark confines of the carriage when he untied the same knot—she was tempted to throw them at him.

She didn't even know why she was so vexed. But her nerves were frayed by the time she stormed up the stairs and into her bedchamber.

Stalking directly to her vanity, she shucked her gloves

and tossed them down beside the black jewelry box. She glared down at the green stones winking up at her.

Then, fumbling at the clasp behind her neck, her hands shaking with annoyance, she muttered, "blasted man" under her breath before she screwed on the pinching earbobs, and strode out of her room.

She didn't get too far. Rounding the corner of the corridor toward the stairs, she saw Savage standing in the doorway of the master chamber. He'd removed his coat and was in the process of rolling up his sleeves as if he had a task ahead of him.

"Ah, Miss Thorogood. If you please . . ." he said, then turned to walk back inside, clearly expecting her to follow.

She did, but only because he didn't seem to have noticed the baubles and it would *please* her to have this over with.

Just as she stepped into the room, he disappeared through the doorway on the far side. Well, she wasn't going to trail after him like a lost puppy. So she called out, "I am wearing your emeralds."

"Are you indeed?"

When his voice reached her, it sounded far too smug for her tastes. Then he emerged from his dressing room, wearing the evidence of a smirk on his lips.

Her ire flared. "As you see."

He prowled closer. There was something altogether predatory in his eyes. It made her pulse quicken. He'd discarded his cravat and his throat lay bare. His open shirt revealed a light dusting of curls that glinted gold in the firelight, and the intimate sight caused an instant rush of heat to the surface of her skin.

She had never seen a man so exposed before. At least, not a flesh-and-blood man. In fact, George hadn't even removed his coat before he'd . . . well . . . she'd rather not think about that.

"I knew they would look lovely on you. That color against your skin is exquisite," Savage said, ambling toward the hearth. "Come closer, so that I may see them in the light."

She stopped in front of him, quite proud of herself for not ogling his fine form. Though, in truth, it was nearly impossible. No marble statue or oil painting had ever ensnared her curiosity so thoroughly. In galleries, she usually averted her gaze, seeking something of greater beauty.

But now, standing opposite him, *he* was the something she most wanted to admire.

Oh, to ogle, or not to ogle? That was the question.

When she reminded herself that she was quite cross at the moment, that was the deciding factor.

She firmly held his gaze. "Well, this should satisfy you, then."

"Should it?" he asked. "I'm not too certain it does . . . *satisfy* me."

Lifting his hand, he traced the border of the necklace, the pad of his fingertip stirring tingles in its wake. And he slowly moved around her, like a lion circling his prey.

The heat of her vexation burned the lining of her throat as she tried to swallow. Some of it even fell into the pit of her stomach, rippling warmly.

She settled a hand over her midriff. "If your primary concern is that others will believe I've earned your disfavor by not wearing the jewels, I'll tell you that their opinions matter nothing to me. And I certainly don't wish to be paraded around, draped with expensive baubles like all your other women."

"Your vehemence on the subject contradicts you, my dear. I think that their opinions do matter to you," he drawled, arching a single brow in challenge.

She huffed, her temper so close to the surface she could almost taste it. "Did you even choose this jewelry yourself? Or did you simply have a clerk box up whatever looked expensive and impressive?" Reading the nonchalance in his expression as a sign of guilt, she pointed. "Ah ha! I'd thought as much. So why should you care at all?"

"Because I am plagued, Miss Thorogood," he said, his eyes flaring as he prowled around her again. "Plagued by a damnably peculiar desire to ensure that other men know you are mine. There's no accounting for it, but there it is, nonetheless."

At his begrudging admission, some of the pique that had been building up came out on a bewildered exhale. "But I'm not yours."

"I'm asking for such a small, trifling thing, really," he continued as if he hadn't heard her. He was standing behind her now, his voice low. "You see, I don't want another man to start wondering if he can kiss you here . . ."

His lips brushed the nape of her neck and a startled squeak left her. But she wasn't sure if she was more surprised by the kiss, or the sudden tumult it caused inside her, awakening every one of her senses in a disconcerting thrill.

Every part that had been roused in the map room became alert at once, the simple touch setting off a cascade of pleasure down her limbs, along her skin, drawing it tight over her frame. It was like a sudden rain shower. She felt it inside, too, where her heart thudded rivers of warm blood that surged through her body.

"I would never give another man leave to do so," she said on a strained breath.

He nibbled lightly over her bare shoulders, all the way to the beribboned edge of the sleeve perched on the crest. "Oh, but he will think about it. With all this creamy skin to tempt him, how could he resist?"

"I'm wearing the necklace now and it doesn't seem to be deterring you. So, I am hardly to blame for the things he does." She felt him smile against her skin and it caused her stomach to flip.

As if he knew this, his large hand stole around her waist and splayed across her midriff. "He cannot help himself when you taste so sweet."

"Clearly, something ought to be done about this man and his wicked ways."

"You think this is wicked? Oh, my dear Miss Thorogood, he hasn't even begun."

He chuckled, the low sound sending a shiver of goose-flesh over her skin. And as the heat of his tongue touched her, a mewl rose in her throat.

The next thing she knew, she was turned in his arms, his gaze like molten jade, his hand at her nape as he sealed his mouth over hers.

She yielded instantly. Blindly, she reached for him, gripping a fistful of his linen shirt. And in that moment, she was forced to acknowledge that she'd been thinking about kissing him all day long. Ever since she'd awakened in his arms. Ever since he didn't kiss her in the parlor, or on the stairs this evening, or in Lord Tilford's map room. The frayed nerves, her irritation, it all made sense to her now.

She'd been craving this.

But how was it possible? Where was the worry? The fretting over how to tilt her head? Was kissing supposed to feel like this . . . so elemental . . . so agreeable?

"This doesn't seem too terribly wicked." She intended to tease him, to continue their banter, but her voice turned husky, and her declaration sounded more like a dare instead.

"No?" he asked, dragging his lips over the most exquisitely sensitive place at the curve of her neck just above the emeralds. "In his mind, he's imagining all the ways he could pleasure you."

"Ha. Take his own pleasure, you mean."

"Hmm . . . I do enjoy your challenges. For the sake of this discussion, however, I am speaking of *your* paroxysm."

She felt the flesh between her eyebrows crease in confusion. "I'm sure I don't know what you mean."

"Carnal bliss, Miss Thorogood? Gasping euphoria? Shuddering ecstasy?" When she merely blinked in response, he tsked, a devilish glint in his eyes. "Well then, it appears a demonstration is in order."

Without warning, he swept her up in his arms and she clutched his shoulders. This was when he would take her, she thought. And the sudden intrusion of the ever-imposing *dreadful ordeal* was like being hoisted out of a favorite chair before the fire and tossed outside into a January blizzard.

"Wait. I don't know if I'm—" She broke off, her mind and body awash in confusion the instant she found herself sitting on his lap in the black chair, her legs dangling over the worn-smooth supple leather arm. "I thought you were taking me to . . . um . . . bed?"

"As pleased as I am by your eager invitation," he drawled sardonically, "this location better suits my current plans."

"So, then, you're not going to . . ."

He shook his head. "Not tonight, sweet."

When a whoosh of relief escaped her, he chuckled. "My poor, wounded ego."

She smiled despite her embarrassment. And she could only feel this way because, in the short time of their acquaintance, she already knew that he was a man of his word.

So when he kissed her again, she welcomed him.

His mouth nibbled lightly against hers, coaxing her to follow every angle and tilt like a ravenous nestling, keeping her needing just one more taste and then another. It was diabolical. He was making her crave the firm pressure, the consuming intensity that she'd only sampled in his study. She knew what he was capable of giving her. But he was holding back.

She wanted to taste the heat of him, to feel the sensuous glide of his tongue. Oh, this scoundrel was dangerous to kiss. The more she surrendered to his tender assault on her senses, to these languid sips, the more she wanted . . . well . . . *more*.

So she held his face and took what she needed. She drew his flesh into her mouth with gentle suction, then feasted on his gruff grunt of surprise. And something deep inside her shifted at the sound, clenching sweetly.

Savage held the back of her nape and made her forget all the reasons she might have been reluctant to be in his arms. Tentatively, she explored the open neck of his shirt. The warmth of his skin and dusting of crisp curls beneath her fingertips fascinated her. She'd never been so bold. But her pulse accelerated at the low purr of contentment he emitted.

Then, as if to show her how lovely it was simply to touch, skin to skin, his hand stroked aimlessly, lazily, along her back and the bare length of her arm in tingling passes that drew her flesh taut and aching beneath the fine weave of her cambric chemise.

He seemed to sense the subtle alterations in her body and moved to soothe her, his hand sliding to her corseted waist, rising up her ribs to pause beneath the heavy swell of her breast. Her heart quickened as his thumb drifted up along the satin of her gown, passing lightly over the center. Her flesh puckered instantly. A spear of sensation shot down to her groin, forcing her awareness on the pulse that labored there as he caressed and kneaded and aroused her flesh. She shifted restlessly on his lap.

As he spread an intoxicating path of openmouthed kisses down the column of her throat, she was barely aware of her dress slackening, the tug of her sleeve slipping from her shoulder, the gentle rasp of his fingertips caressing the vulnerable skin that spilled over the beribboned edge of her neckline. Then he stole underneath to cup her breast, flesh to flesh. And without thought—or an ounce of modesty—

she arched into his palm. Positively shameless! But she couldn't seem to help it.

"You're so charmingly receptive, my dear," he said, his breath hot against her skin. His hand plumped the milky swell, baring the pale globe to the glow of firelight. "Let's see how you react to this."

She gasped as his mouth lowered over her. Her hands flew up to his head reflexively, her fingers weaving into the thick locks as he bathed the tender peak with his tongue. But even then, she did not shove him away. Instead, she held him closer, her back bowing as he traced the ruched center with a tantalizing swirl and then a flick over the taut bud.

Confused by her response, she let a strained sound erupt from her throat as he began to draw on her flesh with gentle tugs, murmuring his approval.

Apparently, she was pleasing him and she didn't even know how she was doing it. All she knew was that she didn't want him to stop.

He whispered endearments against the dampened peak, saying that she was lovely and perfect and he wanted her to bloom for him. His hand coasted over her waist and hips, drifting down her legs in a leisurely caress, and her slippers fell to the floor, one after the other in a muffled thud. Then the pad of his thumb rubbed circles into the arches of each foot, sensations climbing warmly up along the inside of her limbs.

She squirmed in his lap, pressing her knees together, breathless as he shifted to her other breast to lave her flesh with the same thorough attentiveness, his fingers touching and teasing a path along her stockings and pink garter ribbons. And she wondered if all their kisses would end like this.

Until he cupped her . . . *there.*

Prue startled, jolting beneath him. She pulled his head

away, dislodging his mouth from her breast. Stiffening, she squeezed her legs shut tight as she took hold of his wrist.

"Whyever would you . . ." She couldn't finish. She was too confused—gasping and confused as his hand moved in a slow rotation.

"Because you're so warm and soft, especially right here." He made a point of undulating his hand against the tender throb and she made a choked sound. "Surely, your gentleman touched you here, did he not?"

She shook her head. The only time that George had been near that part of her, he'd been rutting over her with bruising force.

"The cad," he growled. "It's barbaric for a man to take his pleasure without seeing to yours. At the very least, he should have ensured your readiness. I will always do so. You have my solemn vow."

"If it involves this, then I will never be ready." She blushed crimson. Possibly purple at the sight of the strong forearm dusted with golden hair enveloped in the green silk of her dress, and the large hand between her thighs.

"But surely, in the darkness of your bedchamber at night, you've put your own—"

"Certainly not," she rasped indignantly, her cheeks aflame with mortification.

Well . . . not entirely with mortification. There was something else, too. Something that felt good. Scandalously good.

He grinned against her burning cheek as if he knew her thoughts. "Mmm . . . your curls feel like silken threads beneath this tiny barrier of lace, so soft, so"—he made a choked sound—"wet."

Wet? She issued a groan of dismay, burying her face into his shoulder. "Let's not speak of it."

A helpless sound left her as his fingers parted the seam of her drawers, slipping into the pale springy curls that guarded her sex. Reflexively, she squeezed her knees together.

"Don't be shy. Open for me," he whispered into her ear. The hot caress of his breath sent tingles adrift inside her, spiraling down into the pit of her stomach and descending lower in heavy liquid throbs. "Let me touch you."

She screwed her eyes shut tight, trying to block out the tantalizing, pulsing sensations as he massaged her mons in a circular motion, his mouth nuzzling that vulnerable place just beneath her earlobe. He really wasn't playing fair.

"Think of this bedchamber," he whispered, "as a haven where you can say anything, try whatever whim takes your fancy, whisper your secret desires. You should never be embarrassed by the things you do, the words you cry out or the promises you might make at the height of passion. It will only be the two of us here and no need to hold back. No one to judge you. No one to shame you for losing control."

"But I don't want to lose control."

"You'll like this, moonflower. It's just a small surrender, really. I only want to feel you come apart in my hands."

Opening her eyes, she looked at him and saw no calculated gleam, only blatant desire beneath a drowsy fan of dark amber lashes. His skin looked burnished over the bridge of his nose and the crests of his cheeks. And further down, pressed against the curve of her hip was proof of his arousal.

Knowing that this impossibly beautiful man wanted her—pale and washed-out Prudence Thorogood—made her feel a bit braver than before. She rested her hands along the taut strain of his jaw and pressed her mouth to his in wordless acquiescence.

His arms surrounded her and they kissed each other as if they'd been starving their whole lives. Ravenous, greedy kisses that tumbled into slow, languorous tastes, deeper and deeper. Arching kisses that ate the sighs from her lips as he kneaded the tender flesh of her breasts, rolling the tips between his thumb and forefinger until she was gasping and writhing.

He lowered his head once more to her breast, hunting for the dusky peak, feasting on her, tugging on her flesh with erotic pulls, slow and deep. And when his hand descended again to the sweetly throbbing juncture, she did not stop him.

She never imagined that surrendering could be like this. That closing her eyes and giving herself over to a scoundrel could allow her the freedom to simply feel the enticing touch of his hand, the thrill of him delving through the curls of her sex, the teasing glide along the swollen seam, the drag of a single finger into the dewy heat.

Still, she gasped at the invasion, acutely aware of the slickness that had not been there before. Had she discovered this on her own, she might have thought something was wrong with her. But the way that he groaned, the sound deep and guttural as if it came from the very core of him, told her that he liked this.

He kissed her again, murmuring against her lips about how wet and warm she was. Wicked things about wanting to taste her and fill her and feel the tight grip of her body over his manhood . . . only *manhood* wasn't the word he used. The actual word was too scandalous even to think, especially when she couldn't think at all as the tip of his finger slowly entered her.

His breath fractured, broken and hot against her cheek. She felt the collection of perspiration on the forehead pressed to her temple. Felt the hardness of him pressed to the curve of her hip. The shallow, burning thrust of his fingertip. The glide of his thumb around an excruciatingly sensitive bundle of nerves tucked beneath her hooded flesh. And *her* breath fractured, too.

She curled toward him, instinctively needing to be closer, to join her mouth to his as he tenderly caressed and probed that snug, aching place. Sensations she'd never felt before gathered in liquid surges and methodical pulses that seemed to match a rhythm of his own creation. She was being sculpted from clay. Designed by his fingers for pleasure and pleasure alone. For all she knew, he held the entire universe in his hands, and he was filling her with stars and shooting sparks that spiraled and clenched deep inside her.

She arched into his touch, body bowing, drawn taut, and she was afraid that she was too full of pleasure. Surely, she couldn't take much more or she might burst from her skin. But he continued to fill her with more . . . and more . . . and more . . . until she tensed, straining against his hand toward an unendurable peak.

Then suddenly she shuddered, violently quaking as she cried out. The strangled sound was ripped from her throat as exploding starlight washed through her in rapturous, endless waves that left her gasping in his arms.

He crooned softly to her. Kissing her damp skin, he kept his finger inside her, gently drawing out every lingering sensation until she was limp and cradled on his lap with her head resting on his shoulder.

"And that, my unexpectedly—perhaps even reluctantly—passionate moonflower, was rapture."

Nuzzling into the warmth of his neck, she expelled a sleepy sigh. "I think it would have been far better for me if I'd never known it existed."

"Ah, yes. After all, it is much easier to resist forbidden fruit if one has never feasted on it before," he murmured sagely, his lips brushing her temple.

Once again, he seemed to have a window into her very soul. Savage may only have wanted to give her a taste of pleasure, but what he'd done was worse. He'd made her feel things—wondrous, scandalous, craveable things. And as she drifted to sleep in his arms, she worried that he could make her feel other things, too.

Chapter 14

Prue awoke on a long, decadent stretch. She couldn't recall ever sleeping so well. But it wasn't until she pushed a fall of bedraggled hair from her face and saw the black canopy above her that she remembered the reason.

She sat up with a jolt, cheeks aflame, the bed empty. Thank goodness. She wasn't certain she could face Savage in the light of day after last night.

Peering through the bedcurtains, she searched the room and found it empty, too. Even better.

But as her attention fixed on the mantel, the bronze and black marble chariot clock—depicting the figures of the three Fates holding the reins of four rearing horses—told her that it was far later than she imagined. Nearly noon!

She never slept this late. In her father's house—as well as her aunt and uncle's—she would have been berated endlessly for this.

Scrambling out of the tangle of bedclothes, she dashed across the room only to look down at herself and—*Holy Pekingese!* She came to a jarring halt at the edge of the rug.

She was wearing her chemise. *Only* her chemise.

Dimly, she recalled Savage carrying her to bed and, when she was still dazed from pleasure, he'd stripped her slowly, promising once more that he wouldn't take her. He'd just wanted to touch her, to see her lovely skin, and to make her shudder in his arms again.

And he had done precisely that. *Oh, had he ever*. Her stomach clenched warmly just thinking about it.

She shook her head. Now was not the time for such ruminations. She was here, she reminded herself firmly, to reclaim her inheritance, not to become distracted by a scoundrel's deftness in the bedchamber. Even if he was exceptionally . . . deft.

Hearing a sigh fall from her own lips, she growled at this unfamiliar side of herself. She needed to remedy this immediately and put her shield back in place where it belonged.

Wanting to leave this room—and the potent reminder of last night—without delay, she haphazardly groped for her discarded clothes on the floor. As she was considering whether or not to sprint down the hall in nothing more than her chemise, the door opened.

Savage's gaze instantly alighted on her, sweeping from her disheveled head to her bare toes. He was in his riding clothes—tailored green coat, camel waistcoat, exceptionally fitted breeches, and boots smeared with mud at the toes. Apparently, he'd already gone out to exercise his horse this morning and was just now coming back.

He grinned wickedly. "You've slept rather late today, Miss Thorogood. Have any interesting dreams?"

She blushed scarlet, her body heating from the memory of the things he'd done to her, his tender ministrations bringing her to a cataclysm—not only twice last night, but again in the early-morning hours.

At some time before dawn, she'd awoken to find herself spooned against his body, wrapped tight as a pillow in his embrace, and the hard length of him pressed against her backside. Still wary of that part of a man's anatomy, she'd tried to ease apart from him.

But he'd stirred drowsily. With his face buried in her unbound hair, he inhaled expanding lungfuls of her scent.

And when he murmured her name with a pleased groan, the sound of his sleepy *"Mmm . . . Miss Thorogood"* made her clench deep inside.

She wasn't sure how simply hearing him utter her name like that could affect her so, but she'd soon found herself welcoming his touch and falling willingly under the thrall of his skillful hands once again.

Her third cataclysm had been even more intense than the first two and swift in coming. Then, completely spent, she'd fallen into a deep and dreamless sleep afterward.

The way he looked at her now made her blush even hotter. However, there was a certain degree of smugness that she really shouldn't abide.

So she straightened her shoulders and tried to look as dignified as one could while clutching one's clothes against a nearly sheer chemise. "I was just going to my bedchamber."

His expression instantly darkened with a frown. "Not like that, you're not."

Striding across to his dressing room, he emerged with a paisley banyan clutched in his fist. He settled the cool silk over her shoulders and took her clothes in hand to allow her to slip her arms into the voluminous sleeves. The garment was so large on her that it draped all the way down to the floor.

Reaching out to pull the lapels closer, he nodded. "That's better."

Again, she wanted to point out that his prudish reaction was rather odd considering the fact that his servants were likely used to this sort of thing. But, to be honest, she wasn't comfortable with parading around in her chemise either.

"Thank you," she said and, without thinking, rose up on her toes and pressed her lips to his smoothly shaven cheek.

Startled by this unconscious act of intimacy, she rocked

back on her heels. Her fingertips flew to her lips as if to guard them as she blinked up at him, only to find that he was just as surprised as she.

Clearly, this tender gesture was not something either of them expected.

So she left without a word, slipping past him and down the hall.

Once inside her bedchamber, she stared at the flushed stranger in the looking glass. Was this what the new Prue looked like—pink-cheeked, tousled and clad in a man's banyan? It was becoming harder to recognize herself.

But it wasn't simply this reflection that was unfamiliar. It was the unguarded feelings blossoming inside her as well.

By becoming Savage's mistress, she had prepared herself for pain and discomfort, and for his remoteness and nonchalance. What she was dealing with instead was comfort in his embrace, exquisite pleasure and a burning desire to know more about him. *Everything* about him. And it was alarming because she knew she shouldn't feel anything of the sort.

This was a temporary affair. He would replace her and she would leave. That was the only way this would end.

Reminding herself of that, she added a mental codicil to the original goal she'd made for herself. She would reclaim her inheritance quickly, before he tired of her and, more importantly, *before* she started to grow fond of him.

⚜⚜⚜

A SHORT while later, Leo rapped on the door of Miss Thorogood's bedchamber.

"Come in," she called out instantly. Then, apparently, having second thoughts, she added, "I mean, one moment, please."

But it was already too late. He'd opened the door and he saw her standing near the trio of mirrors, while her maid busily worked to fasten the last few buttons at the back of her dress. It wasn't scandalous by any means, especially not considering what he'd already seen her wearing and, more importantly, not wearing.

As if she knew his thoughts, her cheeks blossomed with color in the reflection as he came directly to her. He dismissed Dottie, kindly telling her that she could leave the rest to him.

"Are you certain you wish to wear this dress?" he asked Miss Thorogood when they were alone. His tone was grave, his gaze speculative in the mirror as his hands adeptly tugged at the fastenings of the garment with the puffed sleeves and trim-cut waist that flattered her willowy figure.

She frowned. "Does the color not suit me? Truth be told, I balked at first, but Madame LeBlanc assured me that this vivid pink is the very height of fashion."

He pursed his lips and shook his head, all seriousness. "It makes your skin far too radiant and flushed, as if you'd been pleasured all night and more than once. Oh, wait . . ."

She narrowed her eyes at the way he waggled his brows, but blushed anew. "Cad."

He looked at the two of them in the mirror, the pair of them smiling warmly at each other. And in that moment, he could still feel the unexpected kiss she'd pressed to his cheek a short while ago.

He wasn't used to such tender displays. His mistresses tended to be more detached, as he was, indulging in pleasure for pleasure's sake alone. And he wasn't certain he liked this peculiar sense of domesticity that seemed to be invading the perfectly wicked affair he intended to indulge in for the next four months.

Pondering this, he dismissed any concerns just as quickly. There was no cause for concern, he was sure, because he knew himself.

Kissing the nape of her neck, he finished the last button.

"All for the best, I suppose. You might as well wear it. After all, I nearly forgot to mention that you have callers waiting in the blue parlor."

She spun around. "But who would be calling on me?"

"Lady Holt and Lady Northcott."

"Winn and Jane are here?" She swallowed nervously, her gaze darting to the door.

"Apparently," he said darkly. "I believe I overheard them mention a plot to kidnap you from my clutches."

A fond smile brushed her lips. "That sounds like one of Jane's plans."

"Be that as it may, I'm afraid you'll have no time to fall prey to such schemes for the foreseeable future."

Layered beneath his usual veneer of nonchalance, he felt a coiled tension gathering along his shoulders, filling him with the urge to bolt the door and lock them both inside.

"That long, hmm?" Her divinely sculpted brows arched in challenge. "There are some of us, you know, whose *foreseeable future* lasts far longer than a mere four months. Years, even."

Miss Thorogood was right, of course. The future was a long, empty road that stretched out before them. When all was said and done, this affair would be a mere stop—a change of horses, as it were—along the way. Precisely the way he wanted it.

"Such a life sounds uncommonly tedious," he quipped, then checked his pocket watch and turned to leave.

⋰⋱⋰⋱

STANDING JUST outside the blue parlor, Prue took in a deep breath and prepared to face the disappointment of her dearest friends.

Instead, she was embraced the instant her foot crossed the threshold.

"You don't have to do this," Winn said, still holding her

shoulders. "I wish you would have said something before you simply slipped away and made such a decision on your own."

Prue expelled a heavy exhale. Thinking of others and doing what they expected of her had been ingrained in her nature. They didn't understand how important it was for her to make a choice that was for herself and no one else.

"I understand your concern, but it is too late now," she said. "I've already made a public appearance. Even though I don't read the scandal sheets, I imagine my name is there."

Jane, in her usual straightforward manner, nodded. "Quite right. The damage has been done. However"—she paused to lift a hand from the expectant swell of her midriff to point her finger in accusation—"if you think for a moment that we were blind to what was happening to you . . . we weren't."

"And we don't care a fig about what the gossips have said," Winn added.

Prue took their hands in hers. "And all the while you've been suffering by association. I couldn't allow it to continue."

Her friends squeezed her hands in return and, in that instant, she realized that *she* had been the one to reach for them. Which was rather surprising, considering that, in all their years of friendship, any physical displays of affection were always initiated by them.

Prue had welcomed their embraces, of course. She loved her friends. But she was usually reserved and kept herself from giving in to such exhibitions—something she had only learned to do after her mother died and her father remarried.

Odd, that she should think about that now. Odder still, that she hadn't even hesitated to take her friends' hands. It just seemed like the natural thing to do.

Puzzled, Prue slipped free and stepped over to the settee and chairs, where a tea tray waited on a low pie crust table.

Jane eased down onto the blue cushion, with one hand

on the arm of the settee and the other protectively splayed over the child growing inside her. "I suspected that was your reason. Though, to be honest, I'd hoped you were on a mission for more research. Our book could never have enough."

She had to smile. Of course, Jane would think of all the educational aspects of the situation. "*The Marriage Habits of the Native Aristocrat* hardly needs any input from the likes of me."

"I wouldn't be too sure," Jane added with a tone of intrigue. "I've been wondering if we might change the title to *The Mating Habits of Scoundrels*. It would be a scientific study, of course."

"Of course," Winn agreed gaily, accepting a cup of tea. "We'll even put scholarly illustrations in each chapter."

Prue's brows inched toward her hairline. "Of nude aristocrats?"

"No, of monkeys in top hats. That way no one can take offense."

Picturing it, Prue nearly laughed. But it wasn't until Jane withdrew her pocket ledger and wrote down the idea that a giggle erupted. The tea she was pouring dribbled onto the saucer. And when she set down the pot, she realized that her friends were staring at her with peculiar expressions.

Jane closed her notebook and tilted her head in study. "It's been ages since I've heard you laugh. In fact, I cannot even recall the last time. At school, perhaps?"

Prue sobered and quickly cleaned up the spill. First an unconscious display of affection and now giggling? It was as if the tidy drawer where she kept her reserved nature had been opened and rearranged. And she had a vague suspicion just who was to blame.

"Oh, Jane," Winn chided softly, her freckled cheeks lifting. "It doesn't matter how long it's been. All that matters is that she's happy right now, in this very moment."

But Jane's brow knitted with concern as she looked at Prue. "I just don't want you to be hurt again . . . afterward."

"You needn't worry," she assured. "Savage and I are nothing more to each other than a means to an end. I knew what I was doing when I first rapped on his door."

The only problem was, she wasn't entirely sure that was true any longer.

However, she didn't want to think about that now. She wanted to enjoy this moment because it would be the last time that she would allow herself the pleasure of their company. In order for her friends to have any success with their book, any social acceptance for themselves or even their children, then their fallen friend would have to stay out of their lives.

After today, there would be no more visits. No more dinners or teas. No more walks through the park or shopping excursions.

That knowledge brought a painful twinge to her heart. She would miss them tremendously. But it was for their own good.

Chapter 15

It wasn't Leo's habit to spend his afternoons in ladies' shops, perusing hats, gloves, slippers and ribbons. The women of his acquaintance usually needed no encouragement to charge up his accounts. They were happy to take, and to take some more, until the very last day that their contract concluded.

Miss Thorogood, however, was not like other women.

In fact, more often than not, when she politely shook her head at the shop clerk, he found himself being forced to say, "Yes, we'll take that one as well."

Leaving the third shop, she huffed in exasperation as two clerks had to carry out her parcels. "Shopping with you is exhausting. Is there anything you won't purchase?"

Standing in the doorway, he paused to look over his shoulder, eyeing the few hats still left in the window display. Then, with a cheeky grin, he pointed to the brass bell above them. "I won't buy this. I simply refuse."

"Such a pity," she tsked. "That was the only thing I wanted."

So, of course, he was going to buy that bell. If she was going to make a game of it, then he would play, too, and show her how these affairs were supposed to commence.

He turned his head, the mustachioed clerk already flashing his back molars in a wide grin. But then Miss Thorogood took Leo by the hand and tugged him through the doorway. The bell offered one last forlorn tinkle as they left the shop.

"See here, madam. This is no way to treat a marquess," he teased loudly as they stepped onto the crowded pavement.

A few passing matrons and their charges stopped to gasp. Their disapproving gazes whipped down sharply to where Miss Thorogood's glove gripped his in a forbidden public display. Before she could withdraw, he readily curled her fingers around his sleeve and held them there.

Then, to the scandalized onlookers, he shrugged. "There I was, minding my own business, when this woman merely pointed and said to the clerk, 'I'll take that one.' Bought me for a shilling. I feel rather cheap."

"Yes, and there's a viscount in there going for half a crown if you make haste," Miss Thorogood said with a straight face, then proudly lifted her head and towed him toward the carriage.

He didn't mind at all. This was the first time he'd seen a crack in the brick wall she'd erected around herself since her friends had left after their visit.

When they passed the carriage and her determined steps led them onward, past the shops and away from the foot traffic, he eyed her determined profile with curiosity.

"If you wish to have me alone, Miss Thorogood, all you need do was ask. Though, I must say, there is something altogether appealing about being manhandled by you. Nothing a man likes more than a woman bold enough to seize what she wants. Whenever she wants it. Oh, very well, then. Have your way with me."

Once they were around the corner, she stopped and slipped free to face him head-on. "What is the purpose of our outing today?"

"The answer should be clear from the hillock of packages strapped to the carriage."

"But I did not ask to go shopping or to spend your money needlessly on things I will likely never have an opportunity to wear when I am living alone in the country."

Her expression was so proud, her gaze so imploring, her words so adamant that all he wanted to do was take her face in his hands and kiss her.

"I know you did not ask to," he said. "Strangely, that makes me all the more determined to coax you into enjoying yourself while doing it."

She blinked. "So the purpose of the outing was for . . . *my* enjoyment?"

"Of course, since you clearly need a lesson in that. Why else?"

"Well, I thought *you* liked it. After all, you were very determined to spend every farthing you could."

"If I decided to keep my inherited fortune locked in a vault and never spend it, then how would those clerks feed their families? Pay for the clothes on their own backs? You, my little miser," he said with a gentle tug on her pink velvet bonnet ribbon, "are not the only person who refuses to live on the charity of others."

"Oh, I hadn't thought of it that way." Her cheeks colored as she glanced down to the pavement. "I suppose we could shop a bit more. Perhaps at the booksellers and the music shop?"

Even though her acquiescence was a bit reluctant, Leo was relieved. This affair wasn't going at all the way the others had done and he needed it to follow a certain pattern that he was used to.

Setting her hand on his sleeve again, he began walking back to the carriage. "As long as I don't have to balance a piano on top of the driver's perch, you may have anything you wish."

"But you already have a lovely instrument. I've been looking forward to playing it."

"If I had a shilling for every time a woman has said those words to me . . ." he quipped. When she looked up at him blankly, he shook his head. "Never mind. Where would you like to go after that?"

"To collect the rest of my inheritance," she said as if the answer were obvious. "There are still ten more pieces out there, not including the deed to Downhaven Cottage. And I'm afraid they'll be lost forever if we don't act with utmost expedience. Do we have any invitations for this evening?"

Why did Leo suddenly have a sense that there was a ticking clock hanging overhead? "Not until tomorrow evening. My investigator is gathering the names as quickly as he can and I, in turn, am procuring invitations, but it may take some time."

She nodded but her mouth was pursed fretfully as he handed her inside the black confines of his landau. "Not too long, I hope."

"Fear not, you will have it all in four months, as promised."

"Less than four months, you mean. The contract will be concluded in three months and three and a half weeks."

His natural response might have been a quip about how it sounded as though she were marking off the days of a prison sentence. But as he settled his form onto the seat beside her, he felt a pressing need to check the time as if to confirm her findings with the exact hour.

He didn't. Although, when he opened the clasp of his pocket watch, he frowned at finding the hour far later than he'd thought. The minute hand appeared to be moving too quickly, as well. Holding the curved crystal face up to his ear, he wondered broodingly if it was broken.

"How right you are." Snapping it shut, he was determined to take it to the jeweler on the morrow. "However, since we have no fixed engagement to pilfer the drawers and closets of the *ton* this evening, is there anything else that might serve as a distraction from your single-minded plans? Preferably, something that will take your mind off whatever has been bothering you since your friends left."

She blinked in surprise. "How did you know?"

"You've erected so many bricks around you that I'm surprised you aren't wearing a crenelated tower for a hat."

He didn't like that she'd become so quiet and remote. Therefore, he'd decided to do something about it. Only now, he felt as if he'd browbeaten her into shopping.

She nodded and looked out the window. "I'm just going to miss my friends. That's all. They don't seem to understand or care that their positions in society will be jeopardized by furthering an acquaintance with someone who has chosen the life I have done. But I do."

Leo felt the flesh on his brow furrow, but didn't dispute her claim. Much as he hated to admit it, she was right. Had she been a widow or even a woman estranged from her husband, society would accept her place at his side more readily. As the daughter of a respected peer there had been expectations of her. But because she had fallen from the pedestal of purity, she was regarded with disdain.

It was easier for most members of the *ton* to cast judgment. After all, no one liked to be reminded that they were only one slip away from plummeting into disfavor.

He took her hand in his. "Then what you need is a distraction. No more of this shopping nonsense. You should be ashamed of yourself for even suggesting it." He saw the corner of her mouth twitch and took that as a good sign. "So what's it to be, then? Would you fancy a tour of the museum? The London Gallery?"

"Vauxhall," she said, surprising him. "I've always wanted to visit. My mother used to speak of it as if it was one of the seven wonders of the world that she'd experienced during her Seasons. Unfortunately, by the time I became a debutante my father referred to the gardens as *tawdry* and *unseemly*, forbidding me to go."

When the brim of her hat tilted and she looked at him with those beseeching eyes, he knew in that instant that he would take her anywhere she wished—Vauxhall, Paris, the Amazon . . . hell, he'd fly her to the moon in a Montgolfier balloon if he could.

"We'll go tonight, then," he said, and was rewarded with her blossoming smile, eagerness dancing in her eyes. The brooding mood over his broken watch dissipated at once.

✧✦✧✦✧✦

For Leo, Vauxhall had lost its charm years ago. However, as they toured the lantern-lit gardens beneath a canopy of hanging flowers, and the wide-eyed Miss Thorogood was delighting in every banality he'd grown to despise about the place over the years, he was now seeing it with fresh eyes. And at her side in the spectators' box, he'd actually enjoyed the clumsy rope dancers, the tired music and the pitiful fare.

"I did not think it possible that someone could rival my aunt Thorley for stinginess," she said with wry amusement as she held up a vellum-thin shaving of ham at the end of her fork.

"There is a long-standing rumor that they've been carving from the same pig for the last thirty years," he added, earning a laugh from her that seemed to brighten every lantern at once.

He also introduced her to Vauxhall's famous "rack" punch. When the first sip of the sweetened rum and lemon juice touched her tongue, she smiled and he was positively blinded by her radiance.

Had he been able to see clearly, he would have noticed the figure in the crowd watching their box. And he would have been prepared for the unwelcome reunion that would soon follow.

They were walking toward the outdoor auditorium for this evening's play, when a figure ambled along the lantern-lit path toward them. Leo felt his hackles rise the instant he recognized the man in the dove-gray coat and top hat, who carried a signature ivory walking stick in his grasp.

"Why, Lord Savage, as I live and breathe," Viscount Marlow said with a thin, serpentine grin. "And such a lovely new companion on your arm, as always. Might I beg an introduction?"

Leo ignored him and continued onward, keeping to his usual air of nonchalance.

But Marlow wasn't finished.

After he was well behind them, he called out, "I see you have not changed a whit. Then again, the apple never did fall far from your father's tree, did it?"

Leo clenched his teeth. Marlow was only baiting him, as he always did.

They'd been childhood friends—Marlow, Leo and . . . Giselle. The three of them had once trusted each other implicitly, sharing all their secrets and fears. And Leo had once been too naive to realize that it was in Marlow's nature to use those things against a person. Had once been too young and too incensed by Giselle's betrayal to see that she'd been manipulated as well. And he would never forgive himself for pushing her into the arms of the man who'd deceived them both.

But he was older and wiser now, and knew better than to reveal too much to anyone.

Without a word to Marlow, Leo walked on with Miss Thorogood at his side. But he felt her pensive study on his profile and knew what she would ask and what his answer would be even before she uttered the syllables.

"Are you acquainted with that gentleman?"

"Not any longer. And that brief encounter deserves no more thought than one would give to a fly buzzing around horse shite," he said in a tone of finality, closing the lid on the subject of Marlow for good.

Instead of heading toward the auditorium, he took another

path that led them toward the carriage. A sense of anticipation filled Leo at the thought of entering the close confines where it would be just the two of them.

She studied him with a curious tilt of her head. "Are we leaving?"

"There really is nothing left to see. We came, we toured, we delighted, we supped, and now we go."

"I've heard the production of *Waterloo* on the stage is quite a magnificent spectacle. I thought we could use the distraction," she said, but it was clear in her hesitant tone that she thought *he* required the distraction.

Leo disliked having anyone attempt to probe past his defenses. While it was true that her brick wall bothered him, he had no issues with his own and was determined to keep it in place.

The sound of cannon fire that began the play echoed in the distance behind them.

"Well, if it's any consolation, my dear, I know how it ends," he said when they reached the carriage. Handing her inside, he added in a stage whisper, "Wellington wins."

⚭⚭⚭

ARRIVING AT his town house a short while later, they both adjourned to his study as if already accustomed to a nightly routine. *How domestic,* he thought wryly. And yet, he acknowledged a feeling of unmistakable relief at being here with her, where he could leave Marlow firmly in the past where he belonged.

"Brandy, my dear?" Leo asked, much restored to his usual humor now that they were alone.

Miss Thorogood shook her head in answer but watched him with curiosity as he unlocked the hinged door of the secretaire. "I noticed you did not imbibe at Vauxhall. You ordered a red port, but never took a sip."

Standing with his back to her, he stiffened reflexively. This topic was yet another reminder of the past that Marlow had tainted.

"A soured vintage," he said absently, hoping it would bring an end to her inquisitiveness.

Unfortunately, it did not.

"I've also noticed that you have keys for all your liquor cabinets and that your butler decants your wine in front of you at every meal."

"As opposed to doing it myself? Do you take me for a barbarian?"

When he issued an appalled glance over his shoulder, a curl of amusement found her luscious lips. "No. It's just that I've always known wine to be decanted in the kitchen or in the butler's pantry and brought to the dining room in a carafe."

"Grimsby is a fascinating specimen to watch in all his activities. You should see him open a door. An absolute marvel of efficiency. A mere turn of the wrist and *voila*, door open."

"In other words, you will give me no reason behind your preferences and leave me knowing nothing more about you than I did before."

"All I can say is that it's lonely being an enigma."

He heard the sound of her reproachful huff as she wandered about the room.

From the corner of his eye, he watched her trail her delicate fingertips over the tables she passed, touching the smooth marble edges, the finial atop a crystal dome over wax flowers. He wanted those inquisitive hands on him.

She stopped in front of the round-bellied glass cabinet—where he kept his abundant collection of snuffboxes—and turned the key he'd inadvertently left in the lock. He briefly wondered if he should warn her that many of them were inordinately risqué, depicting various acts of fornication, but then decided she should learn her lesson for being such an adorable snoop.

"I have yet to see you take snuff, my lord."

"Never cared for the stuff—or snuff, as the case may be," he said as he poured his brandy.

"Then why do you have so many?"

He shrugged in answer, then he smiled when she gasped.

"They're . . . They're . . ." she stammered.

"Artistic? Imaginative? Well-lacquered?"

"Scandalous."

"Ah. Well, there's that. But not all of them. Some are quite tame. Oh, but not that one, my dear. You don't want to look underneath the"—too late, he watched her eyes boggle—"lid."

She snapped it shut and dropped it on the shelf as quickly as if it were a live beetle. Yet, as she stood in the open door of the cabinet, she eventually prevaricated and chose another.

"There must be a hundred or more. How did you come to have so many?" She tossed an arch look over her shoulder. "Parting gifts from your paramours?"

"A few," he admitted, absently swirling the amber liquid in his glass as he came to her side. "Most are from my travels. The collection began when I was taking my grand tour, shortly after my father died." He frowned inwardly, not knowing why he'd added the personal narrative at the end. But seeing a glance of pity in her upturned face, he quickly asked, "Would you like to travel?"

She blinked. "With you?"

"No, with that snuffbox in your hand. Yes, of course, with me."

Turning away, she chose another from the shelf, coincidentally the first one he'd ever purchased—two gentlemen squaring off with dueling pistols raised. A reminder of his father's infamous legacy.

"I'm sure a holiday with you would be quite the opulent affair," she said with uncertainty.

"However," he added and saw her cheek lift as she chose another with a pair of innocent maidens collecting wildflowers on the top. The underside told a more erotically sapphic story. She closed that one quickly, too.

"After I have my inheritance, I imagine you'll be eager to replace me."

He did not answer directly, but noted with a degree of distraction that his gaze fell on the new rosewood ormolu mantel clock he'd purchased. Paying it no mind, he took a swallow of brandy. "As to your inheritance, it may interest you that I have received an invitation to dine at the house of a lord and lady who are in possession of a certain jade brooch in the shape of a turtle."

She turned with a smile, her eyes bright as a summer sky. "My great-aunt's brooch! Will I be accompanying you?"

"They would hang me otherwise, I'm sure. After all, you're the latest *on-dit* and everyone wants to see you for themselves."

She frowned at this. "Am I so . . . different from your usual mistresses? Is it that I have done something, or perhaps made an error, that has incited their interest?"

"Your only error is in caring a whit about their opinions. You've nothing to worry over," he said. And it was true.

Word had spread about his taking Miss Thorogood over Lady Sutton and people were creating an aura of intrigue that simply didn't exist. His decision had only been as a matter of honor, nothing more.

Her gaze turned speculative for a moment, but then she shifted her attention back to his cabinet of curiosities. Looking down at the enameled box in her hand, she asked, "Do you ever put things inside, like lost buttons, coins . . . perhaps stray diamonds that have spilled from the piles in your coffers?"

He chuckled. "No, they are all empty. And before you say it, know that you will not be the first to compare me to this collection—intriguing, somewhat pleasant to look at, but empty inside."

"But they are not empty at all," she said. "They are filled with the places you've been, the memories of your life. Something lurks in the dark recesses inside each one. I imagine, if you put them to your ear, you'll hear them whisper your secrets."

She did just that with the one in her hand. Her brows inched higher as if she were privy to his every thought.

Leo enjoyed this teasing side of her. And yet, he also became aware of a sense of his own unguardedness.

He swallowed that down with the last of his brandy and put the glass aside. "And what is that one saying?"

"You tell me." She lifted it to his ear, drawing close enough that she felt the crush of her skirts envelop his legs.

His hands settled on the dip of her waist, tugging her closer so that every breath he took was filled with her scent. "Wicked things."

He watched her cheeks blossom to the color of ripe peaches, and his lips brushed the crest of one, then the other. But he wanted to ensure that these tiresome topics were put to bed once and for all. He didn't need a reminder of unpleasant things. And he knew of one sure way to distract her.

Oh, the sacrifices he made.

Slipping the snuffbox from her hand, he returned it to the cabinet before twisting the key in the lock. And, for good measure, tucked the key in his pocket.

"Now, leave all those behind and come upstairs," he said. "We have a certain matter to discuss about the jewelry you're not wearing this evening, and all that lovely skin you've left for me to admire."

Chapter 16

Prue understood that everyone had secrets they'd rather not reveal. Private matters, in her opinion, were like old, festering trunks in the attic—better off unopened unless you really needed what was inside. Which was the reason she hadn't prodded Savage into revealing more than he'd wanted to last night.

Even though she was still inordinately curious about his locked cabinets, snuffbox collection, and peculiar need to watch his butler decant the wine, she left those matters alone. After all, theirs was only a short affair. There was no reason to become too involved in each other's lives.

She only wished she could keep everything that simple.

But the following evening, she realized she was going to have to open one of her own trunks and let Savage have a look inside.

Peering out the window as the carriage drove down the familiar lamplit pavement of Gloucester Square, her throat went dry beneath the ermine collar of her new pelisse. "Savage, before we go inside, I have something to tell you."

"This wouldn't be the same something that stole the color from your cheeks the instant I mentioned where we are going this evening, by chance?"

She swallowed and slid him a glance. "You're too perceptive."

"A soothsayer in a former life," he teased, his hand stealing around hers. She squeezed his fingers reflexively, finding comfort in their shared grip. "I gather you are acquainted with Lord and Lady Caldicott, then?"

She nodded. "The town house directly across the street"—she pointed shakily beneath the swag of silver fringe, her words coming out in a rush—"belongs to my father. Lady Caldicott and my stepmother, Dorcas, are bosom companions. She would often come to tea and sit in the parlor, while Dorcas regaled her with the trials she suffered from such a flawed and ungainly stepdaughter. In fact, it was Lady Caldicott who suggested that Dorcas unburden herself from such baggage by sending me to finishing school. For that, I suppose I owe her a debt of gratitude. If not for her, I never would have met my dearest friends."

Prue could still remember the day that her father had called her into his study. He'd never done so before. Never sought her out or called her down from the nursery to be paraded before him like her half brother, Irwin. She'd felt the heartache of being replaced and discarded as she'd gazed down at them through the stairway banister while he smiled with his new family. The three of them even took trips abroad while she'd stayed behind with her grandmother and governess.

But on her fifteenth birthday, he had wanted to see her. *Her!* And she had been so thrilled that she'd rushed out of her chamber and dashed down the stairs in a graceless disorder of arms and legs. Out of breath and tucking loose tendrils of hair behind her ear, she'd stood before his desk and waited endlessly for him to lift his gaze from the ledger. But when he did, he'd frowned at her appearance and commented on how he'd expected more from her.

He went on to inform her that she was of an age to understand that her sole purpose as the daughter of a peer was to be accomplished, pure and to marry well. She was to exhibit poise and grace and, at all times, be the perfect representative of the family name.

Prue had wanted desperately to please him. *And just look how swimmingly that had turned out,* she thought ruefully.

Savage frowned and angled toward her, capturing her other hand and warming them both between his. "Do you imagine that Lord and Lady Whitcombe will be in attendance?"

Her stomach had ruminated over that possibility, churning and roiling with scenarios. Yet, in the end, Prue knew that her father preferred to avoid unpleasantness whenever he could. He wasn't the kind to leave an old trunk in the attic. No, he sent it away for good so that he would never have to look at it or think about it ever again.

She shook her head. "By now, they are well aware of my involvement with you and will distance themselves to avoid further scandal and damage to my father's good name." Even so, she also knew that Dorcas would be watching through the parlor window, criticizing her every step of the way inside. "I only mention it to prepare you for a chilly reception."

"Fear not, my dear. I've survived my share of those," he said with an almost tender smile. "However, if you would rather—"

"Don't you dare let me balk," she interrupted, gripping his hand with both of hers. "I am still determined to reclaim my great-aunt's jade brooch. I just . . ." She paused to draw in a breath, searching for the right words. Then she held his gaze, gathering strength from it. "I suppose, I just forgot for a moment that I wasn't going in there alone."

"No, you are not alone. And for the record"—he leaned forward and whispered against her lips—"I was only going to offer a brief distraction."

Then he did just that. He kissed her so thoroughly that she almost forgot where she was. Almost.

By the end of the night . . . she wished he had succeeded.

Prue did not like Lord and Lady Caldicott.

They reminded her of Aunt and Uncle Thorley. At least, whenever they spoke to *her*. To Lord Savage and their other guests, they were perfectly amenable. In that regard, they were similar to the Grecian theatre masks, Sock and Buskin, smiling when everyone else was looking but saving their disdainful glowers for her.

After dinner, the gentlemen lingered in the dining room over cheroots and port, while the women retired to the parlor.

That was when Lady Caldicott cornered her.

Prue had just stepped into the garishly bright room with walls and curtains the color of carrots, trying to decide when to steal away to look for her great-aunt's brooch, when her hostess immediately stopped her at the threshold.

"Why, Miss Thorogood, you have certainly exceeded expectations." Lady Caldicott chortled, her lips curling into a sneer that might have appeared a polite smile to the other guests already milling about the room and engaged in conversation.

"I'm sure I do not know what you mean, my lady," Prue answered. However, she had a sense that what was to follow would not be pleasant and steeled herself against it.

"Did you know that, from the very beginning, Dorcas and I knew you would not amount to anything? Such a washed-out creature, you hardly garnered notice. Oh, but you took care of that, didn't you? Then again, what man would refuse what is so freely offered?" She pursed her lips, her disgusted gaze raking down Prue's figure. "Though it is fortunate that Lord Nethersole did not fall for your scheme to become a marchioness by way of entrapment."

Prue stiffened at once, her chin notching higher. "I had no such scheme. Now, if you would excuse me."

She took a step back, trying to leave the room, but she was momentarily caught between her hostess and a large Egyptian urn near the doorway. Then, the horrible woman seized her arm, cinching it tightly to her side.

"The only reason you are accepted beneath this roof at all is because you are a curiosity for my guests. We delight in the ridiculous, you see," she hissed. "And we are all waiting until the day comes when we are driving by in our carriages and see a familiar washed-out face, selling her wares in some dark alley."

Prue's hands trembled, the arm beneath her hostess's grip numb with shock. She was stunned by the venomous attack. It was not the only time she'd encountered scorn for being one of the fallen. There was gossip, of course, whispers behind fans and gloved hands. But this? This was pure contempt.

She hadn't been prepared for it.

Perhaps it was an ignorant mistake on her part. After all, how could her reception have been any different? She knew well that the very society who saw a woman's worth in her innocence and marriageability would be appalled by her agreement with Lord Savage. The same society who applauded George's actions.

She opened her mouth to respond, but her throat was dry and only a strangled sound emerged.

Lady Caldicott issued a haughty laugh. "Even though your protector is something of a celebrated scoundrel, you are nothing more than a whore."

"That is rather the pot calling the kettle black. Is it not, my lady?" drawled a familiar voice behind her, instantly making it easier for Prue to breathe. It had the opposite effect on their hostess, who blanched as Savage continued in a low tone. "After all, I seem to recall a certain fox hunt in my youth where you and my father became separated from the party for quite a while. You were a debutante in your first Season, I believe. And you returned with grass stains on your skirts . . . From a tumble, wasn't it?"

Lady Caldicott's mouth dropped open, her cheeks altering between pasty white and ruddy red as she glanced surreptitiously over her shoulder. "I'm sure you're mistaken."

"And I'm sure I am not," he said, the unmistakable threat hanging between them. All he had to do was speak a little louder and she would be ruined. "I bid you a good evening, my lady."

Savage splayed a warm hand onto the small of Prue's back and escorted her into the hall.

Numbly, she walked beside him as they entered the foyer. It occurred to her that the worst part of this evening was that Lady Caldicott's waspish setdown had taken her unawares. Surprisingly, it had hurt, too.

In those moments, she'd felt vulnerable and small, like a child. Her usual shield had not been within easy reach. But what troubled her most of all was how relieved she'd felt when Savage appeared at her side.

She was a strong, independent woman who was taking control of her life. Surely, after such a short time with him, she hadn't unthinkingly lowered her guard this much. Had she? And if that was the case, then what else might she have left herself open to?

It wasn't until they were inside the carriage and driving away that she remembered the purpose of this horrible evening. "Wait! My great-aunt's brooch."

"I already have it in my pocket, my dear." He reached inside his coat to hand it to her. As her fingers curled around the turtle, he cupped her cheek. "That is why I came to find you, and I'm glad I did."

"I didn't need you to come to my rescue," she said sharply, trying to be strong. But when she saw the shadow of a frown cross his features, she knew he didn't deserve her ire. She was only mad at herself. So, she laid her hand over his. "But I'm glad you did, all the same."

He accepted this with a nod and tucked her against his side as the carriage rumbled over the cobblestone. "Though,

I must say, I had the devil of a time getting into Lady Caldicott's drawers. Thought it would take the king's army and a battering ram to pry them loose."

Prue attempted a smile at his bawdy quip, but she was too preoccupied with her inner battle against the overwhelming desire to rest her head on his shoulder. After all, if she'd learned one thing this evening, it was to keep herself more guarded.

❧❧❧

BUT LATER that night, she could not find the strength to close herself off from him. Not when they were alone in his chamber. He'd told her before that this was a safe and sacred place, and she believed that was true.

However, when he held her close in his chair by the fire, warming her with kisses and shared sips of brandy, she realized something alarming. Something that made her pulse gallop in a panic.

Somehow, against her better intentions, she'd grown fond of him. Terribly fond. *Oh, Pekingese!*

"Did you just say . . . *Pekingese?*" he asked with a curious smile against her lips.

She withdrew with a start. Her cheeks heated and she shook her head. "I hadn't meant to. Well, not aloud at any rate. It's just the harshest epithet I could think of."

"Hmm . . . And why, pray tell, are you cursing when I kiss you?"

"Because I like this," she confessed miserably, her hands fisting in his shirtsleeves. "Quite a lot, in fact. And I like you, as well, which was never my intention."

A small curl of sympathetic amusement lifted one corner of his mouth as he brushed a lock of hair from her cheek and tucked it behind her ear. "Ah, yes. One must always keep a safe distance from troublesome sentiment."

"Precisely." She nodded and turned to press a kiss into

his palm, glad he understood. Then she took a drink from their shared snifter before handing it to him. And with a heavy sigh, she added, "Therefore, there's only one thing you can do to remedy this. You'll simply have to put me through the dreadful ordeal. I'd be sure to hate you afterward."

He went still for a moment, not breathing, glass poised at his lips. Over the rim, his eyes turned almost black, surrounded by a ring of simmering green. And between them, she could feel the frightening potency of his desire.

She swallowed and garnered her courage. "I am in earnest. You may have me if you like."

He tipped back the brandy and drained the glass. A slow, searing, sweet-scented breath seeped out from his lips. Then he set the empty snifter on the table. By the time his gaze returned to her, the pulse at her throat was thumping frantically. It fluttered against the pad of his finger.

He grinned softly. "No need to martyr yourself quite yet."

"But I want to bring you to"—she hesitated before whispering—"shuddering ecstasy."

"Soon, moonflower." His lips pressed against hers in a lingering caress that quickly transformed into something deeper and urgent. And as he carried her to bed, she heard him mutter beneath his breath, "It had bloody well better be soon, or I'll go mad."

She wanted to ask what he meant—what he was waiting for—but feared he would mention some glaring deficiency on her part. So as he held her in his arms and stroked her body, she kissed him back with every ounce of passion she possessed. There was no use fighting it.

Even so, Prue made a new plan. She was going to reclaim her inheritance, take control of her life, and absolutely, positively not allow herself to fall in love with him.

Chapter 17

By the following morning, Leo was in such an acute state of arousal that if he heard one more kitten purr of sleepy contentment from the warm, supple woman in his arms, he was going to lose what remained of his sanity.

As he'd been doing of late, he carefully peeled himself away from his adorable Rip Van Winkle, slipped out of bed, dressed and took his gray for a vigorous ride through Hyde Park until they were both winded from the exercise.

But it wasn't enough. He could still feel her against him, as if her body had left an indelible imprint. Could still smell her sweet fragrance on his skin. And hear her soft words . . . *You may have me if you like.*

And just like that, he was back to square one and hard as a granite monolith.

He cursed. There was no way he could return to the town house in the shape he was in; therefore, he needed something more brutal than a ride to spend his frustration. And he knew precisely where to go.

A short time later, Leo strode through the door of Sterling's gaming hell, tipping his hat to Mr. Finch on his way through the black marble foyer. Climbing the stairs, he pounded on Reed Sterling's office door.

"Go away," a gravelly voice muttered from the other side.

Leo ignored the order, opened the door anyway and saw the former prize fighter in a less than noble position, hunched in his chair and face down on his desk. "You owe me a fight, Sterling, and I'm here to collect."

"Can you not see that I'm sleeping?"

"Is that what you call it? Did you know that civilized people—not apes like you, of course—do that sort of thing in a bed?"

Sterling's blunt-fingered hand absently groped for an object on his desk.

"Are you sure you want to throw that ink bottle at me? You'll make quite the mess," Leo said helpfully as he moved into the room, keeping an eye on that hand as it crawled to something else. He tsked. "The ledger will hardly make a suitable projectile. And now the letter knife? Honestly. How can you be to the point of wanting to stab me already?"

Still holding the bronze hilt, Sterling lifted his dark head and squinted a pair of bloodshot eyes at him. "My wife and I have a pair of newborns at home."

"Felicitations, by the way. I hope you received the gifts I sent."

"Aye. It was so good of you to send that pair of ponies, the circus performers and two crates of whisky to the door," he gritted through clenched teeth. "Ainsley and I don't have nearly enough to do during the day as it is."

"Do I detect a whiff of sarcasm?"

Sterling growled. "As I was saying, we have newborns. In order for Ainsley to rest, I take over in the evenings. But the twins have no concept of day and night or peace and quiet. So, I have not slept in a fortnight. And this"—he gestured with a sweep of his hand over his desk—"was my only opportunity to rest my eyes for a paltry few minutes, until a selfish bastard decided that my closed office door was a welcome invitation."

"I hate to point out an error in such a grand tirade, but I am not a bastard. You and I both know that I would rather not be the legitimate spawn of my father. Then I wouldn't have been plagued for years with guilt over the fact that he shot your stepfather in a duel of *supposed* honor," he said in a melodramatic way to conceal the fact that it was the truth. In fact, he still carried the weight of guilt over things his father had done, but he would never admit it to anyone. Not with any detectable sincerity, at any rate.

"I already told you, he did my mother and me a favor that day."

Leo shrugged as if it didn't matter to him either way. "Perhaps, but I didn't know that."

He'd admired Sterling from the very first time they'd met at school. Reed hadn't been born into the aristocracy like most of the students there. Because of that, he'd been ostracized, insulted and pummeled each and every day. And that was before he went home to face his brute of a stepfather.

Yet, even after enduring all of that, Sterling had never unleashed the rage that had lurked behind his eyes. And in Leo's opinion that proved he was far more noble than any other man he knew.

But Leo wasn't nearly that noble. He certainly wasn't above trying to manipulate the situation in order to get what he needed. Because if he didn't do something to expend some of this damnable tension from unspent lust, he was going to take Miss Thorogood, hard and fast, the instant he walked through his bedchamber door. And after the callous way she'd been treated by her previous lover, he wanted to prove to her that not all men were thoughtless beasts.

So he was taking things slowly, learning what she liked, lowering the proud creature's shield and getting her used to unleashing her passions. During the process, however, he was losing his mind.

Leo dragged Sterling's chair away from his desk, the heavy claw feet scraping across the floor and continued his dramatic soliloquy. "And for years, I had that weighing on me—the sins of my father pressing on my weary conscience—and all because you never once enlightened me. Therefore, you must fight me today. Right this instant, in fact. It's your only way to make amends for being a rotten friend."

Sterling scrubbed his face and growled. "We're not friends. We've never been friends. You've been goading me to fight you for years."

"Merely to settle a debt."

"You tried to ruin my club."

"Because I'm an overindulged villainous aristocrat. Surely, you didn't expect more from me."

His scarred mouth quirked with reluctant amusement. "You did save my life, I suppose."

"Purely by accident, but true nonetheless. So that puts you in my debt." Leo still didn't know what had compelled him to step between a madman's pistol and Sterling. After all, he wasn't the type to do anything remotely heroic. However, that didn't mean he wouldn't use it to his advantage in this particular circumstance. "Now, up, up. Let us be off to your gymnasium. Surely, you still recall how to make a fist and swing those primate arms of yours."

Abruptly, the fighter rose from his chair, his iron jaw set as he cracked his knuckles. "Oh, it's coming back to me."

✥✥✥✥

Two HOURS later, exhausted, perspiring and bruised, Savage returned to his town house.

Climbing the stairs to his bedchamber, he rubbed a hand over his smarting jaw. Damn, but Reed had a murderous right hook. Though, at least now Leo had hope of surviving another night with Miss Thorogood.

As he opened his door, his gaze swept the room, skimming over the trail of discarded clothes leading from the chair to the bed. He paused at the rumpled coverlet and the oval depression in a single pillow—for his head alone, because hers had been resting in the crook of his shoulder all night—and the sight of it tugged a grin to his lips.

Even so, he was mildly surprised to find the bed empty. Miss Thorogood usually slept late. In fact, the more he pleasured her, the later she slept and after last night . . .

No. Better not think of last night.

What he needed was a cold bath to cool his blood. So he strode toward the mantel and yanked the bellpull for Jones. Then, crossing the room, he began shrugging out of his coat, cravat and waistcoat.

He was just unfastening his breeches when he heard a soft, melodious humming from inside his dressing chamber. Curious, he nudged open the door. Then he went stock-still.

Any progress he'd made trying to exhaust himself into a state of abstinence dissolved in a thick liquid rush when he saw Miss Thorogood.

She was wearing nothing but her chemise and bending over to peer into the recesses of his wardrobe. The fine weave of cambric caressed her perfect skin, the hem rising high enough to reveal a scant few inches of her heart-shaped derriere. And as she hummed her merry tune, her hips vacillated back and forth until he was thoroughly mesmerized . . . and heavily engorged.

At first, he cursed the heavens for creating such a woman. Then he praised them. Then he cursed them again. *Bloody hell.* How was he going to survive the day?

"May I help you find anything, Miss Thorogood?"

She jumped with a squeak.

"Savage!" She spun around and summarily fell back into his wardrobe. Batting her way out of the tight row of his hanging clothes, she said, "I was just looking for one of your banyans, but it appears as though they are all in my bedchamber."

He couldn't peel his gaze away from the view of those long, shapely legs, bared all the way up to that little, insignificant hem. His hands twitched, fingers flexing. And before he knew what he planned to do, he was reaching inside for her, pulling her to her feet. Which might have been considered a gentlemanly action, if not for the fact that he didn't withdraw a step.

"Did you . . . um . . . have a good ride this morning?" she asked.

Offering a tremulous smile, face flushed, hair tousled around her shoulders, she ineffectually tried to shield the lovely swells of her full breasts. Cupping them until they spilled over her delicate hands. Splaying her fingers with her taut nipples playing an erotic game of peekaboo. Then awkwardly crossing her arms. She likely didn't realize that her efforts only enflamed his appetite or how close she was to being devoured whole.

Unable to bear the torment a moment longer, he growled, his hand stealing to the nape of her neck as he lowered his mouth—

"Beg pardon, milord," Jones said, having the worst timing ever. "You rang?"

Miss Thorogood squeaked once more and summarily used Leo's body as a shield, pressing her warm, soft places against his hot, unbearably hard ones. He sucked in an agonized—albeit pleasure-filled—breath, his hands splaying into the small of her back. Then again, perhaps his valet's timing wasn't altogether terrible. But any more of her wriggling to get closer and Leo would soon embarrass himself.

"I'd like a bath, Jones. A very cold one, and as quickly as you can manage," he called over his shoulder. Then he reached out and shucked one of his coats off the hanger. "As for you, my little temptress, unless you want to join me in the bath . . . No? Well then, I suggest you slip your arms into these sleeves and take your adorably edible backside all the way to your bedchamber."

LEO SPENT the remainder of the afternoon in his study reviewing his accounting ledgers and correspondence. He also met with Mr. Devaney.

Out of the twelve objects in Miss Thorogood's inheritance, they now knew the whereabouts of nine, three of which were already in her possession. However, the final three—in addition to the deed to Downhaven Cottage—had apparently changed hands several times and still remained elusive.

As for Miss Thorogood, he'd summoned Madame Le-Blanc to create a number of dressing gowns for her. Which should have kept her quite busy and out of his study, ergo out of his thoughts, for a few hours at least. But it did not.

Instead, his irresistible companion breezed into his study at different intervals to show him swatches of fabric and ask for his opinion. And each time, she left her sweet fragrance behind to distract him endlessly.

During the last—not altogether unwelcome—interruption, he remarked that all the silks appeared rather masculine with their dark paisleys and stripes.

"I didn't suppose you would wish to wear pink," she replied. But when his brow furrowed, she clarified with a smile, "Instead of dressing gowns for me, I've asked Madame LeBlanc to make more banyans for you. It's far more practical, considering that you will likely encounter the same problem with your future mistresses."

Any other man would have been delighted to know that the woman in his life was arranging such a gift. But discovering that she had been spending the afternoon planning for the future—when he would be with someone else and she would be gone from him—irked Leo to no end.

Damn it all! She wasn't behaving like a mistress. She wasn't trying to spend his money, unless prodded. Wasn't interested in decorating his house, even though he'd offered several times. And wasn't interested in scheming for a permanent place in his life.

What was a man to do with a woman like this?

He was about to storm upstairs and order the modiste to make a dozen—no, *two* dozen—dressing gowns for her, and not to alter his instructions for any sort of *practical* reason.

But when he stood up from his desk, Miss Thorogood surprised him once again.

She shyly laid a hand on his shoulder, rose up on her toes and pressed a kiss to his cheek. Then she whispered in his ear, "Besides, I much prefer wearing your banyans, because they smell like you."

Just like that, his irritation evaporated. And the rest of the afternoon he caught himself looking toward his study door, his thoughts preoccupied on *his* paisleys and stripes, gliding over Miss Thorogood's silken skin.

✦✦✦✦

THAT EVENING, they attended a casual rout at Lady Babcock's.

After the experience at the Caldicotts', Leo wanted Miss Thorogood to simply enjoy herself with music and entertainment. Among the guests were the more fashionable members of the *demimonde,* whose appearances at any soiree earned a place in the society pages. There were nobles, political figures, noted artists and wits, along with celebrated courtesans—women who had made their fortunes by keeping company with the right men.

It was a world that Leo knew well and he wanted her to see that there were places where she would not be judged for her choices. She would find acceptance here, away from the scorn of society. And, knowing this, he should have been pleased to bring her.

Yet, the instant he walked through the doors with her

standing proudly at his side, a diamond of beauty and refinement, he began to feel on edge, unsettled. That sense of restlessness returned without warning and he didn't know why.

"Miss Thorogood is not to your usual tastes," Lady Babcock said later, as they sat in crimson upholstered armchairs at the far end of the music room, listening to someone play the harp.

"I disagree, ma'am. I've enjoyed the company of many beautiful, accomplished women."

"True," she conceded. "And Miss Thorogood has a certain regal quality about her as well. However, I was referring to her eyes. There is something altogether innocent within their depths."

He shrugged, his gaze resting on Miss Thorogood as she stood near the piano with Mrs. Johnston, skimming through folded pages of sheet music, every movement effortlessly graceful and elegant. "She is young yet and that will change in time."

"But not in four months, I shouldn't imagine. Which still leaves me to wonder why you plucked her from all the roses you might have had instead."

"Perhaps, I'm merely drawn to her thorns," he said, not even able to explain it to himself. "She possesses an inner steel that helps me overlook the single flaw of her unworldliness."

"Only *one* flaw?" Helene laughed lightly. "My dear boy, if I didn't know better, I'd almost think you were besotted."

"But you do know better and understand that I'm averse to such foolishness."

She made no comment but opened her fan. "I'm glad she seems to get on so well with Mrs. Johnston. The two are very alike, both brought up in society but then ruined beyond repair. And it is my hope that Miss Thorogood will be as fortunate to find a man who keeps her quite well. She may even have his children and raise them in a country house where she can assume a married name as Mrs. Johnston has done."

Leo frowned. "Miss Thorogood wants none of that. In fact, she has every intention of retiring from society altogether once our contract is through."

Or once she has her inheritance, he added inwardly, knowing that was the precise reason she'd insisted on adding the "tedium" codicil to their contract. As soon as she had what she wanted, there would be nothing to keep her with him.

Wait a minute . . . *keep her?* Where had that ridiculously errant thought come from? He shook his head, and dismissed the notion instantly.

Obviously, he only meant that he would keep her until the end of their contract because these agreements were a matter of honor. That was all. And if it took the entire duration to reclaim every item, then so be it.

"Do you honestly think that, after spending four months with you, the girl will be celibate for the rest of her life?" She laughed again. "Whatever she claims to desire now will certainly change by then. And I already have a list of gentlemen who want her. All that is required are a few introductions to see if they suit."

Leo needed every single name on that list. He turned his head sharply, eyeing each of the men in attendance. "Are any of them here?"

"Of course. That is the entire purpose of this evening. I like Miss Thorogood and I want to ensure she understands that this life is also her livelihood. So, no more of that poohpoohing the jewels she's given. The gentlemen she takes for her lovers, after she leaves you, will summarily determine the course of her future. And who knows? The first of those men might be here this very evening." She paused to tap him with her closed fan. "Take care with my new chair, if you please. If you clutch the arms any tighter, you'll likely rip them completely off the frame."

He relaxed his grip at once.

"So tell me," she continued in a lower tone, "have you determined if she's carrying another man's child yet?"

He was about to explain that any delay on his part had more to do with becoming better acquainted with Miss Thorogood and earning her trust. Which was true. He would further add that he did not suspect her of striking a bargain with him in order to trick him into thinking another man's child was his. She was always so forthcoming with her thoughts, so honest in her responses. Surely, she wasn't capable of such betrayal.

And yet, if the past had taught him anything, it was never to put too much faith in one person.

Hearing the creak of the armchair, he looked down at his white-knuckled hands as if they were not his own but a stranger's. Frowning, he unclenched his fists. "I have not."

"Well, that certainly explains your surliness," she chided.

"Nothing of the sort. Merely a bit restless of late. I'm considering taking a tour."

"Splendid. Miss Thorogood will enjoy seeing the sights. And just think of all the men on different continents she'll meet."

Leo looked askance at Helene. "That last remark was flavored with a bit too much amusement. Care to explain what you are—"

He didn't finish, because in the same instant the most beautiful voice he'd ever heard began to sing.

His gaze turned to find Miss Thorogood standing by the piano, her eyes closed as if the song was spilling from her lips with a mind of its own. The lyrics told the story of love that had gone, and he could feel the bittersweet ache of every word as if she'd written them herself.

"Oh, my dear boy," the countess whispered in awe, "I am

sure the list just increased tenfold. What man in his right mind wouldn't want such a prize on his arm?"

She was a glittering diamond among bits of coal. A queen among peasants. She brightened the room with her very essence.

"No one," he said, swallowing down the rest of the words on his tongue. *No one else will have her . . . because she's mine.* And the vehemence with which he felt that statement startled him.

Chapter 18

After her song, Prue had to escape to the terrace to dry her tears before anyone noticed. It wasn't like her to weep and certainly not in public. But she had become strangely overcome by a wealth of emotion. Not only the sadness over the poignant lyrics of a love that was lost, never to return, but also of joy over the simple fact that she was singing.

It felt wonderful to sing again. It had been ages since she'd been filled with the desire to do so. Even though she'd always loved it and had been told by a number of women at finishing school that she was quite good, after enduring years and years of criticism, she had lost her confidence in many things and, as a result, her joy.

Tonight, that feeling had returned in a great flood. When she'd heard the applause and shouts of *Brava! Brava!* she'd felt the sting of incipient tears and had whispered an excuse to Mrs. Johnston. The kind woman offered a nod and began to play for their audience as Prue stepped into the corridor and slipped out to the terrace without anyone the wiser.

She needed a moment to gather her composure. It had been such a long time since she'd felt anything so acutely, and now she didn't know how to contain this wondrous surge within her.

Somehow after losing everything, she'd started to find herself again. And she suspected the reason.

Because of Savage, she was learning to be comfortable in her own skin, to trust, to lose herself in rapture . . .

But at what cost? In a few months this feeling would be gone, and so would she. Which made this epiphany utterly pointless.

A rueful laugh escaped her. Just as she was beginning to truly live and looking forward to each new day, he was inside looking for her replacement.

That was the purpose of this party. At least, that's what Mrs. Johnston had alluded to in so many words. She said that polite society could often feel cloistered, especially to those of the *demimonde*. So at gatherings such as this, they were able to speak more freely about their desires, expectations and interests.

When Prue had absorbed this, she'd felt out of her depth among this set. She didn't belong in this circle of fashionable people. They'd lived far different lives than she had done, filled with exotic travels and fascinating experiences. She'd even been privy to some scintillatingly scandalous conversations between courtesans who seemed to know how to pleasure and enrapture every man they'd ever met. And there she'd sat, completely unsophisticated and incompetent.

After all, she'd failed to satisfy the man who'd ruined her. *And* she was unable to entice a renowned scoundrel, even though she was his own mistress!

It was now obvious to Prue that Savage had wanted to come here because he realized his mistake and planned to replace her. Which shouldn't bother her at all, considering the fact that she never desired to engage in sexual congress ever again in her life. And yet . . .

After the time spent with Savage, she did wonder what the dreadful ordeal would be like with him. Perhaps not so dreadful?

She expelled a sigh of utter frustration into the cool night air, glad she was alone with all these confusing thoughts.

"Your performance was positively sublime, Miss Thorogood."

She turned with a start, just as a man stepped out of the shadows near the far end of the terrace. It was *him*, the man on the path at Vauxhall the other night. She recognized the widow's peak of dark brown hair, the piercing blue eyes and the long angular features.

And he was the same man who'd said those curious things. But Savage had made it clear that their meeting hadn't been a welcome one.

"We have not been introduced, sir," she said curtly, her gaze darting to the door. "And for that matter, I do not believe you are among the invited guests here this evening. So if you will excuse me."

The stranger raised his hands as if in self-defense. "You've caught me, I fear. Viscount Marlow, at your service." He bowed, every movement of his lean form exact, precise, as though he were more comfortable in a military uniform than evening attire. "The truth is, I was in the garden next door when I heard a nightingale's song on the breeze and I simply had to come closer. Pray, forgive me for any disquiet my appearance may have brought you." He took a careful step toward her and reached into his pocket for a handkerchief, extending it toward her.

She withdrew a step. However, realizing that her eyes were damp, she slipped her own handkerchief from her sleeve and removed any evidence of emotion.

"It appears I'm bungling this entire introduction." He chuckled, his expression chagrined. "My only excuse is that you have thoroughly enchanted me. It is no wonder that Savage had to have you. I even heard a rumor that he threw over Lady Sutton in order to have you, and that is something he has never done for another woman before."

Lady Sutton? The name instantly sparked a memory of that first morning, when the messenger came and Savage had sent him away without a response.

"You are mistaken," she said. "His lordship would never

do such a thing. He is a man who values his word. Once given, he would never break it."

"Do I detect a tiny flicker of uncertainty?" He pursed his lips. "Well, fear not. It gives you a most charming aura of vulnerability, which stands to reason since you are new to the *demimonde*. Though, I must say, it's quite a rarity that Savage chose you. Ingenues aren't normally his preference. At least, not any longer. His usual tastes bend toward the bold and sophisticated ladies of the *ton*. Not one with such a charming bloom of naivety."

She stiffened. "It is improper to speak of another party when the party in question is not present."

"No need to take offense on his behalf. Didn't he mention that he and I were childhood friends? No? Well, that stands to reason, I suppose. It is in his nature to be secretive, as much as it is to flit from one person to the next without care. He simply replaces those who were once in his inner circle as if they never mattered to— *Oh*, my apologies again. I seem to have troubled you with that remark."

She didn't realize until then that her mien was revealing her thoughts so openly. Taking better care to conceal them, she squared her shoulders.

"I am not troubled in the least." She swallowed down a sudden churning of nerves, then added with all the hauteur she could muster, "If you would excuse me, my lord."

It was only because decorum had been drilled into her that Prue curtsied, and noticed her knees trembling as she did. Before she turned to leave, she saw a gleam in Lord Marlow's piercing eyes.

"It was an indescribable pleasure to meet you, Miss Thorogood," he said to her retreating figure. "Should you ever find yourself abandoned by Savage and in need of a shoulder to lean upon, know that I would be by your side at a moment's notice."

Paying no heed to this last remark, she stole into the house without a backward glance. But once inside, she couldn't shake an unsettled feeling. There was something altogether too intrusive, too probing, in his manner and he seemed to be able to play upon her darkest fears without effort.

Oh, how she wished Savage were here to chase them all away. It was a foolish notion, but she couldn't help it.

Then, just as she stepped into the corridor, he was there.

Savage came from the direction of the stairs, as if he'd gone to the retiring room to look for her.

He pivoted abruptly when he saw her. "And what are you doing in this part of the house, Miss Thorogood? Lose your way?"

No. Just hoping to find you, she almost said. The words were poised on her lips, but she did not speak them. They were far too vulnerable. So instead, she offered, "Just taking a bit of air after my song. It has been a long while since I've performed."

"Has it?" he asked, somewhat distractedly as he prowled closer. But he made no comment about her singing or whether he liked it or not. She hated to admit that she'd been fishing for praise, wanting to know she pleased him, needing reassurance after her encounter with Lord Marlow.

The viscount's hard, penetrating stare had made her feel like a butterfly pinned to a board, helpless to escape. Exposed. And for that reason, she decided not to tell Savage. She simply didn't want to relive it.

Even so, another shiver stole over her and Savage frowned as he reached her.

Laying a hand to her cheek, he drew her face up for inspection. "Your skin is pale and cold. You've taken a chill. That settles it—we're going home at once."

"I'm perfectly hale. There is no need to end your evening's amusement for my sake," she said crossly after detecting an

air of resignation in his tone. "There are sure to be other ladies who sing. Perhaps you might enjoy one of *their* perfor-
mances."

She waited, but still he said nothing. Not one. Single.
Word.

In fact, he said very little at all as they departed, other
than to give his apologies to their hostess for leaving early.
And in the carriage, he seemed too busy glowering at the
window fringe to be much of a conversationalist.

Perhaps he was mulling over the fact that he might have
had any number of the women who'd attended Lady Babcock's party instead of being stuck with her?

That was the crux of the problem. Perhaps Savage had
never truly wanted her. He'd wanted Lady Sutton. And the
strangest part of all was the fact that it actually bothered
Prue.

From the bench beside him, she glowered, too.

Was it possible to have an entire argument with another
person without ever uttering a syllable? Apparently so.

She should be relieved that he wasn't putting her through
the dreadful ordeal, rutting over her, bruising her . . . But,
instead, she felt inadequate.

"Is it true that Lady Sutton was to be your mistress before I arrived on your doorstep?"

He turned sharply. Oh, then he actually was aware that
she was in the carriage? Interesting.

"And where did you hear that?"

She flicked an unseen speck from her crimson velvet
cloak. "I might have heard mention of it this evening when
I was on the terrace."

"From whom?" he articulated on a growl.

"That man we saw at Vauxhall, Viscount Marlow. He
said he'd been listening to me sing from the garden next
door." And here she was bringing up her singing again, and

still receiving no response other than a muscle ticking on Savage's jaw.

"And you failed to mention this to me earlier because . . . ?"

Her chin notched higher. She didn't particularly care for his accusatory tone. "Because we were not formally introduced. I had been alone in the garden at the time and I could not speak openly about such an acquaintance without it reflecting poorly on my character." When he scoffed, she decided to leave out the part about feeling unsettled in the viscount's presence. "Well, is it true about Lady Sutton or not?"

"There was a contract drawn up, yes," he said with a stiff-shouldered shrug. "It was not signed, however."

Her stomach turned at the news. The sick churning feeling quickly spread through her entire body, and she wrapped her arms around her midriff. "You broke your word to her? You *replaced* her?"

"It wasn't like that at all. I'd extended my offer to you first, which was precisely what I explained to her. Taking you as my mistress was a matter of *honoring* my word, not breaking it. It was nothing more than that."

"You make it sound so simple, as if we were all standing in a line with numbers pinned to our hats. 'I'll take you first, my dear,'" she said, imitating his bored drawl and pointing a shaking finger toward the opposite bench as if it were full of future paramours. "'I'll have you next, then you. Fear not, you'll all get a turn . . .'"

"And what would you have had me do? Turn you out when you showed up in that threadbare cloak, looking up at me with those damnably beseeching eyes and asking me to put your name on my list?"

"You said there was no list," she reminded and he grunted in response. "Oh, I can clearly see that you stand by your word of honor, *Saint Savage*."

"I do, indeed, my dear," he said, and his eyes were cold and hard as shards of jade. "That is why I want you to promise never to speak to Marlow again."

Hmph! "Might I have an explanation for this request?"

"No."

"Then I can make no such promise," she said and saw lightning flash. "After all, because of you, the viscount and I are in the same sphere and are bound to see each other. The only way I could uphold such a promise would be to give him the cut direct."

"Then. Cut. Him."

Savage startled her with his vehemence. Clearly, this peculiar request meant something to him. But he was not one to share his reasons for anything he did or anything he demanded of others. So she was left to wonder about the nature of his acquaintance with Lord Marlow.

When she answered, she was more careful and watchful. "Considering my position in society, such an act would not reflect favorably on me or, I believe, on you."

"Now, you're just making excuses. If you're refusing my request then simply tell me directly. The two of us aren't good at pretending, remember?" he mocked.

"It is not an excuse," she said crisply. "Surely, you are aware that I am less than your other paramours. Less sophisticated. Less knowledgeable. Less fascinating."

"You're being ridiculous."

"And you are choosing to be blind, when it is patently clear to society that I am little more than your . . ."

Prue couldn't speak the word *whore* aloud. It was too ugly. But she saw the flicker of understanding in his abrupt frown, nonetheless.

His responding silence—the fact that he never refuted the claim—brought the sting of unwanted tears to her eyes.

Mortified and refusing to reveal how much it mattered, she averted her face as the carriage stopped in front of the town house. When he handed her down, she made a show of needing to fuss with the way her cloak draped over her skirts. They said nothing more to each other as they climbed the steps and Grimsby greeted them in the foyer.

Savage went to his study. She went upstairs to her bed-chamber.

And it was only when she closed the door that she allowed two mawkish tears to escape before she swiped them away. Then she rang the bell for Dottie.

She wanted to hate him for his surly manner this evening, but she knew that this was not the Savage she'd come to know. He was usually generous and affectionate, and more than patient, too.

What had altered that tonight? His desire for another woman? Her own inadequacy? She didn't know.

She didn't like this tension between them. As she undressed and prepared to don her nightclothes, she was thinking of going to his chamber and telling him that. She certainly didn't want discord to be the last thing either of them mulled over at the end of a day.

And even though it was a rather alarming thought, she wasn't certain she could sleep without him. She had already accustomed herself to their nightly routine, lying in his arms and hearing the rhythmic thumping of his heart.

However, whatever plans she might have had altered the instant she saw the bloodstain on the white cambric of her drawers.

"I've already made some rags up, miss, just in case," Dottie said with a matter-of-fact air and slipped the night-dress over her head. "We'll get you all settled straightaway."

A short while later, Prue was tucked into her own bed for the first time since her arrival. "Thank you, Dottie. You've been an absolute gem."

She grinned and shooed her hand in the air as she stepped back through the doorway. "Think nothing of it, miss. I'll just take these drawers down for a good soak— *Oh!*" She yelped in surprise when she saw Savage standing in the corridor. "Beg pardon, my lord. I wasn't looking where I was going."

Prue caught sight of his gaze drifting down to the stained bundle in Dottie's arms. Embarrassment flooded her cheeks in a heated rush. How mortifying!

Unable to face him, she slid down and covered her face with the bed linens. With any luck, she would suffocate to death in under a minute.

When she heard the door click closed, she let out a breath of relief. She was saved from having to face him.

But when she peeked one eye out from beneath the coverlet, she was startled to find Savage standing beside the bed. His back was turned to her as he shrugged out of his banyan to reveal that he was only in his shirtsleeves and trousers.

"Wh-what are you doing?" she stammered.

"I should think it obvious by now, Miss Thorogood. I'm sleeping with you."

"But I'm . . . indisposed."

He turned and there was something almost tender in the way he looked down at her. "Of that, I am aware."

"However . . . ?" she added, and he actually flashed a smile. The surly marquess she'd known all evening seemed to have suffered a transfiguration. Because the man before her now appeared almost pleased. She couldn't imagine why.

"However," he said, "I see that as no obstacle to keep me from holding you."

He hesitated long enough to search her gaze before grasping the coverlet. And he must have read her own yearning in that one eye peering back at him. Clearly, it was the other eye that she should have revealed. It mattered little. Because, in the end, she wanted him beside her.

Gathering her close, he situated her head on his shoulder

and pressed a lingering kiss into her plaited hair. They both exhaled twin sighs of relief, their bodies conforming to the other. Then he blew out the chamberstick and held her in the darkness.

After a few rhythmic heartbeats and when she was on the precipice of slumber, she heard him say quietly, "There is nothing less about you, Miss Thorogood. You are more, much more."

More than what, she wondered sleepily but drifted off before she could ask. And in her dreams, she was thankful that theirs was only a temporary arrangement. Otherwise, she might very well be in danger of allowing her unexpected fondness for this man to grow into something more. Much more.

Chapter 19

"No parcels today, my lord?" Grimsby asked as he closed the front door after Leo stepped inside.

There wasn't a single trace of amusement, either in his tone or countenance, and yet Leo had the distinct impression that the old devil was teasing him.

He supposed it was to be expected. For the past four days, he'd returned from his morning ride, arms laden with offerings for Miss Thorogood to atone for his surly behavior the night of Lady Babcock's soiree.

He wasn't used to apologizing. When engaged in an affair, he always kept matters light and carefree. He never lost his temper or raised his voice. Never spent an entire evening brooding over trivialities like what would happen when their affair ended, or imagined the other men that would follow in his wake. None of that ever mattered. Affairs were for pleasure and pleasure's sake alone. And yet, for reasons unknown to him, he had acted like a churlish beast that night. Ergo the need to apologize.

"Not today," he said, handing his hat and gloves to Grimsby. "Considering the fact that Miss Thorogood threatened to beat me over the head with the next bouquet of flowers or box of confections I tried to give her, I thought it better to return empty-handed this morning."

The butler cleared his throat. Was that a twitch of those low-hanging jowls?

"Anything you'd care to add, Grimsby?" he asked, eyeing him shrewdly.

With an unmovable expression, his butler said, "No, my lord. Other than to say that your watch has returned from the jeweler. I regret to inform you that Mr. Cutter saw nothing amiss and that the timepiece is in perfect working order."

That couldn't be right. Leo knew for a fact that it was running too fast. In all his life, these minutes, hours and days had never sped by as quickly as his watch had recently been making it seem.

Seeing the box waiting on the table, he opened the lid and checked for himself. Well, it *appeared* to match the time on the longcase clock. However, that didn't mean they both weren't running fast.

His gaze drifted from the standing clock to the stairs, and his thoughts were instantly transported to the woman he'd left hours ago, with the face of an angel resting on a pillow amidst a wild disarray of pale silken hair. A man could get used to that, he mused.

But when he glanced down at his pocket watch again, the minute hand had jumped ahead while he wasn't looking. *Nothing amiss, hmm?*

Filled with skepticism, he snapped it closed and fastened the fob chain to his waistcoat before slipping the familiar weight into his pocket. "Just to be sure, I'd like the name of the best watch repairer in London."

"In addition to the two others I've already supplied?"

"Fair point," he said, scrubbing his shaven chin thoughtfully. "Better make it all of Europe this time around."

"Of course, my lord," he said without hesitation and presented the salver. "Two missives have arrived this morning."

Leo picked them up and turned toward his study. The first one was the latest charges from Lady Sutton's modiste. He groaned with exhaustion and didn't even bother to open it. Thus far, he'd paid out an exorbitant sum, and the bills kept coming. She was greedier than he imagined and this was *before* she was even his mistress. He was beginning to wonder if she was worth the effort.

He tossed that one on his desk as he walked to the window and broke the seal of the second letter. The invitation inside stopped him in his tracks.

Grinning, he pivoted sharply on his heel and left the study. Passing his butler in the corridor, he cuffed him on the shoulder and waved the letter. "Grimsby, you've done it again. This is even better than flowers and confections."

"Delighted to be of service, my lord."

Even though his butler wasn't aware of the inside joke that particular turn of phrase inspired, Leo laughed as he bounded up the stairs.

Knocking on the open door of her bedchamber, he saw her seated at the vanity as Dottie put the final comb in her coiffure. Miss Thorogood's reflection smiled at him, her eyes bright. And he felt the instant warmth of it glow in the vicinity of his chest, where other men possessed a heart. Not him, of course. So the glow merely lit the void within.

"Good morning, my dear," he said, coming to her side.

"That will be all, Dottie," she said, and the maid went to gather the discarded night rail and wrapper on the floor behind the changing screen.

His gaze discreetly perused the pristine white cambric, ruffles and ribbon ties. Leaning down, he pressed a kiss to her neck. He reveled in the fact that her hand reflexively lifted to his hair, her fingertips stealing through the locks to hold him against the tender curve for just a moment. And he liked that it wasn't even a conscious gesture on her part because she always emitted a shocked gasp at his audacity.

"You shouldn't," she rasped, the delicate glide of her fingers curving around his skull. "It's far too early. I don't have my wits about me."

"Then it's the perfect time." His eyes closed in utter bliss at the feel of her unthinking caress and the taste of her skin as he nibbled along her clavicle. He moved to wrap his arms around her but then remembered the missive in his grasp. Reluctantly, he lifted his head. "I have a surprise for you."

At once, her expression turned wary. "Not another gift of apology, I trust."

"Grimsby and seven footmen are on their way up the stairs, arms laden with flowers and sweets as we speak."

"Savage, I've already told you that it isn't necessary. I forgive—"

He cut off her reprimand by pressing a brief kiss to that delightfully frowning mouth. "Yes, I know. But in the future, you should learn to use the rare occasion that I am ever wrong to your advantage."

"A rarity, is it, hmm? Well, then it is a lesson I surely will not need to learn in our short time together," she said with a playful push against his chest. But because she looked at him with such fondness, he knew he had, indeed, been forgiven.

Even so, he didn't want to think about how she was always reminding him of the calendar, of each day slipping out of his grasp like sand spilling through an hourglass.

She was right, of course. Soon, they would be nothing to each other but a memory. And he wanted hers to be fond ones.

So he waggled the missive and said, "What do you say to a little larceny this afternoon? It just so happens that we've been invited to tea."

"Is that my surprise?" Her eyes danced like faceted blue jewels in the sunlight.

And in that moment, he had to remind himself that the warm glow inside his chest was only a temporary ailment. Best not get used to it.

⧸⧸⧸⧸⧸

THREE HOURS later, Leo and Miss Thorogood slipped into Lady Gravelle's bedchamber. Only a slight detour from the tour of the garden they claimed to be taking.

Closing the door with a quiet click, Miss Thorogood whispered, "Sitting in that parlor, I felt like the petrified remains of a two-headed goat in a curiosity shop. Do all your paramours spark this much interest?"

They did not. And he was equally dumfounded by this quizzing-glass inspection of his current affair. The only reason he could fathom was because the *ton* was seeing Miss Thorogood as the diamond she ought to have been during her Season and simply wanted her to dazzle their parlors. He couldn't blame them for that.

"No, but we are using it to our advantage. Are we not?" he said, leading her toward the armoire against the far wall.

"True, but it is something I certainly won't miss when our affair is over."

There it was again, the reminder of the imminent end of things. For any other man, it might start to get on his nerves. Not for him, of course. Just for all those other poor sods in the world.

Tugging her to a stop, he leaned in close. "That implies that there will be things that you will miss. What will those be, I wonder." His lips brushed the velvety lobe of her ear and trailed down her throat, her breaths shallow and quick.

"I'm sure I wouldn't know," she said huskily.

"Liar," he chided, pressing a kiss to the crests of her flushed cheeks. "And for the record, my dear, you are far superior to a two-headed goat."

"A three-headed goat, then?"

"Precisely." He grinned and opened the cabinet. "Here, you search the lower portion and I'll take the higher ones."

She began to bend over—then immediately straightened

on a gasp. "Surely it would be better if we weren't standing in the same place at the same time."

He gripped her hips, pulling her back against him, and began nibbling her nape. "I can think of absolutely nothing better than having you right where you are, bent over, face flushed, my name on your lips . . ."

"Savage."

"Mmm . . . That's right, darling, only with a little less chastisement next time."

"You are incorrigible," she said with a breathless laugh as she slipped free. "We don't have time for teasing."

He sighed. "Very well, my little clock-watcher."

She found the fan among a hoard of others in the top drawer of Lady Gravelle's bureau and clutched it to her bosom with a gleeful grin that caused a terrible burning in that void of his.

"This was a gift from Queen Elizabeth to my great-great-aunt, who was one of her ladies-in-waiting. In the safe at Downhaven Cottage, there is a collection of letters that she'd written during her time at court. And soon, the letters and the fan will be reunited."

He should remind her that there was still three and a half months left of their contract, but he didn't want to give her the opportunity to counter that with a tally of days, hours and minutes.

So, he simply replaced her pilfered fan with the extra one he'd tucked into his breast pocket earlier that day.

She arched her brows in question as she gazed at the ornamental fan. "A souvenir from one of your flock?"

"The women I've known are more likely to take anything that isn't bolted down. Except for you, of course," he said with mock censure and tilted up her chin to steal a kiss. "And no, it isn't what you think. There are dozens of these in the garret. Just one of the many things my mother left behind."

"Then surely, you'd want to keep and cherish it," she said

with alarm, laying her hand over his before he could close the drawer.

"Not everyone has the same charming memories of their mothers that you do of yours."

"I'm dreadfully sorry, Savage," she said, her fingers curling into his palm, gripping softly. "How old were you when you lost her?"

He shook his head and issued a casual shrug. "It isn't what you think. She packed a few bags and left when I was an infant."

"Oh." Miss Thorogood's cheeks colored slightly. "Well, there are some women who simply don't take to motherhood. But it's never the child's fault."

"No, it was my father's." He gave a rueful laugh, refusing to be affected by the tender concern in her eyes. "The former Lady Savage took one look at the infant in her arms and decided that he was going to turn out just like his sire. So she took a holiday that turned into a year. Then two years. And then seventeen."

"What happened when you were seventeen?" she asked quietly, cautiously.

"Nothing really. I met her briefly, and only once." He shrugged. "I'd learned that she'd been living in Northumberland with a widower merchant and his five children. At the door, I'd introduced myself. She came to the foyer and said that I resembled my father. I said that she resembled her portrait in the gallery. And that was it."

He left out the part that one of the children had rushed in from the garden, sidled up to her and asked, *Who's this, Mum?*

He also left out the part where she'd smoothed the hair away from the little tot's face, wiped a smudge of dirt from his cheek as any doting mother might have done and said, *No one you need to concern yourself with. Now run along and wash up, son.*

Then, without another word, she took one last look at Leo, turned on her heel, and walked away.

He hadn't thought about that in years. And he didn't care to think about it now either.

"Enough of this maudlin drivel," he said, tucking Miss Thorogood's arm beneath his. "We have a hostess to flatter endlessly about the quaintness of her garden. Then the remainder of the day will be ours to enjoy."

"There will be no more annoyingly prying questions allowed whatsoever. And certainly, no more mentions of our parents," she said with a sheepish grin.

Her nose wrinkled adorably and he couldn't resist pressing a kiss to it before they took the back stairs to go down a flight and pretend that they'd come from the garden.

"What would you say to tickets to the theatre this evening?"

"I would say yes without . . . hesitation," she said, her answer stilted and strained as she looked ahead.

Leo followed her gaze across the foyer to see Lord and Lady Whitcombe in the doorway. The four of them stopped and stared at each other.

Leo suspected that his own invitation to tea had everything to do with Lady Gravelle—an empress of society tittle-tattle—wanting to incite a spectacle and insinuate herself as the creator.

However, there was no scandal to be had that day.

Because the tall, imperial Lord Whitcombe and his short, scowling wife took one disdainful look at Miss Thorogood, turned, then left.

As the butler closed the door behind her father and stepmother, Leo wished there'd been a confrontation. He wanted to tell the *honorable* Lord Whitcombe exactly what he thought of him.

How dare that despicable excuse of a man look at his own daughter with such disfavor and dismissal! She never would have been in this circumstance if not for his own actions. That peer of the realm had decided that her one small, insignificant act—like giving her first kiss to a man in a secluded garden—was enough to end the life she knew? If he had a modicum of honor, he would have accepted his daughter's apology—because Leo had no doubt she'd begged for her father's forgiveness—then quietly removed her from that garden.

He would have protected her. Shielded her with his good name.

Instead, he'd sent her away. Disowned her. Disposed of her rightful inheritance. And left her wholly unprotected from the blackguard who'd taken her innocence!

What Miss Thorogood had needed was someone to rely upon. Someone to help and guide her. Not treat her with callous disregard and then abandon her.

Leo was brimming with a fury that was completely futile. It was palpable, boiling through his veins, tightening in blistering bands along his shoulders and neck. And yes, he realized his reaction was likely more volatile due to the resurfacing of his own memories. But, damn it all, Miss Thorogood deserved better.

"Do you think Lady Gravelle knew—" she started to say, but stopped and expelled a lengthy sigh. "Of course she did. Our hostess likely planned for all of us to meet in the parlor where she would be sitting front and center for the performance."

"If she wishes to be at the center of a scandal, we can be far more creative than this puppet show."

She shook her head. "There's no need. This meeting was inevitable, after all. I am perfectly fine. And besides, there's no more talk of parents allowed, right?"

He resisted the urge to haul her into his embrace and kiss her soundly.

When he thought of all she'd overcome, he marveled at

her strength. How strange it was that he'd once thought he saw a hint of fragility in her gaze. It must have been a trick of the light.

"Right," he agreed, lifting her fingers to his lips.

She nodded. "However, I can honestly say that I wish we'd left a snake in her drawers."

"Doubtless, it would have been the only snake to enter her drawers for a very long time."

Chapter 20

When Prue and Savage returned to his town house, he suggested that she relax in a hot bath before they attended the theatre. Suspecting he made the offer out of some misguided notion of her being too upset from the encounter with her father and stepmother, she squared her shoulders and assured him that she required no such pampering.

"I am made of sterner stuff," she said proudly. "Besides, it is late afternoon and I need to decide what to wear."

Without a word, he took her by the hand and led her to a door on the other side of his dressing room and revealed a vast marble-tiled bathing chamber. A gleaming copper tub waited with curls of fragrant steam rising from a surface strewn with . . . rose petals.

A smile touched her lips as she recalled the first night of her arrival and the petals spilling everywhere. She couldn't resist plucking one from the surface, brushing the softness against her cheek, and thinking about all the things that had changed since then, her fondness for him growing day by day.

"Very well," she said. "Perhaps a bath wouldn't be the worst thing to happen today."

The corner of his mouth quirked in that teasing grin. "If you're unsure, then I would gladly use this for my own—"

"Go. This bath is mine." She gave him a playful shove. But before he could leave, she curled her hands over his lapels, rose up to her toes and pressed her lips to his. "Thank you, Savage."

The door closed with a soft click when he left. She was grateful for the quiet and for the glass of brandy waiting on the table beside various brown phials. After unfastening the buttons of her spencer and draping it over a fiddle-backed chair, she took warming sips in between removing her bib-front muslin and underpinnings.

By the time she slipped into the water, she was heated from the inside out.

A sigh left her as she eased back and allowed the rose petals to caress her skin. Absently, she began removing the stoppers and examining the contents of the phials, and discovering various fragrances. Drop by drop, she made her own scented concoction, the bath oils turning the water milky and slick on her skin. Taking another deep swallow of sweet apricot brandy, she rested the nape of her neck against the smooth lip of the tub and closed her eyes.

For many moments, her thoughts drifted, dreamlike, floating like red petals that brushed against her knees and the very tops of her breasts in whispered kisses against her pinkened skin.

Then she felt one on the crest of her shoulder, the barest of touches, and the warmth of it brought a smile to her lips. She was so drowsy and relaxed, she paid little attention to the fact that her shoulders weren't even in the water and, therefore, no petal could be there. When another kiss touched the side of her neck, she merely hummed with contentment.

This was a lovely dream. She gave herself over to the sensations of kisses sweeping along the curve of her throat, nuzzling beneath her ear, and drawing out another sigh. Her neck arched. Her breasts lifted from the water, nipples pebbling in the cooler air. The shifting water brushed against her, gently lapping over the tender crests in a way that made her taut and tingly.

She pressed her thighs together, her knees sliding as the

undulating warmth of the water seemed to cup her from beneath, plumping her flesh just before she heard a deep, familiar voice murmur, "Beautiful."

Her lips parted on a gasp. Her eyes snapped open to see that she wasn't dreaming at all. *And* she wasn't alone.

"Savage," she rasped, breathless as he bent over her and sealed his mouth around the aching bud. Her hands shot out of the water to curve around his head as he laved her flesh to an excruciatingly sensitive peak.

Any sensibly modest woman would have pushed him away, then tried to shield herself.

But the recently awakened wanton in Prue held him to her breast, her wet fingers tangling in his hair. From beneath her heavy lids, she watched him draw on the milk-white swell, felt the swirling flick and deep suckle that sent spears of sensation tunneling inside her. Prue's body throbbed, longing for the skillful caress of his fingers between her thighs and the rapture they could bring.

He had turned her into this hedonistic creature. She would never have known about shuddering ecstasy or gasping euphoria if not for him. And in a few short months, she would never know it again.

The thought brought a twinge to her heart. The feeling was startling enough that she released him. *Then* she modestly covered herself.

He grinned. Taking a petal from the water, he brushed it against her lips and the shell of her ear. "No need to be shy with me, Miss Thorogood. I merely knocked on the door a moment ago to see how you were faring. Imagine my alarm when you didn't answer. So I peered inside and saw that you were nearly asleep. And knowing how deeply you slumber, my dear, I feared for your safety and thusly swept into the room to employ lifesaving measures."

He spoke with such audacious valiance that it brought a laugh to her lips. It bubbled out before she could think of holding it back, and ended with a small—albeit embarrassing—snort.

"You have the best laugh," he said, his pupils darkening, his gaze hungry.

He caught her lips with his own and kissed her thoroughly, growling as if he meant to swallow down the sound. And it wasn't long before her body was simmering again.

He massaged her, slicking oil over her skin, over her breasts and in between her thighs. Over these days with him, she'd learned that it was no use trying to tamp down the sensations he evoked. He knew her body's secrets better than she knew them herself. So she allowed herself to surrender to his touch.

He bathed her to a tender climax that left her so sated and boneless that when he stood her up, she wasn't overcome with embarrassment. At least, for the first second. But seeing his hungry gaze rove down her body made her abruptly aware that she was, indeed, naked.

She quickly clasped her hands in front of her sex, her skin flushed to the color of the rose petals that clung to her. He merely smiled, kissed her, then picked her up in his arms and strode into the bedchamber.

She startled and clutched at his shoulders. "Savage, I'm still dripping."

Of course, the alarm in her voice had little to do with the fact that she was getting water on his clothes and on the floor, and far more to do with her current state of undress.

Even though she'd been sleeping beside him each night and he'd pleasured her innumerable times, she'd never been wholly, completely, unreservedly nude. She'd always had her chemise. He'd lowered it. He'd lifted it. He'd exposed and touched every part of her. However, there had still been that small scrap of fabric to give her a semblance of modesty. Until now.

"And so you are," he answered with mock surprise. "I'm

going to need to rectify that immediately. Hmm . . . I'd better use this coverlet."

Before she could draw another breath, he lowered her down onto the bed. And by the determined look in his eyes, she had the distinct impression that he had more in mind than merely pleasuring *her* this time.

Her experience of the dreadful ordeal loomed darkly over her, threatening to rob her of any comfort she'd come to feel with Savage.

Seeing him unbutton his waistcoat, she swallowed down a rise of nerves and dragged the bed linens over her, lifting them until they were gripped beneath her chin. "Shouldn't I be getting ready for the theatre?"

"After a near-fatal drowning in the bath? I think not. You might have taken water into your lungs, after all." He peeled away his wet cashmere to reveal that the saturation of water had seeped through to his shirtsleeves. The fine lawn became transparent and clung to his powerful form.

"My lungs are in perfect working order." Her statement likely would have been more convincing if her voice hadn't turned husky as her gaze traveled over him.

"One can never be too certain."

He shucked the shirtsleeves over his head, revealing a broad expanse of shoulders, the light golden furring of hair on his chest and taut abdomen. He was formed with absolutely perfect precision as if sculpted from bronze, his muscles toned from the daily exercise he'd mentioned when he left in the afternoons.

In the evenings, her hands had roved over the sleek skin, but it was something else altogether to see him in the waning daylight. And she was fascinated to find a darker line of hair just beneath his navel, the intriguing trail disappearing into the waist of his trousers like an arrow pointing to a hidden target.

As of yet, she had not encountered that part of him. Like

her, he hadn't slept completely nude. But she had felt him pressing against her.

When his hands went to the fastenings, her heart began to thud in something that felt like a battle between curiosity and panic inside the organ.

Her gaze flew up to his . . . then darted back down . . . then slowly made its way back up. "Are you removing *all* your clothes?"

"So it would seem," he said gravely, but his mouth twitched.

Or, at least, it might have done. She wasn't sure because her gaze lowered again, helplessly drawn to the motion of the wool sliding down a pair of lean, athletic hips, to the thatch of tawny hair and to the—she swallowed—rest of him. *All* of him. Every considerable inch of him, the jutting flesh dusky and dark.

"Believe me, my dear," he said as he gently pried the linens from her grasp, "there's a part of me that wishes I knew of a way to ensure that you are, indeed, perfectly hale that didn't involve the both of us being completely naked for hours. But, alas, I do not. You'll need a thorough examination, after all, and someone to watch over you. And since I'm feeling altruistic, I'm willing to volunteer."

He slid in beside her, gathering her against his body before she could balk. He was warm and strong, his skin sleek and textured with crisp hair that slid against her arms, breasts, legs *and* hips. She felt the imposing length of him pressed along her stomach, his flesh hard and heated. But no matter how warm he was, she still shivered. Apparently, panic had gained the upper hand.

"You've nothing to fear, moonflower. The pain of losing your maidenhead only happens once. I won't hurt you."

He reassured her with a kiss, lingering at her lips until the stiffness gradually left her limbs. The arms she curled protectively against her breasts, unwound and wrapped around his neck. Her fingers found their familiar home inside the wavy locks of his hair as he hummed in approval.

This wasn't so terrible, she thought. In fact, it wasn't at all terrible.

Savage had a way of making her feel that having her body next to his was the most natural thing in the world, naked or not. And she surrendered to the pleasure of his kisses, welcoming his tongue into her mouth with eager suction.

The throbbing ache between her thighs and the sweet clench of her womb was familiar now. It was impossible to keep still. She couldn't stop herself from hitching against him, seeking the bliss that she'd come to crave.

But he was in no rush. He took his time, his hands passing slowly, aimlessly along her body. He held her closely, getting her used to the feel of him, kissing her as he removed the pins from her hair and tenderly massaged her scalp, her nape and shoulders. Then he turned her to lay on her stomach and rubbed away the tension from her back, his open mouth coasting over her skin, whispering how soft she was, how perfect and pale.

Hands splayed over her waist and lower back, he rolled his skillful thumbs into the dip, drawing sighs of pure bliss from her lips. She was so relaxed that she didn't jolt when his palms roved lower still, rising over the swell of her bare bottom, kneading her flesh. He left her limp and languid and tingling from head to toe.

Then he cupped her sex and her breath caught.

The feeling of his hand insinuated between her thighs from this position was strange and new, but not at all unpleasant. She even gave into the impulse to lift her hips so that he could—*Oh yes. That was nice* . . .

"Mmm . . ." he breathed as his finger delved through the curls to slide along the swollen seam. "You're so very wet, Miss Thorogood. Whatever shall I do about that?"

She shook her head in answer, unable to form words as he teased her flesh open and slid his finger into the slick channel. Her greedy, wanton body clamped tight around him in anticipation.

He lay against her side kissing the blade of her scapula, the crest of her shoulder, the base of her nape, then the wing of her brow and her lips. All the while, his finger thrust rhythmically, commandingly, inside her, working her body into a fever pitch until her hands were curling into the linens and she felt the familiar tightness of rapture's approach.

And she was just about to shatter . . . when he suddenly withdrew.

"But, *Savage*." A mewl of protest left her as he turned her unfulfilled body onto her back.

He stalled her argument with a kiss, his powerful form pressing down on her. "This time, I want to feel you come apart."

His words were hoarse, and there was no mistaking his meaning when she felt the hard heat of him poised at the vulnerable nook of her body. Braced on his elbows, he settled over her.

This did not feel at all like it had with Lord Nethersole. For that, she should be thankful, she supposed. Was it because there was no tangle of skirts to hinder her movements? No tall grasses to keep her from shifting beneath the form over hers until she was more comfortable? Until she even welcomed Savage's weight with an unexpected sigh of satisfaction? She didn't know the answer.

Nevertheless, this felt different. Far more intimate, and far more vulnerable.

Savage nudged inside, but her body closed around him like a blockade. And he stopped.

Tension notched his brow with a jagged vein. His breaths

were ragged, slipping out through gritted teeth. "You're so . . . small."

"And you are far too big," she accused, gripping his shoulders, her nails biting into his flesh as he nudged deeper.

"Now is not the time for flattery, my dear. Not when I'm this close to dying."

When you're *close to dying?* she thought, incredulous. What about her? Even saturated with wetness, she felt the burning sting of being stretched and filled as he inched inside the tight constriction.

But she knew that something wasn't quite right the instant he withdrew, then drove inside her, and she felt the rending of her flesh on a single, painful thrust.

❧❧❧

LEO WENT still. The sound of her cry rang in his ears.

That shouldn't have happened, he thought. Then again, he could hardly think clearly at all as he felt the indescribable pleasure of her body, her snug walls cinched around his cock like a vise.

She pushed at his shoulders, her eyes widening. "I don't understand. Why does it hurt? I've done something wrong, haven't I?"

"You've done nothing wrong. Be still, moonflower." He swallowed, anchoring her with his hips. "It won't hurt any more after this."

"You said that about *this* time."

"Well, it appears that I did not possess all the required information," he said, jaw tight as awareness rushed through him.

He cursed and stared down at her with suspicion.

Pale devastation stole over her face as she shook her head. And any fleeting notion that she had plotted to trick him evaporated before it took root. "I'm flawed, dreadfully flawed. I'll never be able to please you."

It killed him when tears gathered in her eyes. He lowered his mouth to hers. "Hush, darling. You are perfect in every conceivable way. And I give you my word that it won't hurt now. Do you believe me?"

"Well, I'm hardly in a position to argue."

Her terse reply brought a grin to his lips as he pressed them against her temple, needing a moment to gather his composure. She felt so good, so right, that it was nearly impossible not to lose control and bring a swift end to their encounter when it was really only beginning.

It was patently clear that her previous lover had not gained entry when he had taken her in a field, rutting over her like a dog and traumatizing her in the process. Then that blackguard had apparently blamed her when he'd ejaculated prematurely.

Nethersole had taken someone pure, sweet and proud, then cast her into the gutter, leaving her to suffer for his own crimes. He should be strung up by his bollocks and left to rot.

That man, however, was no longer Leo's concern or hers, for that matter. And Leo was determined to spend all the time it took to obliterate that memory from her mind, so that all she knew was pleasure.

But his buried flesh was so sensitive that he had to withdraw before he spilled too early and left her with only another memory of pain. She had already suffered the haste of another man, and he wasn't about to do the same.

She sighed in relief, but he chuckled and said, "I'm not through with you yet."

Before she could utter a reply, he kissed her again and felt the familiar jolt tunnel inside him on a bright burst of heat.

He should be used to it by now, surely. But there was something in the way she always welcomed him on a soft sigh. Every kiss was a sweet surrender, the opening of a flower to midnight dew, and it stole his breath each time. He wasn't sure he could ever get enough.

"I like this part much better," she said, her eyes hooded with desire as she looked up at him through her sandy lashes. "Is that a terrible thing to admit?"

"The very worst."

She pursed her lips and smoothed away the errant locks from his forehead. "All I'm saying is that I like the way you kiss me."

"It is too late to make amends. My ego has been mortally wounded."

"Has it?" She tsked. "Such a shame. Shall we order a coffin for it, do you think? Although, I'm not entirely certain there is enough pine in England to fashion one large enough for such an immense—"

"Minx," he chided, cutting her off by tickling her side.

She clutched him as peels of laughter lifted to the canopy before he stopped. And when her bright gaze met his as she smiled breathlessly up at him, he knew that any lingering pain or doubts she might have harbored were gone.

He sank into the cushion of her lips, his skin tingling as her silken hands glided over his shoulders, accepting his weight on her. She arched for his tender attention on that fluttering pulse on the side of her throat. And he delighted in the taste of her skin, the salty essence of the perspiration collecting in the shallow niche below.

Laving her there, he felt a hum vibrate up her body and a twinge of longing came over him. He wanted to be inside her, buried to the hilt when she made that sound. In fact, he wanted to be inside her for every sound, every conversation, every breath.

His pulse quickened as he caressed the round fullness of her breast and he felt her shift restlessly beneath him, saw her lips part and her watchful eyes darken with desire.

Lowering his mouth to the milky swell, he worshipped

the pale center as it budded under the tender flicks of his tongue. Drew on her flesh in a suckling kiss as her fingers gripped his hair. He groaned in pleasure, loving the feel of her hands on him. Loving even more how she'd learned to let go and surrender with him.

Only with him.

A primal surge like he'd never experienced before filled him, his blood rushing hot in his veins as he touched the tender place between her thighs and felt her hips lift to meet him. But he still wanted more of her. So much more.

His mouth trailed a burning path along the downy skin of her abdomen. His tongue skirted the rim of her navel and her flesh quivered in response. Descending lower, he nipped lightly on the flare of her hips, keeping his finger moving along the slick folds. He circled the tender bud until she was writhing, her hips unable to keep still.

Nudging her legs apart, he kissed the lush softness of her inner thigh. He paused to breathe her in, the scent of her musk intoxicating him.

She lifted her head from the pillow, cheeks flushed as she gazed down at him in confusion. "Savage?"

"I'm afraid I have some dreadful news, Miss Thorogood," he whispered against her curls. "But we're not going to make it to the theatre this evening. I'm going to need much more time with you."

Then he opened his mouth over her, holding her still as she gasped and bucked. But as he rolled the flat of his tongue against her, she stilled and her breath came out in a shudder.

He tasted a sharp metallic essence, the last remains of her virginity. Then he tasted *her*, the flavor like cream and salt. Wholly addictive.

"Are you certain . . . you should do . . ." she croaked, her hands fisting in the linens. But her words fell silent as he circled the vulnerable pulse and one finger—then *two*—delved inside the tender sheath.

She answered her own question with a sigh and a *yes* as her hands shaped around his skull, keeping him there.

He could feast on her all day. But the taste of her and the sounds of her whimpers were nearly his undoing. He suckled the bud, laving the tender peak as he felt the first spasm around his fingers. It wasn't long before she stiffened, arching, and a choked cry tore from her throat. He pressed his hips hard into the mattress, fighting release, as she came apart in a sweet deluge of honey.

Greedy, he swallowed down every ounce of her pleasure, kissing and caressing until she expelled an exhausted breath, her limbs falling slack. Then he levered himself over her body. Her skin was flushed, her eyes drowsy but so bright they glowed beneath the heavy fan of lashes. And when he settled between her thighs, she did not hesitate to open for him.

By the time he nudged inside the slick confines, he was shaking with desire. His need had never been more intense. He drove in deep, deeper still, feeling her walls close around him as she gasped.

His breath stuttered, his throat tight as he held still.

He planned to give her a moment to adjust to his size, but she surprised him by opening her mouth on his throat, her tongue tasting him, her lips humming with pleasure. Without warning, his hips jerked inside her. He thrust mindlessly, losing himself in the tight grip of her body. She held him close, wrapping her arms and legs around him, caressing his shoulders and back as he shuddered violently, endlessly . . . until his very soul was wrenched from his body.

And Leo knew he would never be the same again.

Chapter 21

It was a chilly, rainy Wednesday morning when Savage handed Prue into the carriage. He told her that they had an errand to attend.

"Surely, nothing is so important that it requires the both of us to get out of bed at such an early hour," she groused. But it did not matter. He was oddly insistent. "It's your fault that I'm exhausted."

"Of that, I am well aware," he said with an unmistakable smugness and summarily tucked her against his side with her sleepy head on his chest as the carriage rumbled away from her bed.

When the carriage stopped, she was rushed up the stairs and inside so quickly that she didn't know where they were. Honestly, she still longed to return to bed and didn't really care where they were, only that they would be finished soon.

Rain dripped from the brim of her bonnet as she kept her head down as he led her deeper into this place, their footsteps echoing. The sweet scent of beeswax and turpentine lingered in the air.

"It smells like we're in a church," she said sleepily. "But that isn't possible. Surely, a man with your reputation would have been smited by now. Or would that be smote? Smitten?"

"Smitten," he supplied. "And clearly I must have some redeeming qualities because we are, indeed, in a church."

She was still so dazed from a night of hedonistic pleasures

and distracted by watching the last raindrop cling to her bonnet brim—as if its very life depended on it—that she didn't believe she heard him correctly. "Did you just say we're in a . . ."

The words dried up on her tongue as she looked up and saw the two rows of pews on either side.

She blinked. Her gaze snapped up to Savage, who stared stoically straight ahead, and to the long-faced minister in the cassock and then to her right where she saw a burly, dark-haired gentleman with bloodshot eyes and a murderous glower, looking as though he hadn't slept in years. And still it didn't quite register at all until her eyes rested on the aunts and Meg, who were all tearful and smiling.

Prue felt suddenly dizzy. This was one of her peculiar dreams. It had to be. Any moment now Aunt Thorley would make an appearance.

"And why are we in a church?" she asked, her voice threadbare and faint.

"Because you are marrying me."

She squeezed her eyes shut and opened them, hoping to wake up. Oh, where was Aunt Thorley on her chariot when she needed her?

Beside her, she heard Savage expel a long-suffering sigh. "Breathe, Miss Thorogood."

"I cannot." She shook her head. The surrounding church grew fuzzy and dark. Perhaps her lungs were still asleep and she'd left them behind, tucked beneath the coverlet. Oh, how she wished she was there with them.

She felt his hand at her waist, securing her to his side as he strode purposefully toward the vestry as if he owned the place. Once inside, he sat her down on a chair and nudged her forward so that her head was down, his hands running in soothing passes along her back, shoulders and nape.

"Now, take a breath," he commanded, and she did, drawing in one and then another, until the encroaching shadows cleared from her vision. "Better. Cannot have my bride fainting, after all."

Bride. The word was like a face full of cold water.

Slowly, she sat up and saw that he was kneeling in front of her, his hands covering hers, rubbing each finger in a tender massage. Only then did she notice that she was not wearing gloves. She had a vague recollection of standing in the foyer before they'd left and absently wanting to walk back upstairs for her gloves, only to have him say that she wouldn't be needing them.

All at once, this entire morning seemed rather presumptuous.

She slipped her hands from his. "Why are you doing this? Why are we in a church at this despicable hour and everyone in attendance is under the mistaken belief that we are getting married?"

Another long-suffering sigh left him as his gaze held hers. "This is what a gentleman does when he takes a woman's virginity."

"But you didn't."

"I assure you, I did."

"And I know otherwise. I was there when it happened, after all. I bore the agony of it."

"Miss Thorogood. Prudence—"

"Prue," she corrected. Only her father and Aunt Thorley called her Prudence in that superior tone.

"Very well, then, Prue. To put it delicately, my experience is more substantial than yours and, regardless of what you might have endured in that field, which I liken more to an assault," he added tightly, "I am the one who *actually* took your virginity when I broke through that vulnerable barrier yesterday. As you might recall, it did not cause you pain when I entered you the second time."

She blushed at the memory, her body tender in places she'd never been before, where the heat and hardness of him had filled her, branded her, pleasured her endlessly as she'd clung to him, taking all of him and meeting his every thrust with her own greedy response.

Yet, even after all the intimacies they'd shared, she was still not used to speaking so frankly. Especially not in a room filled with statues of saints staring down at her. "It wasn't entirely comfortable either. At least . . . not until the end."

His responding chuckle was tinged with a degree of male pride. "There's little I can do about that, other than to say that you'll get used to me."

She highly doubted that a woman could ever get used to such a man.

As the thought entered her mind, the word *ever* lingered, as in *for*ever. She would be married to him for*ever*, and he hadn't even bothered to ask her.

"There is no reason for this. I am set on a course for my life. All I want is to reclaim my inheritance. I signed a contract to be your *mistress*. I accepted what society thought of me. You did as well. So, there is no need to bring marriage into the bargain."

"Wait a moment," he said, his brow arched with speculative amusement. "Am I to understand that you are annoyed by the fact that I'm marrying you as a matter of honor?"

She straightened her shoulders. "No. I'm angered by the fact that you are reducing my entire existence to the state of my maidenhead"—she huffed, proud that she could say it without blushing *and* with saints looking on—"just like society, just like my father, and just like Lord—"

"Don't speak his name," Savage interrupted on a growl. "Don't ever speak his name again."

His hard gaze was dragon-green, his jaw tight with a ticking muscle at the hinge. Clearly, Savage wanted no reminder of the man who'd unknowingly set this series of events into motion.

She didn't either. However . . . "My reputation has been ruined regardless. You could have simply kept to the contract and no one would have been the wiser. After all, it has been obvious that you haven't wanted me."

"And what could possibly have given you that idea?"

"I've been living beneath your roof, sleeping beside you for a fortnight and you never . . ." Her words trailed off as she looked at his arched brow and it suddenly occurred to her that he'd waited until her courses had come and gone. "I've been such a simpleton! All this time, I thought you were being kind and patient. But you were only making certain I wasn't with child."

"Which, in hindsight, was rather foolish of me," he said with a rueful grin.

But she wasn't laughing. "The very fact that you believe me capable of such a deception only proves how little we know of each other."

He didn't answer for a moment but when he did, his voice expressed a quiet solemnity that she hadn't heard from him before. "Trust is not a commodity that either of us hold in great measure. The difference between you and I is that you possess far more courage. I admire that, as well as the countless other superior qualities residing in you."

Prue felt her lungs cinch and her throat tighten. Savage took her breath away with that forthright statement. Any anger or frustration she might have had evaporated.

He lifted his hand and gently cupped her cheek, his eyes turning the soft color of unpolished jade, and it did terrible things to her heart. "You gave me quite the surprise."

"If I had known, I never would have . . ." Her voice cracked and she didn't finish. She couldn't. A sudden and unexpected surge of tenderness threatened to overwhelm her.

He rose up to press his lips to hers. "I know."

It wasn't much, but with those two words she felt a stirring of hope. "Then we can simply keep our contract in place?"

"Is that truly what you desire?"

She nodded. "It is. I need to have a life of my own making, control of my own decisions, and a home that can never be taken away by anyone. Those are the things a wife never has."

"I thought that would be your answer. Which is why I had my solicitor draw this up." He reached into his inner breast pocket to withdraw a folded packet of papers and presented it to her.

She scanned the document with a pucker of confusion. "Another contract?"

"As you see, it is nearly a mirror of the original but with the minor amendment of our marriage included."

She scoffed. "You equate marriage to a mere triviality?"

He stood and offered an absent shrug, the tenderness she'd glimpsed in his gaze replaced by his usual shuttered cynicism. "Marriages of convenience happen all the time. The parties involved take what they want and, after a time, go their separate ways. It was the same with my parents."

Even though he spoke in his usual unconcerned drawl, she detected a hint of rawness—perhaps even vulnerability— beneath the surface. The only other time she'd heard this was when he'd spoken of his mother's abandonment, and all the things she'd left behind that he still kept in the garret. In that moment, her heart went out to the motherless boy he'd been, and she felt that kindred connection with him once more.

He gave her an alert glance and seemed to know her thoughts because he cleared his throat and continued. "The document states clearly that you will have everything you've asked for—your inheritance, your cottage, and your freedom in four months. And when the contract is concluded, we'll both have everything we could want from each other without any unnecessary complications. We're alike, Miss Thorogood. We both prefer to know what to expect for *our* foreseeable future."

"Unless we tire of each other before the four months conclude," she said, reading that the tedium codicil was still there as well.

"Precisely. Our nuptials are simply a matter of honor. The only difference from our original agreement is that you will also carry the title of the Marchioness of Savage. With that, your position in society will alter—albeit only marginally considering the tarnish the title already holds," he added dryly. "Nevertheless, you'll also be able to maintain your friendships without suffering any guilt over it. And just imagine how much the news will rankle your stepmother. She'll likely have an apoplexy."

"True," she said, almost wishing that she could see Dorcas's reaction. And it would help Prue visit with Winn, Jane, Ellie and Meg without tainting them by association.

But did that mean she was actually considering this most unexpected and peculiar marriage proposal? Apparently so.

She looked up at him with uncertainty. "But even after the contract is terminated, we'll still be married. Are you so sure that you won't want to marry anyone else one day?"

"I cannot think of a single reason I ever would," he said with such utter conviction that it was impossible not to believe him. He searched her gaze. "Of course, you may feel differently. Perhaps, one day, you'll meet a man who can give you everything you ever wanted."

She laughed at the very notion. Savage was already offering her more than she'd ever dared to dream. "No. That will never happen, I'm sure."

"Then, it appears, we are perfect for each other," he said and held out his hand.

∼∽∿∽∿∼

THE INK was still wet on the contract and there was a stain on the tip of her finger as Prue and Savage stood at the front of the church. And she could hardly hear the reverend through the pounding of her heart. Was this really happening?

"Dearly beloved, we are gathered here in the sight of . . ."

It didn't seem possible.

". . . but reverently, discreetly, advisedly . . ."

Then again, perhaps she was still dreaming.

"Leopold Edmund Truman Ramsgate, fourth Marquess of Savage, wilt thou have this woman . . ."

Her gaze lifted to Savage, and she took hold of his hand for reassurance. His responding grip felt real to her. Certain.

"I will," he answered, his gaze tender.

She could get used to that look, she thought. It wouldn't be a hardship. The only problem was, how would she keep herself from falling in love with him and being utterly bereft when they went their separate ways?

"And you, Prudence Wilhelmina Thorogood, wilt thou have this man . . ."

Savage looked down at her expectantly and his brow knitted. But he must have read the panic in her expression because he expelled a patient breath and gently prodded, "Just say, 'I will' and it will all be over soon enough."

She nodded and swallowed to wet her dry throat. "I will."

Then the reverend asked, "Who giveth this woman to be married to this man?"

"I do," a voice answered from far behind her. At once, the familiar tone—layered with coldness and disapproval—let her know that she wasn't dreaming at all.

All the blood drained from Prue's body as she glanced over her shoulder to see her father exit the pew then stride down the aisle toward the back of the church. The heavy wood door opened briefly to a flash of pale gray light and the sound of rain, and it closed again with a hollow slam. Then he was gone.

The remainder of the ceremony was a blur—the ring sliding onto her fourth finger, vows spoken with hushed reverence as if they actually intended to keep them, tearful congratulations and embraces, an introduction to the man named Reed Sterling, their signatures in the registry—and then they were in the carriage.

Her head was resting on his shoulder as he held her hand in his. And just to be absolutely certain, she asked, "Has this morning been a dream, Savage?"

A low rumble of amusement answered her.

Chapter 22

When the carriage stopped in front of the town house, one glance out the window told Leo that the news of his nuptials would likely spread faster than the pox at an orgy. Beside him, he heard an exhausted sigh.

"Please tell me that your servants line up on the stairs every morning and this has nothing to do with what happened at the church."

"I think I should take offense to your tone," he drawled. "You make our wedding sound as though a bolt of lightning tore through the steeple and smote someone."

"So you told your servants of your plans but not your oblivious betrothed?"

Leo knew Prue enough to understand that she did not trust the things that weren't in her control, and tended to shy away from them. That was the reason he'd chosen not to tell her where they were going this morning. After all, she might have decided to flee, even on foot as she'd done in Wiltshire, and he hadn't wanted to take that chance.

"I had to tell Grimsby," he said with a shrug. "Shock a man at that age with such news and he's likely to drop dead at my feet."

And yet, even when Leo had returned from seeing the Archbishop of Canterbury in the middle of the night, the butler hadn't exhibited the faintest flicker of surprise at the news that the Marquess of Savage, sworn bachelor and scoundrel, had procured a special license. He'd merely said,

"Very good, my lord. I'll have Mrs. Crumb prepare the marchioness's rooms."

He wondered what it would take to truly astonish him.

Stepping out of the carriage, Leo extended his hand. "Are you ready, Lady Savage?"

"If I say 'no,' does that mean we can drive around in the carriage until this starts to make sense?"

A less assured man might begin to take umbrage at her reluctance to embrace a life at his side. Any other woman would already be mentally replacing all the draperies and furnishings in his house, ordering dozens of new gowns with jewelry to match, planning grand parties and the like. But she wanted nothing of the sort.

Because Prue wasn't like any other woman.

"Courage, moonflower," he said softly and was rewarded by the feel of her hand slipping into his. He held her wary gaze as he kissed her chilled fingers then lowered her to the pavement.

Together, they endured curtsies and bows and well-wishes enough that it felt like they'd climbed a hundred stairs instead of five.

Grimsby waited beside the open door, jowls unmoving. He bowed to each in turn. "My lord, my lady. Allow me to extend my congratulations and best wishes for your future contentment."

"Thank you, Mr. Grimsby," Prue said and turned to step inside, but Leo stayed her.

He didn't know what possessed him—whether he was bitten by the devil's own mischief or he had to finally see some expression flicker across his unresponsive butler's face—but Leo swept her into his arms and carried her over the threshold.

Once inside, he glanced back to Grimsby but received nothing. Not even a blink. The woman in his arms, however, gave him an earful.

"Savage!" she gasped. "Put me down. I've suffered enough upsets for one day."

"Oh, how you flatter me, my dear," he said dryly and lowered her to her feet.

She had the courtesy to look abashed. "I didn't mean it that way."

"Yes, you did," he said with a knowing grin as he tilted her face up to his. "Remember, there's no need to pretend with me. And while I'm thinking of it, you should probably accustom yourself to using my given name, especially when you scold me."

An impish glint lit her eyes. "That would likely be an overuse of *Leopold*."

"Leo," he corrected, tempted to kiss that smirking mouth, right there in the foyer, with his servants pretending not to watch them as they scuttled past to attend their duties.

They were likely under the misconception that this was a love match. But better that than having the bloodstains on the bed linens lead them all to believe she'd entrapped him, he supposed. No matter how this entire fiasco had come about, he wouldn't want them to think ill of her.

So he gave in to temptation and stole one brief kiss. Well, two—*three*—kisses that ended up leaving them both a bit winded.

Lifting his head, he was gratified to see that she was, indeed, a blushing bride. *His* bride, to be exact. The realization of that fact left him a bit gobsmacked.

Doubtless, the news would throw the entire *ton* on their ears, and was likely buzzing from house to house even as he stood there. "I must leave you now in order to tell Lady Babcock the news. If she reads it in the society column first, she'll never forgive me."

Prue reached for his hand, her grip cold and uncertain. "How long will you be gone?"

"Not long." He warmed her fingers with his own. "Why? Are you going to miss me terribly?"

His teasing brought a soft smile to her lips even as she rolled her eyes and slipped free. "Terribly."

∞∞∞∞

LADY BABCOCK sat in the overstuffed chair in her solar and regarded him over the rim of a teacup as he told her the news.

". . . It was simply a matter of honor," he concluded and wondered when she would gasp, stare agape at him with her eyes wide from shock. Or when she would accuse Miss Thorogood—Mrs. Ramsgate, now—of deceiving him for her own gains.

But she did none of those. Instead, she casually lowered her cup to the saucer and blinked slowly. It was almost as if she and Grimsby had been cut from the same cloth. "For a self-proclaimed scoundrel, you certainly have a low threshold for dishonor. Though, you needn't have married her. A generous settlement would have sufficed, I'm sure."

"Not if there's a chance that she might be carrying my child."

At this, her brows lifted. "Forgot yourself, did you?"

"Merely . . . taken off guard," he admitted with chagrin.

And yet it had been more than that. He'd never felt such an overwhelming surge—a mixture of primal need and something altogether unworldly—rush through him. And the ensuing rapture had been beyond anything he'd ever experienced before. It was alarming to think about how intensely he'd been lost in those moments.

"Hmm . . ." she murmured. "Those who are most guarded are never quite prepared enough, are they?"

"Lesson learned."

"But at what price?" she asked. "You have made her your

wife but, married or not, society will hardly welcome her with open arms. They will see her as a fallen woman who unfairly snared a prime catch."

"There's enough tarnish on my title that few will be surprised by this, and those who are can go to the devil for all I care. If anyone dares to speak a word against her, then they will have me to deal with."

The statement held more force than he'd intended. Even his fists were clenched. Which was laughable because he was hardly one to rush to anyone's rescue.

The countess smiled at him. "So you like her, then?"

He shrugged. "Well enough."

"Sometimes that is all we need," she said with a fond gleam of reminiscence in her eyes. After taking another sip from her cup, she set it down and proffered her cheek. "Give us a kiss. I have a good deal of work ahead of me if I'm going to ensure that my dear boy doesn't hang for murdering someone who might speak ill of her. Fortunately, I still have friends in high places."

Dutifully, he bussed her cheek. "Thank you, ma'am."

"Just do me one favor," she said before he could leave. "Stay at home for the next few days, and simply enjoy each other. It will help her standing in society if everyone believes this is a love match."

"It isn't," he said with utter certainty as he felt the weight of the contract pressed against his heart.

She flitted her fingers in the air. "People tend to make up their own minds about whatever they want the truth to be. Now go. Get back to that lovely girl before she begins to question why she bothered to marry someone so impoverished and unattractive."

❦❦❦❦

PRUE STOOD in the center of the marchioness's bedchamber—*her* bedchamber—and tried to wrap her thoughts around everything that had happened. But her wits were still shredded, her composure hanging on by a thread.

Honestly, none of this could actually be real. Could it?

The room was decorated in a shade of pale blue that was slightly yellowed with age, giving it a greenish cast. The silk wallpaper no longer held the luster that it likely had when the last marchioness lived here, decades ago. But the furniture was polished, the floors cleaned and the rug recently removed for dusting—as Mrs. Crumb had assured her. The brocade drapes were sun-bleached in places and the tasseled tiebacks slightly frayed, but they were still lovely. The two windows were open to draw in the cool autumn breeze and drive out the lingering staleness in the air. And she absently wondered if Savage had ever stepped inside this room or if it was just as closed off as he tended to be.

"It's just so romantic, I could positively swoon," Dottie said as she filled the armoire with the remaining few gowns that had, quite recently, resided in the mistress's bedchamber. "O' course, the other maids and me knew right off it was a love match, what with the way he doted on you from the start, always wanting everything just so. Went down to the kitchens at least three times to make sure the tea tray had sugar and milk and not a single lemon in sight."

Standing at the window, Prue was only listening with half an ear to the maid's wishful thinking. But the last statement was so startling, she could hardly ignore it. She looked over her shoulder quizzically. "He did that?"

The maid's head bobbed in a nod as she grinned and splayed a hand over her heart. "And *oh,* the way his lordship stayed by your side when you had your courses. He never done that before either."

"Never?" she asked, and when Dottie shook her head, she heard a sigh fall from her own lips.

The tender, hopeful yearning to be loved and cherished— the same yearning she thought had died years ago—fluttered to life. No one had loved her since her mother had died. Could it be possible that he might? Or that he cared for her?

No, her mind answered definitively. It wasn't.

After all, Savage had told her himself that he'd married her out of obligation. Though, because of his peculiarly exacting code of honor, it was a wonder that he hadn't been coerced into marriage years ago.

"That'll be all, Dottie," Savage said from the connecting doorway.

Prue startled, her heart quickening as her gaze met his. And as he prowled into the room, she faintly heard the outer door close and knew that they were alone. Just the thought caused a blush to creep to her cheeks. "This is all so new and unexpected, I'm not sure how to act."

"Believe me, I know," he said with a wry grin as he stopped in front of her. "What do you think of your bedchamber?"

"I think you never expected to open the door."

He made no comment, but took her hand and kissed it, tracing the edge of the delicate gold band encircling her finger. "I should have liked you to have my grandmother's ruby cabochon ring, but I no longer have it."

"This is perfect as it is and suits my nature."

"Yes, I'd thought as much the instant I saw it. The grumpy jeweler that I'd awakened in the wee hours of the morning would have preferred to sell me a fat diamond or more emeralds, but I was drawn to this. Slender, elegant and straightforward, like you," he said simply as if he hadn't just made her heart stutter, stop, then start up again.

He had selected this, instead of simply ordering a clerk to fetch him a ring?

"However," he continued, "I did manage to pacify the man when I saw this behind the glass."

He withdrew a slender gold chain from his inner breast

pocket, and dangling from the center was an oval stone with swirls of blue and cloudy gray.

She couldn't resist reaching out to rest it against her palm and examine it in the light. "It's lovely."

"I think so, too." He seemed to find this amusing as a smirk touched his lips. Then he moved behind her, turning her to face the standing mirror and draped the necklace so that the pendant rested in the hollow of her throat. "As I suspected, it is the exact color of your eyes."

Her breath caught as he fastened it. And when he lowered his head to press a kiss to her nape, her heart thudded with almost painful yearning.

It might have been a matter of honor that compelled him to procure a special license from the archbishop in the middle of the night. But then to purchase a wedding ring with such care and to see this necklace and think of her eyes?

The idea of it was too much for her heart to bear.

"The maids believe that ours is a love match," she said quietly, barely breathing as she watched his lips coast along her bare shoulder.

"They were bound to gossip about the blood on the sheets and come to one of two conclusions—love match or deception—which would you prefer? I could accommodate either."

"Oh," she said, feeling rather foolish again. She'd forgotten for a moment that they only had a temporary bargain. In four months, she would still be his wife . . . but in name only.

Which, she reminded herself quite firmly, was precisely what she wanted.

When he lifted his head and his expectant gaze met hers in the mirror, she realized that he was waiting for her to answer. "A love match, I suppose."

"Excellent," he said with a decisive nod, rewarding her

with a kiss to the side of her throat. "We'll need to be convincing, of course. Stay in the bedchamber for days on end."

Thinking of all they had done last night, she blushed and averted her face. Or rather, she arched her neck for him to continue. There was no point in trying to pretend that she was unaffected by the way he kissed and caressed her.

Her arms lifted, her fingers stealing through the layers of his hair. "We could have long conversations. Become better acquainted."

"Much better acquainted," he said against that place just beneath her ear and her pulse quickened.

She felt a series of gentle tugs at the back of her dress. "Surely, talking to each other doesn't require you to unfasten my buttons."

"Merely removing any distractions. What would you like to discuss?"

"What were you like as a . . . *child?*" She gasped as his hands slipped beneath the opening of her dress and beneath her arms to cup her breasts.

"Naughty," he said, kneading her flesh and plucking the crests to tender peaks. "And you?"

Her hands lifted reflexively to cover his, holding him in place. Panting, she let her head fall back against his shoulder. "Obedient."

"Hmm . . . That brings all sorts of wicked requests to mind. Keep your hands right there, darling. Oh, I like it when you obey me. And to be fair, I shall abide your requests, as well," he said, his splayed fingers drifting along her torso to take hold of her hips in a firm grip and draw her back against the thick evidence of his arousal. Then he stole down her center until his right hand molded over the cambric and lace of her drawers against the already damp curls guarding her sex, and her breath hitched. "For example, would you like me to touch you here"—he paused to rotate—"with my fingers or with my tongue?"

A garbled response left her as he slipped a finger through the lace. She was helpless to resist his erotic touch. Her body clenched in the sweetest of aches as he slid in sublime circles and the supple weight of her breasts drew taut and tender in her own hands.

He brought her swiftly to the brink, only to lift away from her, leaving her panting.

"Let me see if I interpreted that correctly," he said as he began to shuck the clothing from her in short order. "I believe that your answer was *both*."

Her head was still spinning, all the blood in her body throbbing low and liquid as he stepped around her and sank to his knees. Then he lifted those simmering green eyes and gave her one last command.

"You're so beautiful, moonflower. So pale and delicate. I want you to watch yourself bloom in the mirror."

Then he opened his mouth over her, kissing and laving her thoroughly as his finger teased through the tender cleft. And in the reflection, she saw a flushed, bare-breasted and wanton creature shamelessly delve her hands through his hair and hold him there.

She closed her eyes, unable to believe that could be her. But that forced all her focus on what he was doing to her body, every sensation acutely heightened.

He devoured her, relentlessly giving her pleasure, his tongue swirling around that throbbing pulse in time with the skillful thrust of his fingers until she was powerless against the plaintive mewls leaving her lips, the tingling spirals that left her trembling. And the instant her eyes fluttered open and caught a glimpse of blue jade against her blooming skin, the wanton in the mirror fractured on a cry as he gripped her hips and held her tightly against his ardent kiss until she was boneless.

He stood and crushed her into his hard embrace, his eyes wild and hungry. Then his hand stole to the nape of her neck and he rasped, "Taste what heaven is like," before he sealed his mouth over hers.

The intimate slide of his tongue against hers tasted faintly of salt and whey, and the sweet-tinged scent of her musk lingered on his skin. She was sure that this was a flavor she should never know. It was wicked and decadent, inciting another hunger. She became suddenly aware of an emptiness inside her, a hollow ache, a longing to be filled as he had before.

"I need . . . more," she heard and was shocked that that whimpered entreaty had fallen from her own lips. She clung to him with something akin to desperation.

"What do you need, my sweet?"

"You," she answered without hesitation and heard the catch in his breath as her lips peppered his chin, jaw and neck with frantic kisses.

His grip on her tightened. "Show me."

She arched inexpertly against him, hips sliding, grinding without rhythm. Her hands fumbled with his cravat, fingers clumsy and shaking. After a minute, a frustrated growl tore from her throat and all she could do was wrap her arms tightly around him, trying to squeeze as close as she could. *"Leo, please."*

He kissed her hard, lifting her against him, and in two long strides, he lowered her to the bed.

Who was this person she'd become?

Prue had always kept herself guarded, afraid of revealing her flaws and imperfections, everything she was lacking. She'd closed herself off from feeling too much because of the pain of rejection that would follow.

And yet, here she was clawing at his trouser fastenings, searching through the seams to find him, to grip him, to swallow down his rough growl as she begged him to fill her and drive away this gnawing emptiness.

Then he drove in and in, shoving deep. Her slick, swollen flesh clamped tight around the burning invasion. But she welcomed the fullness on a choked sob. And when he was buried inside her, he held still, a satisfied sigh rushing from his lungs as if this was exactly what he needed, too.

He gazed down at her as if she was the only woman on earth. And any woman could lose herself completely in such a look. She could even forget the entire reason she'd knocked on his door in the first place. Because why would she ever want to leave this man and live on her own when he kissed her so slowly, so tenderly, that it was as if he planned to keep her right here for all eternity?

"Now, you are well and truly mine," he whispered.

Gradually, he took her hands, lacing their fingers together above her head, their pulses throbbing in tandem. Their breaths spilled into each other's mouths, their hearts locked in a single rhythm . . . then he moved in thick, languid thrusts that eased the frayed edges of this frenzied need and began to soothe the bruised hollows of her heart, filling them, too.

And only later, much later, when their joined cries echoed around them, their bodies still intimately locked, damp and sated, would she dare wonder if a man who'd only wanted a temporary mistress—and a temporary wife—could ever fall in love with her. Because she feared that her vulnerable heart was already lost.

Chapter 23

Leo tried not to pace by the door in the drawing room the following week. It was still early yet. Still plenty of time before dinner *and* for the surprise he had in store for Prue. And yet, it felt far later than the bloody clocks revealed.

"Grimsby, my pocket watch, the clock on the mantel, and the longcase in the hall appear to be running slow," he'd said a short while ago. "Send the footmen to inspect every clock in the house immediately."

His wife had said she'd be down in an hour, but clearly it had been longer than that.

Unfortunately, his butler returned with news that the clocks were all set to the identical time. But it didn't make sense.

"I could send footmen to the neighboring houses to inquire after their clocks as well, my lord," Grimsby offered in his droll monotone.

Leo absently shook his head. "That won't be necessary."

Just as he turned away, he thought he caught the faintest twitch of amusement in the old man's countenance. But when he looked again, his expression was the same as always—bored.

Apparently, the hour just *seemed* to drag on and on. He couldn't fathom why. Whatever the cause, he didn't like this feeling. This waiting. This desire to climb the stairs and knock on her door. She would only laugh again, as she'd done before, and tell him to be patient.

"After all," she'd said, her voice gliding warmly through white glazed pine, "if I'd had to endure a full day with Madame LeBlanc, then you can surely wait a single hour while I dress in one of the gowns you've purchased."

A single hour? Surely, it had been five times longer than that since she'd slipped away into her bedchamber, leaving him alone in his. But looking at the clock once more assured him that it had only been forty-three minutes.

He paused in the drawing room archway to glance toward the stair. *Not* pacing. Just . . . checking.

His diligence was rewarded with the sight of a silver slipper and a ruffled hem descending in a graceful cascade of blue silk, followed by a long white glove, a glimpse of creamy bare skin that made his mouth water, and a slender throat adorned with a blue jade pendant. Her pale moon-silk hair was anchored to one side with pearl-studded pins, then left loose, flowing like a waterfall over the opposite shoulder.

She was incomparably lovely, and it had nothing to do with the gown.

In fact, he preferred her without it. Just the pendant caught in the hollow of her throat as her skin glowed with perspiration, her hair in disarray on his pillow and a rosy flush on her cheeks. That's all she ever needed to wear. Unfortunately, they'd been obligated to make an appearance outside his bedchamber eventually.

He strode out to meet her at the bottom of the stairs. "You're late."

"I assure you, I'm quite early," she said grinning up at him. "Even with the interruption of a strange man knocking on my door, pestering me to check the clock in my room."

"Who would do such a thing? I shall hunt him down and have him flogged this instant."

"Oh, I wouldn't be too severe. Perhaps just send him to bed without supper."

He arched an inquiring brow and paused before they were too far from the stairs. "And would he be permitted to take someone with him, for moral support?"

"No. That would be more of a boon than a punishment. Why? Are you admitting to being the culprit?"

He shrugged. "Must have been a vagrant, then."

After an aperitif in the drawing room, they strolled into the dining room to find every place at the mahogany table set for dinner, and a silver dome perched over every charger.

She gasped in surprise, grinning as she tilted her face up to his. "You arranged all this because of the memory I shared with you?"

"I have no idea what you could mean," he drawled, all innocence.

"Hmm . . ." she murmured in playful speculation. "Are we expecting company, then?"

"Not that I am aware. Did *you* invite anyone?"

She shook her head, but he could see that wonderous light in her eyes. For a while, he'd thought only sweetened tea and larceny could call it forth. But in this past week, he'd discovered all sorts of things that made her look at him that way. And he was becoming a complete glutton for it.

If he wasn't careful, he was going to become one of those silly besotted fools.

"What a mystery," he said. "Perhaps we startled the housekeeper by venturing out of our den on silver polishing day and she didn't have time to store the dishes in the cupboard?"

"Perhaps." Prue began to move toward her usual chair.

He clucked his tongue. "Don't forget, your place is at the other end of the table now."

Her gaze followed his along the vast length. "All the way down there in the darkest recesses of the dining room?"

"Afraid so."

"But won't you be lonely up here?"

He shrugged. "Well, I have Grimsby by the sideboard to keep me company, don't I?"

She pursed her lips, eyeing the two rows of silver domes. "And what if I choose to sit elsewhere? I am Lady Savage, after all."

"Quite true. For that matter, I am lord of the manner and should be able to sit wherever I choose."

She grinned and pointed. "What do you think is under that dome?"

"Boiled pig snout? Calf's brains?" He left her side and walked over to the place setting, lifting the dome. "Worse. Tureen of turnips."

She laughed lightly. "Turnips aren't that terrible, you know. They're one of Aunt Thorley's favorites. Well, on second thought . . ." She helped him replace the cover, then drummed her fingers on it. "If I had the choice, I'd like to sit at the one with the gooseberry tarts that Dottie told me your cook was making earlier."

"*Our* cook, darling," Leo reminded, then exchanged a purposeful look with Grimsby. "And if I *could* find the dome hiding the gooseberry tarts . . . ?"

"Then such a feat would earn a boon from your appreciative wife, I'm sure."

"Excellent." Leo pressed his palms together, chafing them back and forth as he moved around the table. "I think that the tarts are underneath this—" He stopped when Grimsby cleared his throat and subtly jerked his head to the left. "No, this one."

He lifted the dome with a flourish and she clapped, laughing. "Positively astounding, Mr. Ramsgate. What a hidden talent you possess."

"Why thank you, Mrs. Ramsgate. I do believe you have a boon to pay?" He pointed to his lips and closed his eyes.

"As to that . . ." she said softly, and leaned closer so that only he could hear. "I'm quite exceptionally grateful. More than you could imagine. You see, I've been longing for these tarts all day, and the delivery of the boon I have in mind will be rather involved and extensive."

Leo suddenly felt flushed. It was rather unlike him. His pulse even fluttered and he had to hook a finger into his cravat for some air. "If that is the case, then perhaps we should skip dinner altogether."

"I'm afraid that wouldn't be wise," she added with a shake of her head and bit down into the flesh of her bottom lip. "I have a sense that you're going to need your strength."

❦❦❦

TWO HOURS later, Leo flopped back onto the bed and tried to catch his breath. He was sure his soul had just been wrenched from his body, along with his skeleton, and perhaps his brain. At the moment, he was nothing more than gelatin molded to resemble a man.

"What made you think . . . to do that?" he asked, panting for air.

"I saw it on one of your snuffboxes."

His heart hammered hard against his ribs like a wild animal forced to endure a cage. He wasn't sure he'd ever be the same again.

"You took me unawares. I never thought that . . . well that my shy, prim and proper . . . would take charge like . . ." Bloody hell, he was babbling like an untried schoolboy.

She ducked her face against his chest and shyly said, "I just wanted to see what you tasted like. Did I do it wrong then? Is that why you stopped me?"

A laugh that sounded very much like a madman's laugh escaped him. "*Wrong?* No, darling. I stopped you because I was about to bring our evening to an embarrassingly swift end. Seeing you look up at me . . . with your sweet mouth on my . . . and that extraordinary swirling thing you did with your tongue . . ."

He was starting to hyperventilate. And just thinking about it was making him hard again. But after the force of his climax, he'd likely need a day to recuperate. Perhaps a year.

"I just tried to mimic what you do to me."

He didn't know why, but hearing that made him smile. "Yes, well, you're a very quick study, and I only stopped you because I needed to regain a little self-control. I wanted to pleasure you, too, after all."

She pressed a kiss to one of his ribs and peeked up at him. "I wouldn't mind if you'd lost control with me."

If? He worried that it was only a matter of *when*.

"Come here, my little wanton," he said. "Lay beside me and pull the coverlet over us. I would do it myself, but you've drained the life out of me."

"Perhaps you should have tried the turnips. They might have given you more stamina."

"Minx," he chided and gave her shapely bare bottom a playful swat as she covered him in silk, velvet and petal-soft skin.

Gazing down at her upturned lips, he wondered if she was aware that her every smile stole beats of his heart. That was likely the reason the minutes seemed to go missing when they were together, but then were stuffed back into the clock when they were apart. And as he heard his own ridiculous thoughts, he knew he sounded like a lunatic.

He couldn't recall ever feeling this way. It was as if he were being consumed by a terrifying beast with laughing eyes and a grinning mouth that went by the name *Contentment*. He was being gobbled up and there didn't seem to be anything he could do to stop it.

Alarming, to say the least.

He didn't trust this feeling. He was afraid it would make him lose sight of the fact that he was nothing more than a cynical, heartless and selfish scoundrel. And if he forgot that, then . . . well . . . he didn't want to think about the ramifications.

Life had already taught him that he'd been born with an innate ability to drive away the people closest to him. And, if he wasn't careful, he would do the same to Prue.

Her fingertips skimmed through the mat of golden curls on his chest and stopped when she reached a raised scar in the shape of an X. "What's this?"

"A fencing lesson from my father," he answered distractedly.

She gasped and covered his heart with her hand as if to shield it after the fact. "What a dreadful accident."

"It was no accident, my sweet. It was a warning never to leave myself unguarded, even for an instant." He shrugged. "It was fortunate, really. His true skill was in pistols. Crack shot, my father."

"How can you sound so glib? It must have been devastating."

At the look of horror on her face, he touched the rosebud furrow notched above her nose and smoothed his fingertips along her temple and cheek. "It happened long ago."

"But the lesson has stayed with you. Isn't that what you're telling me with your insouciant delivery?"

He tugged her closer and pressed a kiss to her nose. "Such a clever wife. I knew we would understand each other. I just didn't want you to have some grand notion that I'm capable of giving you more than this."

"Believe me," she said ruefully, "I'm the last person who would ever expect more from anyone."

He knew that about her, but seeing a hint of longing in the depths of her eyes made him wish for impossible things, nonetheless. With him, she would never receive what she truly deserved.

However, since she'd made it clear at the church that

she was only interested in a temporary marriage, then he needn't worry about it.

She lifted her hand just long enough to kiss the little scar beneath it before covering it again and resting her chin on top. "So you can shower me with jewels. Buy me a thousand gowns. Pleasure me endlessly. But you cannot"—she paused and he felt a rise of guilt and regret—"drink a glass of wine that I've poured?"

He thought she was going to ask him to love her, and he would have hated to break her heart with his answer. By the sly lift of her brows, she knew she'd surprised him.

"Your cork removal at the end of dinner was quite scintillating. I was actually thinking of replacing Grimsby," he quipped, but she wasn't moved by his humor in the least.

It seemed that it was time for the truth.

Drawing in a breath, he said in the most jaded tone he could muster, "I was poisoned once."

"Poisoned?"

"You know, if you keep gasping like that, I'm going to send for a physician to examine your lungs."

"Be serious for a moment," she pleaded, her voice cracking. "Do you know who did that to you? Please don't tell me it was your father, as well."

"No. He was guilty of many misdeeds, just not that one," he said and was about to leave it at that but . . . *In for a penny, in for a pound* . . . "Her name was Giselle and we were betrothed. She believed she was saving me."

Prue's eyes narrowed and she frowned instantly. "And how would poisoning have *saved* you exactly?"

"It began when I challenged a certain prize fighter, Reed Sterling, to a bout of pugilism."

"Mr. Sterling—the man at our wedding? The one who looked as though he wanted to murder you?"

"Yes, well, that's another story altogether, involving his mistaken belief that I'm determined to rob him of his only chance to sleep." Leo shook his head in dismissal. "As for this particular tale, years ago, I was once rather fixated on the idea of fighting him. So much so that Giselle had been afraid that I was turning into my father.

"The late Marquess of Savage was a man rather obsessed with the need to demonstrate his superiority. This led to many affairs with other men's wives, subsequent duels at dawn and the death of Sterling's stepfather."

"So then your father and Mr. Sterling's mother were . . ." She blushed.

He shook his head and clarified. "My father bedded the other man's mistress, knowing full well what would happen. A challenge was given. According to the gentleman's code of honor, some challenges may be settled by an apology. Of course, my father never apologized. So it was to be pistols at dawn."

"But aren't duels against the law?"

"Indeed, but that doesn't stop a man from wanting justice. Every man wants to uphold the honor of his name," he said. *Or reclaim any honor that he might have lost,* he thought. "In many instances these duels of honor are precisely that, and there is no desire for murder. So the wronged party will take the first shot and aim just shy of his target, ensuring a miss of a vital organ but still making his point. His opponent will do the same. My father, however, always aimed for the heart. On that particular day, it resulted in the death of my schoolmate's stepfather."

Prue laid her hand over his scar. "That must have been awful. Not only for Mr. Sterling, but for you as well."

"It was the first time that I'd been brought face-to-face with the senseless consequences of my father's actions, and I was ashamed of the blood running through my veins. There was no honor in what my father had done. Not only that, but he'd left the man's mistress penniless. And only a coward refuses to take responsibility for his own actions and make amends."

"So in challenging Mr. Sterling to a fight—an arena in which he excelled—it would have given him the advantage. You were attempting to make amends for your father's wrongdoing. It's understandable that you would have wanted to reclaim some of your family's honor," she said guilelessly, apparently having no idea that her swift and accurate insight wasn't something he was used to encountering. "Am I to assume that your betrothed did not agree?"

He gazed at her in speechless wonder for a moment before he was able to respond. Then, feeling like a tongue-tied buffoon, he cleared his throat. "Correct. She believed that if she pretended to be supportive and wished me the best of luck as she poured me—what she referred to as—*a champion's goblet of wine,* then I would fall asleep, miss the match altogether, and wake up the better man."

"What? That's simply ludicrous. If you had missed the match, it would have looked like you'd lost your courage and had no honor at all, which I most definitely know is not the case." She made a point of holding up her ring finger.

With a measure of surprise, he acknowledged that she seemed to know him quite well. And yet, as his gaze settled on the gold band, glinting in the firelight, he wondered if she might be wrong. Wondered if it had been honor that compelled him to marry her . . . or something else.

But he dismissed the thought at once. There could have been no other reason, which was why he'd had the second contract drawn up. He was selfish, cynical and heartless, the type of man who drove women into the arms of other men, time and time again.

"So what happened?" she asked, saving him from the turn of his own thoughts.

"Fortunately for me, I did not drink more than a swallow of the unusually bitter vintage. Even so, when I left, I'd felt somewhat nauseous. At the time, I'd equated the bilious feeling to nerves," he said with chagrin. "Trust me, if you've ever seen Sterling throw a punch, you'd be a bit unsteady, too. But the feeling only worsened and, by the time I was behind the ropes, I could barely stand. And then, to add insult to injury, Sterling took pity on me."

She cringed. "I don't imagine that sat well with you."

"It did not," he muttered. It had been humiliating, the way Sterling had practically carried him into another room and sent for a doctor. "When I recovered, I confronted her. I learned then that she had poured me what she'd thought had been wine laced with a sleeping draught, which had been given to her by a trusted . . . friend."

Leo paused to draw in a breath, remembering the episode.

"James said it would only help you sleep, and that by the time you awoke, you'd see the error of your ways."

"Giselle, if I'd have drunk any more of that wine, I'd likely be dead! That's what Marlow really wants—me out of the way so he can have you! Don't you see? This is all part of his revenge against my father, only I was too blind to see it until now."

She looked at him, her doe eyes round and frightened, her hands knitted in front of the pink sash over her sprigged muslin. "James is your friend. We are doing everything to help you, not hurt you. We're trying to keep you from becoming your father."

"I lost my temper," Leo continued tightly to Prue, the old wound still festering after all these years. "Then she bolted straight into the arms of this . . . friend. So, I confronted him as well."

"Marlow!" he shouted, pounding a fist on the locked bedchamber door the following morning. "I know you're in

there, so there's no turning me away like you did last night. Come out here and face me like a man."

"I do wish you'd keep your voice down. Some of us are trying to sleep," he said drolly. Turning the key in the lock, Marlow opened the door, dressed only in a pair of breeches, partially unfastened. And, behind him, the bed was rumpled with a figure still lying there.

Leo looked away from the bed to deal with Marlow, but caught sight of something pink out of the corner of his eye. His gaze focused on the sprigged muslin and pink sash rumpled on the floor and his heart started thudding painfully in his chest. But he didn't want to believe it.

"Who is that?" he demanded.

"See for yourself, if you like. Though, I warn you, it will come as quite the shock." Marlow opened the door wider and gestured inside.

But Leo couldn't move, couldn't cross the threshold. Somehow, he already knew. "Giselle came to you, upset and in need of comfort, and yet you decided to . . . take her?"

"Surely you don't think this was the first time? I mean, just look at how comfortable she is? Not even stirring at the sound of your voice."

"You're lying. Giselle would never—" He stopped, unable to finish.

"Betray you?" Marlow grinned. "Oh, she's quite capable, I assure you. If you think that whole sleeping draught in the wine was my idea, it wasn't. She was feeling a bit desperate when she found out she was with child—my child—and didn't know how to break the betrothal without causing a scandal. She didn't want to be like your mother and abandon you. She thought it would be too cruel. So she opted to make the broken agreement your idea, instead."

It wasn't true. It couldn't have been true. "This is your doing. Somehow you've tricked her."

"Are you going to call me out, then? Demand satisfaction?" His eyes glittered with triumph and bloodlust. *"Only one of us will walk away. If I die, she'll likely kill herself, as we know fragile women often do. And if you die, then I'll have exactly what I want."*

Leo shoved the memory aside and focused on the black curtains around him. "But it was too late. The damage had been done. Giselle married him, did not survive childbed. And that is the very long story of why I did not drink the wine you poured me."

"Hmm . . ." Prue murmured, her contemplative gaze on the fingertip tracing the furled edge of that scar. "It explains the reason you have your contracts, as well. They help to keep people at a distance, and to protect the heart that you keep locked away like one of your snuffboxes."

His breath stalled, catching in his throat at her all too perceptive insight. And beneath the gentle cruising of her fingertip, his heart beat in a disorderly panicked rhythm.

"What is your naughty fascination with that cabinet?" he asked teasingly as he covered her hand, pressing the flat of her palm against his flesh to quell the sensation. "Though, if your inspection brings about more of the surprises you've just given me, I shall add to my collection without delay."

A soft smile touched her lips at his query as if she knew he was trying to change the subject.

Rising up along his body, Prue looked down into his face, her expression so tender that he wasn't sure he could hold her gaze without losing some part of himself.

"Oh, my darling Leo, I am sorry that people in your past have betrayed you. I understand the scars it leaves behind. And, if I could, I would take all that pain away," she said softly, smoothing the hair from his brow. He tried to look away, but she cupped his cheeks, her hands warm against his skin. "But fear not, I will keep your heart safely guarded as if it were my very own."

Then she kissed him and he was sure that he did lose some part of himself. Whatever it might have been—a chunk of spleen or a piece of his soul—left him like a whisper, putting up no resistance.

Sliding a hand to her nape, he tried to retrieve it. But in the next hour, he'd only ended up tangled in bed linens, exhausted and sated, after willingly surrendering even more.

If he wasn't careful, he'd lose himself completely before he even knew it.

Chapter 24

According to Countess Babcock, attending a card party at Lord and Lady Wade's lavish estate was the perfect event to introduce the Marchioness of Savage to the *ton*. The Wades were famous for hosting fetes that celebrated the latest scandals. It was the place where new rumors began and old ones were put to bed.

In other words, this was where Prue's future in society would be decided.

No pressure, she thought dryly as the carriage slowed to enter the lengthy queue of arriving guests.

She nudged the fringed curtain aside and peered out the window. "It will be an age before we are near the house and the party will likely be over by then. We could simply . . . send our regrets. Tell them we've decided to travel the Continent."

"We could, indeed," Leo drawled, his fingertip lightly tracing the gold band beneath her gloved hand before he brought it to his lips. "Though, I'm afraid if we return to the town house too soon, Grimsby will likely murder us. Between the constant siege of invitations and gifts of congratulations arriving on our doorstep, he doubtless cannot wait until the *ton*'s fascination with us has subsided."

She glanced archly at her husband. "It could be argued that the majority of the letters and invitations arriving are for you alone—some tear streaked from women who are mourning the news and others perfumed and audacious from those who are challenged by it."

"What can I say? Now that I'm forbidden fruit, I'm positively irresistible." He flashed an unrepentant grin, and chuckled when she stripped her hand from his. Tsking her, he leaned in to nibble lightly on her frowning mouth. "In fact, you were saying something just like that this afternoon in my study."

"I believe I said *incorrigible*."

"Strange how the word takes on an entirely different meaning when exclaimed on a sigh of ecstasy, isn't it?"

She blushed, recalling all the wicked things he'd done to her on his desk. As he began kissing her throat, she laid her hands on his chest and lightly pushed him away. "Scoundrel."

"Yes, my darling, but I'm *your* scoundrel," he said and with such tenderness that her heart squeezed on a raw ache.

Then before she could recover, he lifted her to his lap and stole the gasp from her lips in a deep and thorough kiss.

She was helpless to resist. The remains of her ire quickly melted. Her hands slid from his chest to his nape and she swallowed down his low hum of approval as she pressed closer, mouth to mouth, tongue to tongue, torso to torso. She wriggled closer still and was rewarded when he gripped her tightly.

Her velvet rasped against his wool, their hearts accelerating beneath cambric and linen until she forgot all about the purpose of this evening. Until it was just him and her, the way it had been for all these heavenly days together.

Somehow, he'd turned her into a hedonist, forever wanting more. Would she ever have her fill of him?

But then the slow movement of the carriage beneath them brought reality back on a sudden rush. Words like *forever* and *ever* didn't apply to them. Whether she had her fill of him or not, they would go their separate ways in the not too distant future.

Reluctantly, she tore free, pressing her heated cheek against his, her breaths short. "Leo . . . the party."

"We have time for a quick tumble in the carriage . . . for moral support."

"I'm not certain that arriving disheveled will help me face society's scrutiny and speculation." She looked down in seeming disapproval to her bunched skirts and the masculine hand disappearing beneath the ruffled hem.

He looked at her with feigned innocence. "I was referring to myself. After all, how am I supposed to endure an evening of cards when I know that none of the gentlemen at my table will reveal a good hand with a delightful little giggle the way you do. And I can assure you that none of them will gaze upon me with utter adoration for letting them win regardless. My ego is already flagging."

As he lightly stroked her stockinged calf in the sensitive place behind her knee, tingles raced up her inner thigh and made her wriggle again. Against her hip, she found irrefutable proof of his confidence in her response. "Flagging? Hardly."

"I've given the matter a good deal of thought in these past few minutes," he said, his lips finding that spot just beneath her ear that made her want to purr. He wasn't playing fair. "And I firmly believe that my marchioness should always exhibit a well-pleasured glow when appearing in public."

"And wrinkled skirts, no doubt." Prue did her best to ignore the fluttering of her heart at the possessive way he drawled *my marchioness*.

His lips curved in a grin against her skin. "Not necessarily. There are ways to avoid telltale wrinkling."

She felt the warm caress of his bare fingers above the rise of her stocking. Absently, she wondered when he'd removed his gloves. But as his hand ascended and his mouth coasted along her clavicle, she realized she was actually considering his shocking proposal of making love inside the carriage. After all, a stressful night awaited.

Outside, the jangle of carriage rigging, the clomp of horse hooves on the street, and the chatter of arriving guests were all around them. But here, inside these cozy dark confines, it was just the two of them. In here, he was *her scoundrel* and she was *his marchioness*. And she couldn't think of anywhere else she'd rather be.

She arched her neck under his tender seduction, her voice husky when she whispered, "Show me."

But whatever they might have done was quickly stalled when Rogers tapped on the hood. "Lady Babcock headed your way, my lord."

Leo growled an oath beneath his breath and quickly set Prue beside him, smoothing her skirts in place. "It appears as though time is not on our side, after all."

In the next instant, the door was wrenched open and the countess's beaming face appeared beneath a feathered turban. She eyed the two of them and her brows inched higher with intrigue. "And just how are the newlyweds, hmm? Getting better acquainted, I see. My darling gel, you look rather flushed. I do hope my dear boy is keeping you quite content."

"I was about to do just that before your untimely arrival," he muttered, drumming his fingers on the top hat he'd perched on his lap.

"Be that as it may, I thought I should warn you that the turnout for tonight's fete is a little more varied than I anticipated. Because of that, I wanted to offer a united front as we embark on this evening's adventure."

That sounded rather ominous, Prue thought, reflexively squeezing Leo's arm.

His eyes were warm and steady as he gazed down into her uncertain, upturned face while he replied to the countess. "Fear not, ma'am. If you had ever seen my wife march across Wiltshire in the rain with her head held high, then you would know that she can face anything."

Prue's heart stopped ticking for a moment like a stalled pendulum clock. When it started back up again, she was sure the force of it would shatter something and all the love she'd been safely guarding would suddenly rush out. Her chest felt tight, her throat cinched, her eyes hot as if glowing. She was sure that the only way to hold herself together would be to press her lips to his.

Public displays of affection, however, were frowned upon. The last thing she needed was to cause a scandal by kissing her husband in full view of Lady Babcock, the groomsman waiting by the step, and all the arriving guests who'd paused on the pavement to pretend they weren't gawking at them.

So she forced herself to release her husband's hand and face the open door with her chin high and her shoulders straight.

⋯⋯⋯

INSIDE THE lavish ballroom, Prue's reception into society as the Marchioness of Savage was even worse than she expected. Every eye watched her every move, waiting for the slightest misstep. Walking between the tables set up for the evening's play, she felt like a limping mouse in a room full of voracious cats.

That need to be perfect and to find acceptance, if only for her husband's sake, had never been so great. It roiled in her stomach like a storm at sea. And the worst part was, she couldn't even sit beside Leo to absorb his strength.

He was seated at one of the dozen or so square tables on the gentlemen's side of the room with their host. She was at the middle table of the women's side of the room, her back to him.

As Prue took her seat, she soon understood what the final circle of hell felt like.

It was a frigid, wintry place with frosty glares and icicle daggers. Across from her sat her hostess, the formidable Lady Wade, to her left the supercilious Lady Caldicott, and to her right . . . Lady Sutton.

Oh yes, *that* Lady Sutton. The almost-mistress.

If the bated silence as the introductions were made was any indication, then everyone was aware of the suspended agreement between Leo and Lady Sutton. It was so quiet, in fact, that the creak of a single chair sounded like the blaring trumpets of doomsday.

She was a usurper. A thief who'd stolen a treasure she hadn't even imagined she'd wanted. After all, if Prue had known Leo as she did now, she would surely despise any woman who stood in her way of having him.

"It is a pleasure to make your acquaintance, Lady Sutton," Prue said kindly.

The woman's coal-black gaze swept over her and a slow smile spread on her handsome face with her tight, three-word reply. "Charmed, I'm sure."

The first round of Whist consisted of polite, though somewhat superfluous, conversation involving the latest *on-dits* at the other tables. Lady Wade took the trick.

The second involved a patently suggestive retelling of a rumor that Prue had first met Lord Savage *in the flesh on the side of a country road*—Lady Caldicott's trick.

The third was her straight-faced confirmation of that fact, refusing to allow anyone to get the better of her—her own trick.

The fourth was an ever-polite, eyelash-batting congratulations on her recent nuptials—Lady Sutton's trick. "Let us just hope that wedded bliss lasts longer than four months," she added as she gathered the fish tokens.

By the time the next hand was dealt, Prue no longer felt sorry for Lady Sutton.

In fact, from that moment on, the object of the game took on a decidedly bloodthirsty twist. Every trick was a point for either team, back and forth, like subtle lances from the tip of a rapier.

"Hmm . . ." Lady Sutton purred, her claws tapping on her cards. "I wonder what a man does when he tires of the mistress that he made his wife. Shut her up in a country house and resume his affairs by choosing a name out of a hat?"

Prue smiled and laid a card. "I'm afraid I've thrown out all his *old* hats."

But she lost the trick that round. She was too distracted with the memory of her conversation with Leo a few nights ago.

I just didn't want you to have some grand notion that I'm capable of giving you more than this.

After listening to the stories he'd shared, she understood his reason for keeping his heart guarded. Anyone would have done the same.

For the past few days, however, she'd been wondering what it would take to make him want to keep her. It was a silly fancy, she knew. But she couldn't help it.

Since they'd married, they'd been so happy, so deeply and thoroughly ensconced in each other, that she'd started imagining a lifetime with him. A genuine marriage. She could picture spending years and years in his arms, by his side with her hand in his. Perhaps, one day, they might have a little hand to hold and cherish—a boy with a mop of golden curls and his father's devilish green eyes. Perhaps a little girl that they would name after her mother.

But that was a dream she hadn't voiced. As determined as she was to have a life of her own making, her bravery fell short at this. After all, he'd made it clear that their marriage was a matter of honor and nothing more. He was simply offering her the protection of his name before he replaced her.

Distracted by her thoughts, she lost another trick. *Pekingese!*

Lady Sutton reached forward to play a card and a glint of silver drew Prue's gaze to her wrist. And at once, she went still.

She recognized the pink tourmaline dangling from the clasp and the two rabbits facing each other in the center. Her mother's charm bracelet!

"Do you like my bracelet, Lady Savage?" Lady Sutton inquired with a feline grin. "It was a recent acquisition of mine over a hand of vingt-et-un. I believe you are acquainted with the lady who lost it. Lady Whitcombe?"

"Indeed," she said tightly, having no doubt that Dorcas had likely crowed about the object having once been part of Prue's inheritance. And Lady Sutton had worn it on purpose.

She turned it on her wrist, practically purring with delight. "Vulgar little thing, isn't it? I'll likely toss it in the bin later, but I couldn't help wearing it just this once. After all, I've been assured"—she slid a purposeful glance across the room to Leo's table—"that I'll soon have anything I could ever want."

Prue sincerely hoped that Lady Sutton wanted her eyes clawed out because that was certainly something she was about to get.

"What a coincidence. I already have everything I could want," she said and played the final trump card.

But as they rose from their chairs to find another table, Lady Sutton said, "You are clever with your tricks. Or should I say *traps*?"

"I'm sure I do not know what you mean."

"My dear, we all know how you caught a marquess. The only question remains, how long will you be able to keep him? Not long, I imagine." Then she leaned in to whisper. "After all, I have it under excellent authority that he's already wooing your replacement."

"You're wrong about that," she said and turned to leave.

But Lady Sutton took hold of her arm, her grip biting. "Before you become too sure of yourself, you may wish to check his accounting ledgers and see just how many women he's currently keeping in fine clothes."

Prue refused to reveal that the comment had unsettled her in any way. Holding her head high, she shrugged free and walked to the bureau on the far side of the room for a glass of ratafia. But her hand shook as she lifted it to take a sip.

Could it be true? *Was* he already thinking of replacing her?

Glass in hand, she turned to rest her eyes on him at Lord Wade's table. But in addition to her husband, their host and the other two gentlemen—Viscounts Randell and Butterfield—was Lady Sutton. She was casually resting her hand on the back of Lord Randell's chair, which sat directly opposite Leo.

Then she cast a smug glance over her shoulder as if to say, "He'll soon be mine."

Prue stiffened, her skeleton forged of inner steel. And she narrowed her eyes as she looked back at the hoyden. "Not today, Sutton."

She crossed the room and stood by her husband's chair, placing her hand on his shoulder. The gesture was a primitive display of possession. It said *mine*. And he covered her hand with his, lifted it to press a kiss, then set it back on his shoulder.

As she flashed a glance of triumph across the table to his almost-*but not over my dead body*-mistress, Prue decided that she wouldn't give him up without a fight.

Even if she wasn't enough for him now, she was determined to find a way to be, or break her own heart trying.

✎↠∞↞✎

THE FOLLOWING morning, Leo glared down at a new charge from Lady Sutton's modiste.

Damn it all. He wished he would have listened to Phoebe in the beginning and never bothered with the greedy Millie Sutton. He should not have started paying her bills in the first place. At the time, Leo had assumed he'd only pay for the few gowns she'd already ordered, not give her carte blanche to replace her entire wardrobe.

When he married, he thought she understood that everything had changed. Clearly, she needed to be told directly that this would be the last charge he would allow.

However, after watching the way that his father had so mistreated his own mistresses, leaving them without a shilling or place to live even though he'd had means, Leo knew that he couldn't be so callous as to leave her to suffer the wrath of creditors.

But enough was enough. Therefore, he would endeavor to find her a new protector.

Fortuitously, Mr. Devaney came to call at that precise moment.

"Just the man I needed to see," Leo remarked as his investigator stepped into the study. "I have a new task for you, if you are up for it. I need to find a gentleman for Lady Sutton. Preferably a wealthy man who lives far—immensely far—from London."

Devaney looked down at his hat, absently pinching around the edge of the brim between his thumb and forefinger. "As to that, I may have news for you already. But you're not going to like it, my lord."

"If you're about to tell me that she already has a gentleman, I assure you that it will be the best of news."

Devaney slowly lifted his gaze. "Even if that gentleman is a certain Lord Marlow?"

The sound of that name crawled over his skin like insect legs. Marlow was a phantasm, the nightmare that lurked in the shadows—you could never be sure if it would smother you in your sleep.

"And just what is Marlow up to this time?" he murmured more to himself than to Devaney but the other man answered.

"Couldn't say, my lord. But I've also heard he's been making a few inquiries about your missus."

Leo jolted, alarm sprinting through him. "Such as?"

"The names of her family and friends, her schooling . . . just general things that don't amount to nothing."

It couldn't be *nothing* if Marlow was involved. "Keep me apprised of anything new."

Devaney nodded. "I do have some better news for you. I finally discovered who holds the deed to that cottage you asked me to look into. According to my sources, Lady Whitcombe gambled it away at a party. It changed hands a few times at that same party as if it were nothing more than a hot coal, until it finally ended up in the hands of a certain Lady Doyle."

"Splendid work, and much appreciated." Leo shook his hand before Devaney left.

His mood started to improve the instant he thought about how much this would please Prue. He penned a missive to his solicitor, Mr. Godfrey, to inquire about the purchase of Downhaven Cottage without delay. With any luck, he'd have the deed in his possession by this afternoon.

Just after he handed the letter to Grimsby to post, he saw the woman who occupied his every thought and desire, strolling into the study. Closing the door, he stepped around his desk at once to pull her against him. "You are awake rather early, at least for such a slugabed. It isn't even noon yet."

She wrapped her arms around him, her lips quirked,

blatantly tempting him to no end. "If I've turned into a slugabed, then it's your fault."

"I refuse to take the blame. After all, I distinctly recall how soundly you slept on that very sofa before I even kissed you."

"It's still your fault. There's always been something about you that . . ."

"My darling, I will be heartily offended if you finish that statement with a declaration that my presence exhausts you."

"Well," she said with an impish shrug and then laughed when he tried to release her. But she tightened her hold and pressed a mollifying kiss to his chin. "What I want to say is that there is something about you that has always put me at ease, even when I wasn't aware of it. I suppose you might say that I feel . . . safe with you."

Those words, spoken by any other person at any other time, wouldn't have meant a thing. But to hear her tell him that she'd felt so safe that she'd climbed into his carriage . . . so safe that she'd slept soundly at his side even that first night . . . so safe that she had signed a contract to become his mistress even after suffering agony for, what she believed was, her first time . . . so safe that she was letting down her guard more and more each day with him . . . Well, it meant everything.

"Safe with a scoundrel? You are a dreadful judge of character." He grinned and stole a kiss, wishing he could carry her inside his pocket all day.

"Perhaps," she said with a sigh and slipped out of his embrace. Walking to the hearth, she picked up the fire poker and skewered a log. "Though, I must say, after meeting Lady Sutton last night, the same could be said of you. She's awful. I wanted to murder her with my bare hands. Or maim her, at the very least."

"You are quite the Lady Savage, aren't you?" he teased, but spying the recent modiste charges on his desk, he tucked them out of sight and into his drawer. No need to incur the wrath of his adorably jealous wife.

"Apparently so. Which is why I will truly relish stealing my mother's charm bracelet from her." At his murmur of intrigue, she glanced over and nodded. "Yes, I was just as surprised when I saw it on her wrist last night, and she purposely taunted me with it. I want it back as soon as possible. In fact, I'm thinking about barging over to her residence this instant and demanding it."

He was already shaking his head. Considering what he knew of Marlow's association with Lady Sutton, not to mention that she was obviously trying to provoke his wife, Leo wanted Prue to have nothing to do with her.

"Better let me see to it. Wouldn't want you carted off in shackles and irons, would we?" He crossed the room and pulled her into his arms again. If only he had a pocket big enough . . .

She squinted up at him. "And if I'd prefer that you didn't speak with her either?"

He was about to argue that no one dictated his actions. Then he saw uncertainty in the depths of her gaze.

"No need to worry, my sweet. I'm always aware of the dictates of our contract." He pressed his lips to the ring on her left hand and expected her to smile at his romantic gesture. Instead, he saw furrows above the bridge of her nose. Well, if that didn't make her happy, he knew what would.

"Which reminds me," he said, smoothing the pad of his thumb over her brow, "I have just learned who holds a certain deed that you've been wanting in your possession. And I trust that when my solicitor returns from visiting Lady Doyle that you will be the keeper of Downhaven Cottage."

And there was the smile he wanted.

Chapter 25

Prue paid a call at Upper Wimpole Street the following afternoon, taking with her a box of the aunts' favorite confections *and* a heart full of worries. She thought she'd hidden the latter, but Meg had seen through her and invited her to take some air in Regent's Park where they could speak in private.

So, while Myrtle flirted with the nut seller and Maeve fed the geese in the pond, Prue talked about her horrendous societal debut as the Marchioness of Savage.

"Well, I absolutely hate Lady Sutton," Meg said with a stab of her parasol tip to the path at their feet. "The nerve of her implying that Savage would ever cheat on you. I've known him most of my life and, even though I was furious with him for a time, I still know that he always keeps his promises."

"I believe that to be true, as well. Leo is bound by his own code of honor. The only problem is, the promise he made me was for four months," she said, her voice frayed around the edges as she uncharacteristically spilled the contents of her soul.

"Surely, your marriage vows trump that contract you signed."

She shook her head. "He'd had a new one prepared that very morning. We signed it in the church vestry."

Now, she didn't know what to do. How did one convince a notorious rake to spend the rest of his life with only one woman?

Undoubtedly, he'd known far more thrilling women in his life. Well-traveled and experienced women who could keep him enthralled with their conversations and carnal knowledge. Whereas, she had simpler tastes and aspirations. All she wanted was a happy life and someone to share it with . . . and she wanted that someone to be Leo. She wanted that more than she'd ever wanted anything before.

Beneath the brim of her bonnet, Meg's clear blue eyes were kind and hopeful. "Have you considered coming straight out with it and telling him how you feel?"

It seemed like a simple solution . . . if not for the fact that Prue had more experience in losing people's affections rather than in gaining them.

"I'm afraid of driving him away by asking for more than he's willing to give," she admitted quietly.

Her companion didn't say anything for a minute as they strolled among the fallen leaves, the chill of winter's approach becoming bolder. "I understand that fear all too well. After baring my heart to the man I love, he told me I was too young to know myself and then left for the Continent."

Prue felt her heart stop, her stomach churning with icy dread. That was precisely what she was afraid of. Only in her circumstance, she would be the one who went away.

"But I still wouldn't have done it differently," Meg added. "If you don't tell someone how you feel, then how will you know where you stand in their esteem?"

Prue reached out to squeeze her friend's hand. "I think you are very brave, Margaret Stredwick."

"And I think you are, as well."

"Perhaps when I had nothing left to lose. But now . . . ?" She shook her head. "I have everything to lose."

And it terrified her.

Meg's grip tightened. "But you also have everything to gain. And can I tell you a secret?"

"Of course. I've already bared my soul, the least you

could do is bare yours," she said with a grin, linking arms with her as they continued to stroll.

"There's still part of me that is absolutely, positively certain that Mr. Prescott will return one day. He'll proclaim that he loved me all along and cannot live another moment without me." She gave a rueful laugh. "Terribly childish, isn't it?"

Prue shook her head. "Having confidence in one's dreams is something that we all wish we had. I envy your fortitude."

It was easy to picture Meg's dream coming true. She couldn't imagine any man not wanting such a vibrant and accomplished young woman. As for herself, Prue had her doubts.

The years of constant criticism and her subsequent failed attempts to be perfect still sat on her shoulders. Thanks to her time with Leo, the weight of that burden wasn't nearly as heavy as before. Even so, she occasionally heard those whispers, telling her that she wasn't good enough.

But Meg was right. If Prue didn't tell him, then she would never know if there was even a chance for a future.

If not, then she would be living alone for the rest of her life, just as she'd first planned.

"It's like what the aunts say to justify their recipe espionage, that you have to believe something already belongs to you or else you'll sabotage yourself in the process."

So all Prue needed to do was imagine that Leo's heart was already hers.

Simple, right? Hmm . . . she wasn't too sure about that.

"I suppose I could broach the topic at dinner. I'll have the cook make his favorite dishes. And I'll wear that ivory gown he likes. Then, if everything goes to plan, I'll—" She broke off abruptly as she spotted Lady Doyle on the path. The very same lady who held the deed to Downhaven Cottage.

It was as if the Fates were eavesdropping on her thoughts and giving her an opportunity to fulfill the purpose that had brought her to Leo's door in the first place. However, if this was a message from them, she wasn't sure she wanted to receive it.

And yet, Prue was sensible enough to know that it was always better to be prepared for whatever may come her way.

She looked ahead. Lady Doyle was with her daughter and their dye-dipped poodles. The two women were nearly identical in their white ruffled chemisettes over rather imposing bosoms, looking much like pigeons in lavender-and-blue pelisses, walking their matching lavender-and-blue high-stepping dogs.

"If you wouldn't mind, I would like to speak with Lady Doyle for a moment," she said to Meg.

"Of course."

Prue wasn't well acquainted with the lady and her daughter, but since she had been introduced during her first Season, it was deemed acceptable to approach. However, she did so warily. After all, if last night had taught her anything, it was to not assume that everyone conveniently forgot about her ruinous reputation before she'd married.

"Good afternoon, Lady Doyle," Prue called, lifting her hand in greeting.

Coming to a fork on the path, the lady and her daughter exchanged a look between them. Then they turned in the opposite direction, noses high in the air.

"That was rude," Meg said with a scoff.

Prue slowed her step, embarrassed. But, as she cast a look around at the few others milling about in the park that day, she was glad that there was enough distance between herself and Lady Doyle so that it wouldn't appear like a cut direct. Even though it likely was.

"It's nothing," Prue said, adopting one of Leo's shrugs. "Besides, it's getting chilly and I think we should—"

The excited barking of dogs interrupted her and she looked ahead to see the poodles straining against their ribands, pom-pom paws clawing the air as a squirrel darted across the path.

Then the furry rodent stopped and turned abruptly and began to run toward Meg and Prue. A shiver of dread stole down her spine. She had a sense that this wasn't going to end well.

In the very next instant, the dogs broke free, charging forward in a blur of colorful fluff.

Beside her, Meg gasped. "Did they just unleash their hounds?"

"I don't know, and I don't want to find out. I have the worst luck with dogs," Prue said. With her friend in tow, she wasted no time and turned swiftly down the path with quickened steps.

The poodles were giving a merry chase, the squirrel zig-zagging between the grass and the path, but still heading in their direction.

"Quick. Through here," Meg said, tugging her between hedges.

Then they both stopped just short of careening into the pond, teetering on the toes of their shoes, arms waving for balance. But it appeared they'd evaded the errant canines.

"What a relief!" Prue said, hand splayed over the buttons of her spencer.

Meg looked at her, eyes dancing with mirth. "What an *ordeal*! We barely avoided a most flamboyant demise."

On the other side of the pond, Maeve stared at them with her head tilted in question and Meg and Prue began to laugh.

But they celebrated too soon.

In the next instant, the squirrel cut through the hedgerow. The dogs bounded after it, yapping excitedly with razor-sharp teeth. A flock of geese took flight in a sudden calamity of flapping and honking, distracting the dogs with an abundance of quarry. Yet, for some reason, they turned their focus on Prue and Meg.

"Oh no," she muttered.

But it was too late. They charged, rushing around them in a circle. Then they slowed to a trot like show ponies in a parade, their tongues hanging from their panting mouths. To onlookers, these beasts might appear docile and friendly. But Prue wasn't fooled for an instant. Not even when they paused briefly to bow in the grass with their front paws forward, shaved hind ends raised, tails wagging.

"I think they only want to play. Such a good doggie, aren't you?" Meg laughed, already reaching down to pet the purple one. After a tentative sniff, he gave himself over to a good ear scratch.

The blue one, on the other hand, was a bit more demanding. She wasn't going to wait for Prue to decide if petting was something she was willing to do. No, the poodle took matters into her own hands. She lurched forward on hind legs, front paws high, pink tongue poised to lick a face—whether or not that face wished to be licked—and toppled them both to the ground.

The very soggy ground. Prue felt the squish beneath her pelisse.

It wasn't until after the dogs had left a sufficient amount of slobber behind, that they were brought to heel by their owners. Then the two pigeons and two poodles trotted off together to wreak havoc on someone else.

Meg extended a hand to Prue, who was soaked in places that she didn't want to think about. And there was a terrible smell that was likely the fault of what the geese had left behind.

"Oh dear," Meg said, pinching her nose and pressing her lips together to suppress a smile. But her words came out in a laugh as she said, "You really don't have luck with dogs, do you?"

By this time, Maeve had alerted Myrtle and the two aunts were at their sides, quickly escorting the two of them toward the park's entrance to hail a hackney. Unfortunately, there were none to be had at the moment.

"There, my dear," Maeve said with a nod of approval as she slipped Prue's pelisse from her shoulders. "No one will be the wiser."

Regrettably, that wasn't true. The sludge had seeped to her skirt and stockings, and there was an awful smell.

"*Eau du geese*," Meg said, unable to suppress a giggle. "Fear not, we'll see you home without delay."

Just then, a dove-gray carriage pulled to a stop, and out of it stepped Lord Marlow.

"You lovely ladies look to be in need of assistance." Taking in the situation at a glance—and likely with a sniff—he didn't hesitate to offer his carriage.

"You are too kind, Lord Marlow," Myrtle said, unaware of Leo's apparent ill will toward the viscount, and that he'd strictly forbade Prue from speaking to him.

But there was no opportunity to refuse gracefully as Marlow quickly began to hand them inside, each in turn. When it was just he and Prue standing there, he shrugged out of his frock coat and draped it over her shoulders. She balked at the intimacy, but realized he was likely trying to protect his own upholstery.

It wasn't until she looked out the window that she saw Lady Doyle and her daughter watching the entire spectacle.

Prue's stomach turned with dismay as the aunts relayed the story to Marlow, with Maeve offering her viewpoint as if she'd been a front-row spectator to a Greek tragedy.

"And the fact that you never had the chance to speak to Lady Doyle only adds insult to injury," Meg added.

This sparked Marlow's interest, his dark brows lifting toward the brim of his dove-gray hat. "Her ladyship happens to be my neighbor. If there is a message you wish to relay, I would be more than happy to take charge of it."

Prue scrutinized those piercing eyes for just a moment.

In them, she detected no subterfuge, only sincerity. Still, there was something about him that unsettled her. But since he had come to her aid, she saw no reason to be impolite in return. "Thank you, no, my lord. I appreciate the kind offer; however, the matter regards a certain deed she holds and it can wait for another day. Besides, I'm sure my husband has already seen to it."

And yet, there was a part of her that did not know if Lady Doyle had intended to cut her or not. But if she had, there was a possibility that she would never do Prue any favor at all.

"I must agree with you, my lady," he said with a charming grin. "Your husband has always excelled in getting precisely what he desires. There are times when I find myself quite envious of my old friend."

And there it was again—that unsettled feeling as he looked at her.

But she did not have time to analyze it because, just then, the carriage arrived at the town house. Prue bid her friends a good day and thanked the viscount once more.

She did her best to walk through the door with dignity, even though she was stinking and covered in filth from the waist down.

But when Grimsby asked if she required assistance and when one of the maids polishing the banister gasped at the smell, Prue felt like the most ungainly creature ever. Hardly worthy of being a marchioness. How was someone like her ever going to convince Leo to keep her?

Still, she held her head high. "All is well. I merely had a spill. Nothing more."

In her bedchamber, Dottie was blessedly efficient in taking away the offensive garments and all that was left for Prue was to clean off the residual fluids.

Clad in her chemise and corset, she stood in the tub and scrubbed her backside, legs and feet until they were pink. That was how Leo found her.

Startled, she dropped the square of flannel. Reflexively, she crossed her arms to shield herself, hoping to hide her humiliation. But one look at his concerned expression and she knew that Grimsby had told him about the state she'd been in when she arrived.

There was no hiding it. And the instant she thought about everything that had happened—the snub, the humiliation, along with the weight of her impossible hopes bearing down on her—she felt tears gather along the lower rims of her eyes, threatening to spill down her cheeks in a hot deluge.

She'd wanted today to be perfect, and to be brave enough to tell him how she felt. But she couldn't possibly do that now.

"What happened, my darling?" he asked, gathering her in his arms and lifting her from the tub.

In a rush, she told him about the poodles and pond, about Meg and the aunts.

The corner of Leo's mouth quirked when she described being slobbered on by a bright blue beast. Then he sat down on the wooden chair in the bathing chamber, holding her in his comforting embrace. "Are you hurt?"

Shaking her head, she blinked to pull herself together, and tried to pretend that she wasn't an utter disgrace. Pretend that he wouldn't want to replace her. "How did you fare on your errand?"

"Lady Sutton wasn't at home," he said and reached into his pocket for a handkerchief to wipe away the tears that had spilled over. "Why do I have the sense that there's something you aren't telling me?"

"I don't know. I merely fell on my backside. I'm clumsy, I suppose. Just one of my many flaws."

"Now, I know something is the matter because you have no flaws. Not a single one."

A watery, self-deprecating laugh escaped her. "You don't mean that. Everyone has flaws and I have more than my share."

"Well, if you insist, then your belief that you have a flaw is your only one. You are perfect in every other regard."

She was ready to refute that, too. But when she saw that there wasn't a teasing smirk on his lips and no laughing glint in his eyes, she couldn't speak at all for a moment. He looked at her with tender, enduring warmth as if he believed it down to his soul. He touched her as if she were a gift, precious, cherished. And her heart was so full it was choking her.

She took his face in her hands. "I wish I could see myself through your eyes. I wanted today to turn out so differently." She rested her forehead against his. "By tomorrow, all of society will wonder why you saddled yourself with such a creature."

He nuzzled her nose with his and kissed her softly. "I don't care what society thinks. I only care about you, moonflower. Don't you know that yet?"

At the earnestness of his words, the breath rushed out of her lungs. Then she kissed him with all the love that she'd tried to keep safely guarded for so long. It was a desperate kiss, a clumsy kiss, her teeth bumping his. But she couldn't help it. The lock on her heart suddenly broke and the contents spilled out with no hope of ever caging them back in again.

"Easy," he crooned against her lips as he held her face, his fingertips tracing the delicate shell of her ear, feather-light caresses along her brow, through the disheveled wisps of her hair. "Shh . . . We have all the time in the world."

But they didn't. The hours were speeding by, days vanishing before her eyes, and she . . . She needed more.

Shifting on his lap, she straddled him. She couldn't get close enough to stop the torturous, hollow ache that had to be filled. "I need you. I need you so much. I need your hands on me. I need you inside me."

His grip tightened, hands at her nape and on her hip as

she rolled against the unmistakable hardness beneath his fall front.

"Then take me," he growled, his mouth slanting beneath hers, tongue stealing inside, determined to hunt down every raw emotion she had and swallow them down.

She gave them to him, reaching between their bodies to tear frantically at the fastenings of his trousers. His flesh was galvanic, searing in her hand, the mushroomed head thick and dark.

Lost in the frenzy, she lifted. Positioned him beneath her. Then sank down on a slick glide, feeling the satisfying rub of their bodies, inside and out. And they both moaned from the sheer, aching pleasure of it.

She took him, all of him, gripping tight as their bodies merged and filled, lost in a feverish rhythm of her own. But she wanted more than rapture. More than shuddering ecstasy. She wanted every part of him, every breath, every minute, every beat of his heart and dream of his soul.

Her nails bit into his shoulders as she drove down on him again and again, taking all she could. And he arched up to meet her, his body coiled and ready. But he was holding back, waiting for her. She knew the signs—his stuttered breaths, the tight cording of his throat, the lightning bolt–shaped furrow of strain on his brow, his fractured grunt as she tasted the salty bloom of perspiration on his skin. And just knowing that she had brought him to the brink, tipped her over the edge.

The last remnants of her shield shattered on a wrenching sob. *"Leo! I . . . I love you."*

A guttural roar ripped from his throat. He jerked beneath her, driving deep, spilling rivers of molten heat inside her and kept thrusting until she went over the edge again.

And after, when they were both breathless and draped over the chair like wrung-out laundry, he simply held her. But said nothing in response.

Chapter 26

Leo caught himself lingering in bed the following morning, arm bent, head resting in the palm of his hand as he watched Prue sleep. His entire being was absorbed in the fan of cornsilk eyelashes resting above the soft peachy flush of her cheeks, the sound of her even breathing brushing over his furred chest like a feather, the unconscious curl of her fingertips over the steady beating of his heart.

It was almost impossible to believe that this guarded and proud creature loved him.

When lost in the thrall of passion, any number of things could fall from one's lips, whether they were true or not. He knew this because he'd known many women who, like him, didn't know the first thing about actual love—the kind that he'd always imagined was selfless, sacrificing, and all-consuming. No, they had been in love with what he'd given them in the moment, the pleasure and exhilaration of passion.

Soaring to heights of ecstasy gave one a feeling of utter bliss. But those sensations were fleeting. In the end, those climax confessions turned into nothing more than mere words, like a passing greeting or a placating promise. There was no substance to them.

With Prue, however, he'd *felt* the words. When she'd told him, a feeling more intense than he'd ever experienced before had burst inside him like a star, filling him with heat and light until he just couldn't hold back a moment longer.

Contemplatively, he traced the wispy arch of her pale brow with his fingertip. Then he leaned in and pressed his lips to the crown of her head. Drawing in a long pull of her scent, he let it fill every corner and crevice of his lungs. She stirred slightly, curling toward him on a hum of sleepy contentment, tempting him to stay.

Instead, he tucked her in, making sure that no sound or ray of light broached the bedcurtains. Then he rang for Jones.

In the past weeks, his valet had learned to be quite nimble footed when entering the bedchamber and crossing to the dressing room. He spoke only with a bow, his lips moving in a silent "Good morning, milord," before pouring hot water into the basin and lathering up a whisker brush.

Freshly shaven and dressed, Leo went downstairs with a smile, thinking of his wife and having no idea that his day was about to go to the dogs.

It began with the arrival of a parcel.

He was just passing through the foyer after breakfasting when he saw Grimsby turn away from the door. But the sleeve of his coat caught on the latch and he bobbled the rectangular paper-wrapped package. Leo stopped to lend a hand, setting the teacup he was carrying on the rosewood table. But his butler recovered and offered a stoic nod in response.

With the crisis averted, Leo picked up the cup and proceeded to his study. "I imagine you'll be glad when these gifts stop arriving."

"It is no trouble at all, my *lo*—" Grimsby broke off suddenly on an exclaimed *Oh*!

Out of the corner of his eye, Leo saw him stumble over the edge of the rug. He turned just in time to see the package lurch forward, soar through the air, and hit him squarely in the chest. Along with the tea.

The cup shattered. One of the shards sliced into his

palm. Yet, somehow, Leo managed to secure the unwieldy package.

His butler regained his footing and instantly colored. His usual pallid complexion turned a purplish pink in his embarrassment as he rushed forward to set matters aright. "I sincerely beg your pardon, my lord. I'm not normally so clumsy."

"I know, Grimsby," Leo said kindly, ever-fond of the old man. He stilled the hand that tried to sop up the wetness from his waistcoat with a handkerchief. "No need to fret. We'll simply chalk it up to a bit of bad luck. Nothing more. I'll just take this with me."

It wasn't until he was seated at his desk that he noticed the blood on his palm. Unconcerned, he wrapped his own handkerchief around the wound and opened the troublesome parcel.

As soon as he unwrapped and opened the box, he went still, his blood as cold as the Thames in January.

There, lying on a bed of straw was a bottle of wine. A 1787 Lafite, to be precise. The exact label and vintage that Giselle had once poured for him. And tucked beside it was a card that read, *A gift for your lovely bride. I look forward to seeing more of her in the coming months.*

It wasn't signed, but he knew who'd sent it. *Marlow.*

Leo stood and stared down at it. No wonder the parcel had wreaked so much havoc when it crossed the threshold. It was likely cursed.

His blood abruptly turned hot, steaming in his veins. The bastard was clearly enjoying this old taunt of his. But to what end? Surely, Marlow didn't imagine he could lure Prue away from him as he'd done with Giselle? Fill her head with all manner of deceptions and expect her to believe it?

If there was one thing Leo knew, it was that his wife did not take someone's word at face value. A man had to earn her trust. And Marlow would never be able to fool her.

Even so, the very idea that he might try, abraded Leo's temper like sandpaper to skin.

He stormed out of his study, taking the gift with him to the kitchen to dispose of. He didn't want to risk any other member of his staff coming into further contact with this cursed gift.

When he returned to his study, he saw another bill from Lady Sutton's modiste had arrived. He was ready to toss it into the fire. Damn that greedy woman! And looking at the charge, he wondered if the costume had been fashioned from gold thread.

She hadn't been at home yesterday when he'd called, which left the matter unresolved. However, the more he thought about it, the more inclined he was to speak directly to her modiste and inform her that any future bills were to be sent to the lady herself.

As if that wasn't enough for one morning, shortly after that, he received unwelcome news from his solicitor.

Even though several attempts had been made to purchase the deed to Downhaven Cottage, no matter what the offer, Lady Doyle refused to sell. Refused!

Unable to fathom her reasoning, he decided to ride over to the lady's town house to pay a call himself. He was determined to have the matter settled before Prue awoke.

Viscountess Doyle received him in the morning room. A plate of half-eaten trout, boiled bacon, kidneys and poached eggs sat before her and she did not pause in her grazing or make an offer for him to join her.

She cut a slice of bacon and gestured with her fork. "I know why you're here, Lord Savage. But I believe I made myself clear to your solicitor."

"Indeed, my lady. However, I am here to ask you again." He drew in a patient breath and adopted a tone of humility, hoping to prey on her heart, if she had one. Though, if she did, it was likely stuffed behind heaps of ruffles and that monstrous bosom. "Perhaps you didn't realize how important the property is to me. There is no amount I wouldn't offer. Merely name your price."

"It was to be a gift to my daughter. However, the instant I realized that the cottage had been in trust to your *wife* at one point, I refused to permit my Eugenia to be sullied by association."

It infuriated him that, even as a proper marchioness, some members of society still looked down on her as if she were ruined. He had done nothing to squelch the rumors that he had taken her virginity, and believed that would earn her swift acceptance. He refused to let anyone snub their noses at her.

Then again, what did he expect after saddling her with such a sullied title? And he had done little to amend the black marks his father had left on it. But Leo wished he could rewrite history for her. Wished that he was more of the man that *she* deserved.

His teeth gritted together, jaw tight, but he remained cordial. At the very least, he would act the part of a respectable gentleman for Prue's sake. "If you want nothing to do with it, then I will gladly take it off your hands."

"I do not possess the deed any longer," the lady said cutting into her steak, the knife screeching sharply against the glazed porcelain. "Thankfully, the honorable Lord Marlow was only too glad to assist me."

"Marlow!"

She looked up with a slow, satisfied smile. "Oh, yes. Though I'm not at all surprised. After all, I saw your wife climb into his carriage at the park yesterday, looking quite at home in his company. But I'm certain a woman such as she would have many different gentlemen to dote on her."

He tensed all over, fists clenched. Prue would never have done that. She'd given her word to stay away from that blackguard. The idea was preposterous.

There were a hundred things he wanted to say to Lady Doyle, listing a fraction of all the ways his wife was superior to her and that she deserved to be revered like a queen. But he did not bother. Such small-minded people were never worth the effort.

So he turned his back on her and went directly next door to Marlow's.

He stormed past the butler and into the house, where he had once sat and laughed and talked with a friend. But that was long ago.

He slammed the study door behind him. "What game do you think you're playing?"

Marlow calmly closed the ledger on his desk and steepled his fingers. "Is this the part where I pretend to have no idea to what you are referring?"

"I want the deed."

Sitting back in his chair, he pursed his lips contemplatively, taking his time before responding. "I find it quite odd that such a nubile young wife would wish to have a house of her own, do you not?"

"No. It is hers by right, and I"—he swallowed—"trust her."

"You trust her, do you? I believe those are the words every cuckold swears by before learning the truth. Did she happen to tell you of our little sojourn in my carriage?" He stared shrewdly, his gaze dropping to Leo's clenched fist. "I thought not. Well, she was in quite a state and needed comforting. I was only too glad to oblige her, right there on the velvet bench. She even thanked me. Though, I imagine someone of her sweet, biddable nature felt a trifle guilty about it afterward and wanted to hide the evidence with a fresh change of clothes."

Leo knew what he was doing, but he refused to let the insinuation take root. "Stay away from my wife."

"How can I, if she is the one who runs to me? Hmm . . .

that reminds me of someone we both knew quite well."
He turned his gaze to the portrait of Giselle, mounted in
a gilded frame over his mantel like a trophy. And on her
hand, she still wore the ruby cabochon ring that Leo had
once given her when he'd proposed. "It seems that you simply cannot keep a woman in your life for too long. Sooner
or later, they all see you are very much your father's son."

Leo felt the jab of the old wound. He wanted to say
that he was nothing like his father, but it wouldn't matter.
Marlow had a vengeful streak that had twisted the mind it
lived in.

Marlow blamed him for his mother's death. It was because of Leo that they were introduced. Noticing his father's
interest, Leo had warned him to keep his distance, but his
father had seen that as a challenge. And so, wanting to prove
that he could have anyone he desired, he had a brief affair
with Marlow's mother while her husband and son were taking a grand tour.

Then, upon discovering that she was carrying a bastard
child and unable to bear the shame of what she had done,
she'd taken her own life.

"None of this will bring her back," Leo said to him.
"Haven't you had your fill of revenge?"

Marlow smiled. "Not yet. But soon, perhaps."

Chapter 27

The day after Prue had confessed her love to Leo, she noticed a change in him.

He'd become distant, their conversations stilted. But that night, when he held and kissed her, rousing her body to unbearable, shattering heights of ecstasy, again and again, he seemed like a man possessed. It was as though he couldn't have enough of her. And she gave him everything without reservation, telling him that she was his and that she loved him without measure.

The words came easier each time she spoke them. Honestly, she couldn't hold them back if she wanted to. But easier or not, they still frightened her. And she knew she wouldn't feel so exposed and vulnerable if he would only say something in return.

He likely assumed that her declarations had merely overtaken her in the heat of the moment. Hadn't he warned her of that in the beginning?

Perhaps that was the reason he remained silent.

She knew he'd been hurt before and that his own barriers, like hers, had been erected out of a need for self-protection. Still, she wanted him to trust her. To know that she wasn't like the women in his past. And she especially wanted him to realize that she was his wife, not simply a four-month affair.

But the strange daytime distance remained throughout the week that followed.

He left during the afternoons, claiming that he was sparring with Reed Sterling. And when he came home, he went directly into his bedchamber to wash and change clothes.

Prue trusted him. She did. And yet, the lifelong fears of her own inadequacy—not to mention Lady Sutton's taunting words—plagued her day after day.

She'd even gone into his study while he was out and had every intention of checking the ledgers. But just as she set her hand on the drawer, she felt the churning of guilt and wariness in the pit of her stomach, and she stopped.

She refused to betray him. If he was ready to replace her, then she would let him tell her so.

That evening, they were to attend a musical performance. But Prue had no desire for society, and told Leo as much.

"Then we'll simply make an appearance and come home," he answered, turning to adjust his cravat in the mirror and she felt the flesh between her brows pucker.

"Since when do you care about appearances?"

He shrugged. "Merely want to put on a good show. Try my hand at acting the gentleman, and all that."

"I don't know why you'd bother. It isn't as though the illusion of respectability will garner the invitations that we need to steal the rest of my inheritance."

Even though they knew who currently possessed each item, they weren't having much luck finding the opportunities they needed. She was beginning to wonder if she would ever have all of her family treasures restored to her.

In addition to the gold diadem being guarded by a vicious Pekingese and an amethyst ring currently buried inside of a fish in Lady Mumphrey's garden, Prue didn't yet have the century-old reliquary pendant, the family silver tea service, the Rembrandt of her five times great-grandmother (who, according to family lore, had been a bit of a flirt), the ebony casket inlaid with gold, the blue vase that her mother had always filled with jonquils, the silver charm bracelet, or the deed to Downhaven Cottage.

"And once you've collected every item, my dear, do you still plan to retire from London altogether?"

She blinked, startled by the question and by the casual delivery that sounded wholly unbothered by the prospect of her leaving. It felt like a lifetime ago that she'd even considered it. But clearly, he was thinking about it. Was that the reason for his pensive mood of late?

Staring at his back, she frowned. "I do not know."

"Well, until you do, I wouldn't advise only attending parties at houses you intend to pilfer. You'll only raise suspicions."

The *us* and the *we* were glaringly absent in his comments and it caused her heart to twist in despair. Did she truly mean so little to him?

But she did not ask him, too afraid of the answer. Instead, she nodded as if in agreement and they left for the musicale without discussing it further.

Together, they endured an hour of arias from a high soprano. It left Prue with a piercing megrim and a desire to go home. However, the latter had less to do with the pain at her temples, and everything to do with the fact that Lady Sutton was also in attendance.

The instant she'd seen her, that terrible insecurity whispered in the back of her mind and Prue had wondered if her husband had known in advance that the other woman would be there. Was that the reason he'd been so eager to attend?

But she quickly tossed that thought aside, refusing to give the likes of Lady Sutton any power over her.

Wanting to press a cold cloth to the nape of her neck, Prue left Leo's side and went into the retiring room.

The chamber was large and hosted a small balcony that overlooked the gardens, and the curtain-swathed doorway was open just enough to allow a cool breeze. She stepped out for a moment of peace and quiet, her thoughts drifting to Leo and wondering . . . always wondering.

Behind her, she heard the chamber door open and close, then a pair of voices in conversation. She was about to make her presence known when she recognized Lady Sutton's voice. And since she was the last person Prue wanted to confront, she remained concealed on the balcony.

"She is such a cold fish," Lady Sutton sneered. "I do not know what Savage ever saw in her."

"It was likely all a scheme of hers from the start," the other woman said. "I heard she'd tried the same with Lord Nethersole but he saw through her. Though, somehow, she must have put up quite a fuss to have him appear the guilty party, when that can hardly be the case if what they are saying is true and Lord Savage only married her because she'd been a virgin."

"And that poor, dear marquess of mine fell right into her trap," Lady Sutton said with a sigh, and Prue seethed, watching her primp in the mirror through the seam in the door. "I offered my sympathies and promised to console him quite thoroughly. To which, he said—in confidence, of course—that he is already tired of the clinging ice maiden. She bores him excessively and he wishes he'd never married her."

Prue held her breath, hating that the news seemed to fit his mood of late, along with his absences in the afternoon.

"What does he plan to do with her?"

Lady Sutton shrugged. "It doesn't matter a whit to me, or to him. After all, he's the one who suggested a tryst between us, at the masquerade. He told me that he's tired of waiting and that he'll slip away from her side no matter what it takes. And in the gown that I'll be wearing, he'll soon see how my fire is so much better than her ice."

"Hurry, Millie," the other woman laughed. "Let us return so you can signal him with your fan, right in front of her eyes."

Prue waited until they left. When she walked into the chamber, she saw a flash of silver and pink draw her attention. And there, resting on the table, was her mother's bracelet.

She didn't hesitate for a single instant before she picked it up and slipped it into her reticule. Her headache miraculously cleared.

Of course, the evening would have gone so much better if Lady Sutton hadn't stopped directly in front of them and made a fuss over losing her bracelet. She even began to suggest that there had been many missing objects reported among certain houses in society, and that she was just another victim.

Prue felt awash with dread at this, and wondered if her other crimes had been noted.

Leo went still at her side, but said nothing. At least, not at the musicale.

But later, in his study, he certainly had a good deal to say.

Unlocking the cabinet of his secretaire, he casually asked, "So, my dear. Did you steal Lady Sutton's bracelet?"

"No. I simply reclaimed part of my inheritance," she corrected. Retrieving the item from her reticule, she placed it beside his glass.

He stared down at it and a muscle ticked at his jaw. "Now that you are a marchioness and all eyes are upon you, you cannot go around stealing things."

She took offense to the rough edge of his tone and squared her shoulders, still smarting over what she'd heard in the retiring room. "Need I remind you that we have a written bargain between us—a signed contract?"

"A contract which states that I agree to assist in retrieving your inheritance," he enunciated as he gripped the neck of the bottle and poured. "It says nothing about the manner in which I decide to do so. And since rumors have now begun about a rash of thievery, I will not take any risk that will put you under further scrutiny."

"A rather convenient time to develop scruples," she muttered, knowing that he hadn't once been bothered by the notion of stealing from the others on her list. But since it happened to be Lady Sutton, he suddenly didn't want to *take the risk*? Ha!

"Scruples, I find, are kept at the holder's discretion," he said with an air of nonchalance, but his shrug was stilted and tight.

"Fine. I won't interfere with yours if you don't interfere with mine."

He tossed back a finger of whisky and set down the empty glass hard. "Prue, you will return the bracelet."

She glared at him, incredulous. "Even when it is mine by birthright?"

"No, it is not. While you lived under your father's roof, your inheritance was considered his property to do with as *he* chose. As my wife, what belongs to you is legally mine," he said. "Of course, I have no desire to keep these items from you, and so I will not. I am a man of my word."

"*However* . . . ?" she all but sneered, eyes narrowed to slits.

"However," he added tightly, "the means by which they are to be procured has changed. You must accept that."

"I'm not returning the bracelet!"

"Fine. Then I will do it myself. We are to attend a masquerade at week's end, at which time I will slip it into her reticule, unseen."

"Oh? And how do you even know she'll attend? Did you discuss it with her?"

"Don't be ridiculous." He scoffed and poured another drink.

"Or perhaps, you know because you purchased her dress for the event."

He turned sharply. "Where did you hear that?"

But as he asked the question, he glanced briefly toward his desk. As if to ensure that his ledgers weren't on display, perhaps?

"So it's true. You *are* paying her modiste."

"Prue, it isn't what you think," he said flatly. "There is nothing untoward happening between Lady Sutton and myself. I simply couldn't leave her penniless after we'd made a verbal agreement."

Once again, she felt like the usurper. Someone who'd stolen in and taken what didn't belong to her. Not someone who could ever be loved by her husband.

But those were thoughts that the old Prue would entertain, believing herself too imperfect, too unworthy.

The new Prue, however, was fuming. How dare he!

She straightened her shoulders, her chin inching higher. "You must care about her then, if you cannot bear the idea of her suffering."

"Paying her bills was a matter of obligation."

Was that supposed to be a denial of affection, then? It didn't sound like one. "Our contract was, too. In fact, you married me out of a *matter of obligation*. I suppose I should be thankful that I'll soon have Downhaven Cottage. That way, when our contract has expired, I'll live there, just as I'd planned to from the start."

He went still, the look in his eyes guarded as if shades had been drawn over panes of green glass. "Do you want to leave then?"

"If I didn't, wouldn't you send me away regardless?" she asked, her voice breaking as tears filled her eyes.

He expelled a sigh and went to her, his tone softer. "Let's not argue. I do not like to see these frustrated tears or to know that you are distressed over something so trivial.

Come to bed and let me take your mind off all this nonsense."

She pulled away from him at once. "If you dare attempt to make love to me now, then you will soon find yourself without your favorite appendage."

And she left him standing alone in the study, taking the stairs to her own bedchamber where she could have a good cry. Then later, when she heard him in his own chamber and no knock fell on her door, she wept some more.

LEO SLAMMED into his bedchamber, ready to storm through her connecting door. A low growl rumbled in his chest like thunder as he stalked across the room.

Here he was, trying to be a respectable man for the first time in his life. Trying to ensure that she never endured society's scorn again. And all she could think about was their time expiring?

Was she merely ticking off the days of a prison sentence?

He went still as the questions burrowed through his agitation and took root in his mind.

I'll soon have Downhaven Cottage . . . when our contract has expired, I'll live there, just as I'd planned to from the start.

He turned away from the door.

Staring at the empty bed, he wondered if he was better off just staying the man he'd always been.

Chapter 28

Later in her life, Prue would likely think that attending a masquerade at Sutherfield Terrace was a fitting end to how her ruination began. Tonight, however, she would rather have been anywhere else.

Through the almond slits of her ivory domino, she looked down at her pale blue-and-silver gown, heavily ornamented with glittering rock crystals, and thought she resembled the ice maiden that Lady Sutton had called her.

Earlier, Madame LeBlanc informed her that Leo had requested her costume to be that of an angel. "And these," she'd said with an eagerness that thickened her French accent as she settled a diaphanous, shimmering silver cape over her shoulders, "are your wings."

Leo had been waiting at the base of the stairs. His costume was in the same colors, though with form-fitting tights, bejeweled codpiece and tunic.

"I knew you would make the perfect angel," he'd said, lifting her hand to his lips.

She'd felt the warmth of it through the glove and wished they'd been able to settle their differences. It had been five days since they'd argued. Five nights spent alone in their bedchambers. Twelve since she'd confessed her love and heard nothing in response.

Slipping free, she'd covered one hand with the other as if to hold in the heat. "And what is your costume?"

"Is it not clear? I'm *Saint Savage*, of course," he'd said, sketching a courtly bow. He wore a shaped mask that nearly concealed his identity altogether if not for that signature wry curl of his lips and the golden mane beneath the ribbon. When she had not laughed, he tsked and brushed her proud chin with the pad of his thumb. "Let us forget all that's behind us and enjoy our evening together, moonflower. These days at odds have wearied my soul and I would give anything to have you back in my arms as you were."

"Anything?" she'd challenged, looking up at him. "Even my bracelet? Ah. I thought not."

He'd dropped his hand. Other than expelling twin sighs of weariness, they hadn't spoken any more on the way.

When they arrived, stepping through the broad French doors to a crowd of gawking faces *en masque* and lined up on the stairs like a collection of garish and unblinking dolls, she couldn't wait for the night to end.

But Prue should have known better. One should never make such a wish at Sutherfield Terrace. They tended to come true in the worst imaginable way.

The masquerade benefit ball was a complete crush. Instead of being shoulder to shoulder, guests were practically piled on top of each other. It was a tight squeeze just to make it to the ballroom.

She and Leo shared one waltz. It was the very first time they'd ever danced together, and the only time she'd danced in over a year. To say that she was nervous was an understatement. Yet, the instant he pulled her against him and swept her into the dance, it was as if they had been doing this since the dawn of time.

The skill was all his, she knew. He was so solid and sure and easy to follow. With every turn, their bodies were so in tune, so perfectly aligned in movement and form that it was as if they were one—thighs sliding, hips pressing, breasts brushing, fingers gripping . . .

Her lips parted. A fine sheen of perspiration collected on her skin beneath her costume. She looked up at him through the slits in her mask to find slumberous green eyes gazing down on her.

She knew what he was thinking. And it made her breathless and desperate to be unreservedly in his arms again.

Prue couldn't bear their separation and discord. She loved him and her desire to have a life with him beyond their four-month agreement hadn't waned. It went without saying that she didn't want him to slip her mother's bracelet into Lady Sutton's reticule. But was she willing to let a memento from the past ruin any chance of a future with him?

The answer was simple. No.

"Leo, we need to talk," she said the instant the music ended, her hand falling from his shoulder to rest in the center of his tunic.

He pulled her closer and whispered in her ear, "Give me a moment to take care of this errand, then we'll go home and settle matters between us."

Did the words *settle matters* have an ominous ring, or was it her imagination? Either way, her stomach dropped.

Leo drew her hand away from his heart and laid it on his sleeve before escorting her to Lady Babcock's side in the gallery that overlooked the ballroom. Just before he left them, he looked down at Prue, his expression inscrutable as he touched her cheek. "I won't be long."

She nodded wordlessly, her stomach churning with worry as she watched him disappear into the crowd.

Had their argument pushed him so far away that it was already too late to bring them back to where they'd been days ago?

It was possible. After all, a man who was used to keeping women for a few short months at a time likely didn't want to be burdened by strife. Perhaps these days apart had offered him clarity as well, and he'd come to the realization that she wasn't worth the trouble. But if that was true, then why had he bothered to marry her at all?

"I'd wondered that myself," Lady Babcock said. "But then the answer was quite obvious."

Prue hadn't even realized she'd spoken aloud and felt a rush of heated embarrassment rise to her cheeks over revealing such mawkish thoughts.

Standing at the railing, the countess lowered the golden wand of her mask and smiled at her as if they were both privy to the same secret. But Prue shook her head. "Apparently, not clear enough for me."

"It's simple, my dear gel. You never asked for more than he was willing to give. Countless women have, you know. Greedy and scheming, the lot of them." She swept her arm in a graceful arc over the sea of colorful costumes, feathered masks and glittering jewels below. "An unmarried man with title and fortune? What a prize, indeed. So they used their wiles to gain his attention, then proceeded toward their ultimate goal—to lay claim to him as if he were nothing more than a pretty pile of gold coins."

Prue nodded. Though, she'd already surmised that women had treated him like a commodity, it still made her angry. Even more so when she thought about the way that Lady Sutton was sending her bills to Leo, taking advantage of his generosity.

And worse, he was letting her.

"He might be a bit too generous, if you ask me," she said, her hand curling over the rail as she searched for him— and *that woman*—in the throng of disguised faces. But she didn't find either of them.

Helene laughed lightly and patted her hand. "All the better for you, I should think. After all, a man never changes who he really is at his core. That's the truth with all of us. And, in time, our most closely guarded secrets are revealed."

She looked at Prue with a fond smile, apparently not realizing that she'd just confirmed Prue's greatest fear—that at Leo's core, he was a man who didn't want anything permanent.

From the very beginning he'd told her this again and again. And if that was true, then what made her think there would be anything she could do or say to change that?

LEO SAW Marlow across the room before he disappeared in the crowd. Tension built up along his shoulders and neck, squeezing like a vise. Bloody hell. The last thing he needed was to be away from his wife's side with a cretin wandering about.

It still bothered him that Prue had never told him about her carriage ride with Marlow. Keeping secrets wasn't something he thought her capable of. And yet, hadn't he believed the same of Giselle?

All the more reason to settle matters once and for all, he thought and walked on.

Turning the corner, he saw an old friend, Lord Randell. Even though the viscount was a good bloke and they'd shared many laughs, he was usually drunk and *always* chatty. But Leo had been away from Prue long enough. He didn't want to be delayed in conversation.

Unfortunately, before he could slip away, his tap-hackled friend spotted him.

"Aha! And there's the elusive Lord Savage." Randell narrowed his bloodshot eyes and pointed with the flask in one hand, while his other hand was pressed to the ivory pilaster as if trying to hold it up. "See here, old chap. I'm highly offended. Walked right past me without a word earlier."

"Apologies. I've been fighting this crush all evening like a salmon swimming upstream," he said, intending to move on without delay. But then he wondered if Randell might be able to help him. Leaning in, he asked confidentially, "Have you seen Lady Sutton, by chance?"

The viscount chuckled and his one-hundred-proof breath singed the hair in Leo's nose. "As a matter of fact, I saw her with you."

Ah. Clearly, his friend was too drunk to be of any help at all.

"Never mind all that," Leo said and *borrowed* his friend's silver flask, surreptitiously tipping the contents into a potted palm. Then he tucked the empty flask into the breast pocket of Randell's Old Boney costume with a solid pat. "Come on, now. Let's find you something less intoxicating to drink. After all, you're starting to hallucinate."

"But I did see you, Savage," he slurred, tottering alongside him toward the refreshment room where they were serving tea and ratafia.

Leo picked up one of the cups, wishing they served something stronger than green tea. But society matrons believed that black tea, not to mention coffee, was far too stimulating and might incite carnal appetites.

After steadying his friend against the plaster molding of an archway, he handed him the cup. "Here. Drink this."

Randell dutifully downed the tepid brew in one swallow, followed by one loud belch.

"There, Mother Hen. Satisfied?" With a laugh, he swung out to chuck Leo on the shoulder, but missed by a mile and staggered away from the wall. "Damn. You move fast, Savage. I could almost swear you're in two places at once."

Leo gestured to one of the nearby footmen with the empty cup and received a nod of understanding before the liveried man appeared at his side with another. "Yes, well. A few more of these should stop that double vision of yours."

He left his friend in the footman's capable hands and entered the ballroom again. Even though he was a head taller than most present, he still didn't spy his quarry.

He wanted to have this business with Lady Sutton done with once and for all. He would try to speak to her like a gentleman and tell her how things stood between them now.

However, he knew there was really only one language that she understood, and he would speak it if he had to.

"It's STIFLING in here, is it not?" Prue asked from the balcony, keeping her voice as calm and collected as she could manage while in a panic.

"At my age, I'm always too warm," Lady Babcock said with a wry laugh, fanning herself.

Prue attempted a smile, only to have it squirm at the edges like a worm on a hook. She tried not to let her unease show. But Leo was still gone and there was no sight of Lady Sutton either. Were they together?

As she searched the crowd, her pulse rushed faster, her throat tight. She couldn't catch her breath. "I need some air."

Prue didn't wait for a response, but tried with utmost dignity to push and claw her way through the crowd to the terrace doors down below.

A light mist outside kept the party contained to the house and Prue stood beneath the shallow overhang on this moonless late-autumn night. A swirl of fallen leaves skittered across the damp stones as if running from the bitter cold of winter's breath.

She crossed her arms to gather the folds of her cape, but it was too sheer and lacking any substance or warmth. Besides, she wasn't going to accomplish anything out here. She had to find Leo.

Just as Prue turned to head back inside, a figure stepped through the terrace doors—a knight in chain mail and leather jerkin with a sword belt and scabbard slung low around his lean hips. As he lifted the helmet to reveal that widow's peak of brown hair and icy blue eyes, she stopped at once. "Lord Marlow."

"Lady Savage, a veritable angel in my midst," he said with a bow. "I wonder if I might beg an audience for a moment."

She looked to the door and thought of her own important errand. "I'm afraid I cannot. I was just about to meet my husband."

"Coincidentally, as was I. But with such a crush, I believed it would be faster through those doors, there." He gestured to the far end of the terrace with a gloved hand. "You see, I saw him head down one of the corridors a short while ago. Shall we?"

She frowned and wondered if that was the reason she hadn't spotted Leo with Lady Sutton . . . because the two of them hadn't been in the ballroom at all. Then all sorts of questions began turning in her mind, creating a vicious brew of doubt and fear.

"Well, I suppose it would make the most sense. Thank you," she said to Marlow as they headed toward that doorway, and he stepped to the outside edge so that she would remain dry while he took the brunt of the mist that was now a steady drizzle. "What business do you have with my husband?"

"Actually, the matter concerns you, my lady. My neighbor, Lady Doyle, recently gifted me with a certain property that, I believe, belongs to you."

"Downhaven Cottage?"

"The very same," he said with a nod as he opened the door and they stepped inside a long, darkened gallery with windows flanking the far side like mirrors reflecting the faint glow of dying embers in the hearth. "I spoke to Savage regarding the matter, but when I offered him the property, he refused. I am hoping that he has had time to reconsider."

Leo had the chance to claim the deed but refused it? The news was heartbreaking. He knew how much it meant to her.

If there was anything *he* ever wanted, she would go to the ends of the earth for him.

"Perhaps your price was too high," she said, wanting to give Leo the benefit of the doubt.

"Let me set your mind at ease at once on that account," he said as they left the gallery. "It was a wedding gift. I asked for nothing in return."

Prue tried to absorb this information as they entered a vacant arched corridor, lit only by wall sconces at the far end. Faint strains of a string quartet and the din of distant conversation drifted eerily down the bare wood floor and wainscoted walls as their footfalls echoed around them. And there was something else, too. A different sound, like someone crying only . . . not.

Another chill swept over her and she chafed her hands along her arms. "And where, precisely, did you last spy my husband?"

"Though I never saw him emerge, I do know that he was headed in this direction," Marlow said with unswerving certainty. Then just as they neared a pair of darkened doorways, he paused to adjust his costume belt. "Forgive me for dallying, but this scabbard is quite cumbersome. I, for one, am glad that masquerades have gone out of fashion, for the most part. I would hate to endure more of these costumes."

Waiting restively at his side, she heard that strange keening sound again. This time, there was also a hiss that cut through the still air.

But, no. Not just a sound. It was a word.

"*Yes*," the feminine voice said, elongating the final consonant in a way that no one having a mere conversation would do.

For reasons Prue couldn't explain, a chill of dread washed over her. Just where was her husband? And, more to the point, where was Lady Sutton?

Stepping forward, she discreetly peered into one of the darkened rooms and caught a movement. She saw a figure near a window where moonlight filtered in. Yet as her eyes adjusted to the darkness, she realized that it wasn't just one figure illuminated, but two entwined.

Lady Sutton's fall of dark hair stood out in contrast to the pale wall at her back. Her neck was arched in rapture as her arms and legs clung to the man in a pale blue tunic and silver tights who rutted against her. *"Yes, Savage. Yes."*

No! No, it couldn't be.

Prue went cold all over. Cold and numb, her feet leaden. She couldn't stop staring. Couldn't blink. Couldn't breathe. This wasn't happening, she told herself. It was true that she'd worried about Lady Sutton's hold on him, but she never thought he would actually surrender to it. Leo was faithful. He would never betray her, not like this.

And yet, the proof was happening right before her eyes.

Her knees threatened to buckle. The numbness turned to painful pricking in her fingertips and toes, as if she'd been buried in snow and was slowly freezing to death. This felt like dying.

Her heart twisted in agony the moment she knew that she meant nothing to him. Nothing more than an obligation. While she'd been falling in love, he'd been keeping her at arm's length. And now she knew the reason.

"Don't worry, my dear," Marlow said as he wrapped a hand around her waist to guide her away from the tawdry tableau. "I'll take you through this side door so no one else will know of your humiliation. My carriage is close by."

He stepped through, ahead of her, and she paused in the corridor, just long enough to hear her name.

"Prue!" It sounded as if Leo's voice was calling from a

distance, but she knew it was coming from the room where he was with Lady Sutton. He must have seen her. And now he was likely going to try to explain. But she didn't want to hear anything he said.

So, without turning back, she summoned the rest of her strength and hurried after Lord Marlow.

Chapter 29

After Leo had left Randell, he decided that a look over the crowd from above would be his best option. So he headed back toward the stairs that would open onto the gallery.

Several of his friends had stopped him to complain that he'd snubbed them. Apparently, while he'd been focused on this damnable bracelet ordeal, he'd also been quite rude.

But was it any wonder that he'd been distracted? He hated being at odds with Prue. This wasn't how he'd wanted their affair—their *marriage*—to be.

This bracelet and Marlow had driven a wedge between them. But he'd figured out a way to ensure that Prue could have what she wanted, all the while preventing Millie Sutton from wreaking the havoc that she'd intended with her very public accusation at the musicale.

Tonight, Leo planned to ensure that the bracelet was seen in her possession by witnesses. But that would only work if he could find her.

His wife didn't know this yet, but earlier in the week he'd spoken with Mr. Devaney about the bracelet and asked if he knew someone who might be able to make a convincing copy. He did. The duplicate bracelet had arrived this afternoon, while the real one was in a box tied with a ribbon in his study drawer. He'd been waiting all day to surprise Prue. And when this was done, they would put all the strife behind them and everything would return to the way it was. To the way it was supposed to be.

At least that was what he'd thought for a short time . . . until Lady Caldicott had stopped him near the balcony stairs.

She lowered a pair of bronze opera glasses that she'd been using to spy on all the guests. "Looking for your wife, Lord Savage?"

"No need. I know precisely where she is," he said curtly and attempted to move past her on the stair, only to have her lay her hand on his arm.

"Then you're going in the wrong direction, for I just saw her with Lord Marlow on the terrace." She arched her brows with intrigue. "They seemed quite—shall I say—friendly toward each other, dashing through the rain toward one of the doors near the east wing of the house. From what I gather, it's quite secluded there."

His fists clenched at his sides, anger sweeping through him at her unfounded accusation. Leaning in, he growled low in her ear. "I thought I'd made myself clear when you last tried to slander my wife. You should do better to guard your own reputation."

She sniffed with disdain, but looked askance as if to see if anyone had overheard him. "Do you really think anyone would take your word over mine? My husband's title is above reproach, not smeared with scandal and sin. Can you say the same of yours? Or is it solely your fortune and ability to scintillate that has earned your acceptance in society? I think we both know the answer."

He wanted to wipe that sneer off her face. Wanted to test her theory and announce her darkest secret aloud for all to hear. But he was a gentleman—or trying to be, he reminded himself. And a gentleman, especially one who wanted to improve his reputation in society, rose above such pettiness.

"Besides," she added. "It isn't slander if it is the truth. I saw them together."

A sense of unease settled over him at her utter conviction.

And he might have been able to dismiss it, if not for the fact that Lady Babcock had come down the stairs and pulled him aside to relay the same information.

Apparently, Prue had needed a breath of air and, while Lady Babcock had looked on from the balcony and could do nothing about it, Lord Marlow had followed.

He didn't want to believe it. He wanted to think that Prue would have instantly walked away from Marlow and returned to wait for Leo. But he could still hear Lady Doyle's accusation. *I saw your wife climb into his carriage at the park yesterday, looking quite at home in his company.*

Fighting the doubt that was clawing at his peace of mind, Leo pushed through the crowd to get to the terrace.

Rain slanted down from a black sky as he rushed along the slick stones. Thrusting open the door at the far end, he searched the dimly lit room, not knowing what to expect. But the gallery was empty. Stalking through it, he then entered the corridor and followed it around the corner.

By the time he saw the shimmer of her cape, she was a distance away. It appeared as though she staggered and then held on to the wall for support, her head bowed.

Where was the regal set of her shoulders? Her proud grace?

In that instant, he knew something was wrong. This wasn't like her.

Clearly, Marlow was up to something, one of his old tricks. And Leo needed to protect Prue from whatever it was.

He called out her name. But instead of stopping, she quickly disappeared through a side door.

Leo followed. With every step he tried to give her the benefit of the doubt. Tried not to think that she'd kept her last carriage ride with Marlow a secret.

She should have been able to tell him if it was all happenstance and innocent, right?

But he'd learned years ago that he could not always see what was directly in front of him.

Marlow's dove-gray landau was waiting near the gate of the side garden and Leo was drenched by the time he caught up with them.

"What the hell do you think you're doing, Marlow?" Leo growled before the blackguard could climb inside after Prue. Clamping a hand on Marlow's shoulder, Leo spun him around and shoved him back against the carriage, his hand at Marlow's throat. "That's my wife."

With beads of water dripping from a chain mail hood, Marlow grinned. "I think the lady might disagree with that statement. But perhaps that doesn't matter to a man who takes what he wants and cares nothing for the carnage he leaves in his wake."

Leo turned his attention on Prue. In the flickering lantern light, he saw that she was huddled at the far side of the carriage, her cheeks pale and awash in tears. Instantly, he released his hold on Marlow and reached inside, holding out his hand to comfort her. "What has happened, my dear? What has he done?"

She shrank from his reach. "*He* has done nothing but show kindness to me. I wish I could say the same of you."

Leo withdrew his hand, surprised by the venom in her tone. "For the life of me, I do not know what has happened."

"Perhaps you should ask Lady Su—" She broke off on a sob and turned her face to the window, her hand covering her mouth. "Go. Go away."

Damn it all! He hated to see her like this. She was suffering and he wanted to hold her, to soothe her. But he was stumbling in the dark, trying to put the pieces of this puzzle together. "Is this about the bloody bracelet?"

"I never want to hear about that"—her breath stuttered— "bracelet . . . again."

He took Marlow by the cravat and cinched it in his fist.

"Whatever this bastard has told you," he said to her, "it's a lie. He's only trying to manipulate you."

"I wish that were true. But I saw you, Leo," she said, tears glistening in those stormy eyes. "And now I never want to see you again."

"You don't mean that."

She wiped the streaks from her face with the back of her hand and her chin notched higher. "It was going to end for us anyway. There's no reason to pretend otherwise. Goodbye, Lord Savage."

Leo flinched as if she struck him.

She was leaving him? Choosing Marlow over him? It didn't seem possible. She'd said that she loved him. And he—the jaded, cynical rake—had believed her to the very depths of his soul.

Stunned and shaken, he numbly released the grinning viscount. And as he watched the carriage roll away, he realized that he had been blind. Again.

❧❧❧

PRUE COULDN'T stop crying. But no matter how many tears she shed, the image of Leo with that woman would not wash away.

And to think, she'd been ready to forgive him for the bracelet, willing to sacrifice the last memento from her mother just to have him. Only him. He was all she wanted.

But now she knew that every promise of fidelity, every tender look that filled her with so much hope had all been a lie.

When the carriage stopped, Lord Marlow handed her down. "Thank you. I'm much obliged for your assistance in seeing me—" Bleary-eyed, she looked around at the unfamiliar row of houses and frowned. "This isn't my home."

"No, my lady. It is *my* home," Marlow said with his thin smile. "Remember, I brought you here to give you the deed to the cottage? After all, I shouldn't imagine you would want to live with that scoundrel any longer."

At the painful reminder, a shudder racked her but she did her best to compose herself. She no longer had a home, not with Leo. So when the viscount proffered his arm, she took it and went into his house.

He escorted her into the study and offered to pour her a drink. She inclined her head in acceptance, her attention caught by the large portrait of a lovely young woman hanging over the mantel.

"Is that your wife?" she asked, needing to think about something else. Anything else before she went mad from despair. "She's beautiful."

He returned to her with a heavy goblet of red wine. "She was. Giselle died in childbed."

"My apologies. I did not mean to bring up a painful memory."

He waved his hand in a gesture of nonchalance. "It was many years ago."

Prue studied Marlow. He was dressed in a costume of a valiant knight, and had come to her aid. Yet, she still could not escape that unsettled feeling in his presence.

She lifted the glass to her lips, hoping the wine would calm her nerves. All she wanted was the deed, after all. Then she would leave.

Yet, at the thought of walking out the door and facing a life without Leo, her hand trembled. After the barest sip, she set the glass down on a low oval table.

"Do you not care for the vintage, my lady? Perhaps something a bit stronger is necessary after the ordeal you've suffered this evening. Such a terrible thing he did to you, deceiving you."

As he walked toward the sideboard again, another wave of misery brought a fresh sting of tears. Somehow she managed to blink them away. "I would rather not speak of it."

"Of course. Anything you wish."

His words were all kindness. And yet, his manner was curiously flippant. He lacked the genuineness of someone with true empathy. Perhaps that was the reason Leo did not like him and, therefore, refused to accept the deed.

Not that it mattered any longer. Soon she would claim the deed on her own.

Pressing her lips together, she tasted the bitterness of the vintage from her small sip. She never had developed a taste for strong wine. But as she looked down at the glass, a memory returned to her, whispering in the back of her mind.

I was poisoned once . . . Her name was Giselle and we were betrothed. She believed she was saving me . . .

A sudden wave of coldness washed over her as she looked across the room to where the viscount still stood, pouring her a fresh drink. "You're the friend—the one who married his betrothed."

He glanced toward the portrait, still keeping his back to her. "Giselle was always supposed to be mine. She was merely distracted by his charm, until I set her straight on the man he really is. Just like his father."

"Leo is not his father in any way. I know him."

"I'm afraid you don't know him as well as I do," he said, coming back with that same smile as if they were merely chatting about fine weather or something equally inane instead of the thing that scarred her husband and taught him never to trust again. Never to love. And only to seek temporary affections wherever he could.

Like tonight . . . with Lady Sutton.

She shook her head, trying to remove the memory from her mind. But it was impossible to forget. Just like it was impossible to forget how completely she'd fallen in love with him. Those feelings just didn't die in a person instantly. They were still inside her, shivering and shaking from cold, cruel reality.

And yet, it was that very feeling that brought forth the numbness she'd learned to wrap around herself like a shield years ago. She drew in a breath, letting it enfold her with aloofness and propriety.

She straightened her shoulders and smoothed her skirts. Her gaze drifted down to the glass once more. "Were you the one who convinced his betrothed to drug him?"

"What an imagination you have."

"And that was clearly not a denial."

He exhaled slowly. "I don't know what Savage has told you, but I can assure you that I am not the villain. And I certainly don't have to tell you that there are some men who believe they are entitled to take whatever they want, whenever they want it. His father was that way and so is the son. They were cut from the same cloth. You saw it with your own eyes."

She had. Her husband's name had been on Lady Sutton's lips, while her husband had been . . .

Prue took a breath, wishing she could lock the memory away as easily as Leo locked his cabinets. Perhaps she could, if she understood the reasons behind his actions better.

Discovering the answer might be the only thing to keep her from falling apart.

Her cool gaze collided with Marlow's. "You did this to him. You're the one who made it impossible for him to trust."

"As much as I'd like to take all the credit, I cannot. His parents helped him along considerably."

"Then why are you determined to hurt him?"

"You rush to the defense of the man who betrayed you? My, my, you must love him a great deal. Pity, that. He'll never return the sentiment. Like his father, he's too self-absorbed in what he wants in the moment. And he never lets anything stand in his way."

"Is that what this is about—your jealousy? Is that the reason you manipulated Giselle—so that you could take someone he cared about away from him?"

"It's only fair," he said, his voice gradually rising, accusation in every crisp articulation. "He is the one who took my mother from me. He is the one who introduced her to his father, knowing full well what that blackguard was capable of. And he did nothing to stop their affair!"

"His father and your mother were two adults. They made their own choices."

"No!" He slammed his fist down. "My mother was meek and gentle. His father preyed on her weakened sensibilities while my father and I were away on a grand tour. When she discovered herself carrying a bastard child, the regret and humiliation drove her to take her own life," he spat. "Tell me, is that something a *friend* would allow to happen?"

She felt sorry for Marlow. Not only for the loss he suffered, but that he'd allowed the pain and rage he couldn't control to turn into a twisted sense of vengeance. "And you are determined to hurt him at any cost. But I do not understand my part in your revenge. After all, considering the events of this evening, it is clear that he does not care about me."

A slow bitter grin curved his lips. "He married you, did he not? That is more than he's done for any of his other conquests."

"That was only about honor. He did not want to be the man his father was."

"And yet, he cannot escape it." He waved a hand dismissively. "Regardless, his pitiful sense of honor will be bruised enough once he learns that you've spent the night here. Oh, don't worry, my pet. I have no intention of forcing myself on you. You are going to choose to stay—undisturbed and in your own bedchamber, for a single night—and in the morning, I will hand over the deed to the cottage. That is what you want more than anything, is it not?"

She'd wanted the deed from the start. All of this, everything she had done, had been for Downhaven Cottage. And if she agreed, it would be the only thing she would have of her own.

She swallowed. "You don't even know me."

"Oh, I know a good deal more than you think, and I'm quite impressed with your tenacity. Many women who'd been abandoned by their family and cast out in disgrace would have withered away in the country, the bloom of youth and beauty vanishing like petals from the last rose of summer. But not you. Instead, you charged back into town and set it awhirl with your boldness."

"I'm so glad I could entertain," she said with a level glare.

He chuckled and moved closer, his pupils expanding, blue eyes turning dark with hunger. "Such fire. What an enchantress you are, my dear. Do you know, I believe you could use a friend with some influence in society to assist you through this sudden separation."

She took a step back. "All I want from you is the deed to the cottage that you promised me."

"And you will have it in the morning. My proposal is simple—one night for the deed. But if you leave, I'll make certain that you never see it again. Now, surely, one night isn't too much to ask for such a prize," he said smoothly, almost crooning the words as if his tone could mask the threat he delivered. Scrutinizing her, he smiled and nodded as he closed the distance again. "Good. I can see we understand each other perfectly. Come now, let us enjoy our evening together. Here."

He urged the glass into her hand, curling her fingers around the cut crystal. Then he withdrew so she had no choice but to hold onto it, or allow it to fall.

Chapter 30

It took Leo all of fifteen seconds to get his head out of his own arse, stop feeling sorry for himself and go after her.

This was Marlow, for bollock's sake! There was no telling what that devil's spawn was doing to manipulate Prue. And she did not know what evil he was capable of.

Leo would never forgive himself if any harm came to her. It didn't matter that she never wanted to see him again. It was her choice. He'd been abandoned before, betrayed countless times, and he'd survived it. But hell would freeze over before he'd let her go with Marlow.

Trying to leave Sutherfield Terrace proved next to impossible, however. The streets were blocked with parked carriages, facing any which way. And his own was trapped at the far end. It took an eon for Rogers to break free.

An endless interval later, Leo charged into Marlow's town house and found him in the study, standing at the sideboard with his back turned.

"Where is my wife?" he growled.

Marlow didn't even flinch. "I'm sure I wouldn't know."

Leo growled again. He wanted to grab him by the throat, but feared he wouldn't be able to stop squeezing until the life drained out of him. So he paused at the edge of the rug, fists clenched and murder on his mind.

Marlow cast a surreptitious glance to the sofa over his shoulder. And when Leo followed his gaze and spied Prue's diaphanous cape, the viscount clucked his tongue. "Oh, it appears we've been found out. Rather reminiscent of how you discovered Giselle and me, wouldn't you say?"

To hell with controlling his temper. He stalked toward Marlow, his boot crushing something underfoot. That was when he saw the red splatter of wine. The broken glass. And a blood rage pounded thickly in his ears as he wondered what had happened in this room.

This time, he didn't hesitate to take this man by the throat and push him hard against the mantel, the portrait smiling down on them. "I'll ask you once more. Where. Is. My. Wife?"

"Upstairs, preparing for bed. All I had to do was promise her that she would have the deed to her cottage by morning. Who'd have thought that she was willing to do anything—absolutely anything—for it?" Even choking and with his face turning purple, he taunted him with a smile and rasped, "If you don't believe me, simply go upstairs and see for yourself."

Leo shoved him aside and turned to do just that, memories from years ago running through his mind.

But then he stopped. Something wasn't right.

He closed his eyes and took in a breath. That was when he knew Prue wasn't there. He would have been able to feel her presence, calming him, soothing the restlessness inside him. She had a way of changing the air around her, of making everything better, finer, brighter. And none of that was here.

"I don't need to," he said, whipping around to face Marlow again. "I know my wife isn't here."

He snickered and fluffed his cravat, staring at his own reflection in the blade of a letter knife. "Perhaps you don't know her quite as well as you think, Savage. After all, when a woman believes her husband is having an affair, sometimes she just wants to retaliate in kind."

Leo eyed him sharply. "What game are you playing this time?"

"No game," he said, all innocence. "Only what your wife and I saw with our very own eyes—a man wearing your costume, cavorting with a certain jilted mistress of yours in one of the empty rooms at Sutherfield Terrace."

I saw you, Leo . . .

Cold dread washed through him, turning his blood to ice in his veins, sinking like a rock in the pit of his stomach. He suddenly knew what Prue must have thought, especially after the turbulent days they'd had. It was clearly all part of a scheme that Millie Sutton and Marlow had concocted together.

Prue thought that he had betrayed her.

"I should have killed you years ago," Leo yelled, stalking forward.

"I'm inclined to agree," a voice said from the doorway. Leo turned to see Reed Sterling standing there, his shoulder propped against the door frame. "Countess Babcock sent me a missive, requesting my aid in keeping you from the gallows, Savage. However, after hearing all this, I'm more inclined to help you make his death look like an accident. An incredibly painful accident."

Sterling pushed off and began to cross the room.

Marlow blanched, taking a step back until he was against the mantel again. "No one would believe you. They'll think you're simply taking the side of your friend against a respected member of society."

"Friend? Everyone knows that Savage and I despise each other."

"That's not true," Marlow declared, pointing at Leo. "He . . . he took a bullet for you."

"And he's been a thorn in my side ever since he survived it." Sterling cracked his neck from side to side and rolled his shoulders. "Nevertheless, it looks like your days of hiding behind a mask of respectability are over."

Panic widened Marlow's eyes for an instant until he

looked down at the letter knife. His knuckles turned white as he gripped the hilt, brandishing the blade with the slashing motions of a trained fencer. "I'm not afraid of slander from some lowlife gaming hell owner or the titled son of a reprobate and murderer. There's more tarnish on the two of you than a brass pissing pot. Not to mention the fact that Savage married his own *wh*—"

Savage lunged forward without warning. Capturing Marlow's wrist, Leo landed an uppercut that sent the swine crashing into the shelf of liquor. Glass shattered from the force, shards flying in a cacophony of detritus. Then Leo yanked him forward and punched him again.

The knife clattered to the floor. And the viscount shook his head, dazed. But then he charged at Leo on a maniacal yell, coming at him with everything he possessed.

And Leo welcomed it. He reveled in the pain. Then he gave it back tenfold.

Marlow was outmatched. His only real weapons were mind games.

Leo wanted to beat him to a bloody pulp until the life drained out of him on a final death rattle . . . But he wasn't like his father.

So, he tossed him to the floor like a piece of rubbish.

"You bastard!" Marlow spat, wiping blood from his mouth. "You think you've won, but you haven't. I've convinced everyone, including you, that your wife has been unfaithful. That she's been cavorting with me. And if she happens to be carrying a child, then all of society will laugh behind your back for the rest of your life and call you a cuckold. And neither you nor your wife will ever outlive the stain on your family name. A fitting end."

Leo was nearly blinded by rage. He didn't care about himself, but hearing that threat to Prue and suddenly he understood why those men had challenged his father to a duel.

It might have been honor for some of them, but for others

it was justice. It was necessary. It was a need burning inside of them.

It was in Leo, too, hot and scorching like a blazing fire. It was consuming him, shredding his lungs, singeing his throat, scalding his veins. It was in the center of his chest, incinerating the void like a phoenix being burned to ash. And he was convinced that the only thing capable of stopping this terrible, unbearable ache was death.

Preferably Marlow's death. But it didn't matter either way.

All he knew was that someone had to die, because Leo couldn't go on living like this.

"I've changed my mind," he growled. "I *am* going to kill you."

He lunged forward. But an instant before he had Marlow by the throat, Sterling held him back. "We have company."

Leo shrugged him off and glared over his shoulder.

Lady Doyle stood there, and he had no idea for how long or what she'd heard. But her nose was high in the air above the heaps of ruffles on her chest and she sniffed with disdain, storming into the room like an outraged pigeon.

"Don't stop on my account, Lord Savage," she said, surprising the hell out of him. "I should like to see this blackguard castrated while you're at it. Until this evening, I had no idea that the neighbor who I had thought of as a potential match for my very own Eugenia was capable of such despicable actions toward the fairer sex. But I know it all now." She shook her fist at Marlow. Then she looked askance at Leo, somewhat sheepishly, before she took a breath. "I am ashamed to admit that I was eager to believe his machinations. And even though he deserves whatever fate you have in store for him, I should not like to see you hang for his murder. So, if you would come with me, I have news. I know where your wife is."

He stopped only long enough to say, "I'll see you at dawn, Marlow. Bring the deed. I plan to strip it from your corpse."

As he stormed out, he looked sideways at Sterling who was frowning more than he usually did. "If you're worried that I'm going to ask you to be my second. Don't. I wouldn't ask that of you."

"It isn't that." The fighter shook his head. "I just remembered something, and I think there's someone you need to meet."

᪣᪣᪣᪣᪣᪣᪣

A HARD fist pounded on the door at Upper Wimpole Street at three o'clock that morning.

"Dear me!" Myrtle startled, clutching a shawl over her night rail as she jolted from the chair in the parlor where they'd all been since Prue arrived on their doorstep hours ago. "Our caller will likely break through the door. Should we warn Mr. Rivers, do you think?"

Maeve shook her head, her expression as severe as her frill-less nightcap. "Mr. Rivers knows not to unbolt the door."

"Shall I get the pistol out of my valise and shoot the intruder?" Meg asked.

Prue was slightly alarmed that her cherubic-faced friend could sound so cold and bloodthirsty. "But we know it's only Leo."

"Correct. Which is precisely why we should shoot him."

"That will not be necessary," Prue said, holding tight to her shield of decorum to keep herself from breaking.

Myrtle sprang up from her chair in the parlor, her finger pointed up as she hurried to the candy dish. "We can throw all these licorice lozenges that Maeve likes down upon his head."

"Or perhaps we could toss out those horrendous nougats you prefer instead," Maeve added.

Prue stood, feeling restless as another series of thumps fell on the door. "We're not throwing anything outside."

But she went to the window, nonetheless, needing to stop this nonsense before he awakened the entire neighborhood with all his racket. Lifting the sash, she peered down to the two carriages waiting on the street. "I have nothing to say to you, Lord Savage."

Leo appeared out from beneath the portico roof, looking up from the pavement. He was still wearing the last thing she'd seen him in, and it was such a painful memory that she had to turn away because it made her eyes burn with tears.

"Wait," he called. "Please. I have someone here who can set matters straight."

She didn't turn back around. And Meg came to the window to close it for her but then she stopped on an "Oh my goodness! I think you'll want to see this."

After taking a breath to steel herself, Prue looked.

Climbing out of the carriage was a young man about eighteen or twenty with a wealth of tawny-gold hair. He stood beside Leo, both men of the same height, broad-shouldered, lean hips . . . and wearing the exact same costume.

The younger man staggered a bit on his feet as he shielded his eyes from the streetlamp to squint up at her. Then his eyes widened and he grinned. "Hullo, my lady. Blimey, but you've got hair like starlight."

Leo growled, "You're not here to flirt with my wife. Get on with it."

"Oh, right." The man nodded. "I'm Christopher Langhorne. A new croupier at Sterling's gaming hell." He jerked a thumb over his shoulder toward the carriage where she saw Mr. Sterling offer a nod in greeting. "About a fortnight ago, a lady approached me with an invitation to a fancy party. A masquerade. She said she'd supply the togs and that all I had to do was be the man on her arm. But I wasn't on her arm for more than a minute or two before she took me to this back room for a bit of fun. Which we had plenty of. I didn't even mind that she kept calling me a savage. After all, I've been known to bring out all sorts of—" He broke off when Leo smacked the back of his head. "Right, well. It wasn't until Mr. Sterling came to my flat that I found out . . ."

As he spoke, Prue turned away from the window and left the parlor, feeling as though her knees were about to buckle. She clutched the railing as she went down the stairs, her emotions roiling from anger at Lady Sutton's machinations to utter relief that it wasn't Leo she'd seen.

It wasn't him, she chanted inside her head, with every step. He hadn't betrayed her after all.

She crossed the foyer, her hands shaking as she unbolted the door. And then she saw him.

A sob tore from her throat as she rushed into his arms. She clung to him, her words coming out in a rushed whisper. "I'm so glad it wasn't you. I should have known. But when I saw Lady Sutton and heard your name on her lips, I thought I would die. I wanted to die."

"And now you know the truth. The entire sordid production was part of a calculated scheme." Leo steadied her with his hands. But he wasn't holding her, she realized absently. He wasn't hauling her into his embrace and rejoicing as if they'd just survived the worst ordeal imaginable. And then he set her apart from him, looking down at her kindly. "I wanted you to know as soon as possible. I hope the news provides you some measure of comfort."

Without another word, he released her completely and turned to leave.

"Wait." Confused, she laid her hand on his arm, staying him. "Are you not intending to take me home, so we can put this nightmare behind us?"

He shook his head, barely looking her in the eye, his jaw taut with tension. "I have a few matters to sort out before dawn. It would be best if you stayed here."

"Oh." She nodded as if she understood. But she didn't. All she knew was that the mention of *dawn* filled her stomach with dread.

She remembered what he'd told her about his father and the duels he'd fought, along with his own dislike for the sound of flintlocks in the morning.

Her heart thudded ominously, her fingers curling tightly over his sleeve. "You're not going to do anything rash, are you?"

"'Rash'? No."

She searched his gaze and saw that it was cold, like frosted windowpanes. "But you will return later, will you not?"

He inclined his head with utmost formality and turned away.

She splayed a hand over her midriff to quell the turmoil churning inside. Looking past Leo's retreating figure, she saw Mr. Langhorne climb drunkenly back into the carriage, and Reed Sterling met her gaze.

"Will you look after him, Mr. Sterling?"

He glanced toward her husband and said, "I will. After all, my friend has done the same for me."

If Leo had been in his usual humor, he would have offered a quip of denial in response. But the fact that he said nothing as he climbed into the carriage made her worry all the more.

Before he was closed inside, she quickly said, "Leo?"

He turned with his eyebrows arched in bland inquiry.

"You will come back soon, won't you?"

He nodded. "I am a man of my word."

IT WAS well after dawn when a hackney cab pulled up in front of the town house on Upper Wimpole Street.

Prue had been waiting by the parlor window—or fretting by the parlor window if the scattered petals from the flower arrangement she plucked were any indication—all night long. And seeing this unfamiliar conveyance made her heart plummet.

But then Leo emerged and she sprang from the chair, rushing down to the foyer to open the door. He stood on the other side, his face freshly shaven, his clothes crisp, his eyes still cold, shuttered.

He made no move to enter, but handed her an envelope without a word.

She was confused by his demeanor and remoteness. He'd never been like this even when they'd been strangers. "What's this?"

"The deed to your cottage," he said with an air of finality.

"Did you have a meeting at dawn . . . with Marlow?"

He looked away, a muscle ticking along his jaw. "Fear not, I didn't kill him. His solicitor delivered it to me this morning. Marlow has fled London, closed his house and run off with his tail between his legs. Apparently, that pillar of society is unable to face the stain upon his name. I suppose those who are born into it, are much better suited to carry the burden. In fact, I did not know until last night how well it suited me."

"That isn't true." She shook her head. "You are nothing like Marlow and nothing like the man your father was. You are kind, caring and honorable, generous to a fault . . ."

"No need to butter both sides of my bread, my dear. The deed is yours. I won't take it from you," he said. "Now you have what you've always wanted."

She set the deed on the foyer bench and took his gloved hand between hers. "I mean it. You are the best man I have ever known."

"Considering the number of men you've actually known, that really isn't saying much, is it?" His mouth quirked in a wry grin, but it did not reach his eyes.

She frowned and dropped his hand. "Why are you acting this way? You're being so distant. So—"

"Heartless?" he supplied with his brows arched. When she crossed her arms and waited for him to answer her question, he expelled a slow breath. "Very well, my dear, there's no need to prolong this any more than necessary. I've had some time to think and I realize you were right. Not only last night, but when you insisted on the codicil in our contract. You see, I'm finding all this rather tedious and I think it would be better for both of us if we went our separate ways. And you've wanted to live on your own from the start, so think of this as me offering you the perfect opportunity. You didn't even have to endure four full months. In fact, Dottie is packing your trunks as we speak and Rogers is loading them onto my carriage."

"You're . . . you're sending me . . . *away*?" Her voice cracked. She couldn't breathe. Her lungs felt like they were in a vise. Her heart was thudding in a panic, thrashing against the cage of her ribs as if needing to reach out and stop him from withdrawing.

He shrugged stiffly. "You may choose to stay anywhere you like. I just assumed that you would take up residence at your cottage. And don't fret. You're still my wife. You'll never want for anything—carriages, servants, an allowance of twenty thousand pounds per annum—for as long as you live."

She stared at him, incredulous. Did he not know her at all? "I want more than your money. More than *things*."

"Ah, at last your greed makes an appearance." He laughed bitterly. "I'd always wondered what it would take to bring it out. So tell me, what is it that you want."

It terrified her to think about how much she loved him. She loved him so much that she could see herself giving in to living a half-life, just to go with him now. See herself existing on scraps of affection. Willing to change who she was simply to be with him.

But that wasn't the life she truly wanted for herself.

Ironically, he was the one who made her believe that she deserved more. And she wanted all of him or nothing.

"I want everything, Leo. And I won't settle for less." She drew in a deep breath. "But you're right. If money is all that you can offer, then it *is* better this way."

Then she turned and walked up the stairs. And when the door closed below, she felt the finality of it echo inside her heart . . . just before it shattered into a thousand pieces.

Chapter 31

It was better this way, Leo told himself. His life was his own once again, and he was free to occupy himself with the pleasures he'd always known. Or, at least, he would be once he decided to leave the house. And yet, for some reason, he never quite made it across the threshold.

For days, he wandered through every room, looking for things that belonged to Prue, just so that he could send them to her. There was no reason to keep anything around anymore. After all, he knew she was never coming back.

But he made a surprising discovery during his strolls. There wasn't a single trinket, bauble or any bric-a-brac of hers anywhere. She'd left nothing behind.

For that matter, she hadn't even redecorated a single room.

So then why did everything feel different, changed, inexorably altered?

This didn't seem like his house any longer. He was a stranger trespassing through unfamiliar doorways and staring at unfamiliar walls.

"Grimsby?" he called, hearing the steady footfalls walking on the marble tiles outside the parlor. Out of the corner of his eye, he saw the stoic figure move into the room and stand beside him.

"Yes, my lord?"

"Have I always had this chair?"

Grimsby hesitated, then supplied, "For six—no, seven

years. That would have been Lady Thorncastle's contribution, I believe."

Leo wasn't even sure he remembered Lady Thorncastle. Which was strange because he'd always prided himself on being able to recall all his previous lovers. And yet, when he tried to conjure her face, the only one he could see was Prue's.

A sigh dragged the air from his lungs, like a ghost with a heavy chain in the attic. "I need a change of scenery. I'm thinking of taking a tour of the continent."

"I shall have the portmanteau brought down. Will that be all, my lord?"

Leo nodded and heard the butler's retreating footfalls.

A random thought occurred to him as he stared unblinkingly at his surroundings. He realized that chairs were likely the loneliest pieces of furniture. Because the majority of the time, they were always empty.

Therefore, by the end of the week, he had all the chairs carried up to the attic. Though, in hindsight, he should have left the one behind his desk because now he had nowhere to sit.

He'd also had all the settees stored in the dining room. It was crowded in there, but it didn't bother him because he wasn't eating. And the parlors and drawing room were much more spacious now.

However, that created the new problem—the artwork on his walls. He didn't really like any of it. None of it appealed to him, or made him feel any spark of interest. So he had all his paintings taken down and stacked in the dining room, too.

But this only brought another issue to the forefront—the damnable clocks.

They ticked constantly. That *tick-tock-ticking* invaded his thoughts, his dreams. He couldn't go anywhere without hearing it.

Sitting on the floor of his study with his back against his desk, he fished the watch from his pocket and stared down at it.

This had been sent to him shortly after his father's death. It was the only gift he'd ever received from his mother. And inside the lid was the engraved inscription:

Time to prove your worth.

So thoughtful, his mother. *This* was all she'd had to say to him? She'd never bothered to get to know him, only assumed he was like his father. She'd taken one look at her infant son and decided that he was worthless. And then she'd left.

Leo hated this watch and everything it stood for. He hated the time it kept. The minutes dragged on endlessly. Hours were eons. And it was pointless. After all, the concept of time was only a ridiculous construct invented by man to keep track of the empty, meaningless, wasted days of his life.

"Time to prove your worth," he growled and flung the watch across the room, relishing the sound of a hinge snapping, the ping of crystal splintering.

He heard a low whistle from the doorway and his gaze shot over to see Lady Chastaine standing there in a maroon walking costume with her hands on her hips. "Doing a little redecorating, Savage?"

"What are you doing here?" he asked—or *snarled*, rather. "I don't normally take back my old lovers, but I could be persuaded, I suppose. Just don't laugh or sing or tell me stories of your childhood. I don't want to hear anything of the sort."

She shook her head and smiled pityingly at him as she dared to step into the room. "Tempting offer. By the by, how long has it been since you've shaved, or bathed for that matter?"

He scratched his unshaven jaw and narrowed his eyes.

"Then what are you doing here? Low on pin money already? Well then, have a look around and take anything you like. Just be quick about it. I've got plans."

"Oh? And what are those—to while away the hours playing a game of *identify the stain on my waistcoat*?" When he growled at her, she tsked. "I don't need anything. I came to help you."

"And why would I need your help, hmm?"

"A friend might have mentioned something about a certain marquess headed down a path of destruction." She glanced over her shoulder where he could see Lady Babcock bustling about and talking to his servants. "We're here to save you from yourself."

He scoffed. "The two of you are nothing more than a pair of busybodies who should mind their own business."

"So you can simply wallow in misery?"

"I'm not given to wallowing."

She laughed and gestured to the mostly empty room. "Then what's all this?"

"I'm closing up the house and taking a holiday."

Sauntering over in a rustle of petticoats and wool, she lowered down onto the floor beside him and patted his chest. "You're heartbroken."

"Impossible," he growled, shooing her hand away from the aching place that covered the scorched, empty void. "As you know, I have no heart."

She made herself comfortable, mimicking his pose by stretching out her legs and crossing them at the ankle. Then she nudged him with her shoulder. "It might be a bit battered and bruised at the moment. But that's what happens when love hits unexpectedly. It makes you willing to do things you'd never dreamed, like waking up one morning and suddenly deciding to marry."

"That was only a matter of honor," he said, but the words tasted flat on his tongue.

"Or challenging a man to a duel, when you vowed to yourself that you'd never be like your father or those poor sods who'd gone to their deaths after they'd challenged him."

"Go away, Phoebe."

"Then we try to make excuses," she continued as if he hadn't spoken. "We try to rationalize our choices in order to pretend we're in control. And we both know that you like control, with all those contracts that outline every detail of your affairs—who, how long, how much you're willing to give." She ticked them off on her fingers, one by one. "And then there's the fidelity clause. Have you ever wondered why you insist on that in your contracts?"

He didn't answer. He was too busy grinding his molars into dust.

"I believe that the reason is that you've always wanted a genuine relationship, a bond built on trust and affection. You've longed to have someone you could keep close. Someone who is yours and yours alone." She nudged him again. "I suspect you've always had a heart, Savage. You've just kept it locked away, waiting for the one person who had the key."

He sighed heavily, shifting his restless limbs to stand up. Then, he looked down at her and offered his hand. "You disappoint me. I never took you for a romantic."

"Oh, I have my locked doors, too." She smiled wanly and took his hand. Standing, she shook out her skirts. "That was actually the reason I strayed into the arms of another man. After spending all that time with you, I was afraid of falling in love. So I did something drastic to make it stop."

"That's ridiculous. There was nothing to fear. All you'd had to do was adhere to the contract." He frowned at her, irritated. "It would have been over soon enough."

"Oh, I know. You'd made that perfectly clear on multiple occasions," she said dryly. "That is the reason I understand that risking your heart, especially when you've been hurt before, is terrifying. But sometimes, someone comes along who takes us unawares. Then, before we know it, we've already fallen and there's nothing we can do to protect ourselves. So we . . . panic and close ourselves off, the best we can."

Leo didn't want to listen to any more of this rubbish. Trying to shut her out, he turned away and stalked across the room.

Picking up the broken pieces of his pocket watch, he held it to his ear. It was no longer ticking. Broken beyond repair. He could finally get rid of it, he supposed. Finally be done with the reminder of being a man that not even his own mother could love.

But Prue loved you, a voice whispered in his mind.

He tried to ignore it, too. But he couldn't.

He knew with soul-deep certainty that she had loved him. From the beginning, she had accepted who he was, his past, his flaws . . . everything. She'd never tried to change him or hurt him, or take more than he was willing to give.

And in return, what had he done but keep her at arm's length, constantly putting up the barrier of *supposed honor* between them. When all he was really trying to do was protect himself.

Because all along, he'd known . . . he'd known that he loved her, too.

Leo sucked in a startled breath. The sudden glut of air ignited the slumbering ember inside his chest in a devastating conflagration, burning the insides of his veins.

He loved her. And he was forced to acknowledge that it was a love so deep, so unfathomable, that the very thought of losing her at the end of four months had terrified him. He wouldn't have survived it.

So he'd done the unthinkable. He'd sent her away before she could leave him. And worse, he'd done it in a way that was guaranteed to hurt her and to destroy the happiness they'd once shared.

Bloody hell. I've been such a fool.

A charred breath stuttered out of him, his throat raw, chest aching. He bent his head, closing his fist around the watch. The metal bit into his palm as the emptiness he'd been trying to ignore started choking him, singeing his eyes.

He steeled himself, trying to contain the fire, to smother it, to keep it locked away. But his shoulders shook from the effort.

Then a low, guttural sound of anguish slipped out, and it went on and on and on.

After a moment, he felt a hand on his back and dampness on his cheek. Embarrassed, he straightened and cleared his throat.

"So you did something that you knew I would never forgive," he said to Phoebe, trying to pretend that they were still in the middle of their conversation and this was his next line. Trying to pretend that his voice wasn't raw and the void beneath his chest wasn't shredded.

"I had to," she said and stepped in front of him. "Otherwise, I would have suffered the heartache of rejection, knowing that you didn't love me in return." Before he could respond to that, she touched a lacy handkerchief to his cheek and added, "A girl senses these things, after all. There's a certain feeling and a look a man gives her. But I think you already know that."

He offered an apologetic shrug, then touched the tip of her pert nose. "For what it's worth, I hope you find a man who adores you for the meddling little cretin you are."

She laughed lightly. "Thank you, Savage. I hope so, too."

Chapter 32

From the morning room window of Downhaven Cottage, Prue watched the rider approach, his hat tipped low to shield his eyes from the rising sun.

The post was here, she thought without feeling any spark of excitement. The letter she was waiting for would never come.

She let the curtain fall.

She was ashamed to admit that she'd been living for the letters her friends sent, hoping for a morsel of information regarding Leo. But his name was never mentioned, no matter how many times she reread every word.

It did not take her long to figure out that she would go mad if she stayed here alone.

In the beginning that had been her dream. But it was almost impossible to remember the strength it had once taken her to walk out of Wiltshire with her head held high. She'd hoped to find it by returning to Downhaven Cottage. Surely, the reminder of happier times would help to heal her shattered heart.

The first week drifted by endlessly. The breeze coming off the still-water lake was cold and her days were desolate. The second week sat heavily beneath a steady curtain of rain through the cottage windows, and she understood that there was something one felt beyond desolation. It was emptiness.

As she walked through the rooms that had once been

filled with joy, there was nothing inside her heart. Her mind was no different. It held no great plans for the future. Her stomach had no appetite, and there was no flavor on her tongue.

Her life was simply a void.

After three weeks, being at the cottage and staring at her mother's portrait only made her realize how fleeting happiness truly was. Sometimes it died without warning. And other times, it lingered into a slow, fading demise.

She felt utterly stupid and naive to have imagined that Leo had felt the same regard for her. Clearly, he was better at pretending than she might have guessed.

Meg and the aunts had chosen to come with her, helping her with the cottage instead of visiting Ellie and Brandon after returning from their honeymoon. But they would be going to Wiltshire on the morrow. And she would go with them.

She realized that what she wanted from Downhaven was never here. She'd wanted to feel as though she was finally where she belonged, where she could be loved, and where she could be content to live out the rest of her days. But she'd only found that for a brief time with Leo.

"The post has come!" Myrtle said, bustling into the faded yellow room, waving a trio of letters like banners. "One from our Elodie. One from Jane. And one from a certain Mr. Prescott."

Meg, who'd been curled up on an overstuffed chair by the fire, thumbing through pages of an old *Ladies Quarterly*, suddenly leapt up and dashed across the room. "Daniel!"

Eyes dancing, she snatched the letter and tore it open, poring over it on her way to the window seat.

Maeve chuckled as she watched her walk past. "Perhaps, we could read Elodie's letter first. And then Jane's?"

Prue nodded, taking Jane's letter in hand. They listened as Myrtle read Ellie's retelling of the adventures she experienced on her honeymoon. Her friend, who feared a great number of things, was quite proud that she'd bravely taken a ferry and "faced a watery demise," in addition to crossing a footbridge without holding her breath. And the letter concluded with an announcement of "thrilling news," but something that would have to wait until they were all together and could share her joy.

Of course, it seemed quite clear that Ellie would announce that she was expecting a child. The aunts were fairly bursting with excitement, happy tears glistening in their eyes. But at first, they subdued their joy with a glance toward Prue. After all, in a house filled with women, it had been no secret that Prue's courses had come. But she adamantly refused to allow them to pity her for even a moment. She even assured them that it was far better this way, claiming a need for a clean break from Savage.

"I am overjoyed for Ellie, truly," she said.

Then the aunts gave in, letting their expectant happiness overflow as they began to plan the grandest christening breakfast ever hosted.

But that night, when she was brushing her hair at her vanity, she admitted to herself that she wished she were carrying a child, a part of Leo to keep with her always. The sting of incipient tears earned a sigh of self-reproach and she hastily swiped them away just as a knock fell on her door.

"May I come in?" Meg asked, peering inside.

"Of course," Prue answered, quickly schooling her features. "Are your trunks packed for the journey to Wiltshire?"

Coming up behind her, Meg nodded and took long, pale ropes of Prue's hair and began braiding it. But her usual effervescence was absent from her demeanor.

It was only then that Prue saw the red-rimmed eyes in the lamplight, her nose and lips a dark pink that stood out in stark contrast to her porcelain skin. She realized that she'd been a thoughtless friend. "In all our excitement for Ellie, it never occurred to me that you haven't mentioned the letter you received today from Mr. Prescott."

Meg drew in a deep breath and released it slowly as she tied a lavender ribbon to the end of the plait. "There's nothing to tell, really. The letter was short and to the point. 'Dear Miss Stredwick, I have married.'"

Spinning around at once, Prue stood to embrace her friend, who instantly dissolved into heart-wrenching sobs. "Oh, Meg. I am so very sorry."

"How can the man that you're going to love for the rest of your life"—she broke off on a stuttered breath—"suddenly marry someone else? I was certain he felt the same about me."

Prue understood completely. She had thought that Leo loved her, too. In fact, thinking back to the way he'd looked at her and touched her, she'd been sure of it. And she'd even imagined that Lady Babcock had been trying to tell her at the masquerade—that Leo's most guarded secret was that, deep down, he'd always wanted to share his heart with someone.

But that someone was not Prue.

"Clearly, men are like dogs," she said, stroking a soothing hand along Meg's back. "Not the big ones, but those little fellows that bark a good deal to put up a brave front. But at the first sign of tender emotion, they turn tail and run, cowering in the corner beneath a table skirt and waiting for it to go away."

Meg gave a watery laugh and nodded in agreement.

Chapter 33

B_y the middle of the week, Prue's carriage entered the county of Wiltshire. Even if there hadn't been a road sign to tell them, they still would have known because they'd been stopped by sheep crossing the road twice already that day. But now they were on their way again, progressing at a slow, rocking canter.

Meg grimaced, her knitting falling to her lap. "I shouldn't have had that third cup of tea at the last coaching inn. I will surely float away before we make it to the next one."

"That's the reason we knit, dear. It serves as an excellent distraction," Maeve said with an encouraging nod, her needles clacking busily.

"Quite true." Myrtle pointed toward her sister from behind the cup of her hand and added in a stage whisper, "But that doesn't mean she's any good at it. The fringe is always uneven on her side."

For that, her sister poked her with a needle.

A puff of air—which was the nearest thing to amusement that Prue had emitted in weeks—turned to a cloud of mist in front of her. The four of them were huddled together inside, the bricks in their foot warmer having gone cold a while ago. And in the dismal November light leaching in through the fogged windows, Prue studied her own knitting creation and frowned.

This didn't resemble a hat at all, but more like a boot . . . for a giant with a single toe.

"It's a very pale, very fat banana," Meg said with a small laugh and then winced as she clutched her middle.

"This is an abysmal attempt at knitting," Prue said with a sigh of self-disgust and tucked her failure away in the satchel beside her. But she wished she was good at something that she could picture herself doing a great deal of for the rest of her life. Spending all the lonely hours thinking of Leo wasn't productive at all.

"Well, at least yours resembles something." Meg held hers up to the light. It was partly round on one side, angular on the other, with a knotted bulge in the center. "I have no idea what mine is. Although, in my own defense, my mind drifted off to that letter you received from Jane before we left. I'm still flabbergasted by the news."

So was Prue. She couldn't believe that Dorcas had run off with Lord Caldicott and had taken little Irwin with her. Apparently, the two neighbors had been having an affair beneath their spouses' noses for a number of years, which was likely the reason Irwin resembled the auburn-haired Lord Caldicott instead of Lord Whitcombe.

Nevertheless, Prue felt sorry for her father. She knew what it was like to be left with no family and wouldn't wish that on anyone.

As for Lady Caldicott, she might have appeared a tragic heroine in the tale, if not for the fact that her secret affair with Leo's father eighteen years ago had finally come to light. And so had the nine months that she'd spent with her family in the country afterward . . . along with the baby boy that her cousins had raised.

It just so happened that the baby boy turned out to be none other than Christopher Langhorne! No wonder he bore such a strong resemblance to Leo.

Prue wondered how Leo felt about having a half brother. He finally had a family. And even though he'd never said it aloud, she knew that he'd always wanted one.

Of course, Jane likely hadn't written about it so that Prue could have another reason to think about Leo. It was just that everyone was talking about it *and* discussing that night at the masquerade when the two men had been dressed alike.

Lady Sutton and Lord Marlow's scheme had been exposed. And it was believed that they had fled to France together.

Jane had concluded her letter on a happier note, by likening her swollen belly to a Montgolfier balloon and fears that the house would no longer be able to contain her by Christmastide.

Prue glanced down to her flat midriff and sighed.

"What about you, Aunt Myrtle," Meg said cheekily, drawing Prue out of her musings. "Do you have any secrets that would set the *ton* on their ear?"

Myrtle grinned, her knitting needles never flagging. "Perhaps. But shouldn't every woman have a few secrets she never tells a soul?"

"If you're talking about that one summer romance you had with the vicar's son, then I already know. I've known for decades," Maeve said smugly, earning a gasp from her sister and a yank of her yarn. The pretty pink shawl began to unfurl and started an all-out tug-of-yarn between the two laughing women.

Cutting through the merriment was the rumble of thunder in the distance. Prue's ears perked to the sound. She felt the reverberation underfoot as the storm swiftly approached. But as she looked around at all the smiling faces, no one else seemed to notice or be alarmed.

Then she heard a shout—a driver calling to his team— and the thunder stopped. And in that moment, she knew it was not a storm at all.

A shiver of gooseflesh skittered over her skin. And as their carriage slowed once again, she turned her face to the opaque window.

Meg groaned in dismay. "If it's more sheep, I swear I'll murder the lot of them and eat mutton for a year."

But it wasn't only sheep this time.

Suddenly, the door was wrenched open. The aunts and Meg gasped in unison. But all Prue could do was stare agape at her husband. At least, she thought the haggard, bearded man standing there was her husband.

"Leo?" she asked, her lungs laboring, pulse shallow and quick.

"Why aren't you at Downhaven Cottage?"

She blinked. Still trying to figure out if he was actually there or if she'd fallen asleep and was dreaming of him. Again.

"Well?" he prodded, his dragon-green eyes penetrating the gloom.

At his impatience, she snapped out of her fog and squared her shoulders. "I'm going to Wiltshire to visit Ellie. And even though it isn't any of your concern, after that I'm considering taking a tour with the aunts and Meg."

"So you're just leaving?" His tawny brows knitted above the bridge of his nose. "And while I've been through hell, you've been planning a holiday."

"*You've* been through—"

"I see you've moved on quite well."

Her eyes prickled with tears, hands clenching with frustration. "I've had to. Or don't you remember?"

"Of course, I . . ." He raked a hand through his hair and looked around at the others in the carriage as if only seeing them for the first time. He inclined his head. "Ladies, if you don't object, I would like a moment alone with my wife."

Maeve and Myrtle nodded silently, surreptitiously nudging each other with their elbows. Meg, on the other hand, looked fierce as if she were thinking about that pistol she kept in her reticule. But she held her tongue and crossed her arms.

"I'll just be gone a minute," Prue said to them, knowing that Leo could have nothing to say that she had not already heard. He'd made himself quite clear when he sent her away. And she wanted more than he was willing to give.

She would simply have to remember to stay firm and not be swayed by her foolish heart.

But when his large, capable hands settled on her waist to help her down, it was her body she had to worry about. A spear of longing tore through her at the warmth of his touch, her hands curling over his broad shoulders. And as he lowered her to the ground, his scent teased her nostrils, reminding her of all the times her face had been buried against his throat, her tongue on his skin . . .

Better not think of that, she told herself on a hard swallow. She stepped apart from him the instant her feet touched the ground, turning away before he could see the telltale flush of her cheeks.

As he shut the door, she focused on the two dozen fat and fleecy sheep, scuttling along the verge between the meadow and the lane. The driver of a dray was shouting at the shepherd who was trying to dash after his wayward flock, a copper bell clanking in the air.

Then Leo touched her hand. Her gaze lifted to his, her heart twisting with yearning at the tenderness there. She knew she hadn't been imagining it all this time. He did feel something for her. But whatever it was, he kept it closely guarded.

His fingers curled around hers. "It's good to see you, moonflower. I've missed you."

Her throat tightened on a raw ache at the endearment, and she slipped her hand from his. "Is that what you came all this way to tell me?"

In the bleary light beneath the gray sky, his breath misted on a taut exhale and he shook his head. "No. I wanted to find you, and to bring you what you asked for when we last spoke. I have it all with me. Come, I'll show you."

He gestured to the black carriage waiting behind theirs. From the perch, Rogers tipped his hat as they approached. Then Leo opened the door to reveal all her family treasures—the silver tea service, the oil painting, the golden diadem . . . everything.

"How did you . . ." She couldn't finish. She simply stared, slack-jawed and stunned.

"I have been a burglar, a barterer, a counterfeiter, a grave digger, a Pekingese-tamer, and a madman traveling from county to county, chasing a carriage from one coaching inn to the next. But I've managed to collect it all. Even this." He lifted his little finger to show that he had the amethyst ring.

A mortified laugh escaped her. "You dug up Algernon's grave?"

He nodded, searching her gaze with an earnestness she'd never seen before. "It's everything you asked for. And I'm hoping that"—he took a breath—"you will end my misery and come home."

She sighed with disappointment. But seeing the vulnerability in his expression, she lifted her hand to touch his cheek. Then she shook her head. "Oh, Leo. I thought you knew. When I said *everything*, I meant you. The only thing that I want is your heart."

His expression transformed into one of blank astonishment for a moment, his breath staggering out of him in cloudy puffs. Turning his face, he pressed a long kiss into the palm of her hand, his whiskers soft and tickling against her flesh.

"I'm afraid I don't have a heart," he said, and her own plummeted. "It was stolen from me the day that I met this proud, disheveled beauty on the side of the road, being mauled by a drover."

She blinked. Had she heard him correctly? It was impossible to know because her pulse was suddenly rushing in her ears.

"Did you just say that you lost your heart . . . to *me*?"

He nodded. "That day, and every day since. Each time I tried to take possession of it, you would only reclaim it. Like that time I saw you in the rain wearing that maid's cap, or when you decided to invite yourself to a *gentleman's only* party, when you had rose petals in your hair, and whenever you speak or hum or sing . . ."

"You like the way I sing?"

He lifted a hand to tuck a wisp of pale hair behind her ear, his fingertips trailing along her jaw. "I adore it. Especially when you sing in the water closet to cover up the sounds you make."

Her cheeks flooded with heat. "I'm sure you shouldn't mention such a thing."

"And this blush," he continued with a soft grin, "I can feel it glow inside me every time I see it."

She drew his hand down, confused. "But if all this is true, then why not simply tell me? Such a declaration would have been ideal at the church, for example. Instead, you had that second contract."

"Only as a last resort. I had to be prepared, Prue. I had to make you mine, no matter the cost."

His words were so earnest, so heartfelt that her eyes prickled with tears again. They fell in a hot deluge down her smiling face.

"Besides," he added as he smoothed the wetness away with the pads of his thumbs, "that contract was never legally binding. And that codicil was complete rubbish. This"—he took her hand and pressed a kiss to the gold band on her finger—"is the contract that matters, now and for the rest of our lives . . . *if* you'll have me."

Eager to be in his embrace, she moved closer, sliding her hands to his shoulders. But then she felt something between them—a lump pressing against her midriff.

"Careful," Leo said and reached inside his coat and further down to the bulge in his waistcoat that she hadn't noticed before.

Then, much to her surprise, he removed a sleeping puppy. Just a ball of golden fur with a black nose and a pink bow around *her* neck.

"You can name her if you like," he said quietly. "But I must confess, after seeing her prance around with her head held high, I've been calling her Your Majesty. She seems to like it."

Prue was admittedly not the fondest of dogs. But her heart melted the instant those dark eyes opened and blinked sleepily up at her. Gathering the tiny ball in her arms, she felt the swipe of a little pink tongue across her chin. "Wherever did you find her?"

"I was caught by a termagant housekeeper while in the jaws of a rabid Pekingese. The only thing I could think up for an excuse of why I was in Lady Entwistle's dressing room was to explain my longing for a Pekingese of my own. The next thing I knew, the housekeeper was foisting this creature upon me from a newly weaned litter. Not purebred, apparently, and quite the scandal." He waggled his eyebrows with intrigue and Prue laughed. "And now, she's yours . . . but only if you'll come home with me."

"Is this extortion?" she asked, looking up at him slyly through her lashes.

"No. This is madness," he replied, holding her face in his hands. "Though, I've heard that some call it love. And I am desperately, wretchedly in love with you."

She beamed at him, her heart rejoicing. "Of course, I'll come—"

A familiar, deep barking interrupted their reunion.

Both she and Leo turned in unison to see a sheepdog bounding away from the flock in a flurry of white, ropey fur . . . and heading directly toward them.

"No," Leo muttered in astonishment. "It couldn't be the same blasted dog."

He stepped in front of Prue to act as her shield, lifting his hand to whistle.

But even before he could put his thumb and forefinger to his lips, the puppy peeked her head out of Prue's arms and issued the cutest little *yarp* over Leo's shoulder.

The drover instantly stopped, then sat on his hindquarters as his shaggy mop of a head tilted to one side.

Leo and Prue exchanged a look and then laughed. He pulled her into his embrace. "It appears as though you are not the only one who can bring a wayward rogue to heel."

"Perhaps he merely brings out her fire and inner strength," she said, sifting her fingers through his hair, drawing his mouth to hers. And then she kissed him. *Finally.*

Majesty emitted another delightful *yarp* and a happy tail wag, licking them both on the chin.

After a moment, Leo lifted his head and reached into his breast pocket. "I almost forgot, but I have something else for you."

"There is nothing else I could ever want." But then she saw the keys in the palm of his hand. "Are those . . . ?"

He nodded, his expression sincere, tender. "The keys to every lock I have. They're yours now . . . if you want them."

"What's the one with the red ribbon?"

The corner of his mouth quirked. "That's to my snuff-box collection."

"Oh, I'm definitely keeping that one," she said and stole it out of his hand.

Epilogue

Ten months later

"The next time I see that pup, I'm going to murder him with my bare hands," Leo growled as they meandered along the pebbled path on the grounds of Downhaven Cottage.

Prue smiled, leaning heavily against his arm. "I'm not certain if you're referring to your brother or to his new dog."

"Both. After all, just look at our girl." He gestured to the morning room window where Majesty was sitting with her nose pressed to the glass. "She's listless. I haven't seen her tail wag in days."

"She just misses him."

"That mongrel? I won't allow it. If you'd seen the way he was sniffing around her, you wouldn't either."

"I meant Kit," she said with a laugh, using the affectionate moniker that Christopher had been given when he'd come to stay with them in London. And now they were truly a family. "Your brother always hides little treats in his pocket and doles them out when he thinks no one is looking. He spoils her endlessly."

Leo huffed. "The only reason Kit has a dog at all is because he enjoyed the attention from women when he paraded Majesty around the park."

"And since when did you become such a prude, Lord Savage? I shudder to think how you'll be when our daughter arrives."

He splayed a hand possessively over her swollen middle, his green eyes full of tenderness. "I'll keep her in leading strings until she is thirty."

"And if we have a son?" she challenged with an arch of her brow.

"He'll likely be cursed with his father's exceptional handsomeness and have to hold the women at bay with a whip and a chair," he said stoically. But when she narrowed her eyes, he dutifully kissed her. "Very well, we'll lock him in a tower."

Her responding laugh was cut short by a swift and potent clenching of her womb. She sucked in a breath, gripping his arm tightly. The pains had been coming closer all morning. She had tried to hide it, but this one was stronger than the others and took her by surprise.

Leo's face went pale and he was already bending to pick her up when she laid a hand on his shoulder.

"I am fine," she said soothingly. "No need to panic."

"Still, I think we should go back." He lifted his arm in a gesture to Rogers who was following them in the carriage. For the past month Leo hadn't allowed her to step a foot outside without a conveyance close by.

She rolled her eyes. "We are steps away from the cottage door. I can walk. And I'm certainly not going to give birth in the carriage."

"I don't see why not when the babe was likely conceived there."

It was true. When Kit was staying with them, there wasn't as much privacy as before. So they'd begun to take advantage of any time alone they could find. It wasn't long before the excuse of *taking a drive* had turned into a euphemism for a quick afternoon tumble.

"Besides," she said firmly, "Helene told me that walking would benefit me when my time comes."

Leo shook his head toward Rogers, reluctantly giving in. "But we're turning back, regardless. After all, Helene doesn't know everything."

"Hmm . . . I seem to recall her mentioning that plenty of sexual congress would also benefit me. Strange, but I don't recall your arguments against *that* advice."

He grinned rakishly. "Just practicing for our next one, my love."

ᆶᆶᆶᆶ

And in a country estate in Wiltshire . . .

WHEN MEG staggered groggily from her bedchamber that morning, the scent of coddled eggs seemed to rise up from the breakfast room two floors below and smack her across the face.

She instantly dashed back inside, grabbed the glazed chamber pot, and cast up her accounts. Over and over, even when there was nothing left.

"Again, miss?" her maid said with as she rubbed a hand in circles over her back. "It's been nearly a fortnight now. Perhaps it's time to tell your brother or Lady Hullworth."

Huddled over the pot, Meg shook her head vehemently and squeezed her eyes shut tight. "They mustn't know. Especially not Ellie. She would surely imagine the worst."

Then again, the truth was likely just as bad as anything her favorite worrywart of a sister-in-law could conjure. And more to the point, it had actually been a month now since the sickness first began. Meg had just been better at hiding it in the beginning.

Taking a deep breath, she sat up and sagged against the side of her bed. "Besides, this cannot last forever. So there's no need to bother anyone about it."

"I think, perhaps, there is a need." Beneath a ruffled cap,

Bryony looked at her with concern and handed her a square of damp flannel. "After all, you haven't had your courses for two months. Ever since you returned from your holiday."

Meg swallowed. *Her holiday*—when she'd decided on the brilliant notion of having one grand flirtation before she put herself on the shelf. She had been determined to have one scandalous secret to keep with her as she grew old, just like the aunts had done once upon a time.

But somewhere between the Rhine and the Alps, she'd accidentally fallen in love. And now it was becoming clear that she wouldn't be able to keep this a secret for long.

She settled a hand over her midriff and sighed. "I think I might have brought home an unexpected souvenir from my travels."

When a debutante makes passes
at a duke who wears glasses,
she just might end up with more
than she ever bargained for!

Never Seduce a Duke

Meg's story is coming soon!

The Chase by Lynsay Sands

For Scotswoman Seonaid Dunbar, running away to an
abbey was preferable to marrying Blake Sherwell. No,
she'd not dutifully pledge troth to anyone the English
court called "Angel." There was no such thing as an
English angel; only English devils. And there were many
ways to elude a devilish suitor. This battle would require
all weapons, and so the chase was about to begin.

You Were Made to Be Mine by Julie Anne Long

The mission: Find Lady Aurelie Capet, the Earl of
Brundage's runaway fiancée, in exchange for a fortune.
Child's play for legendary British former spymaster,
Christian Hawkes. The catch? Hawkes knows in his
bones that Brundage is the traitor to England who
landed him in a brutal French prison. Hawkes is
destitute, the earl is desperate, and a bargain is struck.

Four Weeks of Scandal by Megan Frampton

Octavia Holton is determined to claim the home she
grew up in with her late father. But she discovers the
house is also claimed by one Gabriel Fallon, who says
his father won the house in a bet. They make a four-
week bargain: Pretend to be engaged, all the while
seeking out any will, letter, or document that proves
who gets ownership. But soon they realize their rivalry
might lead to something much more intimate . . .

REL 0522